Edmond Sutherland was educated at Magdalen College School, where he was head boy, and afterwards read Medicine at Magdalen College, Oxford. Following postgraduate training and research, he was appointed as Consultant Psychiatrist and postgraduate clinical tutor at Birmingham University. He retired from psychiatry in 1985 and studied fine art for several years which culminated in a well-received one-man exhibition in Oxford. He is happily married and has lived in Cambridgeshire for thirty-five years.

I am indebted to my wife, Sheila Ann, for her unwavering support whilst I was writing this book and to Joanne who has been a constant help in secretarial matters.

Edmond Sutherland

WATCHING

AUSTIN MACAULEY PUBLISHERS™
LONDON * CAMBRIDGE * NEW YORK * SHARJAH

Copyright © Edmond Sutherland 2023

The right of Edmond Sutherland to be identified as author of this work has been asserted by the author in accordance with sections 77 and 78 of the Copyright, Designs and Patents Act 1988.

All rights reserved. No part of this publication may be reproduced, stored in a retrieval system, or transmitted in any form or by any means, electronic, mechanical, photocopying, recording, or otherwise, without the prior permission of the publishers.

Any person who commits any unauthorised act in relation to this publication may be liable to criminal prosecution and civil claims for damages.

This is a work of fiction. Names, characters, businesses, places, events, locales and incidents are either the products of the author's imagination or used in a fictitious manner. Any resemblance to actual persons, living or dead, or actual events is purely coincidental.

A CIP catalogue record for this title is available from the British Library.

ISBN 9781398499843 (Paperback)
ISBN 9781398499850 (Hardback)
ISBN 9781398499874 (ePub e-book)
ISBN 9781398499867 (Audiobook)

www.austinmacauley.com

First Published 2023
Austin Macauley Publishers Ltd®
1 Canada Square
Canary Wharf
London
E14 5AA

Thanks also to Austin Macaulay Publishers for their support and editorial expertise. Also, I am eternally grateful for the basic training and education I received at Magdalen College School, Oxford.

Table of Contents

Part One: The Beginning (Chapters 1-7)   **13-70**

Part Two: Mistakes Happen (Chapters 8-15)   **79-152**

Part Three: Professionalism of Secret Services (Chapters 16-23)   **163-224**

Part Four: Explanations (Chapters 24-28)   **233-270**

Foreword

It happened so long ago that no one can be sure whether it is fact or fiction. The traditional version is that a young clerk in Registry mislaid a memorandum from God knows who, about God knows what, probably filing it under WPB (wastepaper basket). This act of carelessness concerning a vital strand of information was lost, and with it, or more accurately without it, the whole edifice of government started to crumble. Heads rolled; bemused executives were tactfully encouraged to leave the service and find gainful occupation elsewhere; there was a mass reorganisation of interdepartmental cooperation. A joint meeting of junior agents from the secret services formed a loose and unofficial committee to exchange information. No fragment of information was to be discarded; every word, hint, rumour, scandal was to be recorded. The committee lasted about 2 years and was abandoned. However, this short-lived committee left one permanent reminder of its existence. A banner still hangs on the wall of registry, proclaiming:

Information Builds Power

Although the formidable Head of Registry, Ms Birkenshaw, commanded the clerks who toiled below this banner to read it carefully, few took any notice of it; and fewer had any idea of its origin.

Except for Lady Eleanor Keenan.

Lady Eleanor Keenan had joined the Civil Service as a minor administrator or manager in 2012, and after a period of quiet observation, she decided to re-establish this small committee. Interdepartmental cooperation was important, was it not? Small amounts of information could be used to complete a complex structure, could it not? It would be of immense value, would it not? And by chance, she had learnt of one, Group Captain Reginald Young, who would make an ideal chairperson. To make the committee official, it requires a name. ANCOM (Ancillary Committee (junior)) was admirable.

And if you're looking for an official title, you can't get much more official than that!

Part One
The Beginning

Chapter 1

The double-decker bus pulled up at a row of shops and the doors opened with an apologetic sigh. This was an industrial estate, built in the '50s and '60s to house workers of Morris Motors and Pressed Steel Fisher car factories, on the eastern suburbs of Oxford. The estate had long lost any charm it may once have had. Stepping from the bus, the stranger was confronted by a row of dispirited shops: a hairdresser (claiming to be 'unisex'), a fish and chip (and kebabs) shop, a beauty parlour (called 'Cinderella's Slipper', with a glass vase of wilting chrysanthemums in the window), a convenience store (its window rendered completely opaque by huge poster advertising the rejuvenating effects of a lager) and a betting shop (its window heavy with venetian blinds for privacy.) Next to the shops was a public telephone box. The pavement was littered with paper, plastic bottles, cartons, cigarette ends and empty drink cans but ignoring that he glanced at an envelope in his hand then walked slowly, appropriate to the summer heat, to the first side street. Anyone watching this scene would hardly have remarked upon a middle-aged man, of medium height, of medium build, carrying a small suitcase with a brown raincoat over his arm; he would have been immediately forgotten. This would have suited Becker well.

The side street in which he found himself was long, straight and uncared-for. On either side were squat, two-storey terraced and semi-detached houses, built with red brick, wooden cladding and little imagination. If this street once had any appeal, it had lost it. The pavements were separated from the road by patches of dry and compacted earth through which clumps of grass struggled to survive. Discarded rubbish was strewn carelessly. Halfway along the street an old mattress sagged against a fence; a sudden gust of wind wrapped a sheet of newspaper round the trunk of a tree and caused a large paper bag to career down the pavement. The few trees which lined the road did their best to survive, but it looked as if they were losing the battle. A solitary, unattended mongrel dog cocked his leg against a wall and urinated.

Cautiously, Becker approached an end-of-terrace house with a stainless-steel numeral screwed to the gate declaring it was number '1'. A featureless dwelling, but with a newly creosoted waist-high fence, a latched gate and a neat square of grass as a front garden. A lady's bicycle, complete with basket over the front wheel, lent against the side wall suggesting someone might be at home. So, it proved. Inside, sitting ladylike, upright and tense, Sylvia (she rarely answered to Sylvie, and definitely never to Sylv) waited at the kitchen table expecting 'her guest'. She was drinking tea and letting her mind roam and wondering what this lodger would be like. Young? Well-dressed? British, for a change? Over the years she had become accustomed to her guests; they reminded her of Aurther, her late husband. After all, it was him that said, "They told him to take lodgers, occasionally." He'd done well for himself; shop steward when he was only 30; went to meetings all over the country, sometimes even abroad; and he'd been good to her with the money. Only went to the pub on a Friday night, not a real drinker. Goodness knows where he got the money for that car, but of course, it had gone now.

The lodgers were always from abroad. Usually nice, tidy, clean men, and the money was useful especially now he upped and dropped dead on her. Only 53 and no insurance. The extra money was a godsend. The doorbell rang, jolting her out of her musings but she took her time to answer it. She walked into the hall, looked sideways at herself in the full-length mirror and was pleased with her slim figure (even at her age), tugged her sweater tight over her hips and made sure her hair was tidy, before opening the door.

She hoisted her welcoming smile. He had a pale face pitted, from adolescence no doubt; forties, slightly stooped, grey trousers, over heavy, black boots; of average height, of average build. At first sight, well ordinary. Except the eyes.

"Mr Becker?" She was rewarded with the briefest of smiles, a nod and an envelope held out towards her. All the time he was looking past her into the hallway, making no eye contact. Taking the envelope, she squinted at the bundle of notes inside; it would be unseemly to count them straight away; instead, she took a step back and beckoned him in, the notes still in her hand.

"Mrs Bryant?" he murmured in little more than a whisper.

A frown flickered across Sylvia's brow; did he say 'Brandt?' Possibly.

"Yes, that's me," and with a little more emphasis, "Bryant! Your room is upstairs." Then rather unnecessarily, "You're alright with the stairs, are you?"

There was no reply, but he followed her up. At the top, he was behind her as she stepped into a room; small, clean, a single bed sandwiched between a heavy dark-stained wardrobe and a chest-of-drawers. A bedside lamp on the chest-of-drawers, an upright chair stood at the foot of the bed next to the window. He pulled the net curtain to one side and looked out at a surprisingly long garden. Tidy enough but uncultivated. Three unpruned trees; two apple and a pear by the look of it but difficult to be sure at this distance. Next door 6 feet bamboo canes supported plants laden with runner beans. Elsewhere, the earth had been dug and raked and from the black soil large onions and lettuces (or possibly late-sown cabbage) grew with regimental precision.

Becker thought of his father's allotment, obsessively neat, all borders sharply trimmed. He knew some of his father's rigid and intolerant thinking had been passed down to him but never questioned it. He dropped the net curtain and turned back to the room but stood still with his hands behind his back.

"It's fertile, the soil. Some say the houses were built on a sewage farm; that's what my Arthur used to say. Not a gardener myself, though." Sylvia nodded towards the garden. Becker remained silent.

"Well, this is it," Sylvia said, again rather unnecessarily. "It's very quiet, most of the time. Sometimes on a Saturday you can hear the crowd at the football. Oxford United you know. Arthur used to go sometimes…if it were a good match…" The sentence tailed off. Becker nodded absently. "They've stopped the kids' joyriding of a night that we used to get, thank goodness!"

He watched her. Still silent. She felt uncomfortable. Then quite abruptly, as if to be polite, he roused himself: "It is nice(?)…It is good(?)…Thank you."

It was at that point that Sylvia became quite sure that her 'gentleman visitor' was not English. She let out her breath, which she was surprised to find she had been holding for some time.

"Right, I'll leave you to it. Will you be wanting anything to eat after your journey?"

"No…thank you," Becker replied, "I go out." (Leaving it unclear whether that was to eat or to do something else.)

"Breakfast about half past seven, shall we say?" A nod in reply. A man of irritatingly few words apparently.

"Very good," she replied rather more sharply than intended. "There's your front door key. The facilities" (with a demure bob of the head) "are just next door. Oh, and thank you," she nodded at the envelope in her hand. At that, she left the room and hurried downstairs. If he wasn't going to eat, she might as well have a glass of sherry, or two, and watch the evening's television.

She settled back into a corner of the settee, stretching her legs out in front of her, arching her back and allowing herself some moments of leisure. Enjoyable. It was true, she had been a bit lonely after Arthur. No children. That factory wasn't healthy, she'd always said so, and what with that shop-steward business, the worry must have played havoc with his heart. There was always some argument about rates of pay, convenience times, shouting matches with the management. But there you are, he wouldn't be told. Have to make the best of it, wouldn't she? There were the regular lodgers (goodness knows how they found her address; she knew he'd had something to do with it. That and the shop steward business.) Anyway, together with the part-time job at the store three afternoons a week she mustn't complain. She'd manage. But, when all was said and done, she was only 49 and still in good trim. Some of the neighbours didn't like her, perhaps she was too good for them, and some of the customers in the convenience store we're not the sort of people she would prefer to talk to. But all in all, she'd get by.

The door banged as he went out, bringing her back to the present. She looked out of the window but couldn't see him; the clouds were stacking up over the rooftops opposite, there'd be a summer downpour and no mistake. He'd be drenched unless he was careful. But that was up to him. This one was foreign that's for sure. German? Polish? Some sort of European certainly. Quiet. But she'd make allowance for the language. Slightly unsettling, with those dead eyes under blonde eyebrows and lashes; a coldness about him. Never quite looked at you. Wouldn't turn your back on him. But she'd never had any trouble with the lodgers before. Why now? She poured another sherry, calmed herself and switched on the telly.

Becker realised he'd need a week or so to roam around the estate, get his bearings. But first find out if the public phone box was working. It was. He dialled a London number and spoke no more than two sentences before replacing the receiver. It was all set then. Time to stroll along the road, have a beer, turn in early. Tomorrow he'd keep his head down. Explore. Wait.

*** *** ***

On a street behind the Tate Britain in London, there stood a double-fronted, two storey, detached house. Prosaically known as 'The House', it was as uninspiring as its name, and at first glance seemed to need some attention, a coat of paint wouldn't have gone amiss. A second glance would confirm this. Any passer-by would be truly amazed at the security measures deemed necessary for such an insignificant building. Inside, there were four large rooms, in each were several desks upon which computers were constantly being monitored by very serious operatives. The basement, central hub of both incoming and outgoing communications, housed electronic communication equipment that would mystify a casual visitor and seriously challenge the world's best hackers.

At precisely 1:30 pm. on a hot and sunny August afternoon, one of the surprisingly heavy doors opened and a well-dressed man of indeterminate age exited and descended the steps. He was the director of this substation, a satellite of Intelligence headquarters at Vauxhall Cross, across the Thames. The man, Phillipson Rice, was born in Manchester of working-class parents, educated at Oxford where he was awarded an Honours degree in humanities and was now director of this department that concentrated on coordinating MI6's information from all over the world. He was six feet tall, slightly stooped and with a plodding '10 to 2' gait. Dressed in a dark blue suit, his coat unbuttoned for it was warm, he made his way along Millbank towards Parliament Square.

Outwardly studious and conscientious, inwardly, this man suffered chronic insecurity; anxiety that a shrink once had attributed to unresolved conflicts with his father in infancy. Or was it his mother? He couldn't remember. In any case, they all said that, didn't they? He had dismissed that pearl of wisdom much as he had dismissed a lot of what the analyst had said to him, and just got on with his life, even though this constant self-doubt continued unabated. And about insecurity, he had once spoken openly to another undergraduate at Oxford of his sexual preference, which resulted in a rebuff, but mercifully no loss of friendship. His academic success at Oxford was noted and following a conversation with one of the Fellows, he applied for a post in a secretive government department (the days of a 'tap on the shoulder' were long gone.) After exhaustive examination, he was accepted and attended a protracted training course in Scotland; he then worked steadily, if unobtrusively, for the service both overseas as an agent and in the U.K. as an administrator. He had just been promoted to Head this moderately large section, at an unusually young age. This promotion augured well for his future; this department carried considerable responsibility.

One of his duties was to attend irregular meetings with representatives of other secret services and similar pay grades in Whitehall; and that was where he was heading.

A pleasant stroll along the bank of the Thames was always spoiled by the constant noise of traffic, jammed head to tail; squealing brakes; crashing gears; the congestion clouded in exhaust fumes. Walking into Parliament Square, he was swallowed up in the crowd. Ice cream was being sold from a van to a long, impatient queue; two coaches had pulled up on the far side of The Square and throngs of tourists were alighting, adding to the crowds milling about. There were people walking in all directions: cameras flashing constantly; unceasing noise.

Suddenly, a convoy of large black cars with police motorbike outriders swept from Whitehall, across the lights and turned quickly past saluting police officers into the forecourt of the palace of Westminster. A minister going to work, perhaps even the prime minister going to work. Crowds pressed forward to get a better look; and just as quickly lost interest and fell back. Rice turned into Whitehall, and approached the Foreign and Commonwealth Office, next to which was the building he was looking for. There was no brass plate affixed to the wall, but an armed policeman was at the large and serious doors. After a cursory glance at Rice's official warrant, the officer opened the door. Rice entered. Inside it was astonishingly quiet.

Rice was disconcerted, as always, not only by reverential stillness and silence but also the uncomfortable proportions of the reception area. The room was small and box-like, the ceiling absurdly high. Clearly some improvised reconstruction had been used to produce this awkward space. A receptionist, whose dyed-blonde hair was lacquered to within an inch of its life, sat at a desk gazing at him without interest. Her immaculate cream, linen suit and white, high-necked blouse were 'ever-so expensive'; her manner was one of perpetual boredom and superiority. This was Clarissa. (Well, it would, wouldn't it? thought Rice.)

Looking at him from beneath astonishingly long lashes, she inquired, "Yes?"

"I have an appointment with Group Captain Young. I've come for the Ancillary Committee Meeting. The name is Phillipson Rice." He laid a card on her desk. She inspected it from a distance and moved it further away with the end of a pencil as if it was contaminated. He went through this silly ritual every time he arrived here. Was it her statement of importance?

"Ah," she sighed. "Just a moment…sir."

With that, she ran a lazy finger down an appointment diary which was only slightly smaller than the menu one would find at a ridiculously pretentious restaurant, and finding something that caught her attention, continued, "Ah, yes, here we are. ANCOM. Would you care to take a seat, sir?" Rice withdrew to a heavily padded chair, sat and waited. As always this gave him time to look about. The internal security guard was the same man, sitting at the same tiny desk, might even be reading the same newspaper, as the last time (and that was a month ago!). Rice was ignored. There was a patch of veneer that had become detached from the receptionist's desk but had not been repaired. Such details were magnified in importance by repeatedly having to kill time and be ignored in this unnecessary manner.

Meanwhile, Clarissa, moving into the twenty-first century, rather crossly tapped her intercom and after receiving an indecipherable squawk in reply, said, "The Group Captain will see you now, sir" and with a wrist so limp it was in danger of disengaging from the rest of her arm, pointed past the motionless security guard to a door which Rice knew led to corridor stretching into the depths of the building. She said, "He'll see you now, sir. First door on the right. It's his office, don't you know. He's waiting for you now."

Phillipson Rice stood. Now he had to pass security. First his name, warrant identification number and time of arrival were recorded in an official ledger, then he was made to relinquish his mobile phone. After this, he was frisked, which sometimes was so intimate as to be erotic. Not so today. The guard stood from his chair, opened the door to a dimly lit corridor and silently nodded Rice through. Rice made his way down the corridor indicated. As usual on this short walk he wondered, *How Clarissa and the security guard coped with so much work, and with such ease!* Arriving at a door he knocked gently. Someone shouted, "Come!" He opened the door and went in.

"Come in. Come in. Why don't you?" A rotund gentleman, of florid complexion, in shirtsleeves, sat behind a large mahogany desk, squinting at Rice over his rimless glasses. Today, Group Captain Young sported a pale blue shirt with wide dark blue stripes, white collar and cuffs but no tie. His braces were bright red.

"Group Captain Young," Rice smiled.

"God no! God no! Well, actually—yes, it is, as you very well know," the man barked rather confusingly, "you remember surely, first names only, here. First names only."

Upon the Group Captain's desk, there were two landlines, one black, one intimidatingly red, a computer screen (totally blank), an ancient intercom and a discarded mobile phone. There was an 'In-tray' with a sign on it reading 'I'm full. Go away' and an 'Out-tray' that was empty. Facing the desk were four, deep, luxurious, wingback armchairs of black leather suitably cracked with age and button-cushioned; none of them occupied. As the reception area had been small, this room was large; the high ceiling much better proportioned to the overall size. Three walls were half-panelled in light oak, and above the panelling, a light-beige plaster. On the plastered walls hung large portraits of dignitaries, some draped in ceremonial robes, all no doubt once important but now disappearing in the mists of time and behind serial layers of thick varnish.

Extraordinarily, among these portraits, though wretchedly out of place, was a rather impressive seascape, all wind filled sails and spume-capped waves, danger and excitement. It hung above the door in the Group Captain's line of vision above visitors. Behind the Group Captain were two tall, sash and case windows on either side of glass-panelled doors, which led out to a cobbled quadrangle. In the centre of this quadrangle, someone had gone to the trouble of lifting a few cobbles and planting a flowering cherry tree. It had not thrived, but no one had bothered to remove it. On one side of the room was a long, highly polished table, and around it numerous straight-back chairs. The carpet was not quite as thick as the one at Claridge's. Overall, the room was an extraordinary mix of senior common room, palatial withdrawing room and gentlemen's club.

"Come in. Come in." Young waved to an armchair. "Now then Phillipson…it is Phillipson, isn't it? Odd sort of name, isn't it?"

"Idiosyncratically minded father, sir," Phillipson replied.

"What? What? Oh, idiosyncratic," said Young as if he had never heard the word before. "Yes. Get your meaning. Bloody awkward fellows, fathers, aren't they?"

Phillipson had no reply to this.

"Tell me, anyhow," Young continued. "All well at Vauxhall Cross, is it? And nothing out of order behind the Tate?"

"I think all is calm. No great panic at the moment."

"Makes a bloody change, what?" Young was gazing above Rice's head at the seascape. "All calm then. I wonder if any of the others will bring along any problems. Hope not."

So did Phillipson but didn't say so.

"Early today, Phillipson, time for a chat before the others get here."

That was something Phillipson welcomed. For months now, ever since he had been instructed to attend the 'ANCOM', he had wondered how such a gathering had come about. "Unusual group that meets here, is it not Group Captain—sorry, Reginald?" After years of working in the service, calling a chairman by his forename still embarrassed Phillipson. Reginald looked over his glasses and desk at Phillipson and, as usual, began stretching his elasticated braces away from his body as if testing their suitability for a catapult. And, as usual, one slipped from his left thumb and delivered a smart blow to his left nipple. He winched.

"Unusual? How, unusual?"

"I wondered how it all started in the first place, Reginald." Phillipson murmured with due deference.

"Ah, see what you mean. Not exactly sure myself, if I'm honest. Seems like about 50 years ago, some idiot made a monumental cock-up: a note landed on his desk, and he did nothing about it, or he did. Idiot filed it in the waste-paper basket; for shredding, if in those days such things existed. Anyway, this note referred to a rumour going about that was in fact not so much a rumour as grade 'A' evidence of treachery. Escalated into a major security whatsit. Chaps across the pond got hot under the collar. Hell let loose. Heads rolled. You know how it is."

Phillipson had some idea of 'how it is'.

"Well, cutting to the quick, some bright spark, name forgotten, thank God, came up with the idea of a joint services committee to be made up of middle-ranking security fellers who would meet on an ad-hoc basis, report minor notes, rumours, slander, what have you, and if it was sufficiently worrying, pass the buck upstairs. That way this committee, ANCOM, might stop further cockups. Get my drift, do you?"

Phillipson did, and so nodded his head.

"Nothing compulsory you understand. As informal as we can make it, But in my humble opinion useful."

Young started experimenting with his braces again which gave Phillipson the opportunity to ask: "Your training in the RAF was helpful, sir…Reginald?"

"God knows how they picked on me to chair this committee, but my time in the RAF, as you say, was useful. Service police with particular interest in counterintelligence. More shenanigans go on than you might expect. Suppose that had something to do with it. Fellow came along, happened to know I was about to leave the service, said he was from Lady Eleanor upstairs, asked me if I was interested. Knew bugger all about it really, but there you are."

"Lady Eleanor, I've not actually met, Reginald."

"Oh Eleanor, she's the one I report to. Fifth floor. Nice enough, easy on the eye if you get my meaning." Young nearly winked but decided against it. "Full training as far as I know; not positive which branch; doesn't interfere that's the main thing."

"And she reports to…?"

"God knows. Up the ladder, way above my pay grade. Bit hush-hush up there. Give her my report after each meeting. No notes as you know. If something is important enough, it'll stick. That's my method. And everything is recorded, anyway. You know about that."

There was a knock on the door. It opened and the other members of ANCOM came in together.

"Been waiting for you." Young looked at his watch then the others. "Let's get round the posh table and make a start. Looks like we've got a full house."

The members had been meeting for so long that they now sat in familiar order. Young was at the head of the table, a representative from GCHQ, the Metropolitan police and MI5 to his left: opposite MI6, Special branch and The Counterterrorist police.

"Right. Who's going to kick off?" Young had their attention. He waited. As usual, there was a pause before one of them would declare a subject he/she considered worthy of note and examination. This informal approach was encouraged by Young; one of the purposes of the group was to identify any events that had, so far, escaped under the radar of the more structured cabinet or joint committee agendas, another was to foster relationships between the security departments. The meetings were continuously taped (as everyone present knew). The final decision on referral was made upstairs. The concept of this low-level inter-departmental group was proposed by Lady Eleanor Keenan and was in fact merely a resurrection of an historical group whose origin was obscure, the one that Young, in his way, had related to Phillipson earlier.

Several topics were raised, and discussions began. Rice had time to observe the group more carefully. Young seemed at ease; Konrad, of GCHQ sat quietly, the ranking police lady Samara Vassell and Nigel Mountford of MI5 lent towards each other making inaudible comments between themselves. Mountford, he noticed, was in the habit of constant movements of his hands, usually in and out of his pockets. Special Branch and Counterterrorism sat quietly listening. Rice listened but was silent.

Nigel took off his glasses and polished them vigorously, even though they were crystal-clear, replaced them and looked round the table directly at each person in turn. When he felt the need to speak his shoulders writhed and he bared his teeth, sucking his breath through them. He began, between these mannerisms, somewhat pompously; "I have received a message directly from the Home Office delivered by internal post marked 'Urgent'. It was sealed. (He was referring to the internal, supposedly secure, post between departments.) He read:

'Police report: enhanced traffic flow on A34 Oxford-Southampton, at junctions Didcot, Harwell and Culham, over the last 3 months. Not substantial, but regular. No known new or major developments proposed at either Culham Scientific Research Establishment or the Rutherford/Appleton Laboratory at Harwell. Due to the Atomic Energy Department's interest in the establishments and concomitant security arrangements, advisable to enquire more closely the nature, purpose and business of this augmented traffic movement. Your early reply to this communique is requested'."

"The missive was unsigned."

With that, Nigel sat at ease, waiting for comments. No one spoke. Somewhere in another room a phone rang persistently. No one answered it. Konrad busied himself by gazing out of the window considering the wide, wide world, or what he could see of it. The Commander frowned at the table. Nigel seemed satisfied that he had successfully relayed to the committee the importance of the message. Rice on the other hand, wasn't quite sure what to make of it. No one was in a hurry; no one seemed worried; no one seemed even much interested. Except Commander Samara Vassell who tapped the table with a knuckle.

"No note about this topic landed on my desk this morning," she complained, and then in a rush, "I wouldn't have had time to read it yet, anyway. I've no time to read traffic reports from Thames Valley Police. It's probably of little interest to me."

"Except in this room." Young said quietly.

She had been taken by surprise. Rice noticed Nigel Mountford smile.

"When did you first hear about this?" Samara was irritated. "When?"

Nigel took his time, leaned forward and eventually preferred to answer another question.

"The missive was unsigned," he repeated.

Samara was not to be put off easily; indeed, she flushed with impatience. *She feels threatened,* thought Rice.

"But when Nigel? When?" she pressed.

"Oh, yesterday I think, some time yesterday." Nigel was off hand. "Well, I said the post came yesterday, didn't I? Why is it important?"

What the hell is going on? Rice wondered. There's some sort of traffic problem near Oxford, admittedly a sensitive area of nuclear research but there's an argument going on between two departments about an inconsequential matter of when a communication had been received. Surely that's not what National Security is interested in, is it? But that wasn't the end of Samara's questions.

"Who delivered it?"

"What?" complained Nigel. "What do you mean? Does it matter?"

"What do I mean?" Samara was sorely tried. "What I mean is, when did the note arrive and who delivered it? Simple enough, isn't it?"

"I've already said; yesterday, and it was delivered by internal courier!"

Goodness me, Phillipson mused.

"So, there we have it," the Group Captain murmured quietly. "Do we hand it on? What do you think Konrad?" At the sound of his name, Konrad was abruptly interrupted in his contemplation of the window and the wide, wide world beyond and, turning to the rest, said:

"Seems trivial to me."

"Why do you bring it here?" Samara asked Nigel. There was an edge to her voice.

"Somebody deemed it important enough to send me an urgent memo, I think that's why." Nigel tucked his glasses into the top pocket of his jacket.

What the hell is going on? Rice wondered yet again.

Young looked around. He was thinking the same thing. "Yes, yes, urgent but why? Anyone?" No one spoke.

Unsure of himself, Rice ventured, "It just seems a little odd. Not a lot to go on but it could be something. Culham, Harwell…sensitive areas, aren't they? Might be something I suppose."

"Brilliant! Quite brilliant!" Young was bullying. "It might be something best passed on to our 'masters and betters' see what they make of it. Let them decide if it's worth calling everyone together for a full session. What do you think? Agreed?"

Everyone around the table nodded. Samara looked irritated. Rice wondered, *What was going on between Mountford and her; it had to be more than an inconsequential matter of traffic near Didcot in Oxfordshire!* Konrad continued to look bored. Nigel smiled.

"Is there anything else?" The Group Captain wanted to know. "Anything at all? Well, if that's all, we can wrap things up. I'll mention this traffic business to Lady Eleanor."

The Commander looked as if she wanted to continue her investigation about timing but decided against it. No one had pressing business. It was an unusually short meeting. The Group Captain pushed his chair back and got up; the others got ready to leave. Rice stood, not quite sure whether to say anything or just leave. He was saved by Nigel.

"Pleasure seeing you again." And with that, the group disappeared out of the door leaving Rice behind. Young sat back down at his desk and called Rice over.

"Rice, word in your ear." (Rice noticed first names had been dropped.) "Nice easy meeting, I thought. My view, a lot about nothing, or more likely, not much about nothing. Sometimes difficult to see the wood, what? See you again."

Philipson Rice made good his escape, retraced his steps to reception, picked up his mobile and passed Clarissa without a word. He stepped into the late afternoon sunshine in Whitehall.

*** *** ***

Phillipson Rice walked briskly, yet thoughtfully, along Whitehall towards Trafalgar Square. The pavement was crowded with pedestrians; one-sided mobile phone conversations everywhere; businessmen going home early or marching to their next appointment armed with bulging briefcases; schoolgirls giggling at a mounted guardsman outside St James' Palace who had dared to wink at them; a gaggle of schoolchildren harassing an inexperienced teacher; lovers' hand-in-hand lost in each other's company; "selfies" being taken outside every building, renowned or not. No one took any notice of Rice. Nor him of them. He worried about the ANCOM. Something about the proceedings had not been straightforward but he struggled to identify precisely what it was.

He turned into Charing Cross Road and as he approached the underground station, he made a conscious decision to dismiss his worries. No doubt they were unfounded, just part of his general insecurity. He thought of his analyst again. Later, on the Northern Line train he sat in a corner of the carriage with a view of the whole compartment and all doors. After years of training and clandestine service abroad, it was automatic. At Camden Town, he got off and climbed up to the High Street and was met with an excitement quite different to Central London. He could be in another City. Gone were the rolled umbrellas and pinstripe suits of the men and the 4-inch heels of the women; here, life was loud, spontaneous and buoyant; the colours primary and strident; the noise of laughter mixed with insistent beat of popular music; occasionally the sharp whiff of unusual tobacco smoke. Everywhere turmoil. The market was louder and packed; customers were spilling out of the pubs, shouting, slapping each other on the back and slopping beer everywhere. Canal boats were moving slowly, low in the water.

Phillipson walked past a coffee shop full of huge, leather-clad, bearded men sitting on stools at a counter around the walls. He passed a second-hand furniture shop, outside which a man resplendent in a dirty vest and with hairy shoulders and chest, a fag hanging from his lips, was selling more small packets of chemicals than wardrobes. He checked behind, looking at reflections in an angled windows but it was only routine. Nothing behind attracted his attention. Further along a group of 'rude boys' loafed about, the arses of their genes halfway to the pavement. He walked behind an old man who suddenly lurched to his right and fell on his hands and knees; immediately three young ladies stopped and helped him up, murmuring encouragement. The old man staggered on, but Rice had noticed the girls' concern. That was part of life here. A huge community. A charity shop tried to attract customers with a display of popular fiction and a risqué dress in its window; the few customers inside looked as if they had the weight of the charity on their shoulders, but little money to spend. Next, was a deserted jobcentre followed by two buildings joined with an arch under which a passageway led to a cobbled courtyard where second-hand bicycles were being sold. Everywhere people were moving.

Rice stopped for a moment and enjoyed the mood, then turned into a side street and enjoyed the peace and quiet of the residential area. He made for his flat (which had been eye-wateringly expensive) and was pleased to be alone this evening often after work if it was after eight o clock he would travel to school and enjoy a drink at this club and he had a friend to stay the night would take a taxi to Camden thus avoiding underground trains which were not always as peaceful or safe as he would wish tonight he preferred to be an his own listen to some music perhaps read a novel.

Just relax.

Chapter 2

Group Captain Young was preparing to leave the RAF in the summer of 2015, after 20 years of admirable police service, having reached his promotional ceiling. He was known for his firm command and special interest in counterintelligence, although this was only a small part of his work. Well respected, he was an amiable companion in the officer's mess and was among the last to leave a party. He had married a young lady with a substantial figure and pleasant personality, who was welcomed into the officers' quarters. She had the added advantage of being the only child of a wealthy retailer (a chain store grocer) who had been knighted in the 2010 list. Neither the Group Captain nor his wife mentioned that 'small matter', but it was well-known gossip amongst the officers' wives. Any apprehension Young had about life as a civilian was dispelled shortly before his discharge from the service when a young man, Jeremy Gould made an appointment and invited him for lunch in a well-known hotel near his RAF base. They met in the foyer.

"Can I get you a drink, Group Captain, before we go for lunch?" Gould asked.

"Thank you. Gin and tonic, just the thing; plenty of ice. Got the afternoon off in any case."

They retired to the bar and settled themselves at a small table in the bay window. A waiter took their orders. Gould chose mineral water.

"As you know, sir I'm from Whitehall. There we've heard you are about to leave the service, sir, after some years of exemplary service." Gould began, although he didn't specify who 'we' were, or how 'we' had obtained this information.

"Yes. Mixed feelings really. Love the service but reached an age where a rest might be welcome."

"Thank you," to the waiter who had returned with the drinks. "Cheers." They raised their glasses. Young took stock. Well-dressed fellow, this Gould, knows his manners spoke well, could take to him. Only thing, Devil was this about?

"Group Captain," Gould resumed, "I work within the confines of Whitehall, a very junior civil servant. General dogsbody really. I answer mainly to Lady Eleanor Keenan…have you heard of her, sir?"

"No. Name means nothing to me."

"Well, Lady Eleanor asked me to contact you with a view to inquiring whether a post of sensitive nature within Whitehall might be of interest to you."

"Sensitive nature? What d'you mean sensitive?"

"The post in mind requires discretion. A degree of confidentiality, shall we say? You see, Group Captain, 'we' (again without explanation) know of your excellent service in the RAF and the discreet nature of some of your work. It's that side of things on which we want to concentrate."

Young began to get the idea. Some form of clandestine operation gathering intelligence. Well, he knew a bit about that. Had done some of it in his time. But full-blown MI5 or MI6 was well beyond his powers. Knew nothing about that, what's more, didn't want to know about that. He said so:

"Get your drift, Gould. But not sure I'd fit the bill. Bit rusty. Not fully trained. Get my meaning?"

"Oh indeed, sir. We are not suggesting covert operations. Nothing like that. It is your administrative abilities that appeal so much to Lady Eleanor. She has heard such glowing reports of your ability to form well-disciplined and discreet groups of personnel; those are the skills that she so admires in you."

"Does she?" Although Young was not averse to compliments, he was suspicious of excessive admiration, especially from someone he had never heard of. But he could live with that! "Mean forming a committee within Whitehall?"

"Exactly that."

"But who'd make up this committee? What would be its aim? Who would be the line manager? What sort of boundaries are we talking about?" Young was so obviously interested that these questions tumbled out in such quick succession and Mr Gould knew the post was tempting the Group Captain. It only required Lady Eleanor to finalise the position and Group Captain Young would be available. Inwardly, he smiled. Lady Eleanor would be pleased.

"Shall we go in and eat?" Gould inquired. "Over lunch, I can let you know more of the post and where you will meet Lady Eleanor. We will, of course, provide transport"

Young got up with new horizons beckoning. Gould got up, congratulating himself on a job well done.

Lunch was taken. Although the courses were hardly exotic, the chef and his staff prepared them with care. The meal was thoroughly enjoyable. Conversation between the two eased and Young recounted some of the more bizarre moments of service transgressions. Gould was pleasantly and politely amused. Young noticed however, that Jeremy (for now he had Gould's forename) was less forthcoming about his own career. He showed some righteous indignation when mention of 'far right movements' cropped up unexpectedly during general conversation and clearly had little time for the vociferous extremists of the American Republican Party. He also thought, *Europe a retrograde step.* (*He probably meant Brexit,* Young thought. Well, that was all right, Young didn't have strong feelings on the matter anyway.) Over cognac (Jeremy drank mineral water) he expressed his views on equality of both race and gender vehemently. "Liberalism is fine in a stable and confident society, but at present, like America, we are hardly stable. Take Europe. Take America. All our concepts of democracy are changing; and not for the better." Young wondered if this was the 'prevailing party line', or whether it was a purely personal conviction. It was not something he wanted to discuss, and in any case was irrelevant. The services were hardly liberal and having been in them for them for 20 odd years, his views had become somewhat rigid. He held his peace.

In any case, it was about 4:00 pm and enough was enough. Time to move on to the future. Or at least his future.

"Will Lady Eleanor be getting in touch?" He wanted to know.

"Oh yes, Group Captain. Through me of course. I will be in touch within a fortnight."

They stood, shook hands warmly (at least Young's handshake was warm) and went their separate ways.

Group captain Reginald Henry Young would have to wait for the call. It came sooner than he anticipated.

*** *** ***

For many, East Anglia is a windy, bleak and uninspiring region of Great Britain, unprotected from blasts of cold air from as far away as Siberia. The population is sparse in the Fens. If the sun shines, the flat land recedes to a remote, level and indistinct horizon and the sky arches above like an immense blue vault. It can feel empty, even forgotten. But when the weather threatens, clouds are mountainous and oppressive and then as sheets of rain sweep across the flat lands the horizon disappears. That can be challenging. There are few visitors, apart from those set on the dubious pleasures of seaside resorts along the coast of the North Sea. Quite coincidentally, in 2015, as Group Captain Young was being recruited into the corridors and rooms of Whitehall, a local retired farm worker here in East Anglia was surprised to witness a large, chauffeur-driven car, with three well-dressed passengers, turn off the A140 Norwich-Ipswich Road and drive into the countryside towards a heavily wooded area some distance away. This was an unusual event but not one that he considered particularly important. Strangers came and went occasionally but the land that had fed him and his family was important, and it was here forever. He loved the land; and the seasons; and the wildlife. Furthermore, his wife and he were fiercely independent and self-sufficient. He was on his painful way to the pub where every day he took his midday refreshment of excellent local ale. Painful, because his arthritis was much worse, even in the summer heat. The wood that the car had made was too far from his front doorstep to worry about and the disused airfield behind the trees was just that, disused, and had been since the war. And let's face it, the war had been over for 'these 50 years since'. He pushed open the door to the bar, and as usual found he was the only customer. Frank, the publican, was a huge man with opinions even larger.

"Same Olly?"

"Same."

The pint glass was filled with strong, clear ale and, as always, with a good head. Money changed hands.

"Saw Summat today," Olly muttered into his beer.

"Yes?"

"Big car. Off towards Fenley Wood. Bloody big car."

"Yes?"

"Know anything 'bout that?"

"Me? Why me? Know bugger all about anything. 'Cept maybe how bad the football was at Portland Road." That was as much as the 'big car' interested them. The chances of Ipswich Town Football Club were far more important. The two of them knew more about football tactics than Sir Alf Ramsey!

The occupants of the car were more than a little interested in a single track road that disappeared into Fenley wood and led to a long-deserted, but substantial mansion well screened from the road. After the mansion had been abandoned many years previously, trees and bushes had grown ever closer, and ivy now covered most of the walls; undergrowth threatened to invade the house itself. Driving past this large house, a visitor would find acres of broken concrete, pitted runways and half-demolished prefabricated huts which were the remains of a WW2 USAAF base. In effect, with the dense woods around, and the open airfield behind it, effectively, the mansion was safe from unwanted or inquisitive eyes or visitors.

The three men disembarked at the mansion, each with maps, house plans and measuring equipment, worked all afternoon then climbed back into the car and made the long return journey to London.

Chapter 3

I took the train from Oxford to Paddington to attend a day of lectures at one of London's conference centres; I considered the whole undertaking a chore essential only because the department in which I worked required my attendance. I don't enjoy these days; generally, I knew no one and spent most of the time watching others chattering and laughing together. The train was half-full of day-trippers going to the capital as part of their summer holiday. They would swelter on the streets of London today, in this weather. I had taken an overnight bag; and I had brought a novel to ease the journey. As it turned out, the novel was so engrossing that we were pulling into Paddington Station before I realised the journey was over. A taxi to the conference centre and I was just in time for the first lecture.

The day followed the usual pattern; speaker, questions, discussion; speaker, questions, discussion…ad nauseam; a break for lunch and another for afternoon tea. I was only interested in one lecture, reporting the latest news of the influence of hormones on brain function and if I were to be totally truthful, I was finding the rest of it boring. It was difficult to stay awake, never mind concentrate. At tea on these occasions, I'm usually on my own and everyone around seems to know everyone else and the noise level rises alarmingly with all their chatter and laughter. Equally embarrassing is trying to balance sandwiches, a saucer and teacup with casual self-assurance which I certainly never feel. I am not the most extraverted of characters! But during this tea break a young lady appeared before me, looked at me steadily and smiled. This, I was soon to learn, was Rachel. The same height as me, she had a fresh complexion but with raven-black hair and intense, brown eyes, a bright and cheerful manner and a mysterious smile, suggesting some private amusement. I guessed she was about thirty years of age, but my estimations were usually wildly inaccurate.

"Hello," she said.

"Oh, oh hello." I feigned surprise as if I was about to rush off and speak to some immensely important person. I don't know why I did that. In reality, I nearly dropped my cup.

"An interesting day?" she was still smiling.

"Moderately." I immediately wondered if this was the correct answer perhaps—'oh yes!'—or, 'absolutely!'—would have been more polite.

"Yes." She said knowingly. "I find it all a bit boring as well."

She had my measure. For the life of me, I couldn't think of anything to say. The silence lengthened and she picked up another sandwich.

"I don't think that we've met before," I risked tentatively.

"No, I don't think we have." We exchanged names and the atmosphere between us eased.

"You live in London?" I asked.

"Yes. Off Kennington Park Road near the Oval Cricket Ground. South of the Thames. Quite a way from here. And yourself?"

"Oxford."

Apparently, she worked as a government funded social-work advisor, concentrating on deprived families but not tied to any locality or local authority, giving her considerable freedom. This involved much travel, even on occasions travelling abroad. The job was only vaguely described, but I ignored that, or more accurately didn't give it a second thought. By comparison, my work as a researcher and very junior Fellow at my old college in Oxford, sounded dreary. We chatted; although what she saw in me, I cannot imagine, I'm hardly the life and soul of any party. Our conversation was cut short by a call to another lecture, but I had been greatly relieved that the tea break had been so unusually sociable. I'd met a pretty, lively and intelligent young lady, who had not dismissed me immediately but seemed comfortable to talk. For the last lectures, we sat together and as the crowd rose at the end of the afternoon, we turned to one another and quietly decided to spend the evening together. A taxi took us to a restaurant she recommended, near her flat, and we enjoyed a meal together. The name of the restaurant for the life of me, I can't remember! What we ate, similarly, escapes my memory; and in any case in the bigger picture, it hardly matters.

Afterwards we shared a taxi back to her flat, during which she made it clear this was the end of the evening and I would return to my hotel. We'd ring during the week.

That's how it started. Two professionals chancing to meet, becoming friends and soon lovers, then meeting regularly at weekends. She spoke little of her colleagues and her job which remained loosely defined, even vague. Whether I gave that much thought remains unclear but certainly I was not unduly worried. Intrigued? Possibly. Suspicious? Not at all.

We kept the weekends free as intervals of relaxation from working lives, alternating between her flat in London and mine in Oxford. Naturally we became comfortable in each other's company and reached the stage of discussing our future together. By the beginning of October, I floated the idea of a holiday, even a long weekend. I reasoned it would give us an opportunity to consider the future; even if it was in a 'make-believe' holiday situation; we could discuss a joint life together, married or not.

Paris was decided upon, something of an adventure (for me at least). We would travel by Eurostar and stay in a tourist hotel and spend the time exploring, just enjoying ourselves.

*** *** ***

As Rachel and I got to know one another during the summer and autumn of 2019, Group Captain Reginald Young was consolidating his position at Whitehall and, at last, was enjoying life away from the service regimentation. He was spending 'quality' time with his wife, Diane at weekends. Their marriage had been comfortable rather than exciting. Always of ample proportions, Diane had, in her youth, been described as 'good fun', a young lady who could wield a mean tennis racket and could down a few drinks at the bar. Unfortunately, her athletic enthusiasm had not responded to Reginald's desperate attempts at impropriety and all advances had been firmly rebuked until the wedding ring was in place. If Flight Lieutenant Young (for that had been his lowly rank at the time) had expected to be overwhelmed by an avalanche of passion and desire in his marriage, he was disappointed. Instead, Diane acquiesced to intimate moments with the passive acceptance of mild inconvenience. Undeterred, Reginald had 'soldiered on' in the RAF (Police Division) and gradually advanced to the rank of Group Captain. His marriage to Diane had settled into one of mutual respect and friendship. Although she was not of passionate disposition, Diane was a caring and devoted wife, admiring his diligence at work and steady promotion.

She had grown tolerant of his mild eccentricities. In fact, she was in most ways, an ideal wife.

Now that Reginald had left the service, they lived near a small Essex village, in a cul-de-sac where large, detached houses stand back from the lane which is shaded by established and mature elm trees. Last in this row of five impressive houses, 'The Elms', as it was originally named, is an L-shaped, mock-Tudor mansion, constructed in the 1930s, built of bright red brick, half-timbered and standing proud above its roofs are several prominent chimney stacks. It is impressive if you like that sort of thing. The house was bequeathed to Diane, who was the only child of an extremely successful grocer, who had expanded his business into a very profitable chain of stores. There is no gate at the entrance to the property, but two gate-posts mark the boundary and nailed to one of them is a plank of wood upon which, in a somewhat shaky hand, 'PLANTAGANET HOUSE' is painted. Reginald had worked on this sign one Saturday afternoon, after having imbibed one or two (possibly more) postprandial gins and tonic whilst Diane was out, attending a 'Bring and Buy' sale at the village church. He had renamed the house in this way for reasons best known only to himself and since that day Diane has never mentioned the sign; she is too polite. Neither has Reginald; he's forgotten all about it. Behind the posts, and the unhappy sign, there is a broad, gravelled drive leading to an impressive oak door set between the arms of the house. Next to the house is a garage spacious enough for two cars. The lane, an apology for a road, is lined with mature elm trees, and presents the visitor with a puzzle, yet unsolved, as it is called Oak Tree Lane. If their dinner guests are not as convivial as their hosts would like, it makes a good talking point. Plantagenet House is situated only two miles from Audley End railway station which is on the London to Cambridge line; thus, convenient for Young's work, now in Whitehall.

After the wide drive and grand oak door, any visitor entering is struck by quiet opulence. Upon parquet floors, thick-pile rugs in discreet colours, are thrown with apparent abandon. If the dining room is large, the withdrawing room (that is the name Diane insists upon) is enormous. The well-equipped kitchen is the domain of Mrs Braithwaite, a local widow, who lives-in since the death of her husband; she cooks and cleans for the Youngs and is 'their treasure'. Reginald is forbidden entry to the kitchen. A conservatory overlooks the garden, which is predominantly grassed but surrounded by well-established herbaceous borders and, in the summer, it is a riot of colour from delphiniums, lupins, begonias, roses, asters and many others the names of which Reginald has forgotten or more likely, never knew. At the end of the garden, willow trees hang branches into a stream of surprisingly fast current. Kingfishers dart between trees and herons stand in water patiently awaiting their next meal. Nestling among the trees is a small wooden hut with a wide window facing the stream This is Reginald's 'Space', ostensibly built for birdwatching, it is in fact his refuge, away from the cares of the world, the chatter of Diane and the orders of Mrs Braithwaite. They own not only the house and garden but a considerable number of shares in the grocery chain, from which they collect profits annually. The profits rise year on year and together with Reginald's pension and his remuneration from government work in Whitehall they have a comfortable life.

But Reginald's real pride and joy is his study. It is an attic that has been converted into a long room, the length of one side of the house. The ceiling rises to a sharp ridge and below which are wooden beams, painted black. Heavy curtains hang on either side of two Dormer windows. The walls are painted cream and there are numerous bookcases filled with books many of which Young has never read. There are several armchairs, and a large desk with a telephone and a laptop. The view from the windows is of the elm trees that line Oak Lane but, in the winter, when the leaves have dropped the surrounding countryside is his to survey.

The final pleasures in the Group Captain's rural idyll are his rounds of golf on a Sunday morning. Whilst his good lady wife worships in the village church, he plays nine holes at the local, private course. There he meets a small group of ex service personnel who play regularly together and whose company he thoroughly enjoys. Any lingering at the bar is frowned upon by Mrs Braithwaite who serves Sunday lunch at exactly 1:00 pm. He is never late for lunch.

Chapter 4

As Rachel and I made our way to Paris that fateful Friday evening in October, at Young's residence the elms separating it from Oak Lane had shed most of their leaves and the summer flowers in the garden of Plantagenet House had lost their self-confident colours. The house and garden were hunkering down for winter. Squirrels had become more adventurous; birds less common; the borders had been tidied and the grass given its final trim. Reginald Young sat in his bird-watching hut ('Reginald's Space') at the bottom of the garden and decided it was time to tell Diane more about his new post in Whitehall.

It was an interesting but hardly challenging appointment. He chaired a committee consisting of representatives from services protecting National security (ANCOM). It was a post commensurate with his rank, and as time passed, he had developed his small committee into, perhaps not an indispensable cog in the wheels of government, but a thoroughly useful and integrated group. He laid great stress on this last feature. Outwardly jovial, some might even say eccentric, he encouraged amiable goodwill within the committee, reasoning there would be greater inter-service cooperation and greater trust if this was achieved. However, unnoticed by those who did not take sufficient interest, he was in fact privately, a quiet, thoughtful and attentive listener. This had not gone unnoticed by those on the upper floors, one of whom, Lady Eleanor Kennan was his line manager and the person that recruited him four or five years previously. She was a slim, attractive middle-aged woman with short blonde hair and an easy smile. He knew she was the daughter of the late Earl of Kingsworth, sister to the present holder of the peerage. She told him, in an unguarded moment, that she had been married to a financier, Patrick Keenan, and that marriage had ended in divorce, but her settlement substantial. She now lived on her own, in a luxury flat in Belgravia. Reginald met her after each ANCOM to discuss the meeting where she took an interest in the proceedings but rarely commented on specific subjects. It was Reginald's belief that she simply underlined topics of current interest, then passed them on for government consideration and action if that were deemed necessary. He had no idea how she was regarded in the hierarchy but knew ANCOM was her brainchild. Otherwise, her position was rather ill-defined. How she had come to be appointed he knew not but presumed her previous experience had prepared her sufficiently well for her present position and she had been thoroughly vetted. Only once in the years he worked here had he seen her irritated or ill-tempered, and that was over an inconsequential matter he dismissed as trivial. Their working relationship was uncomplicated and strictly professional, therefore it was surprising, one morning in October, an invitation arrived via Clarissa, to join Lady Eleanor on the 3rd floor, for morning coffee. This was unusual but hardly of enormous importance, or so he judged. Young took the lift; even three floors are quite a climb for a man of his age even if he did play nine holes of golf most Sundays. Arriving on the 3rd floor he walked to Lady Eleanor's office, knocked on the door, waited and on invitation, entered. The room, smaller than Young's, was nevertheless lavishly furnished, appropriate to her title and position. As was her custom, Lady Eleanor sat in a comfortable chair, legs crossed, glasses perched on the end of her nose. What was not customary was that she had with her a gentleman of mature years who gazed fixedly at Young as he entered.

"Reginald," Lady Eleanor welcomed, "come in and join us." Turning to the gentleman sitting on her right she continued; "This is our liaison secretary and adviser to the Home Office, Sir Brendan Forsythe, to whom I relay the reports from the ANCOM." Sir Brendan unwound himself from his armchair, stood and advanced upon Young. Over six feet tall, his hair and moustache were white and these features together with a pinstriped suit and important tie gave him an air of seniority if not superiority. He reminded Young of Anthony Eden.

"Group Captain. It's a pleasure to meet you." His voice resonated from the depths of his chest. His accent pure public school.

"Reginald, take a seat please." Lady Eleanor indicated an armchair. The three sat around a low coffee table adorned with a tall ceramic vase filled with chrysanthemums. She leant forward and poured a cup of coffee for Reginald. "Milk? Sugar?"

"Milk only, thank you Eleanor." Young sat back and waited.

Sir Brendan spoke slowly and precisely. He came to the point immediately. Reginald was offered a new job, to run concurrently with his present position. The additional work would have appropriate financial recompense, of course.

The position required him to coordinate a series of symposia at a specially converted house in Hampstead. Between each sentence Sir Brendan inhaled through his upper incisors making a strange, whistling noise, quite unusual and disconcerting.

Ignoring that idiosyncrasy, Young listened attentively. This sounded the sort of position he had been hoping for over the last three or four years. Sir Brendan continued; each symposium would consist of a series of lectures and discussions between specially invited experts in that field. This would be meticulously recorded and reported to central government. Young need have no fears; he would be required only to coordinate, not participate in such esoteric discussions. By now, Lady Eleanor apparently had lost all interest in the proceedings. She said nothing, but inspected the ceiling with intense concentration, as if searching for a cobweb the housekeepers had missed; whether she found one or not was not declared.

His job would be to liaise with the leading specialist of each symposium, who would be an eminent person, highly qualified in each speciality. The series of lectures and discussions would last 2 to 7 days, separately each would consider matters of National Security and the most recent research; these developments would be precisely documented. Such subjects as biological warfare, atomic fission and fusion, satellite technology and cybernetics were some of the areas the symposia would cover. A leading specialist in each field had already been appointed and it was with this person that Young would liaise.

"Your role will be to ensure the smooth coordination of this enterprise; you will not be required to participate in such obscure subjects." Sir Brandan assured him and smiled politely. "Like me, I assume you would be out of your depth with the inevitable technical jargon. Each symposium will gather the most up-to-date advances on each subject and advise government of potential danger and appropriate defence."

Young was listening. This was exactly what he had been hoping for. More than excited, he was delighted. But there were several questions which he needed answering. For the moment, those could wait.

Sir Brendan finished with a warning. "The final word on all this is security. If you were to allow me only two words, they are—absolute secrecy." He looked at Young seriously. "The security measures taken at the Conference Centre are beyond my understanding, but I am assured that all in-coming and out-going information is in unbreakable code. The Conference Centre has access to the most sophisticated computers. All reports are marked 'Top Secret and Above'. Absolute confidentiality is essential, and the Centre had been converted with this in mind"

Sir Brendan sat back and waited for Young's reaction. Young wanted to know more of the managerial structure of this new enterprise and to whom he would be responsible. He was reassured those further discussions with him would be arranged before the Centre opened. As a start he would be introduced to the Centre's domestic manager, Ms Stacey Donato. Likely the first series of lectures and discussions would address the role of virology in biowarfare. Professor Linus Bhatti had been nominated as the leader and would be in touch with Young (if Young accepted the job) to arrange dates. More details would be supplied later.

Young spoke. "Thank you for this opportunity, Sir Brendan. I'll give it careful consideration. Will inform my wife of this new offer, but no details, in accordance with your wish for security."

"I think Sir Brendan, that I can assure you of the Group Captain's absolute discretion. You need not worry about security as far as Reginald is concerned." Lady Eleanor expressed her admiration for Reginald.

"That is good to hear," Sir Brendan murmured.

After Young left, Lady Eleanor and Sir Brendan poured themselves another cup of tea.

"Eleanor, I must tell you of my concerns. In truth, they're not my concerns as much as my Chief's worries." (Sir Brendan referred to the junior minister he served.) "My chief is yet youthful, inexperienced in the way of the world and possibly out of his depth in government. It's only his second term in Parliament and he has yet to find the boundaries of his abilities. Can I speak in confidence?"

"You can indeed Sir Brendan."

"To put it bluntly, he is touchy, by which I mean anxious. Must have gone to the wrong School, College, or even University. He's less confident with his colleagues than I would prefer. And now he's been landed with this 'Lawns' business, which incidentally, is costing a bomb. He is unsure whether the product will justify the expense. As I said, he is new to government and overwrought. I tell him that a warm drink of milk before bed is a marvellous panacea for a good night's sleep, but he is resistant to my advice."

"Oh dear." "Lady Eleanor sympathised, not so much with the junior minister, more the courier who carried the news i.e., the wise Sir Brendan, who she knew had other concerns of a delicate nature."

"So be it. Burdens we must bear, I'm afraid. That aside, this is Young, up to the job, is he? No background in the civil service, no training, not sure of the chap myself."

"Sir Brendan, I can assure you that he is perfect for the job. He's had many years in the service of the Royal Air Force and his record is not only unblemished but extremely complimentary. Confidentiality is not a problem to Reginald Young. I have every faith in him. And if I might add, his lack of knowledge of our working practices is an advantage, wouldn't you say?"

"Yes indeed, Eleanor. And I will pass on your excellent reference to my minister, of course."

Young descended to his office completely unaware of this discussion going on above. He was, however, well pleased. He would need to talk with Diane about this (in exceedingly general terms); the possibility of overnight stays in the Centre would need to be introduced cautiously.

So, on the following Sunday morning after an eventful nine holes of golf, Reginald sat in the garden of the beautifully appointed house awaiting Diane's return from her morning devotions. A delicious smell of lunch wafting from the kitchen and Reginald in his 'Space' watched the stream and sipped a gin and tonic. It was the time to tell Diane of his new job and to carefully broach the matter of staying overnight in the Conference Centre, if or when necessary.

Diane joined him, carrying a small, dry sherry as was her want after Church on Sunday morning.

"You're not cold, dear?" she asked. "Winter will be upon us soon. That's why I've put on this old coat, to sit out here. Mary will call us for lunch soon." She referred to Mrs Braithwaite, sighed and settled herself next to her husband on the bench in the 'observation post', as she would have it known.

"Church, ok?" Reginald is solicitous.

"Oh yes indeed, dear."

Young waited for a moment. "Good news at the office Diane." He said at last.

"Really? And what is that? I thought you had something on your mind yesterday evening."

"At last, been offered a job. Seems to carry some weight. Fellow from the Home Office came and offered it."

"From the Home Office? Goodness me, Reginald, and what did lovely Eleanor have to say about that? Is she going to lose you?"

"Didn't say much. It was her boss," he replied, "the job will be over and above the one I'm doing now. In effect, doing two jobs."

"How jolly. But isn't that rather a lot to take on? Don't overtax yourself."

"Appointment, Diane, is really one of management. Liaise with officials and experts who will meet regularly and advise the government."

"I see," Diane said thoughtfully, not seeing at all but not admitting it. "And these meetings will be in Whitehall, will they?"

"Partly. But partly elsewhere."

"I see." This time Diane began to understand the significance. There would be another venue, one she wasn't to be apprised of. Casually, she asked; "Will this other location require travelling, perhaps overnight stays, that sort of thing?"

"'Fraid so, dear. Can't be avoided. Nuisance, but there we are."

Diana was accustomed to Reginald's reticence about his work and admired his caution. Sometimes, however, it became a little difficult. "This management and these meetings, you have made your mind up, presumably."

"I have."

"And the numbers will be small? Selected scientists and government? Any Damsels of the Realm?"

"Not even a Dame in sight!"

"That's nice," murmured Diane, and sipped her sherry.

They turned their attention to the stream below the willows and took time over their drinks. Diane knew better than to ask anything more. Mary demanded their attendance at table. They stood and made their way to the house, hand in hand.

Chapter 5

In early October, Rachel and I travelled to Paris for a long weekend. The Eurostar left from St Pancras where, like seasoned travellers, we boarded the train in good time. For neither of us, was this the first time on the Eurostar. We climbed aboard and settled into corner seats facing one another. Our holiday had begun. The train travelled at a fair pace, and overhead lights came on approaching the Channel Tunnel. As we rattled into it, then through it, Rachel rummaged through her holdall and extracted a book. She settled further into her seat next to the window and kicking her shoes off, tucked her feet beneath her, as many young ladies do. Having made herself comfortable she lost herself in her book. I watched her and found the absorption in her book fascinating. I admired her assurance and was privileged she included me in her world of personal safety. She was totally unaware that I was watching. After I was to learn, the book was 'The Ascent of Man' by Jacob Bronowski, a popular book among scientists but not one I had expected Rachel to read on holiday.

The train clattered through the tunnel and abruptly we were out into the sunshine. France. Rachel looked out of the window, the unexpectedly brilliant light making her shield her eyes. After a glance, she looked across, smiled and returned to her reading. I watched the French countryside rush past; farmhouses, ploughed fields, rural roads, isolated churches, woods; a normal rural landscape but for the innumerable cemeteries and war memorials; terrible evidence of the fighting in Northern France during the two World Wars. Movements in the carriage announced the cold buffet and drink service. Rachel put her book down and we both chose red wine. The interruption allowed me to say what was on my mind. The conversation that followed changed my perception of Rachel, increasing my admiration.

"I've noticed the huge number of cemeteries and war memorials we've passed. An enormous loss of life." I began.

I'm not sure what I expected in return or even if she would reply at all. In any case, she gave the matter some consideration, putting her elbows on the table between us and resting her head on her clenched fists, all the while gazing out of the window. She was somewhere else.

"Without a doubt. But I've also seen plenty of death and deprivation in Africa." (So that's where she had been.) "There I saw plenty of deaths from infections for which no treatments were available. Luckily, where I worked was relatively free from the lethal Ebola; but the population was at risk from many other infections. There are vaccines now that will safeguard the communities against some infections but few available to the rural communities outside the main cities."

"Whereabouts in Africa, were you?"

"Mostly Tanzania, where infections and infestations are common in rural districts. The Western World doesn't seem to extend largesse that far. And it is not just infections; the poverty can be heart-breaking. I visited Kenya on one or two occasions and, can you believe that the poorest live on rubbish dumps and eat what they can scavenge?"

"When was this? What were you doing in Africa?" She'd never mentioned this before.

"Working for a charity attached to UNICEF about five years ago. The whole experience was soul-destroying." Now I understood the clenched fists. She was angry and as well as her fists, her lips were pressed to a thin line.

"I have never been to Africa, but I accept what you say. I was, in fact, thinking of the two world wars and the death toll. From my limited knowledge of history, wars have been fought almost continuously since recording began and for probably a lot longer than that."

"You mean war is inevitable. I might be able to agree with that. But nations ignoring famine and death in huge parts of the world is unforgivable. It amounts to genocide and none of us would subscribe to that, surely?"

"I agree about that, wholeheartedly. But if we think about war for a moment, surely, we are slowly learning. For example, I know a young chap in college whose grandfather was killed at Passchendaele. His father was a conscientious objector in the Second World War; and now this chap buys a white poppy for November the 11th. That's some sort of progress, isn't it?" It was a small example but made a point, I hoped.

"Individuals might learn to hate war," she said, "but over the last fifty years we've had Russia and the Cold War, the Cuban crisis, Vietnam and the atrocities there, now Putin and a different threat; China is rattling sabres at Taiwan, and most other countries, Trump is like a bull in a China shop! Afghanistan seems to be no less of a threat than it was 10 or 20 years ago. The Middle East is a tangle of an Islamic beliefs and interference from 'the great' Nations of Russia and America." She drank her wine and continued to gaze out of the window. Such seriousness on our holiday seemed misplaced and I regretted opening my mouth. "My memories of African poverty, neglect and fear have remained with me as vivid as if it were yesterday. That's the New War." This was a whole new Rachel's that I hadn't, up to now, appreciated.

Further along the carriage someone dropped a lunch tray and some glasses. Rachel sat up and suddenly said: "When we're in Paris I want to go to Notre-Dame."

"Good." I agreed; we were back in holiday mode. I'd learnt more about her. She was not only a passionate believer in equality, but as a Christian the belief was intensified. Or was it the other way round? Either way, it was obviously central to her outlook. Would this intrude into our relationship? Was it an unwelcome visitor? No. It may have taken me some time to recognise its value, but eventually I would come to recognise it for what it was, crucial.

The snack and drinks over, she went back to her book. I watched France go by and thought about the things she had said. The rest of the journey passed in silence. Soon we were pulling into Gare du Nord. We stepped onto the platform carrying two small cases and headed for the taxis. Rachel, in fluent French, asked the driver for our hotel and after a short journey jumped out and paid the driver. I noted her ease with the French language but thought nothing of it. She'd been here before. She was bright. So what?

The tourist hotel was in a narrow side street off the Boulevard de Magenta. It was sandwiched between high houses, the ground floor front rather like a shop window, with at least seven narrow stories above. Opposite stood a row of motorcycles, mostly Vespas and Lambrettas and further down the one-way street, neatly parked cars lined both sides. In my eyes, it was all very French. We signed the register, and a young man carried our cases up to the room. Rachel thanked him, once again in flawless French (as far as I could tell!). I don't think I'd spoken a single word of French since we got off the train. It didn't matter, Rachel spoke the language quickly and without effort. The room (I think on the

4th floor) was perfect. Remarkably quiet, it had a writing desk, wardrobe, two armchairs and a double bed with sheets primly tight and resplendently white. French windows opened onto a narrow balcony from which we had a view of the street and the roofs opposite. A door led to the loo and shower. What more did we need? It was warm(ish) and peaceful. The evening stretched ahead, and we could explore, do what we liked; of course, we ended up in a restaurant just around the corner on the Boulevard de Magenta where the food and wine was as good as we expected, and the service more polite than I expected. But then, Rachel had done the talking! Unsaid, we agreed this was our restaurant and this is where we would eat every evening. Perhaps it's the need for familiar surroundings but I think everybody does this on holiday; choose a convenient restaurant which serves good food and stick with it. We sauntered to the hotel and went to bed early, tired, relaxed and comfortable with each other. Lovemaking was exactly that—loving. Memorable and mutually satisfying. Sleep was welcome, contented and restful. It had been a long day.

I woke with a start. A tentative exploration of the bed beside me confirmed I was alone. Opening my eyes slowly I realised the room was in semi-darkness. Rachel was standing naked with her arms wrapped around her looking out of the window. Beyond her I could see the sky, deep blue but with a glimmer of orange-yellow light just visible above the Parisian rooftop horizon. She was watching the dawn.

"Aren't you cold?" I spoke quietly.

She turned, smiled and without a word came back to bed. We hugged and dozed intermittently, warm and very comfortable, until the aroma of percolating coffee from many floors below us became irresistible.

We showered, dressed and went down.

Breakfast was laid out in the 'cellar', a room with brick walls and arched ceiling painted uniformly pale cream and furnished with separate, small tables on which were laid red and white tablecloths. There were baguettes, cheeses, jams, cold meat slices, fruit and coffee on a central table for self-service. Other visitors murmured quietly. Time to explore. We'd both been to the French capital before, but some places had to be visited, or revisited.

We walked at a leisurely pace to the Isle de la Cite and Notre Dame, stopping at a cafe with tables on the pavement for another coffee.

Rachel put her hands behind her neck, arched her back and tilted her face up to the sun. Even in October it was warm. "That's good. I feel so relaxed." She continued thoughtfully; "I've always felt (frown, searching for the word) alone—no, 'detached'. Yes 'detached', that's better. It was the same even as a child. As far back as that. I've always felt OK in myself but at the same time remote from others. Does that make sense?"

"I think so," I replied. "You've always given the appearance of being self-assured."

"Yes, I've worked hard on that. You know, when I was child, we lived near Aylesbury, a village. There was a huge mental hospital, St John's I seem to remember, and Mum worked there when Dad was away."

"Away?"

"I was young" she went on, "but there were times, I think I remember, he wasn't around. And when he was around Mum didn't like him very much."

"Near Aylesbury?" I raised my eyebrows.

"No. No." She laughed, "He wasn't a Great Train Robber. That was before our time." Again, she frowned. "Whenever he was away, we were always hungry, I remember; always looking out for ourselves. Then Mum and I moved, I don't know why, but it was quite sudden. That was when my school was in a town called Thame, I think. I don't know why we moved there."

"But your mother died young, didn't she?"

"Yes. When I was twelve, I think. I had to go and live with her sister, and my cousins in Southall. London, you know. There was never much money there either, but what I do remember is going to the Borough Market for chips as a treat. The other kids at school were OK, or some of them anyway. All things considered, actually, I did quite well at school, picked up languages quite quickly"

"Your French is good."

"Since school I've expanded on that. I get by in German and Italian, a bit of Spanish. Common Market, thought they might be useful."

I tried to get my head round the change from her childhood to her present assured self, but the jump was too great for me.

"You've made up ground quickly."

"Things weren't all that bad."

I said nothing. Time ticked on, and we had some way to go yet. Rachel pulled out a street map that she always carried. After a while, I said, "Shall we make a move?"

"Right you are," she said, "but on the way back let's make a detour and take a quick look at a garden which is not far from here. Look; 'Anne Frank Memorial Garden'. I'd like to look at that. Shouldn't take long."

We got to our feet and continued. Given the circumstances of her childhood, getting an education and now working for the government needed considerable determination and courage. She was perceptive, quick and outwardly self-confident, and I could now add, determined.

The Notre-Dame standing on the island in the Seine was a breath-taking sight, even so soon after the fire in April. The scaffolding around the roof only made the huge structure of the building more impressive; it didn't appear like a burnt shell but a defiant monument waiting to resume leadership again. Rachel was disappointed but it had been expected. We crossed from the island and walked through the Latin Quarter to a beautiful old parish church on the Boulevard Saint-Germain, the church of Saint-Germain-des-Pres. Inside, the murmur of prayers and whispered conversations magnified the dignity of worship. Even I, a non-Christian, could appreciate that reverence. Rachel sat in a pew, head bowed, deeply absorbed, perhaps praying. I saw for the first time how strong her faith was, and how essential. I didn't interrupt. As I turned away to inspect the stained-glass windows, I bumped into a fellow visitor and apologised for my clumsy behaviour. It was only after a few moments that it occurred to me that I'd seen him before. On the train? In the hotel? In the cafe? I couldn't place him. I dismissed the incident. We left the church and doubled back to the Left Bank of the Seine.

As the parish church had been grand and quiet, the Left Bank was commotion, noise and colour. Rachel took my arm as we threaded our way between the sightseers, looking at the artwork exhibited. Eclectic was the word. Rachel took as much interest in the art as I had been impressed by the church. At last, we got to the Musee d'Orsay where we found the Monets, Renoirs, and Van Goghs. Rachel drew my attention to the time.

The Latin Quarter stretches back from the Seine, a maze of narrow streets leading eventually to boulevards and avenues. What we were after was a small cafe, preferably patronised by locals, where we were sure to get a table on the narrow pavement, and ordered. We were not disappointed. There was no reason to rush. I wondered idly if Andre Breton had started the surrealist movement in this very street. Perhaps. We paid and set off for the hotel. As we did so, I noticed a man behind a Le Monde newspaper in a neighbouring cafe. His coffee looked to have gone cold.

We visited The Anne Frank Memorial Garden on the return walk to the hotel. (I was surprised to see a children's playground in one corner, although perhaps I shouldn't have been.) We sat for a while; no words were necessary. Eventually, we got back to the hotel, organised ourselves and later that evening went for a meal in our restaurant. Tomorrow could take care of itself.

Tomorrow did. Late breakfast, risk the Metro to St Paul station, up to the pavements and hours in Paris flea markets. It's almost impossible to describe the chaos of buying and selling, so many jostling customers around so many gesticulating vendors. So much shouting—and in an unfamiliar language. But marvellous. We had come to buy a small reminder of Paris. Not too big, not too small, not too ornate, not too insignificant. You've done it yourself many times, so you know what it's like. I've never picked up, put down, held up to the light, looked for cracks, grimaced at, and smiled at so many ornaments before. We laughed, frowned, agreed and disagreed. In the end, a modest vase of cloudy blue glass was chosen. Quite valueless, I'm sure, but we'd agreed at last.

Tired, we left. What, at the time, we didn't know was that the following day (a Sunday as it so happened) a meeting here in Paris would have repercussions for us, and possibly for many others, over the years that followed.

The next day, Sunday, we got up late and ate a leisurely breakfast in the cellar. Back at the room we opened the shutters and stood on the narrow balcony overlooking the street below. Not much moved. A cat; a couple of wary pigeons; a chap with a paper tucked under his arm and holding a baguette. On the balcony opposite stood a long, thin and very malnourished fuchsia perched in a pot that was too small for the job. It was the kind of lazy morning that one notices such things. After a while, we went inside, then decided to walk to the Metro and make our way to Anvers Station. Having arrived there, we climbed into the autumn sunshine.

The Sacre Coeur towered above us, domed, white and gloriously mystical. We turned and climbed the flight of steps in front of us.

*** *** ***

After Rachel and I struggled on the steps with increasing breathlessness, we finally saw the magnificent entrance to the Sacre Coeur. We could hear singing from within and could see internal lights through the windows despite the bright sunshine. A service in progress, precluded entry, so we strolled into Montmartre village. The first street was busy; bookshops, galleries, cafes and so on; artists stood chatting waiting for customers; some worked on sketches or portraits. Everywhere was crowded with sightseers and those interested in buying art. We made our way to the far end of the street, and just before it merged into the Artists' Square, we noticed a young chap displaying works from his portfolio. Why we did it I'll never know, but we crossed the street to have a look.

Did Rachel hesitate? I'm not entirely sure. Certainly not enough to stop us casting an eye on the work, but enough for me to notice. Heads together, we were going through his portfolio, when a chap beside me unexpectedly shouted:

"Bugger me! What are you doing here?"

Big, cheerful, full of good humour, Alex Dowson (for that's who it was) hadn't changed a bit. He clapped me on the back, laughed and made it clear he was delighted to see me (and, as it transpired, Rachel.)

"I've just bought some of this chap's work; they're not bad as far as I can see. But as you know I'm no expert." He looked beyond me to Rachel. "Well, I'll be buggered again! Is it really you? Rachel of Mombasa?" He looked genuinely surprised.

"Do you two know each other?" I asked, a rather stupid question given the circumstances. They both nodded.

"Absolutely amazing," cried Alex. "We've not seen each other since Oxford, and damn it we meet each other in Montmartre. Not only that but with the delectable…"

"Rachel," she filled in his memory.

"Right, Rachel! Sorry. Memory, always lousy with names."

"O, K. for everything else! Damn it, you got a first." I couldn't resist it.

"I don't know about you two," he went on. "But I'm famished. What do you say to a plate of something and something else to wash it down? Tell me what's been going off."

And that's exactly how it happened. As quickly as that.

I knew that Rachel had worked for a charity in Tanzania some 5 years previously. What I didn't know was that coincidentally Alex was on a sabbatical year in Africa, and they had met by accident in a beach hotel on a weekend they were both free, in Mombasa, over the border in Kenya. Apparently, although they had been in Tanzania at the same time they had not met there. As we ate lunch and washed it down(!) Rachel learned that Alex and I had been on the same staircase in college; when he graduated, he specialised in biochemical research, and I had followed a career in molecular biology and teaching in college. We had been the best of friends whilst we were undergraduates, but as one does, had lost touch afterwards. It was terrific to see him again after such a long time and we briefly recounted our careers, although not in detail. Then Rachel and he swapped stories about Africa. There was much laughter, and as far as I could detect, no unease. More than a couple of hours passed before we realised the time, and we decided to make a move. It was then that Alex fished out of his backpack the paintings that he had bought and taking one out of the cardboard cylinder said.

"I bought four or five." He leant towards Rachel, "I'd like you to have this one. It looks to me like a 'dream' and that would be fitting for you." (An ambiguous statement if ever I've heard one.) Rachel's protestations were waved away, and he went on, "We'll all be seeing each other again, I'm sure, (and with a raised eyebrow) that is, if you can put up with this character (that was me) for any length of time." After more protests from Rachel, she finally agreed to take the painting. We shook hands, he kissed Rachel on the cheek. And with that, he was gone.

That evening Rachel and I looked at 'The Dream' and agreed that we liked it. A jug with two or three glasses, a handkerchief and paintbrush in the foreground, in the background vague representations of flowers, possibly roses; all in mixed media. There's the suggestion of a dream. It would be another reminder of Paris, together with our vase. Our weekend in Paris had been a sound idea; we were closer, of that there was no doubt, although it remained unsaid. We packed for the morning departure home and strolled to 'our restaurant' for the last time.

In London, we parted and returned to our semi-separate lives. However, our joint future was now a matter of logistics more than anything else. And they were not insurmountable. Life, for me at least, was promising.

*** *** ***

A week after we returned, I received a letter in my college pigeonhole. At the time, it seemed quite an ordinary letter one would expect from an old friend, although I was surprised how quickly it had been written after our chance meeting. Later I would find out that it was a prelude to something I had not expected. Written in his usual excitable style, I reproduce it below, and you can read it for yourself:

Fenland Centre
Wednesday
Oct 2019

Francophiles Unite!
What an amazing coincidence, to meet in Paris, and of all places in Montmartre—even looking at the same bloke's work! After all this time, it must be 5 to 10 years anyway. I'm so glad we met up and bugger the circumstances! And what about that young lady accompanying you? And damn me if I didn't know her already. I hope you didn't mind that I gave her the painting, I thought it suited her perfectly. The others I bought I'm going to keep. And that afternoon! Sitting at a little cafe and sipping cold wine in the warm sunshine. What could have been better? (What was the place called? Francoeur? Cafe de Francoeur? Something like that.) You say you're still in Oxford. I'll come up and see you one of these fine days (and lovely Rachel as well.) It would be good to see the old place again. What's the Eastgate like these days? The Turl? The Bird and Baby? Have they changed much? I miss them, you know. Drop you a note later in the year and perhaps we can meet up; now I'm busy with one thing and another—expect you are as well but look forward to seeing you again.

Best wishes,
Alex.

Apart from the brief and incomplete address, I found nothing remarkable about the letter; and more, it was typical of his rushed style; when I showed it to Rachel she merely shrugged, then said it would be nice to thank him properly for her painting.

I dropped the note on my desk at the flat and got on with my life giving it not another thought. I didn't hear more from him for at least a month—yes, it would have been before the Covid-19 outbreak in China—he wrote saying he was coming to Oxford in late November, early December, any chance of digs? This time there was a mobile telephone number.

Chapter 6

Reginald Young, Group Captain (retd.), strode down Whitehall on a cold November morning, turned sharply into his place of work at precisely 10 am. and climbed the steps. The policeman on duty touched his helmet with respect. The door was opened for him, he entered the ill-shaped reception area and came to an abrupt halt. He was astonished to see his receptionist, Clarissa, who was not normally given to sudden movement either of body or mind, standing up behind her desk and pointing a pencil at him in what he could only assume to be an agitated state. So unusual was her behaviour that it could only be explained by reaction to an unforeseen occurrence of some magnitude; either that or a mental breakdown.

"Oh, Reggie, I thought you weren't coming in." Her voice was more urgent than her usual estuary drawl.

"Not coming in?" He was puzzled. "What do you mean, 'not coming in'?"

"Well, it is 10:00 am."

"Always come in at 10:00 am." He was irritated. What on earth was wrong with the girl?

"Sir Brendan Forsythe is in your office waiting. He's brought his secretary or is it the secretary to the joint committee(?) or is it just secretary(?), or come to think of it, is he the secretary?"

"Good God!" yelped Young, "how many secretaries are here?"

"Just the one." Clarissa reclaimed her seat, much relieved at Young's arrival. "They're all the same person. Just different titles. And I'm not sure which one he or they are today. You know that you're to be shown some Conference Centre or other this morning? Well, he's here to take you."

"Yes. So?"

"I thought you had forgotten."

"Well, hadn't and here I am. So, he's here, is he? Like a chap to be punctual. Meeting booked for 10:15 am wasn't it?"

"Yes. Yes, but he's here already."

"Given him some tea or coffee or something, have you?"

"Of course. Reggie, they're in your office." Clarissa had recovered her composure.

"Good. Must get on, then." And a little unnecessarily; "Know the way." Young marched past the Internal Security Guard and down the corridor to his office, opened the door and went in. This secretary sat in HIS chair behind HIS desk.

"Who are you?" snapped Young by way of reproof, at the same time depositing his umbrella, coat and hat in the hat stand with unnecessary clatter. "And whoever you are, you're early."

The Secretary stood and introduced himself. "Sinclair Cavendish, sir." He was a tall, gentleman, sallow of complexion seemingly afflicted with stomach pain. He was sucking an antacid tablet. He seemed nervous. It was Young's instant assessment that this chap had been promoted well above his intellectual competence.

Sinclair almost whispered. "You're late, sir." He was defensive.

"Rubbish! You're early."

It was at this juncture that Young saw the languid figure of Sir Brendan Forsythe unfold from the depths of an armchair. Young immediately readjusted his manner.

"Ah, Sir Brendan," he declared. "Good morning. Didn't expect your good self." The two shook hands and Sir Brendan returned to his chair and Young took the one adjacent. From behind Young's desk, Cavendish watched the scene unfold with his customary deference.

Sir Brendan addressed the reason for his visit. "As I said to you previously, Young, I want you to visit the Conference Centre and see for yourself the layout of the place, that sort of thing. At the same time, you can take the opportunity to meet the Designated Manager and some of her staff. With that in mind, I've asked Cavendish here, to accompany you to the centre and introduce you. Are you comfortable with that?"

"Oh yes, Sir Brendan. And this morning is a perfect time." Young was accommodating.

"Good. That's settled." Sir Brendan stood and they shook hands again. "Before I go, Group Captain, I want to reiterate the need for absolute confidentiality with regards to this business. It is of vital importance to HMG." Young nodded vigorously.

Sir Brendan left.

Reginald turned his attention to Cavendish. He eyed him with some misgiving. Cavendish visibly wilted.

"Ok Cavendish. When shall we go?"

"At your convenience, sir."

"Well, convenience is now. Prompt. Let's move. This place, conference centre, is it? In London presumably."

"Yes sir. In Hampstead. It's a centre where they will hold several symposia." Cavendish panicked. "Symposia is the plural of Symposium, is it not?"

"Probably." Young was non-committal.

"I think so."

"Does it matter?"

"Probably not." Sinclair mumbled.

What a start, thought Young.

As they walked along the corridor to Reception, Young noticed that although of nervous disposition, Cavendish nevertheless was tall, broad shouldered and carried some muscle.

"Play rugby, d'you?" Young asked.

"Oh yes sir. Second row. Love the game."

Young approved. This chap had gone up in his estimation. Perhaps even Clarissa would take note. They passed her desk; "Just on our way out, Clarissa."

"I can see that, Reggie."

They opened the door, walked down steps and climbed into the chauffeured car. No doubt loaned by Sir Brendan.

On the journey through Central London to Hampstead, Young was told more of their destination. It was a large house (in fact a listed building) with facilities for conferences, space for accommodation and hotel-like catering services, and supportive communication/secretarial staff. He would be given more precise details by the 'Designated Manager' when they got there. Young sat back. This was more his style.

"Like the place, do you?" Reginald enquired of Cavendish.

"Will you, sir, is more to the point, isn't it?"

That seemed to close that line of conversation.

Arriving on a tree-lined road in Hampstead, Sinclair instructed the driver to pull up and wait for him here. They stepped out onto the pavement and walked along another street before Sinclair suddenly darted into a driveway that led to a very large house with a car parking area hidden behind tall hedges. Young followed.

"Carefully does it," Sinclair confided mysteriously.

"Probably," replied Young, having no idea at all what he was on about.

As they approached the entrance, a heavy door swung open and a large man, with a regimental haircut, welcomed them with a smile.

"Group Captain Young and Mr Cavendish? I was advised that you were coming at this time and of course I recognised you, Mr Cavendish, on the CCTV." He nodded to Sinclair before holding the door open, "If I might have sight of your passes, and I'm sorry but any metallic objects; change, pens, watches…Security is tight, I'm afraid. The name is Cobb, gentlemen." *Every inch the ex-W.O.,* Young thought. Passes having been inspected, metallic objects handed over for safekeeping, Cobb retired to his office and stood behind a row of television screens that presumably were monitoring the house and gardens. He spoke quietly into a microphone then looked up.

"Ms Donato will be with you immediately."

The door leading to the rest of the house opened immediately! *(Had the woman been lying in wait?* Young wondered) and Ms Donato stood there, a handsome and confident lady of perhaps 6-ft, middle-aged dressed in an extremely smart tailored, dark grey suit. Rose in her buttonhole. Her hand was extended in welcome.

"Stacey Donato, Manager." Her diction was clipped and precise. "Welcome again, Mr Cavendish, we know each other already, of course." Then turning to Young said, "You must be Group Captain Young," all the while giving him the full-frontal smile.

"It is," Young replied. "Better known as Reggie."

"Quite so," she said, and discreetly but efficiently appraised him. "Mr Cavendish, if you have safely delivered our esteemed Group Captain…" the rest of the sentence went unsaid.

"Yes. I'll be on my way." Cavendish recovered his belongings, backed out of the door which was closed behind him and presumably was driven back to Whitehall.

"Come in. Come in, do." Ms Donato led the way into the house. The Group Captain followed obediently.

Ms Donato and Group Captain Young entered a spacious and airy lounge; Young estimated it stretched the width of the house. There were three tiny pictures in remarkably large mounts and frames. The subject matter was indistinct at this distance but possibly brown leaves. At best 'art decorative', certainly not Art Decor or anything memorable. Several French doors overlooked two terraces, one below the other and beyond, an extensive sunken garden of paths and lawns; trees and shrubs surrounded the lawns. These areas of well-kept grass gave the place its name: "The Lawns." As Ms Donato called him across the lounge to inspect a plan of the four floors of the house, pinned to a notice board, he saw a small bar tucked in a corner. This was something he would not normally miss. It was shut for the moment.

"As well as the four floors above ground," Ms Donato explained, "we have two extensive underground rooms, both fully fitted for lectures and discussions, and all the more secure for being concealed."

They sauntered casually to one of the open French doors which led onto the terraces. They stood together, quietly, admiring the gardens.

"If I might explain my role here," Ms Donato began, "perhaps that will add to what you already know of us."

Young was not a man easily intimidated, but there was something of the headmistress about this Ms Donato; a mixture of intelligence, intolerance and femininity that might be a challenge. But he could work on that later.

"I am the administrator of this government facility. It is my job to welcome all our visitors and ensure a comfortable 2 or 3 days, or longer, stay. We provide full secretarial and computer services as necessary and each of the rooms below ground floor is equipped for lectures, films, slides, discussions etcetera. The government has set up a new specialist joint advisory committee which classifies information from foreign sources on agencies or agents that may endanger this country. This type of information is then divided into categories, and each will be examined, in depth, by specialist groups invited to the Symposia here. After due deliberation, each group is expected to submit a comprehensive Report on significance and analysis of each subject, and if appropriate suggest action. This Report will be sent to Central Government." Ms Donato paused. Whether she was expecting Young to comment or just catching her breath, Young was unsure. But before he could decide, she continued; "I believe that you will arrange the smooth running of our Symposia." Before Young could reply, she went on; "Each conference is completely autonomous; there is no communication between members of different symposia. Further, communication in and out of this Conference Centre is prohibited but if anyone needs to telephone urgently that can be arranged through secretarial staff or myself. We pride ourselves that this Conference Centre is totally secure from electronic and auditory surveillance. It's important therefore that mobile phones, metallic items and computer devices are left with Cobb (or his deputy) at the entrance, on arrival. All visitors will be expected to sign the Official Secrets Act."

Young lent back against an armchair, folded his arms across his chest, and frowned. This was his 'I'm in deep thinking' position, which rarely fooled anyone but was a useful way of giving him time to arrange his thoughts. All at once, as if he had suddenly made up his mind, he pushed himself upright away from the chair and looked straight at Ms Donato.

"That's clear, thank you. You have made my mind up for me. I will certainly participate in helping to make these Symposia as comfortable as possible." (He'd made his mind up a long time ago anyway, and likely Ms Donato knew that. Didn't do any harm to show a little subservience, though.)

"Yes," she said, but nothing else.

They looked at one another. Then quite abruptly Ms Donato smiled (with professional propriety of course,) waved her arm vaguely towards the garden and suggested a stroll.

Young was acutely aware of her presence; not necessarily her attraction, although that no doubt came into it, but her cool efficiency and firmness. She seemed committed to this Conference Centre; determined it should run efficiently. *Was this her first post? Is there more going on here? Does she live in?* Young's mind ran on.

From the terraces, steps and gravel pathways led to the sunken lawns. As they sauntered towards the end of the garden Young idly kicked a pebble and immediately regretted such flippancy. The path led to a secluded arbour where a wooden bench nestled among bushes. A sharp shower in the night had left the trees dripping; there was the smell of damp earth and cut grass; the sound of traffic in the far distance. Young gallantly produced a clean white handkerchief and with a flourish wiped the seat of the bench. Ms Donato didn't smile but sat. There was no small talk.

"I like the place immensely," Young said eventually. "Completely separate groups working here but not overlapping makes great sense to me. And from what you say the support staff is more than adequate."

"Thank you. Can we look forward to your participation?"

"Indeed, you can." Young hoped he hadn't sounded too enthusiastic.

Momentarily she paused and brushing an invisible speck of dust from her skirt said, "It's unusual to have an officer from your service here."

"Is it?" Young felt no need to elaborate.

After a while, they stood, walked back to the house. Young took a final look round the lounge but for some reason he didn't ask to see the lecture rooms nor the secretarial department. The guest rooms and kitchens didn't interest him. He thanked Ms Donato profusely and assured her that he would be looking forward to his next visit and the program of Symposia. They shook hands and Young made his way back to Whitehall. His property was returned to him by the ever-watchful Cobb who also called a taxi. Returning to Whitehall, Young was satisfied with his first visit to 'The Lawns'. A more thorough inspection could wait. Arriving at Whitehall he paid the taxi but did not ask for a receipt.

Once back in his office, Young found a note from Clarissa.

1. ANCOM next week. Have contacted Samara, Nigel, Konrad and Phillipson. Do you want Special Branch and Counter-Terrorist Branch?
2. Mrs Young is in town. Lunch usual place? 1 pm.

Clarissa.

*** *** ***

Young read the note and confirmed with Clarissa that Special Branch and Counter-Terrorist Branch should be invited to the next ANCOM. He sat back and gazed at his seascape above the door. There was danger in the picture, those mountainous waves and thunderous clouds. But the ships were strong. Depending on his mood, those waves were threatening, or the ships were strong enough to reach port safely. Today it was neither one nor the other! Or more truthfully, he couldn't make his mind up which was more likely. He brought himself back to this afternoon. ANCOM next week; Clarissa's got that under control. Stacey Donato: need to make an appointment, look at the place more comprehensively. That could wait. Some things, however, needed immediate attention. He lifted the black phone.

"Clarissa. Call me a black cab for 12:30 pm, please, and reserve a place at the usual restaurant."

By 12:45 pm, they were in one of Diane's favourite restaurants. On a narrow street off Millbank, it was a private dining club on the top floor of a multi occupied building. The restaurant was open to elected members only; Group Captain and Mrs Young were among the elected members. Cosy, oak-beamed, and with subdued lighting the room was hushed. The view of the Thames and the roofs across the river were adequate, nothing more. There were few members dining today. The tables were impeccably laid, the service deferential yet personal. They ordered salmon 'for the lady', fillet steak ("The chef knows how I like it cooked." "Of course, sir.") 'For the gentleman'. Young reluctantly declined a glass of wine opting instead for chilled water. Diane was on the way to one of London's teaching hospitals to undertake a voluntary shift in the gift shop, a task in which she took pride, and one that Young found curiously reassuring. She was looking forward to watching the nurses coming and going off duty, possibly a word or two with a passing consultant—and, of course, smiling with relatives, visitors and now and again patients. She took a glass of white wine. The meal was agreeable, the conversation unimportant, the lunchtime amiable. Outside the traffic and pedestrians went about their business. Reginald and Diane, two taxis having been called for them, went their separate ways.

In his office by 2:30 pm, Young felt satisfactorily replete; looking at the note Clarissa had given him before lunch, he applied himself to matters in hand. He reached for the phone:

"Clarissa, any messages?"

"You've been asked to discuss a Professor Bhatti. 3:00 pm. Upstairs. Third floor. Lady Ellie's office."

"You'll be overheard one of these fine days, Clarissa," Young admonished.

Young looked at his watch. He had time to ring 'The Lawns'.

"Clarissa, get hold of Ms Donato, will you?"

"Who?"

"Ms Donato."

"Who's she?"

Damn it, he hadn't had chance to tell Clarissa about the Centre yet.

"Went to a conference centre this morning with that chap Cavendish. Donato's the woman who runs the place. Stacey Donata."

"Oh, is that the woman at 'The Lawns'? Good job Sinclair left the number for it, wasn't it?"

Young paused for a moment. So, it was 'Sinclair' was it? Interesting.

"Get the number for me, will you Clarissa?"

The phone went silent. It was quiet in the office whilst he waited for the call. After a short delay, the black phone rang.

"Your call Reggie." Clarissa put him through.

Young listened. Nothing.

"Young here," he snapped.

"Ah, Group Captain, how pleasant to hear from you." The confident voice of Ms Donato.

"Ringing to thank you. Meeting this morning." Young explained, rather surprised by Ms Donato's warm welcome.

"I'm so pleased you rang, Group Captain. There's a matter I neglected to mention this morning," Ms Donato apologised. "I hope you will forgive me. My personal secretary will deal with all bookings, invitations, residential matters, travelling expenses, general inquiries etc. for your guests. That side of things. Just ring our number and ask for extension 17. Most probably we will ring you back. Secure line, you understand."

"Right." Young wrote down 17. "And your secretary's name?"

"Harold."

With that, she put the phone down. Young swallowed, looked at the receiver and replaced it slowly. Not the best of afternoons; Clarissa in a mood; Donato possibly over-friendly; and now having to deal with 'a Harold'. And on top of all that Lady Eleanor summoning him. He made his way upstairs.

Young tapped on Lady Eleanor's door, opened it and went in. "Good afternoon, madam." As was her custom, Lady Eleanor sat in a comfortable armchair. She held a cup of tea in one hand and a matching saucer in the other. On the low table before her stood the vase, this time displaying a dozen or so roses.

"Group captain," her voice was cordial, her manner unhurried. "Please, come in and take a seat." She gestured to the silver teapot and bone-China tea service on the table. "Help yourself."

Young sat, leant forwards and poured himself tea, added milk, sat back and waited. The formality of 'Madam' over he could call her Eleanor from now on.

"You're well?" she inquired, gently. "You and your good lady wife. I do hope so."

"Thank you, Eleanor, we are both quite well." Young's bearing had changed. From the affable and cheerful individual downstairs, he had become the efficient, responsive and alert Group Captain here.

"Good." Lady Eleanor placed her cup and saucer on the table before her. "Your reconnaissance at The Lawns this morning, how did it go?"

"Interesting, it was merely a meeting to introduce myself. That's all."

Young was unsure where this was going. His mind darted from one possibility to another; not all pleasant, indeed some small indiscretion might prove to be quite awkward. He waited. "There would seem to be considerable turmoil in the world of politics now. Nothing new there." She poured herself another cup of tea, milk, no sugar; then continued. "We don't have to worry ourselves, you and I, about such esoteric matters. However, shifting allegiances have become somewhat tortuous, and tedious"

"Anything of immediate concern?" Young was relieved the matters were of international policy and not one of departmental interpersonal relationships.

"Put it this way," Lady Eleanor spoke thoughtfully. "Of late our allies across the Atlantic have been getting on well with our Russian (dare I say it?) friends, ignoring of course, the unfortunate occurrences in Salisbury. Russia, and by inference, I mean Putin, claims their Federation wants only sovereignty, prosperity, independence and safety. Quite how these tally with their annexation of the Crimea in 2014 and the unrest with their neighbours, particularly the Ukraine, is beyond me. However, the government is still aware of the increasing threat from the East, perhaps even a resurgence of the Cold War, God forbid! The Americans and Russians are sharing information on space and space development and they're even jointly manning the International Space Station. Nearly in bed together." The Group Captain smiled coyly, as was appropriate.

She went on; "Russia has disavowed communism, so we are told, therefore all is well. But China has not. And there lies the rub. As I say, all this is not our direct concern, but changing loyalties, they impinge upon my equilibrium and sometimes sleep, something I hold precious. Government is concerned that there is mounting menace, possibly an alliance between Russia and China' although there is sufficient threat from each of them to worry us, never mind a joint alliance. Add to that, the menace from the Arab States, at least some of them, and it is true to say international tension mounts by the day. Therefore, there is a need for intense and specific research in areas that have direct bearing upon the welfare and safety of this country. I refer, of course, to think-tanks at The Lawns, among others. You don't mind me calling it that? It is so much more in-house than 'Conference Centre'. I don't know the place myself, but you do now. You are our liaison with the Centre and all that goes on there, do I make myself clear?"

"Certainly, Eleanor. But my exact role? I'm not a scientist."

"Absolutely. What we need is your managerial skills and your ability to direct Focus to sectors that are going to give us maximum understanding of complex problems beyond our precise knowledge and more importantly how to deal with any perceived threat and develop retaliatory action. Not an easy task. But one that is essential. Many and diverse subjects, each led by an eminent person of that field, will make up a lengthy programme of Symposia. The first Symposium is to consider virology, and the person to lead it has been chosen. He is Professor Linus Bhatti, a man of international reputation. Rumour has it that various foreign powers are developing biological organisms to which humans are not immune. Such organisms, apparently in variant forms, even fused organisms, could decimate whole communities, possibly countries, in persons who have no natural immunity and as yet, or no effective vaccine protection. This could lead to not only death, but unemployment, economic and social disaster and so on. Briefly, disaster on an immense scale. It could be extremely dangerous."

There was a pause. Young had noticed that even though Lady Eleanor was not concerned with 'such esoteric matters', she was nevertheless well acquainted with current politics and policies. An interesting dichotomy and one worth remembering.

"My Symposia?"

"You will have a different advisor for each subject. An eminent professor of molecular biology, as I say, Professor Linus Bhatti will supervise the first program of seminars, lectures and discussions. He has already written to scientists with the most up-to-date knowledge of the speciality, and in-depth analysis will be their objective."

"You want me to ensure these Symposia run smoothly."

"Exactly that!" Lady Eleanor relaxed into her armchair and each of them contemplated the project. And if the truth be known their own involvement in it. Young spoke.

"Just two things. Will I have additional secretarial staff? And secondly, when can I meet the esteemed professor?"

Lady Eleanor took some time to reply. "Secretarial staff is at a premium just now. I will see what I can do." In a brighter tone, she continued; "Shall we meet again on Thursday? I'll introduce you to Professor Bhatt. Of course, from here on in, conversation outside government confines is strictly forbidden. Even, I apologise, within the family. So tedious, I know, but essential."

"I understand," Young nodded. He had previous experience of security before, when working in RAF.

"Good." Lady Eleanor even clapped her hands and smiled. "I look forward to seeing you again on Thursday, Reginald."

Well, well, thought Young, *I've been admitted to the parlour!* But just as he was secretly congratulating himself and leaving the room, Lady Eleanor called out to him.

"Lovely girl, that young receptionist of yours. Clarissa, is it? Efficient, I wouldn't be surprised," and as he closed the door, Eleanor smiled. There was no harm in letting him know no she had her finger on the 'pulse'. The Group Captain did not smile.

Downstairs, in his office he considered the program. It was not beyond his capabilities.

*** *** ***

Two days later, on the Thursday as arranged, Lady Eleanor called Young upstairs to her office to meet with Professor Bhatti. Young knocked, entered and said 'good afternoon' to Lady Eleanor. She sat with the professor in armchairs next to the low table laden with the necessities for afternoon tea.

"Reginald, come in and join us. Allow me to introduce Professor Bhatti who will be leading the group considering the latest research on virology, at The Lawns."

Professor Bhatti stood; he was unusually tall and remarkably thin, with a slight stoop as if ashamed of his height. When he smiled, his face and eyes radiated good humour. "Group Captain Young, it's a pleasure." They shook hands whilst Eleanor beamed.

"I will be relying on you to make the seminars run smoothly, with the cooperation and participation of the excellent Ms Donato. We scientists will be identifying the most useful areas of research. I have invited many learned experts on the subject."

Young wanted the lines of demarcation clearly drawn and responsibilities assigned. "My role will be purely managerial, but I will respond to any explicit requests for additional services."

"Quite so." Eleanor was understanding. "The Joint Committee advising our Ministry has been advised by SAGE and others on specific topics. As I'm sure you well know, SAGE stands for Scientific Advisory Group for Emergencies and it collects information for the government, it does not advise on policies. Our task will emphasise innovative research and development."

For the moment, Professor Bhatti and Group Captain Young were comfortable with the proposals. In time, no doubt, snags would appear; they could be dealt with as and when they arose.

"So that is fine." Lady Eleanor was drawing the meeting to a close. "We will kick things off with virology, in the capable hands of Professor Bhatti."

Professor Bhatti spoke. "Group Captain Young, I will give you a list of invited scientists. We have arranged the Symposium for mid-December, and I am pleased to say all that are invited have agreed to attend, apart from one guest lecturer and we are in the process of replacing her. If you would be so kind just to glance at the list and pass it to Ms Donato and her secretarial staff, I'd be grateful. Shall we meet in, say, a fortnight's time?"

Young agreed. The meeting ended.

Back in his office Young felt pleased. His position in Whitehall had been consolidated and ANCOM was working well. Now Lady Eleanor had seen fit to involve him in matters of more consequence. From what little he had seen of the Professor, he liked the man. He was polite, had smiled easily, and was full of enthusiasm and confidence. Lady Eleanor's role was more difficult; less defined; was she merely an intermediary in the management structure, or something else? In addition to that, however, there was an outstanding issue that continued to bother him. He'd heard some time ago, at an ANCOM, Nigel Mountford mentioned a report of increased traffic flow on the A34, near Harwell. Not hugely significant but since that time he had heard nothing further. He wondered (and if he were truthful with himself, worried) about that. Had the report been handed on, as he had fully expected? Had it been followed up? It was probably a small matter that had been investigated and found to be unimportant. He would like to know. For some unaccountable reason, it continued to irritate him. He'd get in touch with Mikhail and ask him to make some discreet inquiries. Tomorrow would be soon enough.

He went home.

Chapter 7

The following day, Friday, saw Young at his desk at a surprisingly early hour. On his way through reception, he caught sight of Clarissa painting her nails. She had looked up casually, acknowledged his greeting and continued her preparation for another hectic day. Young hurried down the corridor and closing the door to his office firmly behind him, he sat at his desk. Not normally a man of indecision, he had, overnight, become uneasy. But about what? Or perhaps more pertinently, about whom? He could not rid himself of a suspicion that something untoward had happened the previous afternoon in Eleanor's office. He knew something was amiss. Something said? Something not said? Something implied? He needed a detached perspective, someone outside Whitehall. His mind wandered to his service in Cyprus.

By the time he was posted there, the civilian troubles that had plagued the island for so many years had, to a large extent, abated. Turkish and Greek invasions had resulted in the division of the island, north/south, and now the two communities lived relatively harmoniously (watched by U.N. peacekeepers.) Britain's presence was now limited to providing a strategic base in the Eastern Mediterranean, the base at Akrotiri manned by the R.A.F. It must have been the summer of 2010 or 11, somewhere about then, when Group Captain, now a service policeman of seniority, was told of stores disappearing from the base at an alarming rate; there were also concerns that some local provisions brought into the camp were of questionable provenance; and more seriously, classified information may have gone missing or worse, been sold, or both. Altogether, these represented significant problems. He reasoned that local knowledge was essential and with this in mind, he set about finding a Greek-Cypriot local who would inform him of unusual trade, or movement of supplies on the island. He made journeys from the base to different towns, finally choosing Ayia Napa as the most promising place to start these inquiries. It was about 130km from the RAF base, an hour-and-a-half drive, and a thriving tourist resort. Far enough away from base to afford him some anonymity and crowded enough to make surveillance difficult. Better yet, it reputedly harboured gangs and criminals and possibly criminal gangs! If there was anywhere in Cyprus that attracted villainy, it was here. Young was looking for a local lad who had a wide network of contacts and might be privy to some less than straightforward transactions. For example, the movement of illicit goods, or money, or even better, information, would be immensely helpful. Someone who might overhear conversations that were not intended for official ears. Young, dressed in civilian clothes, used taxis for the journeys between the base and Ayia, and he made it his business to make friends with one of the drivers, Mikhail Stephanopoulos. It was a happy coincidence that the two met. During WW2 Mikhail's grandfather had joined the Cyprus Regiment but unfortunately and bravely had been wounded. Being injured in wartime service for Britain was considered honourable and a strong allegiance to this country was created.

Mikhail, furthermore, was an interesting character. Born in a small village in the Troodos mountains and brought up in a fiercely patriarchal family and society, the youngest of three brothers but older than his four sisters, he was a handsome, intelligent and friendly young man. Village life was unsurprisingly parochial and rather dull for this spirited lad and as soon as he could drive, he followed his brothers to Ayia Napa where he could have greater freedom and join them in their taxi business. He was a taxi driver in and around Ayia by day; and had a good time by night. The seaside resort bustled with excitement during the season. Intoxication was common, although excess frowned upon, and for young men and women life was a riot of parties and careless evenings. Mikhail joined in, with enthusiasm.

After friendly and increasingly confidential conversations, Young decided this was the chap to give him local information about unusual supplies of goods, just possibly discussions of information from the base. That was the start of his association with Group Captain Young. From then on, Young used other drivers and as far as the other drivers were concerned, whatever friendship that had developed between himself and Mikhail petered out.

On a warm evening, in midsummer 2011, had you been strolling along the main road in Ayia, you would have been overwhelmed by the constant movement of happy, often slightly inebriated, holidaymakers wandering in and out of the brightly lit shops and tables of the never-ending line of tavernas. If you continued to watch carefully, you might have noticed one or two residents of serious disposition, sitting at tables and taking an inordinately long time to drink their small lagers. Occasionally large cars would drift along the road and stop; the occupants might lean over and speak quietly to these serious men, after which the cars would continue their slow journeys and the men would get up and move off. You would need to be very observant to spot such brief conversations and you would have had to be extraordinarily patient and perceptive to notice a middle-aged man of robust build in lightweight jacket, open-necked shirt and casual slacks, carrying a newspaper and weaving his way slowly through the crowds, looking with interest at young ladies, shops and the nightlife. If you had seen him, you might observe him stop at a taverna (Paxos by name although miles from that tiny island) to give his legs a rest and take some refreshment. Like everywhere else, the taverna was packed and the gentleman asked Mikhail, the taxi driver that we have just got to know, if he would be kind enough to remove his leather coat from the second chair at his table, for the gentleman to sit. Mikhail willingly complied and the gentleman placed his newspaper on the table before ordering a gin and tonic. He took his time to enjoy the drink. Neither spoke. Ten minutes later you would then have seen the gentleman rise, leave and absent-mindedly forget to take his paper. Nothing extraordinary, you might think and of such trivial importance as to be dismissed from your mind. And that of course was the object of the exercise. Totally unimportant and easily forgotten. Perhaps a quarter-of-an-hour later Mikhail would leave. He would take the newspaper.

This was the method Reginald and Mikhail had devised to communicate with each other. Within the paper, there was a hand-written list of questions concerning Cypriot illegal markets, trouble on the border with the Turkish North, gang cooperation or otherwise and even conversations overheard between residents and persons from abroad of dubious demeanour. The answers would be returned to Reginald by Mikhail at times stated on the list of questions. They would meet at different tavernas, at different hours, and on different days of the week and even use different items to carry the questions and answers (books, magazines, shopping bags etc.) It might not have been the most sophisticated of operations, certainly not one that would have been taught on the Secret Service introductory courses in faraway Scotland, but it served the two very well and as far as they knew no one had been any the wiser. Mikhail was rewarded for his efforts and Reginald obtained useful information. It is no exaggeration to record that during their cooperation, fewer stores vanished from the base, goods that were brought in were lawfully obtained (mostly) and information security tightened.

It is extraordinary to report also, that in the three years of association, Reginald and Mikhail, spoke so infrequently they could have been Trappist monks. The silence was broken when Young informed the lad that he was to be leaving the service within months. They had met at the Taverna Paxos, possibly chosen by Young for sentimental reasons. Who knows?

"Mikhail. Bad news. Being posted back to Britain in a couple of weeks. Then it's Civvy Street for me. Done enough for Queen and Country, what?"

"I'll miss you, Reginald." (Much the same as virtually everyone in Cyprus, Mikhail's English was nearly perfect.)

"Yes, bit of a wrench. Unfortunately, it means the end of our financial arrangement. Can't help it."

"I'm sorry you're going. It's not just the money, I liked being useful." (Much the same as virtually everyone in Southern Cyprus, Mikhail was loyal to Britain.)

"Helped me enormously, Mikhail. Very much hope you'll consider coming to Britain. If you do, here's my mobile number." They chatted for half-an-hour or so, shook hands warmly and parted.

Almost five years later, as it happened on his way home from Whitehall to Plantagenet House, Young's mobile buzzed. After all this time, it was Mikhail telling him he was in London, working for his brothers' private car hire company in the capital and giving his number. Subsequently they had kept in touch.

The day after meeting Professor Bhatti, Young decided the time had come to ask for the assistance of his erstwhile friend, Mikhail Stephanopoulos. He used his mobile to arrange a rendezvous in the Embankment Gardens at 4:30 pm, 'or thereabouts', and therefore at 4:20 pm he stood from his desk, put on his overcoat, walked down the corridor and, saying good evening to Clarissa, he took an unhurried stroll along Whitehall, then left along the embankment towards his usual underground station, changing course to enter The Gardens, where he immediately spotted Mikhail sitting on a bench reading The Evening News. The usual tangle of black curls fell over Mikhail's forehead above his handsome face. He wore his beloved leather jacket and smiled as soon as he saw Young approaching. Reginald joined him. Not given to overt displays of affection, nevertheless Young shook hands cordially, and even pressed the young man's shoulder.

"Mikhail, how are you? Really good to see you. Settled? Work OK? Brothers?"

"Good to all those. They call the private hire company the 'Two-and-a-half Brothers'. It will become the 'Three Brothers' as soon as I get married!"

"And when can we expect that?"

"Not yet!"

"Intend to stay then, do you?"

"Yes, I think so." Mikhail ran his hand through his hair. "I certainly like London."

"The weather?" Young looked at the slate-grey sky.

"It takes a bit of getting used to, but I'll manage."

"Brought you these. Not sure you can get them in this country." From his briefcase, Young produced a pack of 100 Karelia Blue cigarettes.

"Thanks. Thanks very much." (Mikhail had given up smoking but he was too polite to say so.)

They were silent, both gazing across the grass, and now empty flower beds. Their contact in Cyprus, because of necessity, had been irregular but mutually beneficial. It would be different in Britain. Neither of them knew how it would pan out exactly.

"Point of all this is that sometime soon I may well need your services again. Think you can manage that? Fit it in with your work, that sort of thing? Normal money. Yes?"

"Fine but I'd need some warning. But yes, I think it is possible."

"Would I ring you directly or is phoning the taxi firm safe enough?"

"It would be safer to ring me directly."

"Ring you direct then." Young murmured. "There's no rush now. I may want you to give me some information about a person's behaviour away from the office. Perhaps, might mean tailing someone over a weekend."

"Like I say, I'll need some warning."

"Let you know well in advance." Young smiled, stood up and they shook hands again. "Contact you in a couple of weeks or so. OK?"

"Sure. No problem."

Young left the Gardens and walked to the underground station. Mikhail made his way back to the car hire firm. A brief chat but both were satisfied.

Arriving home, Young found Diane waiting for him expressing effusive gratitude for the excellent lunch and offering him a gin and tonic with plenty of ice. Her work at the hospital charity has gone well and she had seen two consultants, one of whom had passed the time of day with her. Even a television crew! (Unfortunately filming in another part of the hospital.) She was looking forward to a light evening meal, a good book and bed at 10:00 pm. Diane was satisfied with her day. Young still worried. He slept fitfully.

The following week passed without serious incident. He called the Customs' Office in Lowestoft and spoke with an old mate, who'd been a Flight Lieutenant when they were both in the Service. No luck. He'd try later. Then he rang a policeman in Amsterdam who also knew from his previous experiences and spoke to him briefly. He made a fruitless search on the internet for the history of Stacey Donato. With Cobb, he was more successful. (Dennis Arthur Cobb; retired Warrant Officer, royal artillery. Just as he thought.) He found time to visit Lady Eleanor and talk in general terms about The Lawns and the possible mileage that might be made from the Programmes there. She was in a good mood. Nevertheless, he returned to his desk still puzzled.

However, by Friday, the weekend beckoned as a welcome relief. He'd been unable to identify the source of his unease. It was a state of mind he did not welcome or relish. To declare that he was overwrought would be an unwarranted exaggeration; to say he needed a weekend's rest was undeniably true. He looked forward to a quiet weekend.

It didn't start well. The train from Liverpool Street was packed. He found himself pushed against a door, hanging on to a rail to steady himself all the while becoming increasingly irritated. At Audley End, he stepped down onto the platform and felt the sudden chill of a November evening but outside the station, mercifully, the only taxi was available. He climbed in.

"Sorry guv," the driver said over his shoulder, "heater on the blink." Well, it would be, wouldn't it? The taxi eventually turned into Oak Tree Lane and pulled up at the door of Plantagenet House.

"Put the fare on my monthly account," Young called, in truth a little more abruptly than was strictly necessary. The taxi-driver accelerated away, in truth, a little more abruptly than was strictly necessary. Young opened the heavy, oak door and immediately his spirits lifted. There was a rich, fresh and perfumed smell of furniture polish and an accompanying aroma of food cooking in the kitchen. That together with the warmth of the central heating, cheered him to the bone. Home at last he hung his coat on the stand, opened the door to the lounge. Immediately he saw his wife immaculately dressed to impress, reclining among the cushions of her favourite armchair. She held a large glass of red wine by the stem. This did not augur well. In fact, it was always a sign, if he was not mistaken, that a guest, or worse guests, had been invited for the evening, possibly even dinner.

"Reginald, there you are. Good day at the office dear? Pour yourself a drink darling. I've asked Charles and Alice to dinner. That's a pleasant surprise, is it not?"

Young poured himself a stiff gin with a splash of tonic, no ice and collapsed into his own chair. Charles and Alice were, of course, the Reverend and his wife! Bang went his evening of gentle relaxation, for no sooner had he made himself comfortable than chimes from the hall announced the arrival of their guests. Reginald reluctantly (it must be said) sat up. "Don't worry, dear, that will be Charles and Alice. I'll go to the door and welcome them." Diane left the room. Young groaned, He heard his wife open the front door. "Good evening, vicar—and of course, Alice!" He heard his wife enthuse. "Come in please. Oh Alice, what lovely flowers, you shouldn't have. I'll get Mrs Braithwaite to put them in water straight away."

The vicar, who was extraordinarily tall, came into the lounge followed by his astonishingly diminutive wife, where Young, now upright, acting the perfect host, shook hands and invited them to sit on the divan. The difference in height between the vicar and his wife was so remarkable that the mechanisms of intimacy between the two was a matter of bewilderment for the older choirboys who hotly debated the issue long into the night. Young's thoughts, however, were on another idiosyncrasy of their spiritual leader. Namely, the well-known fact that his dentures were ill-fitting, so much so that his sermons, often extremely long and boring, held fascination for the congregation only because of the independent and random activities of his teeth. It was claimed in some quarters that certain wags laid bets on the exact time of an oral catastrophe during a sermon. With all this in mind, Young went to the drink's cabinet. "Dry sherry Vicar? And Alice, sherry?" Two glasses poured, Young handed one to Alice and one to the vicar. Then with malice aforethought, he offered the vicar a dish of peanuts. An awkward silence followed, broken by a warning cough from Diane. Young sat down again.

Conversation was slow and strained, Diane valiantly raising one acceptable tropic after another, while Young surreptitiously refilled his own glass regularly with grim determination. Not a moment too soon the lounge door opened, and

Mrs Braithwaite announced. "Dinner is served." Whereupon they all stood and moved to the dining room with a degree of relief. There, they stood as Charles said Grace (in Latin of course) and then enjoyed an excellent meal. Mrs Braithwaite was a very good cook, and the vicar was especially appreciative of the cottage pie (hazardous mastication of steak avoided) and his wife demonstrated a voracious appetite which made Young wonder if she was stocking up for the rest of the winter. After the meal, they all returned to the lounge and at precisely 10:30 pm. Charles checked his watch and instructed Alice that it was time to leave their hosts with grateful thanks. Young hid his relief with a remarkable display of disappointment that even Diane, who surely must have known better, almost believed. At last, the front door closed behind Charles and Alice and Young hurried back to the lounge for a nightcap.

"That went well," he beamed, hoping to divert Diane's opprobrium at his lacklustre performance during the evening. But she was not fooled.

"You might have been more communicative," she sniffed. "I think I will go up. And don't you think you've had enough to drink for one night?" It was most unlike her to be overly critical. Left on his own downstairs, Young helped himself to another nightcap and having swallowed that, slowly followed his wife upstairs. It was not the evening he had hoped for.

Part Two
Mistakes Happen

Chapter 8

During the autumn and into November and December members of ANCOM had slowly become more confident as a group and inter-service exchange of information easier. Again gradually, members began to invite colleagues with special information to attend some sessions (with Young's prior approval.) Two weeks before Christmas, the last scheduled meeting of the year was convened. As usual Samara Vassal and Nigel Mountford arrived together. (Young noticed.) Konrad Taylor of GCHQ and Phillipson Rice of MI6 together. (Young noticed.) Adrian Orwell (Special Branch) and Les Morgan (Counterterrorism) drifted in late.

"All present, and correct? No guests?" Young asked unnecessarily, looking round the polished table. "Get on, shall we?"

Konrad leant forward. "Personally, I'll be glad of a break over the Festive Season. I'm not on call this year. But I look forward to a fresh start here, next year." Murmur of agreement went round the table.

Young shot up in his seat. "Good God! Festive season?" He barked. "Must do something about that!" (It seemed improbable that he meant to move Christmas to another date, more likely he had forgotten to get any presents.) Young was smarter than he appeared; his main reason for the outburst was to maintain good humour in the group, even Christmas cheer.

"Two weeks." Mountford intoned gravely, sucking air through his bared teeth, as if he were announcing the date of an execution, not tidings of great joy. The others nodded solemnly.

"Steady on, not that bad. Diane will enjoy it, so will you lot. Only me who's forgotten." Young looked round. Samara was more settled, enjoying the closer attention of Nigel Mountford who considered himself superior in years, service and confidence to the others. No one had yet dared to disabuse him of those beliefs. Rice seemed totally at ease, but Young wondered if there was an irritation between the sister intelligence services. If there was, he was sure the

Americans were sniffing about somewhere. Whilst Young was considering America, Konrad coughed gently into his fist, a sure sign of an impending contribution.

"We have come across reports, mainly from across the Atlantic," he said, "there is a substantial increase in telephone communications from a province in mid-China called Wuhan. Nothing conclusive but it may be of interest."

"Why?" Asked Phillipson.

Young noticed the question and how quickly it had been asked.

"That's rather the point. There is a BSL-4 facility there," Konrad replied. "In our language, that means a Biological Secure Laboratory at the highest level of security i.e., 4, actually one of a string of such places across China. It is believed, in such laboratories, scientists are not only investigating viruses but experimenting with them; possibly producing viruses of increased lethal properties; perhaps even combining viruses together to form more virulent organisms. If they could fuse lethal viruses with airborne viruses, they could make ideal biological weapons. Any unusual activity is monitored."

The longest contribution from Konrad ever, Young thought. *He must be excited!*

"America has four or five of these BSL-4 facilities, doesn't it?"

"At least, that number." Phillipson contributed and Young noticed it.

"There is no suggestion at present that China has developed a new biological weapon" Konrad added.

"Right. But we'll have to take note." Young was watching everybody closely. No one seemed inclined to add anything, so the matter was put to one side. Perhaps a mistake. Other business concerned some Russian incursions into British air space, growing unrest on Russian NATO borders. Young noticed there was still no mention of traffic numbers on A34. The committee broke up towards 4:30 pm and everyone shook hands, Christmas good wishes were exchanged, and they all departed.

*** *** ***

As members of ANCOM left the building in Whitehall they quickly dispersed into the hordes of pedestrians arbitrarily pushing each other in all directions and apparently moving quite haphazardly. London was heaving with late shoppers, people on their way to or from pubs or parties, or just desperately trying to get home and out of the pandemonium.

But at Paddington Station, two travellers arrived at 6:30 pm. from Oxford. The purpose of their visit to London was vastly different. I was one of the travellers on my way to Rachel's flat where we would spend a quiet weekend, enjoy a good meal and drink one or two glasses of wine. We would enjoy each other's company and I might well learn more details of her occupation of which I had learnt little.

The other traveller arriving from Oxford at 6:30 pm was Ernst Becker. His motive for being in London was very different mine. First, he walked to the nearest public telephone, made a short call and hurried away he turned into a litter-strewn passageway and to a cafe whose lights were barely visible from the main concourse. Pushing the door open he found a room hot and steamy containing about 10 Formica-topped tables, a dozen customers and a transistor radio playing at full blast.

He surveyed the scene with little enthusiasm. This must be the traditional British café, basic and hygienically dubious. Furthest from the door at chest height a counter rested on a display unit filled with tired sandwiches and unappetising-looking cake. Behind this counter but just visible through the display unit and steam, an enormous brown enamel teapot was occasionally lifted with a grunt, by the surly girl who was serving. A beaded curtain separated the eating area and customers from the kitchen from which the sound of crashing dishes and frying pans could be heard above the shouting, laughter and occasional oaths of the kitchen staff. Intermittently, the girl behind the counter turned her head and shouted an order over her shoulder. She invariably received no reply.

Becker stood at the counter patiently waiting until she deemed the moment propitious to take his order, a full English breakfast (at 6:30 am!) He turned and walked to an unoccupied table against a wall where he could watch the entrance. No one took any notice of him. After only five minutes, an enormous plate of fried food appeared on the table, together with a boiling-hot mug of tea. He had just started on this when two men came in, collars turned up against the December cold, collected two teas from the counter and joined him. The three men talked quietly. Becker continued to eat, hardly looking up. Anyone would have had to be extremely observant to notice a membership card (for a rather exclusive club) pass over the table under one hand and into Becker's pocket in a flash. After a while, the two men left, leaving Becker to finish his meal. He ordered another tea, sat back and waited for time to pass. Eventually, after looking at his watch, he stood and made his way slowly out of the café. Still with time to kill, the club didn't open until 8·00 am, he sauntered slowly to the underground station and took the train to Piccadilly Circus. The train was not crowded but he made sure not to make eye contact with any other passenger. At Piccadilly, he climbed the steps and joined the crowds gathering for a night of entertainment. Under the huge flashing, neon advertisements the pavements were massed with jostling revellers. There were sad, solitary figures as well; a homeless lad who couldn't have been more than sixteen; an old man, legless under the influence of alcohol staggering about begging without expectation of success. The noise and traffic were horrendous. Becker darted into a side street where it was at least quieter. As he made his way cautiously further into Soho a young bully of a man barged into him and continued walking without an apology. Becker reacted with explosive anger and without a moment's hesitation seized the youth's shoulder, swung him round, grabbed his throat and punched him once in the face, very hard. The youth sat down abruptly. Becker left quickly before a scene developed and disappeared into a crowded public house. This was typical of his impulsive reactions and might result in unwanted observation, even arrest. He had been repeatedly warned about this in his training.

The pub was warm, brightly lit and busy. The drinkers were concentrated round the bar and Baker had to push his way through to get service. The barmaid looked at him and waited. Her blouse revealed in impressive cleavage, her lips painted bright cherry red, and strands of dyed blonde hair fell provocatively across one eye. Becker barely registered her.

She bent across the bar. "Pint darling?"

"Uh-huh," Becker muttered. He leaned an elbow on the bar trying to avoid a wet mat and puddles of beer, at the same time averting his face. The barmaid gave up any attempt to have a conversation. Becker sucked the froth from the top of his beer, collected his change and went to a table well away from the bar preparing to mark time. Only half an hour until the clubs opened but gradually the pub was filling up and getting more boisterous by the minute. Eventually, what Becker was trying to avoid happened. A feller sat at his table.

"Having a quick pint before going home?" the man nodded at Becker's grubby raincoat and assumed working clothes; he would have been surprised had he glanced down for he would have seen Becker's shoes which were new, unmarked and highly polished. This man was not what Becker needed. If he moved to another table and ordered a second pint, the man might take umbrage and remember him. Best to smile, reply quietly and leave without hassle. The man most likely would forget the incident completely post up.

"Yes," he finally said, "just a quick pint then I must get home," and before the man could say anything else Becker got up. 'Curious' the man thought as Becker left, 'was that a German accent?'

Outside Becker gave the man no thought. He was still too early for the club, so he decided to wonder and gaze into shop fronts but keep moving. His coat collar turned, up, head down he should be able to waste half an hour without arousing interest.

At 8:15 pm, he made his way to the club and found a large man blocking the door, inspecting membership cards. He gave his Becker's raincoat a reproachful frown but let him through the door. Inside, he deposited the offending coat with the cloakroom attendant and walked through the next door, now resplendent in new sport's jacket and patterned handkerchief showing from his top pocket. He later discovered that this was the first to several rooms of which the club boasted. This one had subdued and hidden lighting, the decor blue and white; all seats were button-upholstered in luxurious blue leather. The walls were adorned with large black and white photographs (or reproductions) of famous models taken by only slightly less well-known photographers. Around the room several pairs of well-dressed men and women conversed quietly, occasionally chuckling modestly. Becker approached the bar. The bartender was at once in attendance, young, lightly bronzed with an open next silk shirt.

"Sir?" His fingernails were highly polished and his manner solicitous. "A drink sir? A new member if may be so bold? I don't remember having a previous pleasure."

Becker nodded and ordered Scotch and water then signed his name below as this was his first bar charge in the club: JAMES DEACON. He carried his drink to the end of the room. Two heavy curtains hung below separate arches. Above one, in beautifully painted gothic lettering; **Apollo/Pan** and above the other **Aphrodite/Artemis.** This made no sense to him, but he guessed (correctly as it turned out,) that Apollo as the best bet. He found himself in a comfortable 'snug', a smaller room dimly lit this time in pale green, around the walls were buttoned-green, thickly padded banquettes and, as to be expected, low tables situated conveniently. Only two men sat together in this room. He heard music; classical, tranquil and tuneful. Here another bartender could have been the identical twin and the first he had encountered.

"Good evening, sir. Are you dining with us tonight?" Perhaps this was the anteroom for diners only and Becker suddenly felt uneasy. Had he made an important mistake?

"No. No." Becker we short. "I can wait here? A friend."

"Of course, sir. Please sit anywhere." The barman indicated the whole room with a sweep of his arm. Becker had not wanted his presence associated with anyone, but it was clear he had to explain himself somehow.

"I'm just waiting."

"Good." The man and moved along the bar, flicking some hair from his forehead with one hand and a speck of dust from the counter with another and then unnecessarily arranging some bottles. He now regretted coming through the curtain and finding his presence so conspicuous. But it was too late. He pulled out his mobile and busied himself with improvising emails. Head down. When he next looked up, two more men had come in and further, Phillipson Rice was at the bar chatting in low tones to the barman who was obviously talking about Becker, for he inclined his head towards him, and Rice now turned to look at Becker and smiled. He came over and joined Becker.

"A new member?" Rice asked affably. They shook hands and by way of introduction he continued, "Phillipson Rice."

"Carl Deacon." Becker replied. This was going to test his self-discipline and resolve; not the new name, or Rice, but the ambience of the club itself!

"It's lovely to meet you, Carl." Rice continued conversationally. "I try to drop into the club twice a week or so living in London it's no trouble and I find it so convenient comfortable and restful. And of course, there is always the opportunity to make new friends." The sentence faded away and Becker wondered if there was an invitation there. He couldn't be sure, English not being his first language. "Yes," he replied, "it was recommended by a friend, and I thought I would drop him and find out for myself."

Rice picked up his drink (a cocktail?) and finished it. "Another James Deacon?" Becker handed over his glass. "Scotch and water please."

As Rice collected the new drinks Becker viewed the room with more confidence. Rice returned. "We have three floors at the club. Above us is the dining room where all are made welcome, and the cuisine is excellent. Above that there is an overnight accommodation for out-of-town members. I'll let you into a secret; I've never stayed here since I joined the club!" Becker mumbled something incomprehensible and dipped his nose into his glass of Scotch. "Angus tells me that you will not be dining with us here tonight, Carl." Angus of course the barman. "Actually, I'm not eating here myself. I've already eaten and quite honestly couldn't touch another thing. What are your plans for later this evening? James?"

"Oh, nothing particular." Becker was vague. "I'm open to suggestions." Better hope that was not too obvious! There was a short silence as Phillipson mulled the matter over in his mind. The silence between them then lengthened, and abruptly Rice said; "Your accent, it's continental, is it not?"

"I am originally from Potsdam, northwest to Berlin. It was of course eastern Germany, but I don't remember that. Germany is all the same Republic now, in any case. I have been living in this country for several years." Becker was not altogether being honest. "I like this country. I might stay."

"Your papers? No problems?" Becker merely shrugged. He was keen to leave now but Rice was making no effort to move. Becker suggested another drink albeit reluctantly. If Rice noticed the hesitancy, he didn't comment on it but seemed to be deep in thought. By the time Becker returned, Rice had made up his mind.

"Do you live in London, Carl?"

"No. Not London."

"How is it that you joined the club then?"

"Two reasons; I am often in London, and a special friend of mine, someone with similar…tastes, recommended this club as an excellent rendezvous in which to make friends. And they have accommodation here."

"They do. As I said." Rice dropped his voice to a whisper, "It's terribly expensive. Why not stay at my place tonight, Carl?"

Now Becker must not seem too keen, but this invitation was exactly what he was angling after. "Perhaps if it is convenient to you, I would love to."

"That's settled." Rice pressed his invitation. "I'll just ask Angus to order us a taxi and then we're all set."

"Excellent. I'll collect my coat."

On the way to Camden and Rice's flat, there was little conversation. Becker was thinking back over the encounter at the club. His training was for moments such as these. Had things gone smoothly? Had there been any unnecessary incidents that might be remembered? Overall, he was satisfied (the altercation with the bullyboy was quite separate); there was always a degree of risk which was inescapable and by the time the taxi arrived at Rice's address, Becker had reassured himself that he could complete his assignment safely. Rice had mentioned there would be no visitors over the weekend and was looking forward to a weekend of relaxation and satisfaction…Rice had been in the secret services for years and was trained to be cautious, but not once had he had any suspicion of Becker either in the taxi here nor in the club. "Here we are, guv." The driver pulled up outside the flat. "Cash? Very good and thank you sir." The tip was modest but appropriate and forgettable.

Becker followed Rice as they climbed the stairs and let themselves into the flat. With the lights on, Becker saw a moderately sized lounge with doors leading, he assumed, to a kitchen, bathroom and a bedroom. The flat was furnished throughout a long couch taking up much of the lounge. There were shelves crowded with books and a small desk in one corner with a laptop. Landscape reproductions in frames around the walls. Curtains were drawn at the windows.

Rice went into the kitchen and indicated to Becker that he could take his coat into the bedroom. The room had bedside tables reading lamps and a large double bed covered in pale yellow, silken bedspread two or three pencil drawings of young men in various stages of undress graced the walls. Becker hurried back to the lounge and accepted a strong Scotch, the strength of which he had never tasted before.

"I'll freshen myself up with a shower." Rice smiled, going into the bedroom and leaving the door wide open whilst he undressed in full view.

"What are your pastimes?" Rice wanted to know.

This caught Becker unawares for none of his unsavoury pleasures were suitable for flirtatious chitchat. "I follow football." He managed. There was a long silence but eventually Rice walked naked from the bedroom towards the bathroom. "Will you…" The question was cut as Becker, with speed few would associate with him, was behind Rice, a garrotte around the neck and was pulling with all his strength and a good deal of pure hatred. Visceral revulsion overwhelmed him. In seconds, Rice's knees gave way and Becker felt the weight of Rice's body as he slumped to the floor. Becker was breathing hard but otherwise calm. He hardly looked at the corpse as he dragged it behind the couch and out of sight. Rice no longer existed and never had, in any real sense, for Becker. The murder was as quick as that.

Becker felt nothing except perhaps relief that the mission had been so easily accomplished. Rice ceased to exist as soon as he was dead and the body out of sight. In many ways, Becker was an ideal assassin. Cold, with no feelings at all for his fellow mortals, he was on the one hand superficially engaging and on the other emotionless, ruthless and without remorse. After he killed Rice, he didn't give him (or the act of murder) a single thought; his mind moved immediately to his present situation. It was far too late to call a taxi he would be remembered at this time in the morning. He would make himself comfortable here. First another Scotch. Then settle in the lounge feet from the corpse and sip his drink savouring the sharpness. Sometime tomorrow he'd go through the flat, make it look like a break in; take the laptop, it might be useful to the boss. He walked into the bedroom, pulled back the satin cover and climbed between the black sheets and was asleep within seconds.

Saturday morning tucked away from the bustle of Camden market and the Lock, the immediate area around Rice's flat was peaceful. Becker washed and dressed without haste. No one knew he was here; he'd given a false name at the club and his description and even fingerprints or DNA would be no good to the police because as far as he knew, the police had no record of him in this country nor was his data on any international list. Mrs Bryant would not miss him until Monday evening at the earliest, she would just assume that his trip to Birmingham (!) had gone on longer than expected. He was not sure of the agenda for Rice, but it seemed unlikely his absence would not be noticed much before late Monday evening. Why not have some breakfast. He found some bread to make toast, butter and marmalade. It would have to do in place of croissants. He couldn't find any fruit, but he could make coffee. He sat at the kitchen table gazing out of the window giving not the slightest thought to the body of dead Rice in the lounge.

Eventually, he decided to complete his task; he opened the laptop made nothing of the stored information but pushed it into a briefcase. Somebody might make something of it later. The papers in the desk appeared unimportant; he ignored them. He went quickly along the bookshelves, but they held only textbooks on economics, politics and would you believe it (philosophy!) No interest to him whatsoever. At about 11:00 pm, he finished and let himself out of the flat made his way to Camden underground station and so back into the crowds of central London.

The crowds in central London were intent on Christmas shopping. Regent Street was ablaze with lights, shop windows were crammed with presents and promises, parents were by turn happy or harassed sometimes both at once. Children gazed expectantly into the faces of innumerable Santa Claus; some even had a shrewd suspicion that there was something was not quite right. There was only one Father Christmas, wasn't there? One or two bravely pulled at the beards! No one took any notice of Ernst Becker as he left London.

Chapter 9

In December 2019, the population of Britain made a momentous decision. On Thursday, 12th of December, Boris Johnson and the Conservative Party won a general election with a parliamentary majority of 80. This had been won largely because of anticipation of Britain leaving the European Union and the promise that we had won back our Island and now could make our way in the world, unencumbered by the ever-growing bureaucratic machine of Strasbourg and Brussels. There was optimism everywhere, or nearly everywhere! Boris Johnson became Prime Minister and continued expressing his forthright views on the success that Britain could now expect in world trade.

In the corridors of Whitehall, optimism was more subdued.

At Plantagenet House, Group Captain Young's wife, Diane, was volunteering her time and energy to various church activities, for Faith was a major part of her well-being and Christmas was a busy time and an important celebration of course. Reginald, whilst discreetly supporting her activities, retreated to his study at regular intervals to read his emails and the latest information from the services.

In Norfolk, between Ipswich and Norwich often at night, large, articulated lorries were arriving at the mansion secluded in the woods off the A140. The building and cellars were being converted into biologically secure laboratories; the work being carried out to the highest specification. Entry and exit to the grounds were rigidly controlled, admission severely restricted.

Rachel and I decided to stay in Oxford for two weeks over Christmas and we were looking forward not only to the celebration but also a visit from Alexander that we had met in Paris. Work was to be adjourned for the vacation.

Of ANCOM, Nigel and Konrad were on leave. Samara had drawn the short straw and was on duty over Christmas. Special Branch and Counter Terrorist Branch representatives were, as to be expected, on stand-by duty. Clarissa, if not exactly unhappy, was on her own and sulking in her own flat and singularly bad-tempered back home with her parents on Christmas Day. Par for the course.

For days, Rice lay dead and unattended in his flat.

Quite remarkably, in the weeks before Christmas, the absence of Phillipson Rice from his desk at 'The House' went unnoticed, or if noticed no one deemed it sufficiently noteworthy to make enquiries. It was not until Boxing Day that the occupants of the flat below Rice, became aware of an offensive odour; it was not until the following day, when they could get no reply from ringing the bell that Rice's disappearance was reported to the police. Even after the Camden Police Station was notified it was yet another 24-hours before the door to his flat was finally broken open and his corpse discovered. By that time, decomposition was well advanced and the fetid stench, characteristic of human decay after death, sent a young Constable downstairs and outside in a great hurry, to vomit copiously into the nearest gutter.

Now, at last, there was a widespread investigation, not only at 'The House' but within the local Camden Constabulary. And matters of course were complicated. Rice, admitted the intelligence service reluctantly, was not all that he seemed. There are aspects of his life that couldn't possibly be shared with the police, and this confused the issue. Tempers became frayed and little headway was made in the search for his killer. This did not prevent the local CID examining the flat in minute detail and their observations were duly recorded. This would at least help in the long run.

Rachael arrived in Oxford seven days before Christmas, and we drove straight from the station to my flat, which was the first storey of a house that at one time belonged to a college, I believe. The house, adjacent to the road over Shotover Hill, was sheltered on 3 sides by tall trees and shrubs (huge rhododendrons that flowered magnificently in springtime) but left an unobstructed view of Oxford City. One of Rachel's pleasures whilst staying here was to stand on the balcony and look at the city of Oxford and the colleges silhouetted against the setting sun.

Work in the colleges had wound down for the holiday. Rachel had taken leave. Time was ours. I was relieved to get away from the college and the laboratories, and we spent time driving to the villages around Oxford which were at their best over Christmas; devoid of tourists; festive; mulled wine in all the hotels and pubs; open fires; decorated trees; lights suspended from genuine oak beams. And nowhere any haste.

We called into college on the way home some 5 days before Christmas, and I found a letter from Alexander in my pigeonhole. (I had telephoned my address to him, but he still insisted on writing to the college, for reasons best known to himself.) At the flat, we read it.

Hi gang,

Sorry no can do. Been struck down with the dreaded winter lurgy.

Confined to quarters. Bugger, isn't it? Be in touch New Year.

Alex.

And that was that. No Alex at Christmas apparently. I rang immediately but it went straight to voicemail, so I left our best wishes and said we looked forward to seeing him in the New Year. What more could I do? All I knew about his circumstances was that he worked for a private Chemical Company somewhere in Norfolk. I think he mentioned a village on the coast somewhere as a bolthole, but I couldn't remember the name even if I'd ever been given it. The reunion would have to be postponed.

Rachel and I resumed our rapport as if we'd never been apart. Every evening was spent discussing this and that, really nothing of much consequence, at ease in each other's company. We had made up our minds to marry sometime in the New Year and I suppose my parents (who still lived in Stornoway) would have to be told, and probably invited, but that decision could be deferred. There was a celebration of Midnight Mass in Christ Church College chapel (which also serves as Cathedral), and Rachael wanted to attend. I drove to the college, but for my part, I walked in Christ Church Meadow, well wrapped up. The grass and the trees were heavy with frost, the moon bright and the air cold. Floodlight Oxford was spectacular especially from this distance, the spires and towers a warm yellow against the cold, black sky. For both of us, the midnight excursion was thoroughly enjoyable, within the cathedral and out in the meadow. We returned to the flat and slept soundly.

Christmas day was planned; after a lazy start, exchange of presents and a light breakfast we'd drive out to lunch at a small pub in a village only ten miles or so away. Alex and I had played many games of cricket for the college on the village ground and where we had drunk innumerable pints with the landlord, his wife and a few of the regulars. After this time, apart from the landlord who I spoke to on the phone when I booked Christmas Day Lunch, I was not sure how many of the crowd I would know.

On a cold Christmas morning, except for the captivating lights and carols radiating from a church, there can be few sights more welcoming than a thatched, country pub promising warmth and good cheer.

The first person we saw walking into the pub was the self-styled squire; tall and gaunt, he was not advancing into old age easily.

"Well, I'll be damned, if it isn't that fellow who's off drive was always suspect. What's happened to your mate? Alan? Alf? Damn good wicket keeper that chap."

"Alex."

"That's the one."

"Down with the winter bug I'm afraid."

"Should come here. Got the cure for that sort of thing here," he proclaimed, raising his glass of scotch to prove it. "And what a charming young lady." He stood and bowed to Rachel.

Sitting again on his barstool, he resumed serious application to alcohol. His obsession with all things cricket was challenged only by his veneration of whisky (preferably single malt), the latter winning the contest for his affections. Nevertheless, he continued to lecture anyone within earshot on the inadequacy of present-day cricket coaching of the forward defensive shot. "Firm wrists. Essential," he harrumphed. "No one teaches that anymore. Just look at the England side. Need I say more?" But he always did say more, a lot more. His wife, who had heard it all innumerable times, stoically drank her rum and coke, ensuring as the party progressed there was less and less coke in the mix until she no longer cared. She had nurtured four children almost totally without her husband's help, or even interest, (except in the nets where they were a great disappointment to him. "Damn it, all gals, d'you see.") If the children had left her chronically tired, her husband left her chronically bored. She was therefore chronically cross. It must be said, however, that the 'squire' was greatly frustrated by his physical limitations that distressingly hampered his cricketing expertise on the field of play. His right leg had been amputated some years ago due to alcoholic overindulgence which had caused severe circulatory damage. This had not only restricted his mobility but also his ability to play cricket. For example, his wrists were fine when he played his forward defensive shot, it was his balance that was the problem; he tended to fall over. It had to be pointed out however that this was not only due to his anatomical handicap. He usually batted at the tail end of his side's list of batsmen and on some sunny afternoons had to wait hours in the pavilion for a call to the crease. His unsteady walk to the wicket had to be seen to be believed. Bowlers had no need to worry, in fact it had been known for fielders to give him directions to the wicket. Another well-known side effect of excessive alcohol consumption, double vision, further impeded his performances. If he got to the crease successfully and remained on his feet, often his bat was aimed not at the deliveries to him, but at the two unfocused balls his eyes erroneously perceived. His batting average was not impressive. He had turned down the suggestion to act as scorer because it was 'beneath him', which, in a way, was a blessing in disguise, because normally by mid-afternoon he was totally incapable of coherent speech, never mind accurate numerical calculation. The suggestion was quietly dropped.

"Look who's here, Tom!" The 'squire' addressed the landlord. "And a fair maiden with him."

Tom, the landlord, stood close by, his paunch an object of wonder. It had been developed over countless, dedicated years of serious beer-drinking. His wife disapproved of his paunch and so did his general practitioner but for different reasons. Both had now abandoned their repeated attempts at measuring its circumference; one, because she didn't possess a tape measure long enough, and the other because he couldn't believe the landlord was still alive. However, Tom was a jolly chap, the conventional 'life and soul of the party', universally liked (or tolerated) by all his customers (well, he was the landlord.) I'd heard it whispered by regulars 'in the know', that Tom's wife was conducting an illicit affair with the local undertaker. This information had forced Alex to opine; "It gives a whole new meaning to being laid out." Whether Tom knew of his wife's aberrant behaviour or not was a topic of endless speculation in the village. Whichever the case, it didn't interfere with running of the pub nor consuming a substantial proportion of the profits.

Sitting next to the open fire the village schoolmaster, on holiday and therefore permitted to enjoy his Christmas, was keeping an eye on the proceedings. Later, his guard would drop as the beer flowed, and he would tell his unlimited stock of jokes, not all of which would pass broadcasting censors unchallenged, and some that would shock parents of his charges, though probably not his charges. Rumour had it that he had left his previous school employment abruptly and under suspicious circumstances, some even suggesting that there may have been repeated deficiencies in the teacher's tea fund, which would have carried a lesser retribution than the real malfeasance. However, that might have been a vile slander; no one was sure. Anyway, his wife had retreated from most social contacts, let's face it, all social contacts and village activities for the last five years. She was not present today, lying down in a darkened room, suffering from one of her frequent migraines.

Most of the others present were unremarkable regulars from the village. Farmers, or farm workers, but I also saw a nurse I knew with her husband and raised a hand in acknowledgement. These villagers were the 'bread and butter' of the pub, who not only brought in ready cash but gave it character; a cheerful atmosphere that some village pubs had, and some didn't. I knew the regulars would welcome a young lady like Rachel, and within seconds, she was surrounded by a merry gang, all intent on impressing her with their wit and charm. We both loved it, especially Rachel who was never one to reject flirtatious banter. The doors were locked at 1:00 pm so everyone could settle down to enjoy themselves.

Mid-afternoon the Bell above the bar was rung and we all made our way to the large room at the back, where two scrubbed, wooden tables had been set for about 30 places. Labels showed the seating and Rachel, and I were paired together. Traditional Christmas lunch was served. As courses followed, one after another, the noise increased and the laughter became less inhibited, although on reflection this may have had more to do with the consumption of wine and beer than the excellent food. After the dishes had been cleared, there was mercifully only one toast to our host. It was proposed by the squire, of course, enunciating every word with the exaggerated care of a habitual and excessive drinker. (His wife was sound asleep throughout the entire performance.) Slowly we all dispersed into the afternoon. The lunch had been entirely successful.

Back at the flat Rachel and I pulled up the 'drawbridge' and subsided into armchairs. Who could have forecast the scare to come?

Chapter 10

On the evening of 31 December 2019, Britain prepared to celebrate the New Year. The streets of London were thronged with merrymakers hell-bent on recreation; Piccadilly Circus was packed, many revellers climbing the famous statue. Trafalgar Square and Leicester Square were seething and swaying with jubilant crowds; in Soho, sex workers of both genders were doing a roaring trade. Clubs and pubs were uncomfortably packed, but no one cared; even waiting hours to be served with more alcohol was tolerated, although towards midnight with rather less composure. The Lord Mayor of London, Sadiq Khan, had promised a Thameside firework display the likes of which had not been in London before. Literally thousands gathered on both embankments from Westminster to the Eye Wheel and beyond. Spectacular had been promised, sensational it was. The weather was perfect and only a light breeze disturbed the curtain of smoke from spent fireworks; and that curtain was constantly changing colour behind the dazzling explosions of yet more fireworks around and on the neon-lit Eye. The scene was astonishing. Thousands of candles were held by those among the crowds, and lasers swept across the sky.

Many millions more watched on TV and on social media.

Elsewhere, more genteel celebrations were under way. Diane and Reginald Young at Plantagenet House, on the stroke of midnight, raised their glasses to toast the Queen, Commonwealth and the New Year, strictly in that order. To have a drink on New Year's Day as Big Ben chimed 12 was obligatory in their lives, no matter where they were in the world. And sure enough 'our marvellous workmen' had made sure that even with the repairs currently underway, Big Ben did not fail them. What a country! Happy New Year!

Rachel and I watched the London celebrations on television and then went out onto the balcony and, arms around each other's waists, enjoyed the comparatively modest display of fireworks and floodlights over the city of Oxford. 2020 was to be the year of our marriage and our expectations were high and happy. Sinclair had broached the idea of a New Year party to Clarissa by saying; "Do you know Bamburg Castle on the Northumberland coast?" (Clarissa's eyebrows shot up to her hairline.) "Well, just north of that but also on the coast is the home that Mummy and Daddy inherited." (Clarissa's eyebrows returned to their usual position.) "What do you say, we pop up there for Hogmanay?"

Clarissa did not need to think. "Of course," she cried, imagining oak beams and a multiroom mansion on the coast of Northumberland. "Of course. I would be delighted to come."

"Right-ho! We'll drive up."

And so, it was arranged. The journey was long, but the luxury of Sinclair's new Jaguar XF 300 Sport eased the tedium. *'If you could see me now, Reggie!'* thought Clarissa perhaps, slightly unkindly. It turned out that the 'inherited home' was not quite Bamburg Castle, but it was certainly big. And crowded. Mummy (of English descent, and an accent to prove it) and Daddy (of Scottish descent, and a kilt to prove it) welcomed Clarissa and introduced her to several characters in evening attire, whose names she forgot immediately. One group of intense young men, dressed in kilts, were discussing Scottish independence aggressively, which surprised her as we were still in England, weren't we? Incomprehensibly, a couple sat cross-legged on the floor crying. No one took any notice of them. On a chaise longue, another couple seemed purposefully intent on furthering their physical relationship rather than joining the party. No one took any notice of them. A dachshund had sneaked into the room undetected and had become amorously attached to a kilted gentleman's leg; fortunately, the gentleman was in such an advanced state of intoxication that he took no notice. Clarissa, who was still relatively sober, remembered there was a Cavendish tartan (made official in 2019) but she could see no one sporting it tonight. It had to be said however that Sinclair was rather vague about the exact pattern and Clarissa was not too interested in expanding her knowledge that far north of the border (they were still in England, weren't they?) At midnight a Piper skirled his pipes (or whatever it was they did!) and everyone then sang 'Auld Lang Syne' and after that some of the more excited partygoers shouted, "Lang may Yer Lum reek" which was met with a mystified silence from most of the company. Guests were invited to 'Tak another dram' and then carry it to a long trestle table where two handsomely attired waiters were serving dishes of haggis, with mashed neeps and tatties. Clarissa viewed these dishes with some misgiving but was relieved to see plates of sausage rolls, chipolatas, vol au vents, cheeses, bread rolls, olives, salad—you name it, there it was! All accompanied by as many drams as you wished. She had only just filled her plate with fare of which she was familiar, when a huge, bearded specimen, complete with kilt, drew up in front of her and towering above her, helped himself to several of her sausages while shouting at her in a language or dialect she couldn't understand; presumably a Scottish accent or it might even have been Gaelic for all she knew. As he edged ever closer, she tried to back away, only to find herself trapped against a wall. Fumes of whisky engulfed her. For a second, she panicked, but Sinclair materialised, interposed himself between Clarissa and the drunken highlander and all was calmed.

"Fun?" he inquired.

"Absolutely," she answered in a voice that may have belied her momentary loss of self-assurance. She wondered at the same time, how long it would be before they could decently retire for the night. Good God! Some of the men had started dancing and jumping about so that their kilts exposed more of their hairy legs than Clarissa was prepared for. It was all quite frightful to a 'gal' who had been accustomed to the gentility of a finishing school. She hunted desperately for another dram, and thankfully found two.

In Norfolk, Alexander was still unwell and bed-bound at the medical facility of the private laboratory in which he worked. At first, he ran a high temperature and suffered a sore throat and his muscles and joints ached painfully. No more than typical symptoms of influenza. However, the Company he worked for was so concerned, their doctor was called urgently lest this was more than just a winter cold. Alexander hardly registered the doctor's visit and was asleep most of the time. Although the doctor confidently affirmed that 'sleep was the best medicine', his condition after four or five days began to cause alarm. The laboratory in which he worked contained highly toxic substances and further, experimented with lethal and contagious viruses. Accidental contamination was always a possibility. Intravenous fluids. Analgesics were prescribed but by midnight on New Year's Eve Alex was unconscious. On the firm's orders, two staff were dispatched to Alexander's cottage on the Norfolk coast where all possessions were removed and the tiny, now empty house secured with padlocks. They missed the painting on the far wall. Becker caught the night ferry from Lowestoft to Rotterdam. No one took any notice of him.

*** *** ***

The first day of the year is traditionally a general holiday, but Group Captain Young retired to his office in Plantagenet House and Diane applauded such diligence. He considered the death of Rice; it was a mess, that was sure, and he was uneasy about letting the police take a free hand, but that seemed to be the way Eleanor wanted it. She made up her mind to allow the police force a free hand to investigate Rice's death and would hear of no interference. He felt it unsatisfactory. He worried that he had to wait for police conclusions and powerless. That did not sit well with him. Then, the other thing. The department placed much importance on the success of the symposia at The Lawns; the 'consideration of recent viral research' was so much Greek to him. But with such significance attached to the symposium, he had best be on top of the administration and management was what Eleanor wanted him to do. Tomorrow, without fail, he would ring Professor Bhatti and then Stacey Donato.

The next day, Group Captain Young returned to his office in Whitehall and as planned, rang Professor Bhatti and decided to meet that afternoon. Then he contacted Stacey Donato to check on accommodation for the forthcoming symposium.

Meanwhile Konrad in Cheltenham, pondered over a couple of reports from the World Health Organisation (WHO) relating to China. These would require specialist knowledge to make sense of them, but others in his department had already flagged up the reports as important. He needed to get in touch with Young. By January the 6th, 2020, Konrad was sufficiently intrigued by these reports, to ring Young directly. Clarissa answered.

"Reception."

"That you Clarissa? Can I just mention, I need a word with Reggie?"

"He's busy with Professor Bhatti at the moment, but as soon as he's free I'll speak to him." Clarissa made a note in the diary.

"Thanks, say it's quite important, will you?"

"Yes, I will, and I'll get back to you as soon as I can."

She sat back reflecting on the days spent in Northumberland. The family home was not Bamburg Castle, but it was substantial. Mummy and Daddy held no titles but were obviously loaded and Sinclair well-mannered and diverting enough to be interesting, even if he wasn't ambitious. She might be able to light his fires. Now, there was a challenge! She would see…

By 4:30 pm, Young and Professor Bhatti had concluded their discussions which included the list of topics for the forthcoming symposium. The date for the start of the conference was January 27th, three weeks hence and invited specialists had already been contacted. Gratifyingly, almost all had responded with acceptance to the symposium. Neither saw attendance as a problem. Young was left to ensure appropriate accommodation was provided for the guests at The Lawns.

Professor Bhatti wished Clarissa 'Good afternoon' on his way out, and she in turn walked along the corridor and knocked on Young's door.

"Konrad phoned today and said he'd like to meet with you concerning a couple of matters he'd stumbled across. I said I'd ask."

"So happens free tomorrow morning, aren't I?" Young was not particularly excited. "Could fit him in then. What d'you think?"

"Sounds OK." Clarissa had thoughtfully brought the diary. "I'll pencil it in."

"Nothing else?" Young asked.

"I don't think so."

"Oh, by the way, Clarissa," Young changed the subject. "You haven't told me of your adventures in the North. How were they?"

Clarissa sat back, crossed her shapely legs and gave Reggie an abbreviated version of the events. "It was super. Sinclair was the perfect gentleman and his parents so-o generous. We had a super time, if perhaps a little Scottish for my liking. I don't enjoy the sound of bagpipes as the others did and one or two of the gentlemen were rather forward in their advances. Oh, you should have seen the dancing! Those men!"

"Hell, d'you mean?"

Young detected that some of her pre-journey enthusiasm had evaporated. But he chose to ignore it.

"Well, as far as I'm concerned, kilts and reels don't mix."

"Dammit young lady you're blushing."

Clarissa was. Now that she was thinking more vividly of the whirling dancers, her blush deepened.

"Saw more than you bargained for."

"Oh yes, I did. A lot more! Can we leave it now Reggie?"

"Otherwise damn good time what?"

"Oh yes, a really good time indeed." Curiously, she was blushing even more now.

Young and Clarissa eyed each other speculatively but said no more. And with that Clarissa returned to her desk.

Tuesday morning, January 7th, 2020, Konrad arrived to see Young. Clarissa welcomed him, spoke to the Group Captain on the phone, and invited the member of the ANCOM to proceed to the office. She would arrange coffee.

"Reggie, Happy New Year. Sorry to trouble you." Konrad perched himself on the edge of one of the armchairs. "Good break?"

"Fair to middling. You know how it is. Yourself?"

"Good, yes good. My wife's expecting our first any day now, so it's all hands to the pump."

"Congratulations. 'Fraid my wife and I have not been so blessed." Young paused and looked at the turbulent seascape. "Think sometimes we've missed out. Not sure."

There was silence for a while and Konrad eased himself back into the chair, the door opened, and a member of the catering staff brought coffee…Young continued to gaze at his oil painting but suddenly jerked himself upright and spoke.

"Now then Konrad, what's this all about?"

"Most probably nothing, really. I just thought you ought to be aware of one or two messages that have come my way. At the tail end of last year, there was a statement from a place called Wuhan in China about a case of 'viral pneumonia', remember? Nothing to get excited about except there is a highly secret and seriously guarded bacterial and virology laboratory built there. If you remember, I mentioned at one of our meetings that the Americans had picked up some increased telephone traffic from that area earlier."

"Remember that, yes." Young frowned.

"Well, on 30th December there was a media statement from Wuhan that there was a 'cluster of viral pneumonias' in the area, apparently of unknown origin. On January the 1st, WHO requested more information from China, but it wasn't until the 3rd that China provided some information i.e., 'a cluster of pneumonia cases'. On the 5th, that was Sunday, WHO issued general advice on the treatment of viral pneumonia. Now it's not for me to comment on virology, but it does seem that something odd may be happening, if WHO is troubling itself."

"Yes." Young pondered at length. "Not much to go on though."

"I quite agree. I just thought it was part of our remit to highlight any unclear or puzzling information."

"It is." Agreed Young still frowning. Something was bothering him; at first sight it seemed a big jump but why this sudden interest in The Lawns, Professor Bhatti and the symposia? A long shot but…"Right, Konrad. Quite right to bring this up. Better keep an eye on proceedings."

"Certainly. Probably nothing."

"All the same, Konrad, think we better call a meeting together. What do you say, later this week? Say the 10th? No rush is there?"

"None at all." Konrad was pensive.

They finished their coffee, made polite noises at one another and Konrad took his leave. Young had noticed that Konrad was not the 'gazing out of the window and dreaming' person he had been but was focused. Something had caught his attention and no mistake. Young's attention was caught as well.

He called Clarissa and asked her to arrange a formal meeting of ANCOM on Friday, 10th January, and arrange for him to visit The Lawns. She rang back to say that Stacey Donato was on leave but would be back by Tuesday the 14th of January and would 12 noon be acceptable to him as a provisional appointment. He said it would.

*** *** ***

After the Christmas break, Rachel returned to London and work, and I returned to college. We both needed to get back into work, and so we agreed to suspend further weekends together for a few weeks. Every evening we phoned and had a short chat, but we had no definitive date in mind for a reunion. One thing did worry us however and that was the continuing silence from Alexander, and we decided that if nothing had happened in a couple of weeks we would investigate.

*** *** ***

Friday, January 10th, Young was in his office when a tap on the door indicated the presence of Clarissa who entered, complete with huge diary and benevolent smile.

"Reggie, just to remind you, the meeting of the ANCOM is at 10:30 am."

"ANCOM. Today?"

"Reggie, come on, you arranged it."

"Just joking. Just joking."

"I'll send them in when they arrive. And organise some coffee." She left, unsmiling.

Young was not as relaxed about this committee meeting as he would be normally. He had worked assiduously to integrate the individual members into a united group that would present strong agreement on information of interest; draw together operatives from the intelligence services, GCHQ, Special Branch, Counterterrorism and metropolitan police to a single influential unit. Difficulty had arisen with the death of Rice, a complication he could well do without. Eleanor had told him to leave it to the police, but Rice had leaked the puzzling traffic congestion, she said. It was unsatisfactory as far as Young was concerned.

At precisely 10:30 am, a loud knock on Young's door encouraged him to yell; "Come." But considering that a little abrupt he added quietly, "Come in," by which time Konrad and a colleague were already in the room. Perhaps showing a display of some tension, Young jumped up and proceeded to the polished table and sat at the head with his back to the windows.

"Come, sit down, why don't you? We're going to be around this table anyway so might as well start here, what? Now who's this young man you've brought, today?"

Konrad and his colleague followed the Group Captain to the table, then sat together on Young's left. "I brought along Michael. He's rather new at Cheltenham but extremely bright and I thought this might be a learning opportunity for him. Further, I think he may well have something useful to add to our discussions."

"Good. Good. Hello, name's Reggie."

"Good afternoon." Michael spoke for the first time and was formal.

"Don't stand on ceremony here" (pause) "nor sit on it either!" The Group Captain Young waited for the laugh; there wasn't one. "Looks like we're the only ones…"

Just at that moment, another knock and the door swung open admitting Nigel and in his wake Samara, accompanied by a tall, heavily built man in a dark suit.

"Come in. Join us."

Samara came to the table and introduced her colleague as Detective Superintendent Brian Franklin. "I thought, this morning, we might be touching on the unfortunate death of Phillipson Rice and so I've brought along the Superintendent who is overseeing the investigation into his murder."

This was, of course, exactly what Young did not want. Nevertheless, the bloody man was here, and the committee would have to listen; hopefully, comment as little as possible. The three pulled up chairs and sat opposite Konrad and his colleague Michael. Young made the introductions, then taking a deep breath, decided to get the discussion started; but before he could say another word the door opened yet again, and coffee was brought in.

"Thanks. Help yourselves."

Finally, they were joined by a member of Special Branch, today Young noticed, in mufti.

At this stage of the proceedings, Samara plucked up courage and re-introduced the Superintendent. "I thought that he would be able to give us the latest information. Detective Superintendent Franklin manages Major Investigation Teams, one of which is investigating Rice's death. He is more hands-on than me." She had the committee's full attention but Michael, the new boy from GCHQ, knew nothing of the murder; that would soon be rectified. He sensed a certain hesitancy in the members but at the same time their faces were attentive and expectantly focused on the Superintendent. Before Young could explain that the police investigation was not their concern, the door opened and yet again the committee was interrupted. Lady Eleanor walked in and unhurriedly sat at the table and helped herself to coffee. Slowly she looked at each of them in turn and finally and more intently at Group Captain Young. The room was still.

"Good morning." She purred. "I have met the lady Commander, Konrad, John from Special Branch and Nigel before, but I am at a loss to place this young man (gesturing at Michael) and another, I am sure, esteemed member of this committee (smiling at the Detective Superintendent). Young, now thoroughly watchful and not a little uneasy, leant forward and introduced Michael, new from GCHQ, and Detective Superintendent Franklin."

"Good morning," Lady Eleanor greeted each in turn, "and thank you Reginald. I hope you don't think that I am interfering, but your committee has highlighted such useful snippets of information over the last few months that it has drawn appreciative murmurings from those on high and my reports to the Sir Brendan need to be substantial and well-informed, with a more intimate knowledge of your membership and working practices. I hope you understand."

"Of course." Young kept his thoughts to himself but was sure that she was here to hear the latest on Rice and would without doubt have been made aware of the Detective Superintendent's attendance. She was also adept at obfuscation. Konrad saved him.

"Before the Detective Super (and this was to be the generally accepted abbreviation to be used for the policeman) starts, I would like to bring to the committee's attention some disturbing facts that have cropped up with regards the outbreak of a viral influenza in China."

Young was eternally grateful. "Certainly, Konrad. Matter of some urgency, isn't it?"

"Please. I hate to interrupt quite so quickly, but I would like to know if the Chief Super has been cleared for this meeting." Eleanor would not let go.

"Oh certainly," This was Samara. "Before we came, Brian was cognisant of the confidentiality of this meeting and had previously signed the Official Secrets Act, in any case."

"That's good to know." The Baroness smiled. Young thought to himself. *Surely she's satisfied now.*

Konrad started again. "Michael here, works with me at GCHQ and has a special interest in WHO, and reports from that body. Perhaps, Reggie (deliberately addressing Young and not Eleanor) if you don't mind, I'll ask Michael to let us know about his disquiet with some data he has received."

Young nodded his assent and privately noted that the Baroness had been disregarded. Michael leant his elbows on the table, and with remarkable confidence in one so young, started to speak.

"I think the first thing to say is that, at present, no one can be sure of the seriousness of this reported outbreak of viral pneumonia in China. Just a little background might be helpful. The common cold and influenza are caused by a virus rhinovirus. Almost twenty years ago in 2002 there was a serious outbreak of respiratory infections, again in China, which was discovered later to be a mutated form of a different virus, namely the coronavirus, named SARS, that is merely an abbreviation for or a South Asian Respiratory Syndrome. It is important for two reasons; the first is that it is much more severe than the common cold and can be fatal and the second is that it is easily transmitted from human to human in respiratory droplets. Another coronavirus mutation was found later in the Middle East and appropriately called MERS, an abbreviation for Middle East Respiratory Syndrome. This one is not nearly as potent as the SARS."

Most of the members were lost but the next sentence brought them back on course quickly.

"Now the big problem is that just last month, in December, in a place called Wuhan in central China, another new mutation of this coronavirus might be causing rapid and widespread respiratory infections, although the exact nature of the virus has yet to be determined."

"So, a nasty little virus called coronavirus might have changed enough to harm us humans."

Young was trying to keep up.

"That's right." Matthew was keen to explain his interest. "How did this virus change into a deadly human threat? Was it natural evolution? That would take a very long time. Or was this virus manufactured in a laboratory? If it was manufactured, why was it manufactured? One answer is for use in biowarfare. That apparently is now possible. What brought this to my attention is that WHO is taking this seriously. On 5th of January just 5 days ago, they gave the first intimations that this disease outbreak was due to this new coronavirus. They also issued risk assessments and advice on what they had been told from China. Today they've published technical guidance on how to contain viral illnesses, to detect it, test and manage potential cases."

"Right," said Young, "but what's that got to do with us? This virus is in China, isn't it?"

"That's true. But what may concern us is that although there is what is called a 'wet market' in Wuhan which may have been the original source of this virus, worryingly there is a high security virology laboratory in the same area; and a leak from that facility cannot be ignored. And it may well spread out of China."

Young spoke. "You mean this just might be a man-made type of virus." Now, Michael had the committee's undivided attention. Young went on. "So, if it is man-made, we would want to know why it was made. And that makes it very much our concern."

"Precisely." Michael sat back. "One last point. No matter whether it is man-made or has jumped to humans from a fish market or an animal (say a bat), it's bloody dangerous and we have no natural immunity."

"It could spread world-wide?"

"It could, and that would be catastrophic."

"Thank you, Michael." Young said somewhat uncertainly. "Not sure how exactly we put that together for our 'master's and betters'. Clearly, it's important.

May have to ask you for a written précis. Would that be possible?" Young enquired.

"Certainly."

Lady Eleanor looked at the table. She did not speak.

Heads nodded. This was so far from the Detective Super's normal day that he must have wondered what he'd wandered into. But Samara brought him back to familiar ground. She spoke directly to the Group Captain, "Shouldn't we listen now to the latest on the investigation into poor Rice's death?"

Young was not going to answer that with Lady Eleanor sitting there. But no one even looked at Eleanor, so Detective Superintendent Franklin began.

"As far as the pathologist can tell us, Mr Rice was murdered on or about the 11th of December. He was at the time in his flat, and there is no suggestion or evidence that there was a break in, or a stranger had forced a way in. We therefore assume that Mr Rice invited the perpetrator of this deed into his flat. The next point of interest is that he had undressed and was preparing for a bath when he was assaulted from behind and strangled with, what the pathologist assumes, was a leather belt or something similar. We have investigated the background of Mr Rice and know that he was a member of a club in Soho which catered for those amongst us who are of lesbian or gay disposition." (Young inwardly squirmed at the phrase) "It seems further, that on the evening of the 11th of December he drank in this club where he is a regular and is remembered by the barmen. One of these barmen can also remember that he met a man of quiet nature, well dressed and possibly with a mid-European accent. There seemed to be no altercation nor argument and the two are thought to have left together on friendly terms at about 11:00 pm. There was no further sighting of Mr Rice that evening, and if they travelled to his flat by taxi, we have been unable to trace the driver. Our forensic specialists have found only evidence of Mr Rice in the flat, apart that is, from several unrecognised fingerprints. Similarly, DNA found cannot be identified on our database."

(*And all this from memory,* thought Young, *not a notebook in sight!*)

"One other line of inquiry has been shut down. We were made aware that his line of work was confidential. The Home Office had…" Before he could go on the Lady Eleanor interrupted.

"Thank you, Superintendent. I think that is as far as we can go on this matter today. You have been extremely clear in your summation of the investigation so far."

All heads turned to Young for confirmation. He nodded.

Lady Eleanor stood up and smiled at each of them in turn. "We all think your work is valuable and I commend you to continue with it. I hope I have not interfered today. That was not my intention." And then turning, she walked slowly to the door and left.

It was for Young to sum up as best he could. "Michael, thank you very much for your excellent dissertation on something that might develop into importance, possibly world importance. I look forward to receiving your précis. And thank you Chief Super. There's just one other thing; sometime soon we will have to look for a replacement for Phillipson. I'll speak to Eleanor about that. If there is nothing else, I think we can call it a day. Thank you all."

The room emptied, leaving Young still at the table gazing fixedly at the turbulent seas.

With the benefit of hindsight, we can see now, the warning of impending danger posed by this new coronavirus was to an extent marginalised. ANCOM took it more seriously than many other organisations but did not consider it important enough to give maximum promotion.

On Tuesday, 14th January, Young, looking forward to his visit to The Lawns and of course, his meeting with the charming Ms Donato, arrived for his appointment at noon in good time. Arthur Cobb, bespectacled, big and well-dressed, welcomed him courteously and relieved him of his mobile phone and miscellaneous metal objects then asked if he was carrying any recording equipment about his person. When assured that Young was not, he allowed him in and told him Ms Donato awaited him in the lounge. Young walked down the short corridor and entered the spacious room overlooking the garden, where Stacey Donato was waiting. Her smile was warm, and she walked towards him tall and elegant, extending her hand:

"Group Captain! Come in please. I am so delighted to meet with you again."

Young smiled and shook hands, at the same time noticing her long, raven-black hair and what a wonderful contrast against her impeccable, pale blue suit. "This lady," he mused, "is imposingly attractive."

"I have to apologise," she murmured, "when your assistant phoned, I was away on short leave. My secretary made this appointment and I hope it is not too inconvenient"

"Good heavens no." Young assured her, "Perfectly convenient."

"Good. But unfortunately, my secretary also forgot that we were having a security meeting here today, and in less time than it takes you to blink, the participants will be recessing for lunch and beverages." A shy smile. "Not necessarily in that order."

Young smiled, as an experienced man-of-the-world would. Whether Donato recognised this attempt at intrigue was not made clear.

"Might I suggest that we adjourn to my flat where it will be (pause) quieter. Trust me."

Young swallowed and followed her upstairs. (Perhaps she had noticed!) This was a very different Stacey Donato than the one he met before.

The flat was, as Young imagined it, large, with several rooms; the lounge where he was taken was sunlit by picture windows overlooking the garden. The walls were painted in pastel green, the furniture of light pine, contemporary in design but by no means avant-garde. The carpet was deep-piled off-white, the armchairs well-cushioned and covered in floral material and in the middle of the room a long, low glass-topped table supported a tall ceramic vase containing a large bunch of roses. Comfortable but not ostentatious.

"Please." Ms Donato indicated an armchair. "Can I get you tea, coffee, or something stronger? We have about an hour before we go downstairs again."

"Coffee, please." Young played it safe.

After Ms Donato left to make coffee, Young wandered round the room, hands behind his back, viewing the framed paintings on the walls. A couple of 'pretty' watercolours and a much larger and more challenging mixed media on paper (original, if he were not mistaken), with a signature that was flamboyant but illegible. Her desk held a reasonably sized computer, a printer and a landline phone, above it hung a large calendar covered with notes above a photographed reproduction of an impressionist painting. He moved on to the bookcase where he found, to his surprise, copies of the New Oxford Annotated Bible, the Qur'an and a dictionary/thesaurus. There was a row of the Hilary Mantel trilogy, a row of Ian McEwan, some large art books and more. On the bookcase were two photographs: one of a teenage lad in the countryside leaning on a gate and smiling at the camera, and the other, a more composed picture of a dark arched bridge under which was a river in deep shadow, posts silhouetted black against a brilliant sunset. After looking at the photograph for several moments, Young saw that between the posts were two figures, apparently stationary and looking across the water, also silhouetted against the evening sky. It was quite impossible to make out who the persons were, or even their gender. It was at this point Stacey re-entered the room and placed a tray with two coffee cups, percolator, silver milk jug and sugar bowl on the glass topped table.

Young turned and felt the need to explain his interest in the photographs although there was no hint of annoyance on Stacey's part.

"I was just admiring the photographs. Particularly the one on the right, with the bridge, river, figures and sunset. Quite startling."

"Yes, a friend of mine who is a semi-professional photographer took that. I quite like it as a matter of fact. The other one I snapped; it's of my son before he went up to university."

"A handsome young man," the ever-chivalrous Group Captain replied, making a mental note at the same time: *Oh yes! A son. And no wedding band.*

"Shall we?" Stacey made herself comfortable and indicated the coffee. Young sat opposite and accepted coffee. "Milk, no sugar, thank you."

They faced one another outwardly at ease. At last, Young resumed; "I wanted to come over and remind myself of the layout here; before we have our first symposium on the 27th. Get the feel of the wonderful facilities and make sure you are happy with the numbers attending the symposium."

"So wise. I like to think this is a well-run establishment, efficient both in hospitality and secretarial services. As a sensitive government sector, I think the security is as impregnable as the present technology allows." Stacy crossed her ankles.

"That's good to hear. Had no doubt of that, and anyway that is not my concern. My role is merely to promote the work here and hopefully assist others to inform government of prudent action. That's all. However, I do have a question for you…"

"Yes?"

"…how are the conclusions here relayed to the government departments?"

"Oh, that's easy. We have a secretarial service that ensures all discussions, contributions, analyses and recommendations made here are encoded and sent electronically to central government. Unfortunately, we are not yet in the age of quantum computers and unbreakable codes are not at our fingertips, but our procedures are as secure as we can make them, and all messages are completely obliterated after a limited period. I hope that puts your mind at rest."

"It does."

Young was not sure how to proceed, or even proceed at all. However, for the moment he sat tight. Eventually she said, "We will be meeting again soon then." They sipped their coffee.

"Of course. Accommodation for five days is arranged. I think that's what you requested." Stacey looked at him directly.

"Five days will take care of it perfectly."

Young noticed for the first time the scent of roses. *How on Earth do you get scented roses in the middle of Winter,* he wondered.

"The roses are beautiful," he nodded towards the glass-topped table.

"Quite lovely, aren't they?"

Stacey said no more, which left Young at a loss for a suitable riposte and in danger of having to take his leave and he was too comfortable for that. Saved!

"As I think I mentioned before," Stacey breathed, "it is unusual for us to entertain one from your service."

The question was left in the air and Young considered his answer with care.

"I was an administrator. Flying was not my thing. When I retired, I was invited to take up this position in Whitehall."

"I see," she said, "that goes a long way to explain the apparent anomaly."

Silence again. This was beginning to get tense. At last, Ms Donato reverted to her managerial role. "I think, if you have finished your coffee I need to go back down and get on. Is that acceptable?"

"Of course." Young said. "Sorry to have taken up too much of your valuable time." They went downstairs and Young took his leave.

After he had left, Ms Donato considered the man. Pleasant enough, well-mannered, not the world's rival to Einstein, but quite inquisitive. Harmless? (I think. I think.) In the taxi back to Whitehall, the Group Captain considered Ms Donato to be two things; attractive (and she knew it,) competent (and she knew it.) He looked forward to further encounters.

Chapter 11

On Tuesday January 14th the day after he had enlisted Mikhail's assistance and been reassured by the cooperation of Superintendent Franklin, Young approached Whitehall in an optimistic frame of mind. He smiled at the officer on duty outside, Clarissa at her desk and even the internal security guard at the inner door. He strode down the corridor and entered his office with elan. Sitting behind his desk soon changed all that. It was immediately obvious that nothing had changed fundamentally. The style atmosphere of the Whitehall officers was matched only by the infrequent and hurried steps of important persons passing his door. The telephone rang far away then stopped abruptly; whether it was answered, or the caller had given up in frustration was unclear. After a while, the staccato sound of a secretary's heels could be heard approaching his door, passing without stopping, and on down the corridor. That was followed by a heavy silence. He waited for the next sound.

His internal telephone rang. "Reggie?" It was Clarissa.

"The same."

Short pause while Clarissa thought about this answer. Finally, she decided. "Reggie! Message from a guy called Mikhail, sounded foreign, he said 'started today'. Mean anything?"

"Yes."

Another pause, this time rather longer as Clarissa waited for more information but when it was not forthcoming, she put the phone down. Young went through his messages: nothing there: nothing from The Lawns. They seemed to be functioning perfectly well without his assistance. Nothing new there. On the spur of the moment, he stood, grabbed his coat and left.

"Going out for a while," he called to Clarissa on his way past.

And that's how it began. The brew of excited anticipation and intimidating boredom was a heady mixture that was adversely affecting his equilibrium. He couldn't settle. He took to wandering slowly away from the office and Whitehall, head down, hopefully inconspicuous, absorbed in his own thoughts and unheeding of other pedestrians. Today, his first day of such inconsequential meanderings, he found himself on Westminster Bridge leaning on the parapet watching the grey/brown Thames drift by. That was how his mind was, drifting, sluggish, aimless. Big Ben was partially hidden behind scaffolding and the Palace of Westminster seemed shrouded in the greyness of the day. One or two small boats chugged about, up and down stream or crossing from one bank to another. Not frantically busy, not inspiring, going about their business unenthusiastically and mildly irritating, on the edge of his awareness. The footfall behind him was continuous, often hurried, sometimes even urgent. In his preoccupation, he ignored the activity. He had become sure, but it had to be said on meagre evidence, that all was not well in his department. Another complication. Konrad and that fellow Matthew had raised the possibility of something catastrophic peeping over the horizon. That was a much bigger picture. All in all, it was thorny, but he could do no more than wait. In 10 days, perhaps, Mikhail would produce something concrete to go on; something to get his teeth into.

He must have been leaning there for some time, for a policeman approached him and asked if he was well in himself.

"Oh, quite well officer, thank you." Young straightened up quickly and moved off in the direction of Whitehall.

Another day, he found himself in a small art gallery off Regent Street. Everywhere here was white and bright. Small oils each delicately illuminated hung, widely separated, on white walls. Two or three small standing exhibits were placed decorously around the room. One looked like a broken tree branch with side branches, painted black and stuck into a lump of white painted concrete. What was he supposed to make of that? A skeletal hand? An appeal to a God? A shape? It was entitled 'No.17', which only added to his bemusement. In the end, he realised it was a broken tree branch stuck into some concrete. Here it was 'Art'. Did that make him a philistine? Probably. A woman with carefully arranged untidy hair who was reading catalogues suddenly looked up at him as if he had said something. Perhaps he had. He hoped it wasn't an obscenity. He hurried over to gaze at an artist's intense interpretation of a bowl of flowers and after a while he became aware of a person standing next to him.

"Beautiful, isn't it?" the person breathed into his ear.

Startled, he looked. He had an impression of a middle-aged lady dressed in a twinset, with pearls, permed hair and perfume.

"Yes," he managed, before bolting for the door. He'd heard of these cruising middle-aged ladies with hopeful thoughts. He found refuge in a bookshop and proceeded to wander around, looking at books without much interest. True, there was a section entitled 'Erotica' but he scampered past it lest anyone accuse him of being one of the 'dirty mac brigade'. At least, he was not accosted by any unaccompanied middle-aged women but after about half an hour he couldn't help but notice a store detective following and watching him with suspicion. He grabbed a book, took it to the till and bought it before leaving and hurrying back towards his office. Not all was lost, at least he had a book to read this afternoon. Inside his office he sat to his desk and opened the book eager for a diversion. It was a heavy tome on Quantum Theory. Apparently, all was lost. He had nothing to read this afternoon! He opened a drawer, threw the book into it and shut the drawer quickly but firmly.

And so, the days dragged by. He would either hide in his office or his Club, tending to wander less frequently, apprehensive lest sympathetic policemen, predatory middle-aged ladies or suspicious security guards approach him. Elsewhere, evidence was mounting of an imminent global event perhaps of frightful proportions.

It was not strictly the concern of GCHQ, but Konrad and Matthew, possibly with the encouragement of ANCOM, were sensitive and eager to learn more facts about this curious pneumonia outbreak in China's Wuhan province. It was just about possible that this was a virus that had accidentally escaped from a laboratory intent on manufacturing agents for hostile use, and that would be their concern. China released details of the virus' structure, and on January 12th, WHO issued detailed instructions on the control of viral infections worldwide. Further, there had been 6 deaths in Wuhan and cases now reported in Thailand, South Korea and Japan. It was also and even more worryingly reported that there was human-to-human transmission. WHO of course was not the only global organisation that was concentrating on this possible epidemic. There were international conferences in Switzerland, Germany, America and countless other countries all attended by world experts in the subjects associated with virology, epidemiology and treatment. In Britain, the Scientific Advisory Group for Emergencies (SAGE) met frequently, with the aim to advise the government. Whether the government heeded the advice was another matter. Many

Pharmaceutical firms were working to produce a vaccine as fast as possible. (AstraZeneca, Pfizer, Moderna and many others.) The race was on to produce a vaccine to protect as much of the world's population as possible before it was too late. The other thrust of research was to produce and test antiviral drugs to treat the illnesses directly. Antibiotics like penicillin only killed bacteria; this was a virus that was unaffected by antibiotics. New antiviral agents were needed, but so far, they seemed far off. Matthew placed his findings before Konrad, who informed his boss whilst at the same time making sure that he would tell Young's ANCOM of the growing world-wide concern. Elsewhere the populace took little notice. Slowly but surely, a false belief (or hope) in the public's mind grew that this was 'like flu' even 'only a new flu'. A costly misunderstanding.

*** *** ***

By the evening of Wednesday, January 15th, in Oxford, I had still not heard from Alex and had become bothered. He had told us that he had the 'winter lurgy' but that was before Christmas, and it seemed unlikely that 'flu had incapacitated him for so long'. On the other hand, Alex was notoriously erratic in his behaviour and perhaps a better offer had come along. (Well, there are ladies in Norfolk aren't there?) But more seriously, I couldn't get hold of him on his mobile. It didn't go to voicemail. It had been shut down. Surely even Alex would remember to keep it switched on. Deciding what to do was difficult. The best plan I could come up with was to phone Rachel. I phoned Rachel.

"Rachel Harding."

"All well?"

"All well." Our usual abbreviated greeting had developed naturally.

We gossiped for a while in a light-hearted way as usual. I'm not sure why I didn't mention it immediately; probably putting off and dodging a decision to contact the police. Reluctance to contact the police was learned behaviour from a childhood in Stornoway. In Scotland, talking to third parties concerning private matters was considered disloyal no matter how appropriate the circumstance. But after a few moments I told Rachel I still couldn't get hold of Alex in Norfolk, that his mobile was shut down and I couldn't even get voicemail.

"What do you think?" she asked.

"Well, it's nearly a month now since we've heard anything. I can't imagine what has happened. I'm wondering whether to ring the police."

We talked this over and, in the end, agreed that it wouldn't be wasting police time, that we were both quite concerned, and it might well be in Alex's best interests.

"I don't know his address." I suppose I was putting off the inevitable yet again. "How will they find his address?"

"Quite honestly I have no idea," she replied. "I expect they have ways and means."

After a few more moments, we rang off. With her help, I'd made up my mind. Sort of! After 10 minutes I rang the police.

"Constable Mundy. Can I help?"

"To be frank, I feel a bit foolish." I started.

"Can I be a judge of that sir?"

"It's like this…" And I went on to tell him the story of a chance meeting with Alex in Paris, of 'flu before Christmas, an expected reunion cancelled and now his mobile shut down. "I suppose what I'm reporting is a missing person."

"Your name and address sir?" I told him.

"And the name and address of this person who seems to be missing sir?"

"Alexander Dowson, about the same age as me, roughly 30, but his address I don't know."

"You don't know it sir?" The pause made me feel guilty. Goodness knows why. The silence grew embarrassing. In the end, he said, "Perhaps it would be best if you came down to the station sir and gave a formal statement. If that would not be too much trouble. You'll find the police station on St Aldates about half a mile past Christchurch Meadow. Is that convenient sir?"

"No trouble at all constable. Will tomorrow morning be soon enough?"

"I think that would be ideal sir."

I assured him I would be there at about 10:00 am.

On Thursday January 16th, I walked down St Aldates, passed Christchurch College and approached the Oxford City Central Police Station. It is a straightforward building; there are no frills, and it has precious little character. It is a utilitarian structure. Inside, it's not much better. But as you would expect of a police station it is polished, clean, careful yet surprisingly quiet, almost as if everyone is on their best behaviour, even drunks in the cells.

The duty Sergeant was expecting me, and I was taken to a small room, where I was asked to make a statement. I repeated the information I gave the evening before and was told enquiries would be made. They had my address. Yes. Could

I give them my phone number? Yes, and I did. Was I intending to leave the area in the foreseeable future? No. Very politely they asked me if I would be good enough to let them know where I was going, if I changed my mind. Yes. And that was that.

Outside, I knew the matter was now out of my hands and in some respects that was a relief.

The days after I'd visited the police in Oxford, and they had presumably started enquiries about Alex, I began to prepare lectures and tutorials for the approaching term. I rang Rachel twice over the weekend, but she was out, and I had to leave messages. That didn't worry me. It was just one of those things. It had happened several times before.

When I got home on Monday evening, 20th January, there was a recorded message on my phone from the Oxford police. They had contacted Norfolk, and would I be kind enough to ring Inspector Leeder (a Fakenham number, wherever Fakenham was!) and at my earliest convenience. Tomorrow would have to do.

Somewhat intrigued and not a little worried by the message from the local Constabulary, I rang Inspector Leeder in this place called Fakenham on Tuesday morning. Eventually I was put through.

"Leeder."

I gave my name and address. "Inspector. I'm ringing as you requested concerning my friend Alexander Dowson."

"Thank you." The answer was crisp if not exactly loquacious. I don't know what sort of accent I was expecting but what I heard was clipped Oxbridge. "I fear," he continued, "I have to trespass upon your time and for that I'm sorry, sir."

"How's that?"

"The laws in Britain covering the privacy of an individual are quite strict, and rightly so. A warrant has been granted to trace Mr Dowson's mobile phone and we have traced it. But now we're confronted with another problem of privacy. The phone has been located in a cottage situated in a small village on the North Norfolk coast and the premises are locked, and surprisingly padlocked on the outside. We must show need for entry into the building, but we may require someone who knows the man of the house. And of course, that would be your good self."

"I see." Now, this had become seriously worrying. "Do you mean for identification purposes?"

"Quite, sir. I apologise for the urgency, but I feel the quicker we are inside this cottage the quicker we will be able to assess the seriousness of the situation. Is there any possibility that you could come to Fakenham this week?"

Now this was serious. "I can come on Friday, if that is soon enough. I've no idea where Fakenham is."

"Friday will be fine. From what you say, Mr Dowson has been missing for some time now. Another two days is not going to change the situation materially. You have a Satnav, sir? Or if it is impossible for you to make the journey, we could send a car."

"Of course. I can drive." He didn't think I was being obstructive, did he?

"Very good sir. If you could come to the police station at Fakenham. Shall we say 3 pm? I think you should make it from Oxford by then."

"I'll try." I disconnected. He would call Rachel later in the evening, perhaps put off their weekend reunion. She was out again. I left a message.

"Materially?" Strange word to use.

I drove away from Oxford at 10:00 am, Friday 24th January. Estimating it would take me 3 to 4 hours, with a stop for a quick lunch. There was little traffic on the roads to Northampton but once past there, the A47 was slow. I got caught behind a huge lorry which did little to ease my journey or my anxiety about what would be found in Norfolk. Past Peterborough, the A47 is a reasonably fast road to King's Lynn; but then a right turn onto the A148 brought me to another difficult stretch of road which seemed to go on for hours but in fact only took 45 minutes. By the time I reached Fakenham police station, I was a little fractious! Inside, I asked for Inspector Leeder and got shown to his office. As I walked in, he stood offering to shake hands. I discovered he was not a big man, thin faced, hollow cheeked with pursed lips and what seemed to be a perpetual frown; his dark brown hair was receding alarmingly for one who appeared so young. He was drinking what I assumed to be tea from a large white mug upon which was printed 'Inspector;' probably an unwanted and rather embarrassing gift from his wife on his promotion. Introductions completed, I declined a cup of tea and we got down to business.

"You are concerned about a friend of yours, Alexander Dowson, sir?"

"I am. I invited him to Oxford in early December, only to receive a note telling me he was unwell. Seasonal 'flu as I remember."

"Unusual that, is it? I mean the note, sir?"

"I'm not quite sure what you mean, exactly. I think if I could give you the background it might help."

"That would be helpful." He sat back and placed his elbows on the desk and clasped his hands together. He waited.

"We were at college together, Oxford, same staircase in college—it must have been 10 or 12 years ago. We were the best of friends but after finals, like so many others, we drifted apart. He moved to the University of East Anglia to take a higher degree and I stayed in Oxford lecturing and giving tutorials. With research into organic chemistry on the side." Leeder said nothing but waited for me to continue. "In the autumn of last year, we met by accident when I was on holiday in Paris with a young lady, in fact my young lady, Rachel."

"Unplanned, sir, this meeting?"

"The meeting? Oh yes, completely accidental. In Montmartre to be precise, looking at artwork in the street. I don't know if you have been there but it's well worth the journey."

"No sir, I haven't been as far as Paris, I'm afraid." Somehow, I had expected this reply.

"And, can you believe it, Dowson and Rachel had already met."

"Some coincidence, sir."

"Funnily enough, that's exactly what Alex said! They had both been working for charities in Africa several years previously in Tanzania but had met on break weekends away in Kenya; once or twice I believe."

Inspector Leeder said nothing for a while. He thoughtfully straightened a folder before him on his desk. I carried on. "Cutting a long story short, we invited him to Oxford in December, but he wrote us a short note saying he had 'flu'. And couldn't come. That was the last we heard from him. I've rung his mobile several times and went straight to voicemail; but recently his mobile has been switched off."

The inspector said nothing for a while and then; "This young lady, Rachel, and you live together, do you sir?"

"Not exactly. She lives and works in London, and I work in Oxford." Then, as if I had to explain myself, I added; "We intend to get married later this year."

"So, your fiancé. And her full name and address please?" He wrote the answer down in the folder before him. "And how well did she know Mr Dowson do you think?"

It was quite clear where this questioning was going and although I realised, he was only doing his job, it, of course, irritated me. "As I said, they met in Tanzania or at least on occasional weekends in Kenya. Nothing more than that as far as I know."

"A charity you say."

"Yes. UNICEF, I think. Or attached to that organisation."

Again, Leeder I said nothing for some time, but then quite abruptly; "What do you think has happened?"

"I have no idea."

"Chance, I guess," he said.

"I have no idea."

"Right." This Inspector Leeder was patient if nothing else. I could see the drift of his questioning which made me cross as well as uneasy and he was still looking at me steadily. After some time, I got fed up with this.

"As I said, I have no idea where he is. He's just dropped off the radar as it were."

"Quite so, sir. Well, from this end we have traced his mobile phone. The difficult part was when we got to the address. It's a cottage in a tiny village on the North Norfolk coast, not far from here, probably about 15 miles. When we arrived earlier, we could get no response hammering on the door and we found it to be locked, but as well as that, curiously padlocked on the outside." Leeder pursed his lips and was clearly unhappy. "We looked through the window, of course, but as far as we could tell, through cobwebs and dirt the inside was completely empty of furniture and personal belongings. Odd that wouldn't you say sir?"

"Sounds as if he's left the cottage and moved on." I suggested cautiously.

"Yes, indeed sir"

"I don't really know his circumstances in Norfolk." I said, "As far as I know he works for a private chemical firm and we met as I say, and said twice before, quite by accident. I have no real knowledge of his life in Norfolk. Nor his work."

"But he knew the young lady," he glanced down at his notes, "Rachel?"

The silence between us became uncomfortable. Now he was staring out of the window saying nothing. He continued to frown. A motorcycle accelerated past and then the noise gradually subsided, and it became eerily quiet again. He asked; "What does Rachel think sir?"

"I have told her that there has been no contact and that I was coming here today, but that's all. I've no idea what she thinks."

"Right." He sat up straight, picked up his mobile and stood up. He'd decided! Striding to the door, he opened it and called for a Sergeant Eyles. "Everyone ready?" shouting as if to awaken a platoon. He received an affirmative answer.

"Ok, sir, let's all go over to the cottage. I've got a people-carrier we could use, and your car is probably as safe here as anywhere." A slight smirk. A slight joke? I got up and follow him.

Detective Sergeant Eyles introduced herself as Glenda. Well-built, young and with attractive blonde hair, she was about 6 feet tall, with the handshake like a vice. Her associates, two uniformed constables, carried between them a bag from which metallic sounds reverberated. Glenda handled the people-carrier expertly. The van was spacious enough but with a curious antiseptic smell about it. The journey took only half an hour on the winding, hedge-enclosed byways of Norfolk and the village was, as Leeder said, tiny. It was adjacent to the sea or may have been once. A nature reserve and marshland now separated it from the Wash. There was a through road that snaked between small houses that were built of brick and flint-pebble. I was told the cottages were originally built for fishermen but now as Norfolk had become a tourist attraction, the prices of houses (used as holiday homes) had made them too expensive for the local inhabitants and many had long since departed south. This had caused bad feeling and occasionally emotions boiled over. There were a couple of shops, a house with a picture window, advertised as an Art Gallery and at the end of the village, surprisingly, a newly built community hall. The Cottage we were looking for was tucked furthest from the main road at the end of a terrace of tiny cottages set at right angles to the road and approached by a pebble path which was overgrown by grass and weeds. A tall fence opposite the houses cast a dark shadow across the path and there was still frost clinging to the tall weeds in the late afternoon.

The five of us walked up the path to the padlocked door, and without a word of command the two constables prised the padlock away from the wood and then used an Enforcer to burst the door open. We entered as a group. Inside it was dark with a stale smell of an empty house left vacant for some time. The electric light still worked and although not bright it was enough for us to see that we were in a small, square room, painted a dull grey and empty of all furniture and belongings. Leeder looked about with his usual flown.

"What do you make of it Glenda?" he asked.

"Not a lot," came the reply; then; "been empty for some time I would say."

"Mm." Leeder was non-committal. "We're told that his mobile is here, turned off. We'd better find it and take a careful look around." And then, as an afterthought, "Don't touch anything."

Some wooden steps led up to a half loft and a bedroom of sorts, again empty of all possessions.

"Take a good look around, will you? Outside as well." The constables moved off with Glenda and searched the garden and as best they could in waist high overgrown grass and weeds. Even when Alex was here it was clear he was no gardener. After half an hour's searching fruitlessly outside and thoroughly inside, it was decided nothing, more could be done today. "At least, we know that your Mr Dowson is not here. Chance a guess." Leeder stated the obvious. The house was relocked, and we piled into the people-carrier and Glenda drove back to Feckenham.

"I'm not sure now—" Leeder muttered, half to himself and half to me "—except, of course, the whole setup. How do you see it, sir?"

The question was put to me, but Glenda answered. "Have you got the registration number of the missing bloke's car? Does he own the cottage? Has he bought it? Or is he renting it? We'll have to find out those things."

"Yes. Yes." Clearly Leeder did not like sergeants to form questions. "We'll start a major operation on this missing chemist—he is a chemist?"

"Of sorts," I replied.

"Ok. Chemist. Unusual for these parts."

At the police station, Glenda joined Leeder and me in his office. Tea was brought in. Leeder reckoned we had done as much as we could today.

"Couple of things," he started. "You know, in a way, I'm relieved the cottage and garden are deserted but at the same time it adds a problem. Where has he gone? Is he still alive? What's the meaning of all this?" He looked at Glenda then at me. Glenda and I said nothing.

"I'll have to speak to the super later," he says. "It's too late in the day now. You've been on the road all day. No need to drive back to Oxford tonight. Can I book a room for you? Brought the necessary overnight gear with you?"

"Yes, to the first. But no to the second. I'll manage if the shops are still open."

"Don't worry, Glenda will look after you."

It turned out that Glenda was an efficient escort and shopper, and we chatted amiably as she shopped for me. It was only later, when I was in my single room, it occurred to me how easy this had been. Was it too organised? Was it too convenient? Tomorrow would tell.

The hotel Glenda Eyles took me to was on the outskirts of Fakenham. I asked her to come in for a drink before she left and she agreed to have one soft drink before driving home, which she said was 5 or so miles away. We made ourselves comfortable at a table in the small bar near a window overlooking a patio and garden. For such a confident sergeant, she was a remarkably diffident young woman. Still living with her parents, she was unmarried. Her main recreation was tennis but that was limited to summer for there were no indoor courts within easy reach. Her life was fairly circumscribed outside the Force. (She didn't volunteer the information, but later I learned her mother suffered from early onset Alzheimer disease and with her elderly father she was the principal carer in the household. Police and nurse seemed incongruous; but within this young lady, I decided, not at all!)

"Your fiancé, you must have known her for a while?" she spoke quietly.

"Still at work, are we?"

"Not at all." She blushed. "I was just making conversation really."

"Of course, I'm sorry. I'm not used to 'fiancé'. Not a word Rachel and I use."

Sergeant Eyles moved in her seat and crossed her legs. "When do you plan to get married?"

"God, we haven't got round to any definite date yet. Sometime this year, I suppose. I can't see why not."

I welcomed the sergeant's courtesy, being here in Norfolk on my own. In fact, I began to enjoy myself. She was cheerful; smiled occasionally; conversational. But at the same time there was a reserve about her, especially at a personal level. I wondered how one could sense such guarded remoteness without words being spoken or attitudes being obvious.

I suddenly blurted out; "Is he always like that?"

"Is who like what?"

"Leeder. Pedantic." If I was hoping to strengthen my bond with the sergeant in this way, it didn't happen. Loyal!

"He's careful. A touch insecure, maybe." That's as far as she was going. "He'll ring the super and that'll give him confidence."

"Right. And I'll see him tomorrow presumably."

"Yes, He works some weekends, and this is one of them. I'll come and pick you up around 9:00 am. Will that be alright?" She stood up to leave and we shook hands. All very correct.

"I enjoyed talking to you, Glenda." I said.

"And you," she replied and walked out of the bar. I saw her drive off through the window and went to find some supper.

I slept surprisingly well, considering. The following morning, on the dot of 9:00 am Sergeant Eyles pulled up at the hotel and we returned to the police station. Leeder was waiting for us in his office.

"Hotel up to standard, sir?" Leeder inquired.

"Yes. Thank you."

"Just a few words then we'll let you get on with your journey." I looked around the office. I saw no change from yesterday. I looked at Leeder. He stared back at me. He then remarked.

"To get back to this inquiry. You say you knew this chap Dowson about 10 years ago at college."

"Yes."

"And then lost touch."

"Yes."

"And then bumped into him, as it were, by accident in Paris last year, accompanied by your fiancé"…he shuffled some papers about and finally came up with, "yes, here we are, Ms Rachel Harding."

"Yes, that is what I said."

"You added, I think sir, that she already knew Mr Dowson from charity work in…" and to save time by shuffling more papers, I add. "Tanzania."

"Yes indeed, sir, Tanzania." He looks at the wall all behind me perhaps searching for a map of Africa to locate the exact position of Tanzania! "How long ago did she come across Mr Dowson in Tanzania, did you say, sir?"

"I didn't."

A pause, which lasted just a little too long. Sergeant Eyles crossed her legs and moved in her seat. Leeder remains silent, then.

"Well, roughly?"

"I have no idea, but I can guess; perhaps 5 years ago."

"And did she know Mr Dowson before…Tanzania?"

"If we are to be precise, they met in Kenya. I don't know for sure, but my impression was that they not met before."

"Got on well did they, sir?"

"Yes, yes I think so." At this point, I remembered our meeting with Alex in Montmartre. Was there a slight hesitation in her step as we approached him? Or was that my imagination? Whichever, I'm not mentioning that to Leeder. Then I remembered Dowson giving her a picture and saying something like 'That picture describes you'. But that was merely a friendly gesture…wasn't it? I'm certainly not going to mention that to Leeder, although I am not altogether sure why not.

"Is your marriage planned?"

"We haven't got round to a date yet but certainly this year sometime."

"Sort of partially arranged is it then, sir?"

"Something like that."

Sergeant Eyles smiled; we went through this yesterday evening.

"I think that's all, sir." Leeder closed the file in front of him. "Thank you for your time and patience. We will be in touch with you if there are any developments and I would be grateful if you would contact us if you hear from Mr Dowson—or indeed if Ms Harding has any news of him. Thank you, sir."

"Please," I said, "I only want to help." Sergeant Eyles accompanied me to my car.

We smiled, shook hands. I left. The whole episode in Norfolk was unsatisfactory. Nothing had come to light to ease my mind. Were they suspicious of me? Of Rachel? I thought perhaps they were.

Chapter 12

In Lady Eleanor's office, Young waited for her to begin. On the table between them today stood a tall ceramic vase of exquisite design, artfully filled with stems of Evergreen.

"Reginald, how are you?"

"Well, thank you. And yourself, Eleanor?"

"Oh, you know, overlooked and overworked. Never mind." A patient sigh. "Tell me how things are progressing with you."

"There are three matters for us, I think. Preparations are complete at The Lawns. Professor Bhatti will have the symposium up and running on Monday and Ms Donato is her usual competent self."

"Good. I like that young man Bhatti. Ms Donato I have not met her yet, I must get round to it."

"Then there is this business of the outbreak of pneumonia in China. Not directly involved of course; kept abreast of the news from Konrad Taylor at GCHQ. Seems to be getting serious."

"Really?" Eleanor raised her eyebrows but not her voice.

"Call together ANCOM ASAP." *(Good God,* thought Young, *hell sort of language is that for me?)* "Then report to you Eleanor."

"Thank you."

"Finally, can I ask if the unfortunate Mr Rice from MI6 has been replaced?" Young asked diffidently.

"Yes indeed. We are now to welcome a Mr Stratton, a Mr Hugo Stratton, to be precise. I'll appraise him of the time and date of your next meeting."

"Shall we say next Thursday. The 30th at 2:30 pm?"

"Fine, I'll let you know."

Obviously, that was the end of the meeting and Young withdrew and descended to his own office. After 10 days or so cooling his heels, Young sat with increasing impatience. He opened his laptop and his spirit rose. An email from Superintendent Franklin.

1. Investigation continues Rice murder. Man met in Soho club prob European. DNA from hair not recognised in Brit. or Interpol. Trawling CCTV Soho/Camden. Yet no sighting of pair. Poss. one leaving club? Too dark; impossible to be sure.
2. Rice worked at 'The House', part of Vauxhall Cross and MI6. No queries from them. We have no further information on Rice. Hasn't travelled abroad for years.
3. So far dead ends.

Young read this slowly, then again. It was unlikely they would find the murderer soon but at least they were still interested. Good. He rang Clarissa and said he'd like a meeting of ANCOM on Thursday the 30th, 2:30 pm. He said that a Mr Hugo Stratton would be the new member in place of Rice and informed her that Eleanor upstairs was dealing with it, and she could expect Stratton on Thursday. He was about to replace the receiver, Clarissa spoke.

"There's been a message from customs and excise at Felixstowe. Know anyone there? Been bringing in illicit gin, have you?" Young looked at the ceiling, sighed but said nothing. "Do you want me to ring them back Reggie?"

"No, it's alright Clarissa, I know who that'll be. I'll get him on my mobile."

"Right." She rang off.

Young was pleased that Gordon Baxter had remembered him. Young hadn't seen him since a posting in the north years ago, but he clearly recalled the happy-go-lucky Flight Lieutenant, who could sink a few pints and was damned good company. If Young remembered rightly, Gordon had intended on his demob to join civil aviation as a pilot but for some reason that fell through and now, he was in customs and exercise. And Lowestoft of all places! They'd often been in the mess bar together and later went out into neighbourhoods, if the truth be known, to keep an eye on the local talent. In that respect, Gordon hit lucky. Marjorie, yes that was her name, a lovely girl, a comely barmaid, full of fun. Not one of the world's great thinkers but then who was? They got married in the end, must have been 20-25 years ago. A couple more suited to family life he could hardly imagine. Young used his mobile.

"Gordon? Reggie Young here. You called, you old rascal. How goes it? Why the phone call?" It all came out in a mad rush.

Gordon Baxter's voice was as clear as a bell when he spoke.

"Reginald! How are you doing? Still ploughing the straight furrow? Didn't I hear somewhere on the grapevine that you'd married the lovely Diane?"

"That's right. And yourself?"

"Marjorie and I parted ways a couple of years back. She took the boys with her. Bloody disaster really. But there we are."

"Oh my God! Sorry about that. Thought the two of you were made for each other."

Young was astounded by this news. *Gordon's marriage had been set in stone,* he thought. He'd heard that Gordon was good at his new job and kept his eyes and ears open but a divorce! Gordon seemed anxious to get on, so Young ventured.

"Anyway Gordon, you rang."

"Yes, I'd heard you were padding the corridors of power in Whitehall…"

"Not quite that, Gordon," Young interrupted.

"…well, whatever. I thought I'd mention something," Gordon said. "Here goes. What with Brexit and one thing and another things are quite chaotic, but for some reason this one business has stood out to me. There's been quite a lot of traffic bound for Norwich and the north, nothing new there. Mostly lorries, small vans, cars. Nothing unusual about that. Papers all in order and so on and so on. However, a few unusual items have started to come through recently; some chemicals and medical equipment from Africa can you believe? Slightly unusual. Oil and medical supplies are high on the list of imports from China but not Africa! Licences OK, but here's the thing. We took a closer look at one of the smaller vans that came through searching for immigrants as an excuse. Found nothing except glass containers with a water-based emulsion destined for a Norwich store, a small place on the A140. Didn't want to make a fuss seemed harmless enough but there's something else. The police have reported to us an abandoned car found in Felixstowe registered to an 'Alexander Dowson' who has disappeared. We had a memo asking to keep an eye open for him, but no Alexander Dowson has gone through this Port, I'm pretty sure. Might have had a different passport I suppose but…Anyway, get this, this same Dowson picks up the glass containers from this place on the A140. Or more precisely a storage company on the edge of Norwich. I rang the local police, and they knew of the place but had not been made aware of any odd transactions. Said they'd keep an eye on it from time to time—they usually do that anyway, these places store anything! But they've not reported back, and I haven't had the time to take the matter further. Know of this Dowson, do you?"

"Can't say that I do." Young tried his memory, usually pretty good on dubious characters but nothing rang a bell here. "Tell you what though, Gordon. Happen to know a superintendent CID quite well. Mention it to him. He should have a copy of missing persons. See what comes up."

"Probably nothing, Reggie, but I thought I'd just let you know. Tell me what transpires will you? In any case the next time you're over in East Anglia drop in and see me. A lot of catching up to do."

"Yes, to both of those things and I look forward to seeing you."

They disconnected and Young sat back pondering this information. Meant nothing to him now but he'd see Franklin.

*** *** ***

I came to know later this was the first time my world and Young started to converge.

*** *** ***

Young fished out his mobile and thankfully Mikhail answered immediately.
"Park? 10-minutes?"
"See you there."

Young wanted to catch up with Mikhail and find out what Eleanor had been up to. He was still shrugging into his coat and scarf as he walked briskly past Clarissa in reception.

"Going home early?" she sniffed.

Young ignored her and swept out of the main door into Whitehall and hurried along to Embankment Park. January had turned cold and there was a sharp breeze off the Thames making matters worse. Young made it to the meeting place in record time only to find Mikhail had beaten him to it. Wrapped in his usual leather coat with a scarf around his neck, he sat waiting on the bench, shivering.

"You know what? Let's stroll along the embankment, try to shelter out of this wind and wrap our hands around some hot coffee. What do you say?" Young had realised, a little belatedly, this was no place to sit on a freezing cold January afternoon. Mikhail got up and they made for the Embankment and hopefully an outdoor coffee seller. They soon found one.

"Two coffees."

"Sugar?"

Mikhail took sugar, and Young, gritting his teeth, did not.

Young trusted this lad both in Cyprus and latterly in London, but this was a whole new ballgame. In fact, it was possible that National Security was at risk, God forbid. It would be prudent to be economical with information. Young began. "Tell me Mikhail what's happened to you over the last few days and your new assignment?"

Michael pulled out his notebook, opened it and started to read. "Right. Couple of weeks ago I made a start. She lives alone in Belgravia, big flat, drives a Volkswagen 4x4. I made searches into the family background. (Young was surprised at this; it was over and above his expectations of Mikhail.) She's the daughter of the late Earl of Kingsworth. Briefly married to a financier called Keenan, separated from him some years ago. No children. One older brother; taken the title. No special friends living in the neighbourhood. Went to St Hilda's College, Oxford, second in modern languages. Travelled widely in Europe, and I think, Russia, Hong Kong and just possibly China. As far as I can make out, she has no political attachments. Weekdays to and from Whitehall government offices by chauffeured car. Doesn't use her own except for weekends, and I think sometimes in the evenings. But usually, she shuts the front door and stays in."

"Mikhail, I congratulate you, you have been busy and very thorough. Much more than I expected. Can you destroy that notebook?" Young nodded at the book in Michael's hand.

"It's written for me only, but with my shorthand writing no one would be able to read it."

"Just the same. Destroy it will you?"

"Sure."

"So, straight to bed in the evening do you think? No clubs? No bridge nights? No boyfriends? No political meetings?"

"Not as far as I can find out. However, last Friday, which would be the 17th, she drove to a hotel near Bedford. Stayed the night."

"Did she now? Meet anyone as far as you know?"

"That was my first weekend trailing her, so I had to be careful. I think she met a woman about 8:00 pm and they had supper together. I didn't risk going into the dining room. No idea of the name. Better luck this weekend if we're lucky,"

"We're lucky? Who's this we?"

"Going to take Rose, my intended. And her brother. Never mind she doesn't like the idea. If you're trailing somebody, it's best to go as a threesome. Less obvious. You can get closer."

"Is that right? Would never have thought of it. Wonder why all the way to Bedford?"

"I don't know. Probably find out more this weekend."

"If she goes."

"If she goes."

"Anyway, Bloody good work Mikhail. Meet next Monday afternoon, 3:30 pm? I'll be walking along Whitehall near the Whitehall Theatre. Can you pick me up in your car?"

"See you there."

They went their separate ways.

On the way home, Young called into the office. Just as well. As soon as he had stepped into reception Clarissa cried; "Thank God your back. I need a word." She followed him down to his office. Safely inside: "That Donato woman rang. Wants to talk to you today rather than next year! And Lady Muck upstairs wants to see you. I thought you'd gone home."

"Gave an excuse, didn't you?"

"I wasn't sure what to say, to be honest with you Reggie."

"Clarissa, you're all of a flutter." Might be romance.

He suddenly asked, "How's Saint Clair?"

She looked at him. "What's that got to do with anything?"

"Nothing really," he replied airily. "Nothing."

She returned to reception. A few moments later the phone rang. "Donato on the line." Click. Donato spoke. "Group Captain," she sounded breathless. If he hadn't known better, he would have put it down to anxiety. But Donato? Not her! "To what do I owe this pleasure?" The ever-gallant Captain asked. If she noticed his manner, she didn't respond. "Just to remind you everything is ready for Monday. I've put aside five days as suggested. Only one has not been able to attend, but she has forwarded a comprehensive paper." Then a little too quickly perhaps, "And a list of possible researches that might be undertaken."

"Excellent."

"We look forward to Monday, then."

"Absolutely Stacey."

Young put his phone down and gazed at the seascape. The Lawns was set up; ANCOM was working; those side of things were fine. Also, he had realised Whitehall was different to the RAF service, outwardly more relaxed, without the rigours of service life, something that was taking time to get used to. At first, it had been unsettling but now he had more time to think matters through. Like now. Long hushed corridors, closed doors, everyone going about their own business without a glance at him as if he were not included in their important work. Occasionally a well-dressed gentleman would emerge from one door then disappear through another without a word. There were muted conversations; tapping of unseen computers; mysterious bulky folders held close to the chests of hurrying young ladies. In the RAF, there was regimentation, always noise. Always shouted commands and the constant stream of aircraft taking off and landing. In part, his mildly eccentric or jocular behaviour was a reaction to his apparent exclusion. He was easier, now, in his own mind and had become more relaxed. But, as he became accustomed to this new pace of work, he had time to assess, carefully, the actions, even motives, of others. And now this is where he felt all was not well. But how? What was it? He didn't know. Yet.

With a sigh, he pushed back his chair, mounted the stairs to find out what Ellie (Clarissa!) wanted. Unsurprisingly it was to make sure all was prepared at The Lawns. He assured her all preparations had been made, descended the stairs, collected his coat and scarf and went home. A curiously mixed day at the office.

Still in a contemplative frame of mind, as he travelled to Plantagenet House, he again went over the day's events. A replacement for Rice. Possibly Eleanor's reluctance or misgivings? Baxter's phone call! The disappearance of…who the hell was it? Dyson? Dawson? Ah, Dowson, that was it. Africa? Chemicals? Now bloody Eleanor off to a hotel in Bedford. Anything in that? The Lawns up and running no problem there. Before he knew what was happening, they were pulling into Audley End station. Taxi home. Weekend.

The following day, Saturday, Reginald let drop casually into the conversation with Diane that the symposium was due to start on Monday somewhere in London and might, just 'might' you understand, must stay overnight in the capital. No, no he was not allowed to tell her exactly where but if she needed him (he gave her the number) this would find someone who would be able to get hold of him. The information had resulted in tight lips but no more.

He didn't think nine holes of golf on Sunday morning would be appreciated, so he retired to his office when Diane attended church. On her return, he did not inquire into the vicar's health, nor the sermon and whether there had been an accident or not. In the evening, he packed an overnight bag and retired early. Sleep was difficult.

Chapter 13

On Tuesday and Wednesday morning, Young called in The Lawns making it a matter of routine rather than for any apparent reason. Stacey Donato was polite and as he watched her attentively but could not discern any signs of defensiveness or distrust. Her demeanour was as it had been recently; courteous, absorbed but neither brusque nor cautious. On each occasion, he stayed for only a few minutes before leaving to travel to his office.

At the same time, Konrad's message was still on his mind, and he had to prepare himself for Thursday and the next ANCOM. The Lady Eleanor-Donato association seemed a long way from global epidemics or even pandemics (although the word had not yet been mentioned, certainly not publicly.)

In Plantagenet House, Diana noticed his thoughtfulness but wisely said nothing. She was so pleased that this new business, that she was not allowed to know about, had not kept him away overnight. So far.

Young hastened past Clarissa, barely acknowledging her and hurried down the corridor to his room. It was Thursday afternoon, the day of the ANCOM and he was late. As he barged in, the members of the committee, sitting round the long table sipping bottled water and chattering, fell silent and turned, as one, to look at him. It was the abrupt silence and the upturned ring of faces that was unsettling, even hostile; the sudden silence and cessation of movement seemed critical. Among them, Lady Eleanor frowned and ostentatiously looked at her watch. It was 2:35 pm.

"Sorry. Sorry." Young took his place at the head of the table. "Meeting went on longer than anticipated." (The staff at his gentlemen's club were discreet, weren't they?) *Dammit,* thought Young, *just the meeting when her ladyship turns up.*

"Perhaps we can begin." Eleanor spoke with studied restraint, the tone of which did not escape Young's notice. "I have introduced the new member, Mr

Hugo Stratton who is replacing the unfortunate Mr Rice from MI5. This, Hugo," she just nodded at Young, "is Group Captain Young."

"Good afternoon, sir." Hugo Stratton was dressed in a three-piece suit, with a guard's tie, Young noticed. "Pleasure to meet you, sir."

"Hello." Young was recovering his composure. "Informal here, old chap, first names only. Reginald—sometimes Reggie. Hello, Hugo, is it?"

"Sir." Nod of the head.

Good God, Young thought. *First Lady E., now this upstart. Or perhaps a slow learner.* (In fact, Stratton was neither.) *Time to get a grip.*

"I assume that our leader, Lady Eleanor, has told you our function, and that we're pretty informal." If Young was hoping Eleanor had not prepared the young man from MI6, he was disappointed.

"Oh yes, sir…sorry! Reginald. She has told me all." *(Was that a barbed remark?* Young wondered.)

Lady Eleanor interrupted, "Hardly your leader, Reginald. More an interested observer."

Everyone around the table smiled with her Ladyship. Except Young.

"Good, good. Well, unless anyone has pressing business," Young paused for comment, and as no one spoke he continued, "we'll ask Konrad to tell us of his worries. Or will we be hearing from Matthew today?"

"I think my colleague from GCHQ would be better informed on this matter than I am, so I'll ask him to address the meeting, if that's alright." Konrad glanced at Matthew and sat back. Young looked around the table; Konrad and Matthew as to be expected sat together; Vassell was next to Mountford, the hands before them on the table; chap from the Terrorist Branch (must try to remember his name! Morgan, that was it); and the self-contained Adrian Oakwell from Special Branch; Superintendent Franklin that he had invited specially; and of course, finally, Madame herself.

Matthew lent forward. An intense young man, he was eager to make his message clear, but diffident in this unfamiliar situation. He wasn't sure to whom he should address his report. But decided on Young. He began rather hesitantly.

"At GCHQ, we have been listening to messages from China, WHO and of course communications from MI6/5." Here, he looked across at Stratton, who appeared to be scrutinising his fingernails with a degree of concentration that Young found irritating. Matthew went on: "This new pneumonia virus made its appearance in China, and 4 cases were reported on the 30th of December last year. Today, only 31 days later, there are now 7,834 cases worldwide, by anyone's standards that's a lot. And 170 deaths. It is likely that it will not be long before it's in Britain."

"So…" Mountford, after baring his teeth and sucking a breath through them, was thinking aloud, "this new 'flu has spread quickly and it's out of China. And might, at some future date, appear in Britain."

"Exactly that." Matthew was now resolute; he must get the next point over at all costs. "This is not a 'flu-like infection, it's a new viral infection which is like the SARS-1 pneumonia of 2002 to 2004. That one was serious enough, but this one seems worse. Even more contagious and therefore more lethal."

Again, Mountford spoke. "Ok, it's not 'flu', but it's like 'flu!' Either way, that's for the medics, SAGE, whoever. Not us. What's it got to do with us?"

"With respect," Matthew now spoke directly to Mountford, "this is not 'flu-like' but 'SARS-like', which can be deadly."

"So is flu. Bad in 1918–1919, wasn't it?" Mountford was not to be bullied and considered he had scored a point.

"I think," said Matthew with studied patience, "we must let the Medical Profession sort out the details. However, what I must stress is that this is contagious and dangerous. And there is another aspect of this outbreak which may concern us directly as a committee, tasked with focusing government attention on menace from foreign powers."

There was no doubt that Matthew had the committee's full attention now. The debate about the exact nature of the pneumonia was obviously not for them. What was for them this was.

"In the SARS-1 outbreak of 2002 to 2004 China was, even for them, reluctant to share information with the rest of the world. In fact, we had little information before the epidemic spread out of China to Hong Kong and elsewhere. Fortuitously, that epidemic petered out. This time although China is more open and has confirmed that this virus is SARS like, and of the same family of viruses. But they are still slow to give us details. This new virus is more easily transmitted and even more importantly transmitted from human to human. This makes it extremely dangerous. Conveniently called SARS-2." He let that sink in, and then; "Today, WHO declared a Public Health Emergency of International Concern. A pandemic will inevitably be declared."

If it were possible, the committee were now even more attentive. Now, the coup de gras; "This outbreak began in Wuhan city of China. It is in that city that there is a highly secretive and sensitive maximum-security laboratory that we believe is experimenting on viruses and just possibly altering and making them more lethal."

"Bugger me," Young couldn't help himself as the penny dropped. "You mean the Chinese might be making this stuff."

"Possibly." Matthew sat back.

"Does that mean it's being manufactured…and could be used for military purposes?" Mountford was sceptical. "Bit science fiction, isn't it? Bit like the conspiracy theories the Americans keep coming up with."

"Is it?" was all Matthew said.

The committee took its time to digest this. Young asked Konrad: "Anything in it d'you think Konrad?"

"It can't be ignored, that's for sure. I think I'm with Matthew here. I'm worried."

"Wait a minute." Mountford was sharp. "We don't know a lot about this yet. OK, sounds bad, but as far as manufacturing the wretched stuff, where's the evidence?"

"I agree," piped up Matthew. (*Now, there's a surprise,* thought Young, but said nothing.) "We need substantial evidence." he went on. "But with so little from China, short of breaking into the laboratory, I think we're stymied."

"Precisely." Mountford looked smug.

"However," and now came Matthew's warning, "if it does prove that this virus is so lethal, and contagious, no matter how it developed, we're going to require an immense amount of money, time, and scientific expertise to produce vaccines of the quality and quantity that will prevent a global disaster."

"Exactly my point. That's for the scientists, isn't it?" Mountford said. Samara Vassell, sitting next to him, nodded vigorously.

"Of course." Konrad came to Matthew's aid. "But the very least we should do is make a noise so loud that the Prime Minister and his government will understand the urgency, that is, if they don't already!"

"You think that no one has noticed this disease spreading about?" Mountford was unnecessarily sarcastic. "Of course, they have!"

"I don't think there's any doubt about that." Matthew was conciliatory. "But the more noise everyone makes the better."

"We would have to be careful how we broached the subject." Lady Eleanor was thinking politically. "On the one hand, this matter is of course extremely important, on the other we don't want to be treading on too many important toes."

"I agree. Personally, I've got better things to do with my time." Mountford was adamant and his neighbour, Samara, nodded vigorously yet again.

"Have you?" Muttered Matthew, surprising Young, Konrad Taylor and, perhaps, even himself.

Following a gentle tap on the door, Eleanor's secretary entered and leaned over to whisper in the ear of her Ladyship. She, in turn, looked a little startled but nodded her head. The secretary withdrew, closing the door behind her.

"Reginald." Eleanor spoke almost apologetically. "I have been called away rather suddenly and it's something that I can't possibly ignore. With your permission, I'll go and attend to this matter which shouldn't take too long. When you finish here, I wonder if you would come upstairs and have a chat with me."

"Of course, Eleanor."

Young had watched Lady E. carefully through the meeting. He had detected no sign of unease and he wasn't even sure the Eleanor/Donato association had anything to do with Matthew's worry about this damned virus.

Eleanor stood, murmured her apologies and left the room. This was an interruption that Young could have done without; now he needed to get the committee back concentrating on what Matthew had been emphasising as quickly as possible. Looking round the table it was difficult not to notice serious disagreement. Whilst Eleanor and her secretary had been whispering, Young could not help but note that Vassell and Mountford were in deep conversation and Hugo Stratton was leaning towards them listening; Konrad Taylor was apparently congratulating Matthew on his presentation; and further, the other three members, Superintendent police, Terrorist Branch and Special Branch representatives were to all intents and purposes, if not exactly excluded, then were at the periphery of the group. Young didn't like this one bit; but was not sure why not. How much had Eleanor influenced this separation? Had Eleanor's departure reinforced some split between the members or was the division more fundamental? As her Ladyship was the link to ministerial levels, surely it was in her interest to present a united and balanced assessment of their work. Young tapped the table and the conversations died away. Choosing his words carefully, he spoke quietly; "As I see it, there has been a conflict of priorities. Nothing else." (He was trying to keep personalities out of the equation.) "GCHQ has presented a case for the extreme caution regarding this new viral pneumonia, and that is based upon the evidence that they have gathered; some of it scientific. Others" (again he mentioned no one person) "feel that their expertise lies elsewhere. I must agree. However, I also feel that we must present to Government that we are seriously worried. We may well add that we agree great importance should be given to scientific exploration. And I would like the whole committee's agreement."

He judged that he had gone as far as he could. He wanted the committee to continue in its present form, as that could give balanced advice from their level. Nevertheless, he saw no advantage in prolonging the discussion, certainly if it was to become acrimonious.

"Frankly," said Mountford, "I think that you have summed up the situation very well. Can I just repeat though, in my opinion we must leave science to the scientists."

With that, Young decided they had enough and drew the meeting to a close. As they all got up to go, he called to Superintendent Franklin that he'd like a word. After the rest had departed, Franklin and he made themselves comfortable in the deep leather chairs.

"Quite a meeting." Young murmured.

"A trifle tense, was it?" Superintendent Franklin smiled.

"Just a little!"

They sat gazing out of the French doors into the shadowed courtyard, both welcoming a moment's relaxation.

"Tea? Coffee?" Young offered.

"No, I think I'll pass on that if you don't mind."

"Not at all." Young was still considering the differences that had occurred. Not the differences of facts, they were indisputable, but differences in reaction to those facts. And that was much more sinister. He pulled himself together. "Now let's consider Phillipson Rice. Any headway, Brian?"

"Not as such. We're gently working on the club in Soho and I'm not altogether sure that the meeting there was by chance. We know the foreign bloke with a mid-European accent was called 'James Deacon!' That's as much of a giveaway as I've ever heard. Foreign chap, accent to match, called James Deacon? I think not."

"Well, that's something anyway." Young turned this over in his mind.

Franklin, as if he had read Young's mind. Franklin said, "Of course those blokes in the services get themselves about a bit." Brian Franklin surprised Young, but not sufficiently to drop his guard. Although, come to think of it, he trusted this chap, Brian Franklin. So, where's the problem? The Superintendent went on; "I get the feeling that I'm not always in the picture." The Superintendent left it there.

"Yes." Young ran his hands through his hair. "Look Brian, something else has cropped up, and I want to share it with you. Sorry. Sorry. Sounding like I come from California, what? Well, I don't think so, so I'll tell you about it!"

Brian Franklin made the American connection and smiled. He approved of Young's preferred language.

"Used to know an officer in the RAF, works now in customs and excise, Felixstowe. Spoke to him the other day and he was mildly worried about a fellow gone missing—his car found abandoned in Felixstowe, but as far as he can tell the chap hasn't gone through the port."

"Yes?" Franklin was listening.

"Fact of the matter is, some merchandise, possibly unusual, has been going through the port bound for Norwich or thereabouts. And this fella comes from the same area. Odd."

"Name?"

"Alexander Dowson."

"Just a moment." Franklin pulled out his smartphone and worked it quickly. "Yes, Missing Persons Unit has flagged him up. Dowson, Single, aged 32, Norfolk, chemist. Nearest police coordination is a place called Fakenham, Inspector Leeder."

"That's him. Got an address, have you?"

"You mean where Dowson was last seen? That seems to be very odd. He was reported missing by someone in Oxford who didn't know his address. The local police managed to track Dowson's mobile but have subsequently reported him missing."

"That's helpful. Thought I'd mention it."

"Ok then, Reggie, I'll let you know if anything odd turns up. But if that's all and if it's alright with you I think it's time that I got back."

"Certainly Brian. Sorry to have kept you, and thanks for your help."

They stood, shook hands and Franklin departed.

The broad staircase was uncarpeted and dark except for one landing where there was a small window overlooking Whitehall which gave a glimmer of light. The climb seemed more arduous than usual and at the top Young stopped to get his breath back, then knocked on her door.

"Come." Lady Eleanor commanded.

She was, as usual, sitting at the low table still adorned with the tall vase and evergreen branches. She pointed to the chair opposite. He sat.

"Well now, Reginald," she began, "a more than usually lively meeting."

"Yes." He placed his elbows on the arms of the chair and waited.

"I think we have a division of opinion."

"Yes."

Eleanor flicked a stray hair or particle of dust from her skirt, neither visible to Young. She folded her hands and placed them rather deliberately on her lap. Young was aware of her displeasure.

"Do you think that dipping into the vernacular is an appropriate response to the facts as they were reported in your committee?"

"Possibly not. But I was shocked." Young replied briskly.

"Weren't we all?"

"Eleanor." Young wanted to make his point. "I think this is not just a disagreeable outbreak of a virus but one which is potentially of global importance; and it may even indicate an intention of biological assault. I want everyone to wake up."

"Oh! So, the outbreak might be from a laboratory. Accident?"

"You heard what was said, no one is sure yet." Young had to be careful now; he wasn't certain of Eleanor anymore. "Have the feeling, nevertheless, that unless we're careful not everyone will recognise the potential threat. And I mean threat to God knows how many lives." Lady Eleanor winced at the mention of God.

"Can you explain yourself, Reginald?" She asked mildly.

"If this matter is neglected, not taken seriously, and dismissed as a pesky 'Flu epidemic, our response may prove inadequate. And if this virus is man-made, or a virus deliberately modified to be more lethal, then the source of that manufacture is very much the government's concern."

Eleanor had now ostensibly turned her attention to the evergreens.

"Lovely, aren't they? I do so love this time of year, don't you? The stillness of autumn and those vibrant colours, wouldn't you agree Reginald?"

Young was appalled. How could this woman, who presumably was able to bring influence, be so blasé about this potential threat? Perhaps many in Whitehall would take the same view; oh, don't worry, this was something doctors can sort out, not us; leave it to someone else. He was almost speechless.

"To get back to your worry" (Young noted the 'Your') "what I'll do is this. I will forward a memo to Sir Brendan (you remember him, my boss) and a copy to the Department of Health stressing the committee's discussion. How's that?"

"Thank you," Eleanor, "was all he could manage."

That seemed to close the conversation and Young left, shutting the door quietly. In his office, he gave himself time to calm down and order his mind. He remained deeply worried that many influential figures might not take this business seriously. If that attitude found its way to the higher echelons of government, goodness knows what might happen, or more likely not happen! There was a positive, at least for him. He was going to take this Eleanor/Donato association very seriously. And was there any link to Felixstowe, chemical companies, even this missing chap Dowson?

Tomorrow was the last day of the symposium at The Lawns. He would make his way over there and find out how it had gone. Relaxation was the last thing on his mind.

*** *** ***

When Brain Franklin had returned to his office, after attending ANCOM and spoken to Young, he rang Fakenham police station and asked for the duty Inspector. He was put through to Inspector Leeder. The conversation was short, but he gathered that this Alexander Dowson had bought a cottage on the North Norfolk coast, but had abandoned it and apparently disappeared himself, possibly from Felixstowe. The bloke from Oxford who had reported the missing Dowson had been interviewed and although he seemed to have no idea where Dowson was, there was an element of suspicion surrounding his girlfriend, a woman named Rachel Harding from London, Kennington to be precise. Leeder said his Superintendent was called Fitzwilliam who worked from Norwich headquarters. Franklin put the phone down and wondered. Nothing substantial, but interesting. He left a message for Superintendent Fitzwilliam at Norwich headquarters. Asked to be called back.

Chapter 14

As usual, on arriving at his office on Friday morning, Young made himself comfortable at his desk, hands behind his head, he considered the perils on the high seas. None of those magnificent galleons had sunk, yet. These thoughts were interrupted by a tap on the door and the entry of Clarissa, complete with bleached-blonde hair, a powerful perfume and an excited smile.

"You are positively glowing, I see," Young remarked dryly.

"Oh yes, oh yes." It was obvious that she was bursting with news but couldn't wait for Young to ask. "Sinclair has asked me!"

"Asked you? Asked you what?"

"Asked me to go with him on his Old Boys rugby tour."

"Play rugby, do you? Not an Old Boy, are you?"

"Goodness me, no. Just going on tour with him."

"What are you going to do then?"

"Watch him play rugby I suppose." (She nearly added 'silly', (but thought better of it.)

"On your own?"

"No. There are 15 in a team, I think, and all the wives and girlfriends are going as well. So, we'll all be watching. We're going to tour Scotland, playing Old Boys from other public schools. Hugely exciting. And Scotland is a long way away."

"Know that."

"We will have to be staying in hotels."

"Imagined that. So what?"

"Well, he's only booked one room for each Hotel."

"Ah, I see." Young nodded. He now understood the excitement for what it was. "Well played."

"How do you mean; 'well played'? I'm not going to be playing."

"Quite." Young was losing his patience. "Didn't mean that, but never mind. Think you'll enjoy it, the rugby I mean?"

"Well, I've got the others to talk to haven't I?" She sniffed. "It'll mean that I take all next week off, but I have squared it with my supervisor. She's going to employ a temp. for reception, so you'll be OK."

"Hope it all goes well for you," Young smiled. "But I think we need to put our minds to some work. Back to business. Sit yourself down."

Clarissa lowered herself carefully into one of the voluminous, leather armchairs and in the process nearly disappeared. Young took no notice.

"Perhaps you could arrange another meeting with Superintendent Franklin at his office and I'd like to have a chat with Professor Bhatti after the Symposium finishes…Shall we say Monday?"

"I'll arrange those before I go off today and leave them in the appointment book." Clarissa climbed out of the chair with some difficulty and straightened her skirt before leaving the room. Young relaxed. And his mobile came to life.

"Young."

"Group Captain. Ms Donato here." Formal to a fault, Young noted. "As you may remember this is the last day of our first conference and to mark the occasion, we have decided to hold a, shall we say 'Celebration?' 'Farewell?' dinner this evening. 8:00 pm. Casual attire, of course." Here Young realised there was no direct invitation, only invitation by inference.

"I would be pleased to attend, thank you." Touch of sarcasm. "Lay a place for me."

"I'll tell the staff to expect you."

"Thank you." Young put the phone down. *She couldn't help herself,* he thought, *even if that officiousness was injudicious.* It was not the attitude that was unnecessarily abrupt but the change in attitude from 'shall we go up to the flat?' to 'is there any need for you to be here?' It was the change of manner that aroused suspicion, not the manner itself. They rang off.

*** *** ***

During the afternoon of the same day Norwich police phoned Superintendent Franklin in his office in Holborn. Superintendent Fitzwilliam rang. Franklin answered the phone:

"That you Brian? Caroline Fitzwilliam from Norwich."

"Thanks for ringing back. I thought the name was familiar. We met in a previous life, didn't we? Hendon, was it?"

"We've met before, certainly not at Hendon, I left there before you started shaving! It was much later, business in Cheshire. Murder of a prostitute. Big job, remember?"

"Of course. That Caroline Fitzwilliam."

"Know a lot of Caroline Fitzwilliams, do you?" Caroline spoke drily.

"OK. OK. Not that many!"

"How's life treating you, Brian? Still married? Children are grown up now?"

"Olga died a couple of years ago. Breast cancer."

"Oh, shit! I am so sorry, Brian. I didn't know."

"No reason you should have done. Left a bit of a gap, I have to say."

"I bet." There was a short, tight silence. Franklin broke the tension. "And you Caroline? Still fancy-free, are you?"

"If you're asking whether I'm married or not, I can tell you. I'm not! But this isn't the reason I'm asking."

"Go on."

Caroline hesitated to get her thoughts in order, then: "We've lost a young chemist, Oxford educated, latterly of East Anglia University, Alexander Dowson by name. He was buying a house on the Norfolk coast, mortgaged, which has been deserted and left completely empty and padlocked, looks like for some time. Next, his car turns up in Felixstowe apparently abandoned, no sign of Dowson. The port authorities claim he has not passed through the port so, again, he has disappeared. I've got an officer, Inspector Craig, looking at the case. Conscientious but not exactly dynamic. He's reached a dead end. We've made extensive enquiries through income tax and government sources. I can find no employment for this lad Dowson, his mortgage company reports he's up to date with payments but has no idea where the money is coming from, and his bank is similarly in the dark. I heard that you're interested in this case but I'm not clear how you got involved. Tell me?"

"Difficult, Caroline, difficult. All I can say is that Whitehall told me about this disappearance and some movement of a strange cargo through Felixstowe docks addressed to a place near Norwich. They thought that this fellow Dowson might be implicated. But how, God knows. And if Whitehall knows, they're not telling."

"Like that, is it? We thought as much; if not the cargo, then some form of employment of Dowson that's not straightforward. But here's the good news. The officer at Customs and Excise Felixstowe, noted the address of the package that contained these dubious samples. Nothing contravening the import laws, certainly not drugs, but something he wasn't sure of. Bright sort of chap at customs, Gordon Baxter. He used to be RAF."

"Was he?" Franklin sat up.

"You sound interested."

"Not really," he assured her in an off-hand tone of voice. "Funny though, I ran into an ex-RAF Group Captain the other day."

"Know each other, did they?"

"I'll ask him." Franklin avoided answering her directly. He needn't have bothered because she went on:

Caroline Fitzwilliam had noticed the avoidance but didn't comment on it. "So, we are finding out all we can from Inland Revenue, the bank, car tax and insurance and so on. Not much more we can do within the prescribed limits. Of course, now I've spoken to you. I realise there may be avenues of enquiry that are less prescribed."

"Look Caroline, can we just leave it there for the moment."

"Certainly. I know what you're talking about."

"Just one thing, Caroline." Franklin had been wondering for some time where this cargo had come from. "Any idea who sent this load through Felixstowe?"

"Well, we know it came from Mozambique of all places but there was no address or sender's name."

"Is that unusual?"

"To be honest I'm not sure. My guess is the country of Mozambique would not frequently send cargoes to Britain, but to make sure I'll speak to Gordon Baxter at Border Control and find out. Anything else?"

"Sounds like you're doing your best to trace this Dowson and so on. No doubt the cargo will sort itself out when more is known about him."

"Probably. Pleasure talking with you again, Brian. And I'm so sorry about your wife." Caroline Fitzwilliam rang off.

Franklin was not much further forward, but at least he was sure Norfolk was on the ball and there might be a connection through the RAF with Baxter-Young worth following up; the package would no doubt sort itself out. He could leave it for now.

* * *   * * *   * * *

By the time he arrived at The Lawns, the lectures and discussions we're over for the day and he was able to sit with the contributors for the celebration meal. This was the first time that he had visited the dining room and found it much to his liking. There were two long windows, heavily curtained, and stretching the length of the room, a table with chairs and elegant carvers. The table was set with placemats and silver cutlery. Professor Bhatti welcomed the Group Captain and beckoned him over to sit beside him at the head of the table where he was introduced to notable scientists on both sides. The four-course dinner was served at a leisurely pace and with professional efficiency, during which the conversation became increasingly lively. Young found that reassuring. There were a few members who had formed small groups, eagerly debating some aspects of their work, but the majority were merely enjoying the final evening. Young spotted Stacey Donato at the far end of the table, dressed, this evening, in a spectacular crimson dress that matched her raven hair admirably. He raised a tentative hand and received a nod in return. Those on either side of her seemed keen to engage in conversation, which came as no surprise to Young. There was enough wine, but not an over-abundance, yet Young had no doubt he would be leaning on a bar gossiping with one or two of these scientists before the evening was over. Perhaps even chatting idly to the delectable Donato.

At the end of the meal, Professor Bhatti rose and spoke of his gratitude to the participants and for his admiration of the wide-ranging discussions that had followed. He summarised the week's work and remarked upon how instructive it had been; finally, he thanked Stacey Donato and the staff for the excellent accommodation and amenities. He suggested that everyone should adjourn to the lounge and, thought Young, *to the bar.*

As he had anticipated the delegates continued to unwind in the lounge and one or two even joined Young at the bar. These academics were judicious in their consumption of alcohol but nevertheless were enjoying themselves. Young particularly noticed two enterprising fellows eagerly vying for Donato's attention but receiving little response.

"I hear you were in the RAF." A tall, cadaverous-looking gentleman peered over his half-glasses at Young. "Fine service!"

"It is." Young agreed, surprised by this sudden approach. He was engulfed in severe halitosis; no wonder the bloke wasn't talking to anyone else.

"Absolutely. My grandfather was in bomber command in the last big one. Before your time, I should think." (He did not make clear to which 'big one' he was referring.)

"Yes, probably before my time. Proud of my service, though. I presume you're not in the services."

"God, no! I turned my hand to molecular science. Specialised in cellular mechanisms of living organisms."

"Really? You've lost me."

"Oh, once you're into it it's quite straightforward."

"Really?" Young had no desire to 'get into it' and looked around desperately for rescue; his eye fell on Prof. Bhatti who was not drinking but talking to an engaging but serious young lady; pretty, open-necked blouse, trim skirt and high heels.

"Excuse me," Young said to the lofty academic. "I must have a word with the Professor," Young nodded at Bhatti. "Catch you later." And with that Young scuttled off leaving the scientist looking around for possible beneficiaries of his wisdom, if not his breath.

"Ah, there you are, Group Captain, escaped from the good Professor Piper I see." Professor Bhatti was smiling. "An extremely gifted scientist, but perhaps a little intense! Have you met Jill; she and her associates transcribe all our recorded deliberations. Then I have the enviable (?) task of summarising them for departmental perusal."

"Jill" Young smiled, made a small bow and shook the damsel's hand.

"Pleased to meet you, Group Captain." However, she indicated that she had an urgent message for the Professor, "The order of lectures today didn't seem to fall into a logical sequence, so I am not quite sure how we are to proceed." She spoke quietly, just above a whisper.

"Don't worry your pretty head." Bhatti stretched forward and laid a hand carefully and lightly on her shoulder. *Heavens,* thought Young, *I didn't know he had it in him!* "We'll sort it out into some sort of order later, don't worry." Bhatti was reassuring.

"Thank you very much Linus," She didn't look at Young nor did she retreat out of Bhatti's reach. "I'll just get on with the others then."

She trotted away and both Bhatti and Young admired her walk.

"Lovely, isn't she?" Bhatti said and raised an eyebrow. "So accommodating."

"Is she though?" Young straightened his shoulders and inquired. "One of the flock of secretaries is she?"

"Goodness me no, she's in charge of the secretarial staff. She looks after the others, keeps them up to scratch, that sort of thing."

"And Ms Donato, does she feature in their work at all?"

"Apart from being the administrator for all the auxiliary services here, I don't think so. She doesn't have direct access to the transcripts if that's what you mean. They are transmitted securely to Lady Eleanor at your end, after I have put them into some sort of order and summarised the main concepts and recommendations."

"And the agenda for each day?"

"It's put up on the notice board over there for all to see."

"Right." Young casually looked across at the notice board. "So really it is only the titles of the lectures which are advertised, not the contents."

"Goodness no, the contents are strictly confidential." Bhatti was looking around, whether or not for other maidens was not made clear to Young. In any case, it was time for him to make it back to the bar.

At the bar, he ordered another gin and tonic and looked round, hopefully for Stacey Donato, but couldn't immediately see her. He thought nothing of it; perhaps a call of nature? A phone call? Who could tell? There was plenty of time and he had warned Diane that duty might keep him overnight in London. So, there were no anxieties there. Better still, Prof. Piper, he of impressive elevation and unwelcome breath was talking to (or was that at?) two colleagues who from the expression on their faces Young judged to be wearied and perhaps disinterested. He turned back to the bar and found another G&T waiting for his attention. Graham, the custodian of liquid refreshments, gave him a lopsided smile and then attended to another order. Young moved away from the bar.

He noticed that numbers were dwindling quickly, and scholars had started to depart for their rooms. He couldn't see Donato anywhere and consequently the evening had not panned out quite as he had expected. Hoped? It was only 9:30

pm but he could make his way home to his ever attentive and ever observant wife, even though she didn't expect him. It would be a lovely surprise for her.

Chapter 15

Arriving home from The Lawns and the completion of the first successful symposium, Diane was pleased to see her husband.

"I wasn't expecting you, dear." She spoke to him from the depth of her armchair, holding a glass of red wine delicately in her left hand and with a book laying on her lap, the other hand holding the pages open.

"Finished early Diane. Thought I'd make it home for this evening rather than rough…it in London."

"Quite dear. How wise." Young poured himself a gin and tonic and settled across the room from her. It was warm and peaceful, and he felt tired. But sleep was not in Diane's mind:

"I met a most delightful gentleman this afternoon in the hospital shop. Plastic surgeon. Consultant. Very eminent, I'm told. Such a gentleman."

Young metaphorically girded his loins. No ordinary surgeon for Diane!

"He complimented me on the excellent display of goods in our shop. Oh, and that voice; you should have heard it." She was so excited she lost the place in her book 'So melodious'.

"Melodious? Singing, was he?" Young couldn't help himself.

"Don't be silly Reginald. Anyway, I plucked up courage and asked him if he and his wife, I assumed there was a wife, if they would care to join us for an evening meal here at Plantagenet House. Well, you never know, do you dear?"

"You mean one of us might require plastic surgery?" Young, feigned confusion.

"Reginald don't be so silly. He graciously declined the offer but said that he looked forward to meeting with me again. He might accept an offer later on. That would be nice, would it not?"

"Yes." Young said, fervently hoping that the eminent surgeon would not accept an offer of an evening meal. For God's sake, what do you talk to a plastic surgeon about? Young smiled weakly and asked, "Is there another G and T going?"

The evening drifted by in much the same way, and they retired to bed early and slept soundly. Luckily, Young did not have nightmares about skin grafts removal of unsightly growths or anything else that he could remember.

In the morning, Young woke up and needed peace and quiet to think through these awkward situations in Whitehall. It was Sunday and Diane dressed carefully with church in mind and after breakfast departed for morning worship; she would listen attentively to the sermon, and just possibly, watch intently for any random dental activity. Young retreated to his office.

After a while, it became progressively more obvious to him that the problems in Whitehall needed to be dealt with independently. ANCOM had reached the stage of becoming seriously worried about this pneumonia outbreak in China, and its spread throughout the world and inevitably to this country. Many international meetings had expressed anxiety over this epidemic, but it would add to the pressure on government if strong and united representation were made to the Department of Health, the Home Office and possibly even the Ministry of Defence from ANCOM, Professor Bhatti and the Symposium. And therein lay the second problem; one which required careful investigation at a different level, one that he knew fell within his domain.

He would meet with Brian Franklin, Konrad Taylor and Hugo Stratton and possibly Nigel Mountford of MI5. This small group would examine the transfer of sensitive information from The Lawns to Sir Brendan Forsythe and enquire more thoroughly the relationship of Eleanor and Donato. Plantagenet House would be an ideal venue for the meetings if Hugo Stratton could make their deliberations secure. Reginald would speak with Diane on her return from church and he thought she would welcome his colleagues into their home. The meeting of the group, of course, would be in his study.

On Monday morning, February 3rd Young approached his office in Whitehall with some determination. He was looking forward to tackling the issues. The ANCOM and setting up the small group. As he opened the door to reception he came to an abrupt halt, for sitting in the chair normally occupied by the smiling Clarissa, there was a lady, of short, cropped hair, thin lips and a frown. This was not what he had become accustomed to. The lady's heavy horn-rimmed glasses gave her a look of menace, even malice.

"Good morning." Her manner was assertive, even unfriendly. "Group Captain Young I think."

For a fraction of a second, Young wondered whether to challenge this assumption but discretion got the better part. Regaining his presence of mind, he remembered Clarissa was, of course, watching rugby in Scotland and enjoying Highland hospitality in freezing conditions; this must be the temporary replacement.

"I am Ms Harper-Fowles' temporary replacement." The lady announced.

"Who's Harper-Fowles?" Young asked apprehensively.

"That would be Ms Clarissa Harper-Fowles, your receptionist."

"Oh, Clarissa. Know who you mean. And you are her 'temporary replacement'. How temporary? How long?" There might have been an edge of panic in Young's question.

"For the week that she is away."

"Got you. And the name?"

"My name is Guthrie."

"It's a pleasure to meet you, Miss Guthrie."

"Likewise, Group Captain. But I do favour Ms As far as I can make out from the appointment book, which I have to say, is difficult to decipher" (sniff) "you are free this morning, but Professor Bhatti is expected at 3 pm."

"Excellent. Must get on, lots to do. Be in the office, anyone wants me." And Young escaped past internal security and to his office.

Safely in his office, Young decided to get started straight away. As he pulled his mobile out of his pocket to start getting his small group (splinter group? subgroup? minority group? Perhaps best without a title?) together, but before he could use his mobile. The landline called his attention. *What now?* he thought impatiently.

"Yes?" He was terse.

"Is that Group Captain Young?" A female voice, not Guthrie that was for sure, had been rather annoyingly put straight through.

"Yes." He was hesitant.

"Glenda Eyles here, I'm sorry to disturb you."

"Glenda who?" Young was not familiar with the name.

"Glenda Eyles. I work with Inspector Leeder, but I'm afraid he's taking a week's holiday. I'm general dogsbody while he's away. From Norfolk; Fakenham."

At last, Young realised where this phone call was coming from, although he'd never heard of Glenda Eyles, whoever she might be. Come to think of it, when Young asked Franklin about the missing Dowson he'd mentioned Fakenham (in Norfolk was it?) and some inspector of police. Buggered if he could remember the inspector's name though. This girl had said 'Leeder', so that must be it.

"I'm Detective Sergeant at the same station. Inspector Leeder spoke to Superintendent Franklin, but as soon as he mentioned 'sensitive' he was told to ring you, even given your number. But Leeder's been called away suddenly, so I must do it. We've traced Alexander Dowson's place of employment, and that is what is so sensitive."

"Sensitive? In what way, sensitive?" Young asked.

"Perhaps not sensitive I think a better word might be secretive."

"Goodness me! Whatever do you mean?" Young had enough on his plate without secret establishments in the depths of Norfolk. Hell's sake, what was this about?

"His place of employment is not far from Norwich, a bit north of Ipswich. Off the A148 to be precise. It's heavily guarded and entry seems to be difficult to obtain."

"Is it really?" Young mused. "What's this all about then? Bloke is—sorry, probably was—a chemist. What's secretive about that?"

"The Inspector doesn't know. But we've passed it up to our Superintendent. She thinks London should know. That's why he rang Superintendent Franklin."

"Got you. Better give the matter some thought. Perhaps I can ring you back in 2 or 3 days' time. Alright?"

"Oh yes." Young could almost hear relief in the voice.

"Let's leave it there for the moment. Get back to you, probably Friday."

"Thanks, Group Captain."

"Oh, call me Reggie." Where did that come from? Young asked himself.

"Oh. Before I go. Just one more thing; I took it upon myself to drive out to the village he lived in and had a walkabout. There are a few shops and an art gallery for tourists, a fishing tackle shop and a typical village store that sold everything from postcards to buckets and spades, to tins of beans to model ships. You know that sort of shop. I talked to the assistant, a young girl but bored, and bought some groceries. Apparently, Dowson was a regular customer at weekends; quite talkative, something of a comedian and I think there may be more to the two of them than meets the eye, if you know what I mean. Trouble was, I noticed a wedding band. But it's got nothing to do with me. Anyway, she could be smitten and he's an attractive chap, I'm told. It's not much of a surprise; the whole village has a population of only about 500 so choice is limited. If there was something going on, then it took a knock because one Saturday he walked in with an impressively good-looking woman. The girl thought the woman was a bit old for him, but that just might be a biased judgement! They were close anyway, and here's the best bit, the woman was staying at his cottage."

"Well, bugger me!" Young was all ears. "Know anything about this woman? Name? Car?"

"'Fraid not. I think it might be advisable to have forensics take another look. Any signs of a second occupant, although I have to say they're thorough usually. I'll have to ask the boss first, but maybe get them to take another look."

"Excellent, Sergeant excellent. Can I leave it with you for a moment? I've got a lot on my plate." Young was most impressed with Sergeant Eyles.

"Right, you are. Speak to you Friday." She rang off.

An interesting morning's work. Young decided to take time out in his gentleman's club and get some peace and quiet. He scampered past Ms Guthrie, guilty, like a schoolboy playing truant and hurried along to his club near St James.

Inside the club it was warm and quiet. The bitter blast of a February wind and the incessant noise of traffic on Whitehall were securely excluded by closing the door behind him. He made for his favourite room, euphemistically called the library, which was in fact a refuge for the members of the club. The walls were lined with heavy, leather-bound tomes no one ever read, armchairs were scattered around the room and next to them, were small tables upon which drinks could be placed within arm's reach. Minimal movement had replaced unnecessary activity.

Young settled into his favourite armchair and called for a gin and tonic and whilst the wine butler set about this task, he looked around the room. It was amazing how relaxing it was just to sit here, a perfect interval of peace in the middle of the day.

Farthest away, a retired Brigadier who was of immense age and suffering from terminal boredom, slept soundly beneath the spread-eagled pages of 'The Times' newspaper. He would occasionally utter a strangled war cry to which no one took any notice, and then would resume his afternoon slumber. At about 4:00

pm, he would suddenly awaken and shout 'Pass the port, damn you', upon which the elderly wine butler would disappear into the cellar and reappear with a tray upon which a bottle of vintage port and a glass would wobble alarmingly.

Young continued his inspection of the room. And sure enough, there was Clive, a member of enormous wealth and little conception of reality. This young man had taken the consumption of alcohol to a whole new level; he was already on his third bottle of Burgundy this afternoon. It was rumoured that occasionally he fell 'off the twig' and had to resort to the convalescent care of a very expensive private clinic. Whether this was true or not it did not seem to interfere with his daily inebriation. He waved a hand in the general direction of Young, but this was no reliable indication of his awareness of another's presence. Young ignored him.

Finally, in his surveillance of the room Young spotted the most important man. The elderly wine butler who sat at his desk in a corner, motionless except when called into service. His knowledge of the wine cellar was only matched by his expertise in selecting winners at Newmarket (and elsewhere); indeed, the gratuities he received often depended upon the accuracy of his forecasts.

He should have retired 10 years ago but was so loved by the members and so nagged by his wife at home, that he preferred to stay on; in perpetuity, if necessary.

Young returned to his place of work at about 2:00 pm, only to find Ms Guthrie was unexpectedly absent from her desk. For this, he was profoundly grateful, only for his good humour to evaporate when he opened the door to his office and found her sitting as primly as was possible in one of his armchairs. She was tight-lipped and the practised frown in place.

"At last, Group Captain," she looked at her watch. "I have a message for you."

Young beetled around his desk and sitting down looked at her expectantly.

"Lady Eleanor Keegan has phoned several times. She requires your presence in her office."

"Is that all?" Young spoke with a nonchalance he certainly didn't feel. "Better make my way up there then."

"I would think so." Ms Guthrie stood, adjusted her glasses and took herself off.

What have I done now? Young wondered. *She couldn't smell my breath from there surely to goodness.* That to one side, he needed to be alert with her ladyship and mounted the stairs thoughtfully. "Come in." Her response to his knock was imperious. "Reginald, there you are. Come and sit. Tea?"

"Thank you, madam, but no." Then Young added quickly; "I've a meeting at 3 pm with Professor Bhatti."

"Professor Bhatti, a very learned gentleman, I think you will agree. I will not delay you long so there is no need to fret."

"Anything I can do." Young relaxed, the urgency must have been Ms Guthrie's unpleasantness and not her ladyship's impatience.

"A small matter. As we approach the end of the financial year, those who must account for government spending have reviewed each department's expenditure for the year. Ours seem to have increased, not substantially you understand, but enough for them to notice. They have asked for my opinion on the matter, and I would be grateful if you, at your convenience of course, would arrange for clarification of any expenses incurred by ANCOM. This is a mere routine matter, nothing more."

"Of course, Eleanor. I'll get one of the secretaries along the corridor to look into it. Anything more?"

"Only to ask if all goes well with the committee's deliberations."

"Couldn't be better. I think the committee has bonded really well and is feeling confident as a group." Young was deliberately, if misleadingly, cheerful. "Anything else?"

"No, nothing. Give Professor Bhatti my regards."

"Of course, Eleanor." On his way down the stairs, he realised that subsidising Mikhail might be showing up on his expenses. He would have to deal with that himself. Plenty of time yet.

Reginald was looking forward to the visit from Linus Bhatti. Liked the man. Had a predilection for a pretty face. Man after his own heart and as Lady Eleanor had mentioned, learned as well. At the top of his game, personable and cheerful. At 3:00 pm on the dot, Ms Guthrie announced the Professor and left immediately. Young stood from his chair.

"Linus, come in and sit comfortably." Young indicated one of the arms. "See if I can rustle us up some tea, what do you say?"

"That would be welcome, Reginald. Thanks."

Young rang and asked Ms Guthrie to organise tea.

"One way or other things went well at The Lawns?" Reginald inquired.

"They certainly did. Stacey (Young noticed the 'Stacey') was quite charming, and the hospitality was that of a 5-star hotel."

"Jolly good. Place seemed well run. Meal on the last night was first rate but I think Ms Donato left early."

"Did she? I didn't notice."

Young weighed up this remark. If true, the Professor did not know of any possible meeting Donato had in the hotel later; alternatively, he could be deliberately forgetting her departure. Bhatti continued; "We covered a great deal of ground, concerning recent developments in biological mutations and their applications. Lines of enquiry which has yielded some fascinating papers and discussions about the work involved in altering viruses or even combining viruses together to make them more lethal or more infectious or both! It would be remiss of this country to fall behind; there is evidence that other countries are forging ahead with similar research, and we see the primary aim is to develop rapid response vaccinations for any new lethal viruses. We have also drawn up a comprehensive list of suggestions for the development of aggressive biological application."

"And these recommendations will be passed to…?"

"In the first instance, Lady Eleanor and from there to ministerial level which will also have input from the crisis committee, COBRA and its scientific subcommittee. SAGE."

"Is it possible for me to have sight of these recommendations? Not the scientific details of course they would not only be lost on me that are really of security above my grade."

"Of course." Linus Bhatti made a note.

Young tilted his chair back, gazed at the ceiling and realised that all this would require considerable thought. The big questions for him; were the recommendations drawn up by Bhatti et al. get passed to the government departments in full? Get passed on at all? Or even if they did get passed on, were they passed to anyone else?

Tea arrived and this gave Young the chance to get his ideas together. One question straight away. Was Bhatti suspicious of Donato? He considered inviting the Professor to his small enquiry group but decided against it for the time being.

They chatted amiably and clearly Professor Bhatti was happy with the outcome of the symposium and with the recommendations that were going to government. After about half an hour, the good professor left.

Young fished out his mobile and contacted Mikhail. "Whitehall Theatre, 10 minutes?"

"See you there."

Reginald was loitering outside the Whitehall theatre when Mikhail drew up in his car, leant over and opened the door. Mikhail spoke quietly. They drove to Fulham and found a parking space remarkably only yards from the café (Muriel's Cakes). Inside, about 15 mothers and toddlers were making more noise than Reginald would have thought possible for such a small number. They took a table screened by net curtains in the window.

"Tell me." Reginald spoke just above the whisper.

"Lots. Went to Bedford again. I was with Rosie and her brother, so Keenan didn't suspect. Bar 830. Same woman turned up about 915. Super about 9:45. Now it gets interesting."

Reginald sat forward.

"About 15 minutes later a chap turned up. Called Meisser or Nesser. Can't be sure."

"German?"

"Well not from the Isle of dogs that's for sure."

At that moment Reginald's concentration was diverted; a pair of large brown eyes were staring at him over the rim of the table; steadfast; embarrassing; chocolate smeared across the forehead, above those eyes. A chair was scraped back, and a young, untidy looking mother came to retrieve her child.

"Come along Tony. Don't bother these gentlemen." She eyed Young suspiciously and returned together with child to their own table.

"You are saying," Reginald prompted. Mikhail went back to the weekend in Bedford.

"Right." Mikhail composed himself. "This woman, Stacey is a looker I can tell you. Got registration of her car; Stacey Donato. Handed over a thick folder to this Meisser/Nesser guy. God knows what was in it."

"Brilliant, Mikhail. Brilliant!"

"Oh. I booked another night at the hotel. Just me and Rosie. Hope that's OK."

Reginald slipped him a thick envelope full of money. They finished their tea, and on the way-out Reginald waved to the little boy. His mother frowned.

Mikhail put the notes in his pocket. They returned to Whitehall, but on the way, Young nodded at Mikhail's notebook, from which he had been refreshing his memory. "Destroy your notes Mikhail, there's a good chap."

Reginald re-entered the offices of Whitehall and Mikhail drove away.

Part Three
Professionalism of Secret Services

Chapter 16

As soon as Young arrived in his office on Tuesday 4th Feb, he dealt with his in-tray before bracing himself for the walk to meet Hugo Stratton in Vauxhall Cross. His internal phone called for his attention.

"Young."

The disembodied voice of Ms Guthrie sounded in his ear. "Your car has arrived, Group Captain."

"Car? What car?"

"The car to take you to the audience with Mr Stratton."

Audience? Car to take him? "I thought I was walking."

"Not now." Ms Guthrie rang off.

Young pulled on his coat and puzzled, walked past Ms Guthrie and out of the building. A rather athletic looking gentleman, with close cropped hair and dressed incongruously a three suit, jumped from a black car at the kerbside, opened the rear nearside door and invited the Group Captain in.

"You're here for me?"

"It is Group Captain Young, is it not?" Young nodded. "Then I am here for you sir."

"Damn decent of you." Young said as he got into the car; although if the truth be known, looking at the muscular chauffeur, he had little option. Hugo Stratton was sitting in the back of the car.

"Hugo!" Young exclaimed.

"Come. Make yourself comfortable." Stratton nearly patted the seat next to him. "Not far."

The chauffeur got in the driving seat, and they pulled out into the stream of traffic making its way towards Trafalgar Square. Circling Nelson's Column, they swept past the National Gallery and St Martin's church and re-entered Whitehall driving towards Westminster Bridge and across the Thames.

"Not going to Millbank, then?" Young was lost. Normally in charge in Whitehall, he was now being driven away in the company of a very silent and very still Hugo Stratton. It was as if roles had been reversed and Stratton was in charge. Young needed to assert authority.

"Not going to Millbank, then?" He asked again this time brusquely.

"No. I'd like to show you a house the service has rented from an industrial entrepreneur who now resides in the Bahamas and is sympathetic to our purposes. Quiet. Discreet."

"But not what I was expecting." Young blustered without much vigour. He felt intimidated, empty. A feeling quite new to him. He could demand they stop the car and let him out, but there was little chance of success in that; or he could make a show of bravado, but that might be interpreted as aggression. He was experiencing remarkable uncertainty.

This was, of course, what the silence of the journey was designed to produce.

They had reached Streatham, at least Young thought that's where they were, but then turned off the main street into a jungle of side streets and pulled up eventually at a large, detached house set back from the road and with a service road at the rear. They parked in the service road. The chauffeur led the way through a kitchen, where two young men who were busy cooking completely ignored them, then upstairs, ushered him into a room poorly lit by one standard lamp. Stratton closed the door behind them, and the chauffeur was left sitting outside in the hall. As soon as Young's eyes became accustomed to the shadows, he recognised Nigel Mountford and Konrad Taylor sitting to either side of a rather handsome, middle-aged lady, not unlike Diane in appearance and dress; a lady he had never met before.

But it soon became apparent that any resemblance to Diane was merely a superficial likeness. This lady radiated authority.

"Come in. Come in, why don't you?" The lady called out. "Take a chair, Group Captain. It's good of you to come and see us."

"Had no option." Young muttered. Nevertheless, he sat on the hard-backed chair. He tried to take stock; there were the three he knew from secret services, but this lady was new to him. The floor was wooden and without carpets; the furniture, what he could make out in the gloom, was sparse and five uncomfortable chairs were arranged in a loose circle. One remained empty; for him, he presumed. His inspection was interrupted.

"My name is Marcia," the lady announced. "Good afternoon, Group Captain."

If Young had felt rebellious, or nervous, or purely numb in the car, he was in the middle of nowhere now. In all the years of RAF service, and even in his time at Whitehall, he had never been in a situation like this. He was confronted by three colleagues, who turned out to be anything but colleagues, all of whom were deferring to this lady.

"Your name?" He asked.

"Marcia," she replied.

"Yes, you've said that. But what comes after the Marcia?"

"I'm sorry. I am not at liberty to admit my surname."

Hell's this all about? Young racked his brains. *Out of my depth but buggered if I'm going to admit it.* Young's thoughts were bouncing about with no coherent design. Then without warning he became aware that the room was absolutely silent. There was no sound of traffic outside, no movement inside the house. The four were looking at him unmoving and patient. There was no anger. But no comfort. The silence lengthened. It was quite disorientating. Why on earth were they going to these lengths, he was on their side wasn't he?

Suddenly Mountford thrust his hands deep into his pockets. The movement seemed to inspire Marcia to speak.

"We're here to discuss a subject that has occupied you for some months. We recorded your appointment as chairperson to a small group within Whitehall after you left the RAF; we know it as ANCOM and our three associates here are, as you well know, members of this group. Our primary interest is with the person who resurrected this bygone group, namely Lady Keegan. We need not amplify the reasons for our interests but let us say we made a careful note of her office. We were surprised she reintroduced cooperation within our services at such a low level; wondered quite what purpose it served."

Young interrupted, no doubt stung by the implied humiliation and degrading of his contribution to National Security. "Surely collaboration between services is always beneficial."

"That is the conventional view, I grant you. However, times are changing rapidly," Marcia continued, "and there is now much more natural cooperation between our agencies, how shall I put it, a holistic approach? Boundaries have become blurred, and rivalries moderated. Mr Mountford and, originally, Mr Rice was pleased to attend your group, as of course, was Mr Taylor and Mr Stratton."

Marcia now paused; she would need to choose her words carefully. To imply they were there only to observe and report back would be counter-productive; she still required the Group Captain's assistance, even if he did not yet realise it.

Young, remembered Mountford, Rice, Stratton and Taylor as volunteers from the services, nothing more. He now appreciated there was more to their attendance than he imagined. This came as a shock; it exposed his naivety. In the space of ten minutes, his assumptions about ANCOM had been completely undermined. ANCOM was a very small cog in a very big wheel. He felt proportionally diminished. Young looked round again, perhaps for support, who knows? Hugo Stratton had not moved or spoken since sitting down. Nigel Mountford, as usual, had an air of superiority about him; but his movements were to ease his buttocks occasionally on the hard chair, needless adjustments to his tie or plunging his hands in and out of his pockets. The window was behind Konrad so instead he gazed fixedly at the standard lamp. Marcia continued.

"Group Captain, you may remember some time ago, Mr Mountford let slip that there were some difficulties with traffic in the vicinity of Harwell in Oxfordshire, on the A34 to be precise. In fact, he had been given false information deliberately. Are you with me, Group Captain?"

"Remember the traffic problem. Yes." Young was feeling used. From what Marcia was implying, the traffic chaos at Harwell was a complete red herring. Why? Did they think someone in his group was untrustworthy? He leapt to the defence of his group. "How do you know the information was false, and furthermore why did Nigel use my group for your benefit?" Young was hanging on to Nigel's first name as if it represented a friend.

Marcia smiled. This was exactly what she wanted. The Group Captain's curiosity, even if it was defensive. "Mr Mountford was completely innocent of any dishonesty to your group. He believed the traffic information to be entirely authentic. Indeed, when he reported this incident to us, we also believed it to be genuine. It was only later, when Commander Vassel could find no confirmation, that we realised the intelligence was false."

"So, who provided the information to Nigel?" Young was immensely relieved to understand that Nigel Mountford had not deliberately misled ANCOM.

"How perceptive of you, Group Captain." Marcia's smile broadened. "That is something we turned our minds to immediately. In the end, we realised only one candidate was possible. There was only one person who had full access to the deliberations of ANCOM and could insert bogus intelligence. If not that person, then someone in her direct line of management."

Silence. More of a pause for information to be absorbed and hopefully understood. Young frowned; "You mean Lady Eleanor or above, Sir Brendan or above and so on."

"Precisely." Marcia was pleased that he'd made the deduction; he would be less defensive now. And it looked as if he had not yet equated his own position with this difficulty. "And then, one of our own, poor Mr Rice, was unfortunately killed. That left us with a considerable problem; his death, it goes almost without saying, was a terrible blow to us, and we are profoundly sorry. But was his death a pure coincidence? In this case perhaps an unfortunate result of his sexual proclivities? Or was his death arranged by a foreign agency? If so, why? What possible reason was there for a foreign agency to take such a risky measure? Quite the reverse one would have thought. That's what gave the game away. And more, Group Captain, we are in a powerful position. We know with absolute certainty that Mr Rice in particular, and no members of ANCOM, even yourself, disclosed that false information to any foreign agency. We have been assured, beyond all reasonable doubt, that no information of that nature has ever been divulged abroad. And yet, this is the clincher, Lady Keenan let it be known that this false information had been delivered abroad. There could not be clearer evidence of her involvement."

The emptiness that Young felt when he had come into the room had waned but was replaced with anger and then disappointment that those, he thought he could trust might have just been using his group for their own purposes, unknown to him. This was a world of deceit at a level he had never experienced. He had met plenty of miscreants whose word could not be trusted but these professionals were intentionally misleading those around them, apparently not for personal gain but because of an abstract concept of loyalty; this was something else, and although he had vague ideas about the Secret Services, he had never come against their machinations so closely. The silence grew longer, and Young's temper gradually subsided; if Keenan had used him and his group deliberately to direct attention away from herself that could only be because she was involved with another much bigger betrayal.

And the penny dropped! Marcia recognised the change in Young and judged the time just right to him to move on.

"Group Captain, I see you have been disappointed with some of the revelations you have heard this afternoon. I can only say that nothing was done by any of the services represented here today that was anything other than duty to our country as we saw it. We hope you appreciate that."

"Hear what you say. And certainly, value the security of our country. It's the methods that are new to me."

"Quite so." Marcia soothed.

For the first time, Stratton spoke. "Reginald, believe me. None of us enjoy what we do. Forget what you read, see at the cinema, watch on television. Our world is much dirtier than any of that. Our motives are sometimes obscure but our actions often far more crucial than the public realises. And occasionally the outcome is disastrous. Poor Rice, for example."

"Yes." Young moved in his chair, eased his back, eased the tension. Mountford ran his fingers through his hair, adjusted his tie and finding nothing else to do with his hands pushed them back into his trouser pockets. Konrad continued to gaze at the standard lamp.

"I think that brings us to the two final points on our agenda this afternoon." Marcia straightened her skirt and sat up straight. "First, we know of your association with one, Mikhail Stephanopoulos. A useful contact from your days in Cyprus, we think."

God, thought Young. *What else do they know?* Eventually, "How?" He asked.

"Do you remember the infant who came to your table in 'Muriel's Cakes'?"

"You don't mean you use toddlers?" Young couldn't believe it.

"Goodness, no. But you might remember his mother who rescued him from your table…"

"Yes, I think so. Woman, as I remember, thin, not happy, bit scruffy."

"That's the one. A lovely lady; quick thinking and very dexterous. You didn't notice the microphone she attached to the underside of your table by any chance?"

"No," was all Young managed, quite overwhelmed.

"We know, through that, that you and your friend Mikhail are interested in the association between Lady Keenan and Ms Donato."

"Donato? Of The Lawns? You surely don't know her." Young looked up at the ceiling. For help? For inspiration?

Mountford supplied the answer. "Remember Mr Cobb, do you, at the door?"

"The security man?" Young spoke hesitantly. Mountford readjusted his tie, crossed his legs then uncrossed them again. "One of ours," he said.

"Not Cobb surely. Service man. Dammit, a warrant officer. Not one of your brigade."

"He is now." Mountford crossed his legs again.

"Good God," was all Young managed.

Marcia spoke again. "We know of the Donato-Keenan association, although yet, not all the details. But we have been interested in The Lawns since its conception some two years ago. Extremely sensitive information is to be discussed there, not the sort of information that should go missing! We believe that is the big betrayal. The traffic and Rice we're only a smokescreen. Poor Rice. Which brings us to the final point of this afternoon, Group Captain, and then we can all go back to the securities of our offices." Marcia had waxed eloquently because she was now sure that the good Group Captain had seen the advantage of their future joint endeavours.

"It has also come to our notice that you are concerned about a certain Alexander Dowson. Again, I believe through a useful contact from your service days."

"Gordon Baxter?"

"The exact person to whom I refer."

How did this lot know about Gordon, or come to think of it, Alexander? Young gave up. Marcia now made clear how and why Dowson was of interest. "We have been taking considerable interest in the development of a chemical facility in Norfolk. We believe that within the facility experimentation with unpleasant viruses is taking place and these viruses are to be found naturally occurring in some West Coast states of Africa. This is unusual; it is more usual to find lethal viruses flourishing in Central or West Africa but the bugs our friends in Norfolk are interested in come from East Africa; Tanzania, Kenya, Mozambique, Ethiopia, even as far north as the Nile Valley. And Mr Dowson works (or just possibly worked) in this Norfolk facility."

"Yes," Young said slowly. "His name has been mentioned to me."

"Quite so. He is, we believe, on the police 'Missing Person List'. And this is very convenient to us. We do not want to attract attention to ourselves or show any overt interest in the Norfolk operation; not just yet!"

"I understand." Young could see the way this was going.

"And this is where you can be of immense help to us. If you would pursue Mr Dowson, preferably with assistance from the local police, we would be most grateful. If those enquiries were centred around his house on the Norfolk coast, well away from the chemical facility, so much the better."

Marcia was an excellent judge of timing. She was convinced Young would be unable to resist this opportunity so soon after his world had been turned upside down.

"I had intended to visit Norfolk soon," Young conceded. "This would fit in very well."

"I am so pleased," Marcia looked around at her colleagues. There was palpable relaxation. Mountford stopped fidgeting; Konrad had lost interest in the standard lamp; Stratton said nothing. Well, he wouldn't, would he?

"As is its usual habit, time marches on." Marcia looked at her watch for the first time since Young entered the room. "I believe we all have offices to go to, which offer far more comfortable surroundings than this rather spartan attic. I think we have covered all we intended for today. Shall we meet again in two or three weeks? Do you all agree?" There were murmurings of agreement and the men got to their feet. If Young expected handshakes, he was disappointed; Stratton suggested they collect the chauffeur and leave.

"Where can I take you?" the chauffeur asked on your way down the stairs.

"Whitehall," Young replied. "Lots to do." What he meant was he needed time to recover.

As was to be expected, they drove to Whitehall in complete silence. Young thanked the chauffeur and returned to his office. It was quiet in his office. He contemplated the seascape vacantly. Was that an impression of a distant coastline? More likely wishful thinking. He stared at the picture for a long time. No one interrupted him.

Chapter 17

Safely past Guthrie, and comfortable behind his desk, Young had almost totally recovered from the impact of yesterday's revelations. It had taken the previous evening's warmth of Plantagenet House and the companionship of his wife to come to terms finally with yesterday's encounter with Marcia *Noname*. And, come to think of it, his altered relationships with Stratton, Mountford and Taylor. Sleep had been difficult and repeated excursions to the lavatory inevitable. But strangely, with a frosty dawn and the intermittent stirrings of birds in the trees around, the new day had brought a new resolve. He looked forward to the day and realised, quite remarkably, that this was an unusual sensation. Over breakfast he recognised that he had acquired a new sense of purpose.

He was well-pleased that he could adapt to change and was not too old or to set in his ways to adjust to sudden reorganisation. He would tick off the various programs that were uppermost in his mind now. The threat of COVID infection might overwhelm the world but was outside his remit and although he was involved with The Lawns and symposia, the first of which had focused on biowarfare which must have touched on manmade or man-altered viruses. Come to think of it, Young had not seen either the program or any summary of the proceedings from the symposium. He must check on that. The possibility of a Keenan–Donato malfeasance was under observation by the extremely competent secret service, and he could rest easy on that score. Next, was the research development in Norfolk that may or may not by experimenting with noxious viruses. Again, that was not his concern. What had become clear to him was that whatever expertise he commanded would be best applied to the disappearance of a chemist from the coastal village in North Norfolk. What the connection there was between all these was unclear.

However, the parameters of his investigations had been fixed and he was pleased to work within them.

Having made up his mind, Young rang Superintendent Franklin.

"Franklin." He had been put through at last.

"Brian. It's Reginald. Fancy some lunch?"

There was some shifting of papers, and a muffled conversation before Franklin came back on the line; "Thank you."

"My club? Wait for you in my office. Shall we say 1:00 pm?"

"Very good. Better need to be back by two, two thirty at latest."

"Not a problem." They disconnected the line.

It wasn't far to Young's Club and the short brisk walk eased the stiffness of his morning's desk-bound duties. The air was still on the brisk side of cold, but the walk eased the stiff tegs that had been desk-bound all morning. The uniformed doorkeeper bade the Group Captain 'welcome' and Young proceeded to sign in the superintendent as his guest.

The dining room had on its high ceiling ornate plaster corbels, multi-bulbed chandeliers hung down, their light reflecting from the gold embosser damask wallpaper covering the walls. This room was markedly different from the library. It radiated opulence, near ostentation, the tables were discreetly separate, for privacy, and the cutlery highly polished.

"No ladies?" Franklin looked about the half-empty room.

"No, not so far. Any day now, no doubt." Young opened his linen napkin with a satisfying crackle of starch, whilst Franklin looked around at the splendid space. "Now listen, Brian. What are you drinking?"

"Water for me, Reggie, on duty; no option." Franklin the careful policeman.

"Oh, then I'll just have a glass of Bordeaux. That'll do me." Young was disappointed, he would rather have ordered a bottle, but never mind. Franklin commented on the quietness of the room only a few yards from the traffic of Whitehall. Young nodded.

. "Beef is good." Reggie recommended. "But order what you like. Once upon a time it was considered that food in the gentlemen's clubs should reflect the austere cooking of public schools, you know boiled cabbage with everything, but not today." He handed Franklin the typed menu, which was not exhaustive but, he assured the policeman, extremely well cooked no matter what you chose. "Haven't really got to know one another. Not had a proper chat."

"That's true." Franklin inclined his head. "It's been all work really. Tell me about yourself."

Young was taken aback. Used to asking questions rather than the other way round, he took his time to answer. "Married 25 odd years. Happy. Settled. No children. Was in the RAF for about 20 years, their branch of the military police. Reached the ceiling for promotion. Retired. Offered a job here in Whitehall. That's about it."

Franklin observed this was a list of activities with little reference to relationships. He would have to judge the nature of the man as time went by. The waiter arrived without a sound and Young asked for a glass of the red and, and of course, the beef. The policemen ordered beef, water instead of wine. The waiter disappeared without a sound. He could have been a passing apparition.

"Live in London?" Franklin asked.

"No. near Cambridge. Get off the train at Audley End. Know it, do you?"

"Can't say that I do."

"Small, detached house" Young was modest. "Call it Plantagenet House."

"Odd name." Franklin frowned.

"More of a whim, really. Richard Third lost his crown to the Tudors don't you know, started the Henrys. Henry is my middle name. Bit of a joke really."

"Oh, I see. Bit of a joke!" Franklin's frown deepened; history was not something that he had excelled at in school, and it held little interest for him now. Best say nothing. He couldn't imagine many would understand the joke.

"And married, you say?"

"Diane? Quite like her myself. Get along well enough."

Praise indeed, thought Franklin.

"And you Brian? Can't be all work surely."

Brian Franklin was always careful with his answer to that sort of question. He was as honest a cop as the next guy, but home life was a bit harrowing over the last two years. His wife had died. And just after that, the children had grown up and left to start lives of their own. All the family plans he had made had collapsed. There remained a sadness within him which was constant and his obsession with work probably eased it.

"My wife died two years ago."

"Sorry. Had no idea. What a bloody thing!"

"Yes. We had so much to look forward to…" Franklin didn't finish the sentence.

Fortunately, the waiter arrived. Beef. Jug of water. Glass of wine. Accompanying vegetables. *Not the moment to tuck in with gusto,* Young thought. However, Franklin sat up, smiled then said; "Let's eat, shall we? I'm quite self-sufficient now the children have grown up. I have the house to myself and live a relatively quiet life."

"And work." Young reminded him.

"And work." Franklin agreed.

Despite the sadness of the moment, both men managed to enjoy the meal and even ordered a selection of cheeses. Young decided the first glass of wine should be accompanied by another. He ordered another! Eventually, pushing their chairs back they rose and ambled into the library, sat facing one another in armchairs and enjoying a cup of coffee. Looking round, Young saw the usual persons in attendance. The brigadier was not yet demanding his port. The undersecretaries were missing but another pair had replaced them. The wine butler sat motionless. *One of the best ways to get to know a colleague quickly was to have a meal with him*, Young thought, thoroughly relaxed. They ordered coffee.

Franklin was wise enough not to offer to pay for the meal. They had given themselves time to consider things and at the same time come to some sort of understanding of their separate responsibilities. He wondered how Young felt about his position in Whitehall. He had years of active service (presumably) and now was stuck behind a desk, in a position with no power and an unclear, at best, objective. That couldn't be easy. Not a job for himself, he was much easier with clear-cut interactions and directives.

"This morning we have been able to clear up at least one or two points." Young was positive. "I think the committee has grasped the seriousness of this developing pandemic—it's only a matter of time before it does become a pandemic—and without jumping to conclusions has noted viral manipulation in laboratories. Only hope the politicians can understand the dangers and relegate their obsession with economy, industry, finance—and I suppose necessarily votes."

"Thank goodness I'm not concerned with that. In fact, I'd hate to be in government. Half the time they are warding off unnecessary criticism and this must surely interfere with concentration on matters as serious as this one."

"Well said, Brian. Couldn't agree more. But let's not get drawn into the philosophies of politics!"

"Absolutely not, but it's another factor in slowing down any reaction to danger."

Young considered the situation. "I suppose it's part of my job to sound an alarm or get Lady Eleanor to do that." Young leant forward and lowered his voice. "There was something else, Brian, thought I might mention it."

"Yes?"

"This business with the chemist missing in Norfolk. Any further forward, are they?"

"Not that I'm aware of. I've spoken to the Norfolk police on a couple of occasions but there's no breakthrough yet."

"Somehow it bothers me." Young was being cautious. "An old friend like Baxter, ringing me out of the blue odd. Something's going on."

"I'll let you know of any changes, but as of this moment this chap, Dowson, was it…is missing. Full stop!"

"Like to be kept in the loop as it were, Brian."

"Leave it to me."

Franklin looked at his watch. "I'll need to get back. Sorry, and all that."

"Not at all Brian. Better make my weary way back, anyway."

They left the club and went their separate ways. If nothing else, Young had got to know Franklin better. That would be useful.

After lunch, Young decided. To visit the lawns. Outside the club, he waved down a black cab and was soon at The Lawns being frisked by the stone-faced Cobb.

"How are you, Mr Cobb?" Young was cheerful.

"Well, sir, thank you. Ms Donato is in her office and will be down directly." Young resisted the temptation to ask where her office was. He went to the lounge and relaxed in an armchair viewing the lawns and herbaceous borders still shining with frost. The good lunch had left him in a congenial mood.

"Group Captain." Donato was standing over him. "A pleasant surprise."

Young stood, extended his hand and replied that he was pleased to meet her again. They sat in chairs facing the French doors and garden.

"I've dropped in just to ask for went well last week. Heard from Professor Bhatti the lectures and discussions were productive. Were any snags with regarding accommodation and so on for the visitors."

"Not really. When young lady turned out to be a follower of veganism rather than a vegetarian as we had been told. But her dietary requirements were met with ease. Chef was very accommodating. Otherwise, it went without a hitch."

"That is good to hear."

There was a pause. Young sat back. He placed his hands on the arm of his chair and looked at the ceiling. (Surprisingly, a thin crack ran across one corner.)

"Can I offer you some coffee, or should we have a drink from the bar?" Donato was solicitous.

"Let's have a drink." he said, perhaps slightly too quickly.

Donato went back to the bar. "Wine? Red or white?" *No vintage here, then* thought Young. "A glass of red would be most welcome," he said.

"I'm looking forward to reading the Professor's summaries," Young continued. "Have you seen them?"

"Goodness me, no. There was a list of subjects and speakers on the notice board over there, but not the content of the lectures or discussions. I fear they would be meaningless to me."

"Same here. Afraid lost with science. My view, not comfortable with the subject. Past me by."

Young had already noticed the list had disappeared. That didn't mean anything, but Donato had handed Keenan a list, or a menu, or a sheaf of paper or something of the sort when they met in the hotel in Bedford. Young knew someone else was there as well.

"We are now anticipating the next conference," Donato continued. "This one is to be a completely different subject. 'Cybernetics' I think it's called. Something to do with communications." Donato pulled a face.

"Best of luck." Young was at pains to express his ignorance also. "How on Earth these bright boys can get their minds round subjects like that beats me." Young shook his head.

They finished their drinks and stood together. "Well, that has put my mind at rest," Young said, "your services seemed to have been excellent. To be expected, of course." "Thank you." She didn't display any modesty, false or otherwise, because it was a compliment that she was expecting. When all said and done, she had been managing much larger concerns than this. In the past few years.

"I'll be in touch again quite soon, no doubt, Ms Donato."

"I look forward to that Group Captain. And remember, it's Stacey!" He returned along the corridor to his mobile. "Get me a taxi. Would you, old chap?" the expression on Cobb's face did not change. "Which regiment were you in?"

"Engineers, Sergeant-major, later on."

"Thought as much. Action?"

"Oh yes, sir."

Young's taxi arrived.

Young asked the taxi driver to drop him short of his office. And as he walked down, Whitehall pulled out his mobile and got hold of Mikhail. He wouldn't be overheard here, surely. But at the same time, it felt stupid. Secrecy was not his middle name.

"Mikhael? Reginald. Got some work to do."

"Go on." Sounded as if he was eating. He probably was.

"Need to go to Norfolk this weekend. Leave Saturday should be home Sunday. That, OK?"

"Can I bring the intended?"

"No. Rather, you didn't. On this occasion, we need to be on our own. But sometime, love to meet Rose."

"You mean Eunice."

"No. You're intended. You told me, Rose."

"That's as may be. It's Eunice now."

"Is it? Well, make your excuses. We need to be on our own."

"Okay." Mikhail continued eating. He didn't seem bothered.

"Saturday morning. Pick me up outside Whitehall theatre? 9:30 am?"

"Sure." Young put the mobile away, climbed the steps, and hurried past Ms Guthrie.

The rest of the afternoon passed without incident. He asked Miss Guthrie to arrange for ANCOM on Tuesday, next week. He would need to adjust to the new relationships. But. But continue to encourage discussion on the COVID-19. Reinforce government awareness of the threat. And with that in mind, he decided to slip upstairs and let Lady Eleanor know how well the committee was going, how members had applied themselves and mention the symposium. Emphasise the increasing likelihood of a threat of pandemic. He would amble to the secretaries along the corridor, sort out his expenses. The coming weekend was likely to be expensive.

Young got home at 7:00 pm. Listened to Diane's description of assorted incidents. In and around the charity shop and enjoyed a glass of gin and tonic. As it happened, Diane was in a pensive mood. When he mentioned that he might be away for the weekend. "Saturday night?"

"Almost certainly." She murmured that he should not overwork himself but remember what 'the doctor had told him'. Trouble was, he couldn't remember what the doctor had said; in fact, he couldn't remember going to the doctor at all. Well, not recently, anyway. Perhaps she meant something else.

Chapter 18

With hindsight Friday, 7th February was crucial to many we know from this saga.

If we start with myself, that day I was as unhappy as I can ever remember. The next day, Saturday, I planned to go to London and talk with Rachel in her flat. She had been out of touch now for weeks. Had she moved on from our relationship? I was terrified. What if she wasn't there and couldn't be contacted? Like Alexander had disappeared? Would she be safe? A possibility I was unable to contemplate. Had she bolted with him? Another possibility too unpleasant to think about. It was like being in an impenetrable jungle with no escape. Completely lost. No conceivable solution. And tomorrow it had to be confronted.

I drove to college but realised I was in no mood to prepare tutorials or work in the laboratory, and luckily no lectures were booked, I decided to walk along a lane behind the college to the Cherwell River and the towpath to the University Parks. It just so happened that Rachel and I had taken the same route one end of summer evening the previous September.

She had gone before me through a gate, and I had noticed she was so tall that her shoes had only modest heels. She had been laughing; dressed in a colourful summer frock; happy. Today, I noticed the gate creaked and the hinges were mottled with flaking rust. The Parks in February were scruffy; clumps of trees stood bare, frost-covered and cold, the paths between them streaked with ice. A mist hung over the river like a shroud.

Don't be ridiculous! That's my dejection, not the natural condensation of cold air over the river. I felt angry with myself, born of frustration I suppose.

The walk from the Parks, passing Keble College to the 'Lamb and Flag' pub is about 100 yards, no more. That day it took forever. Rachel preferred the 'Bird and Baby' across St Giles, but I'd walked far enough far enough for a while. I went into the 'Lamb', ordered a pint and sat sipping it in a corner. No one bothered me. As I sat there, I resolved to confront the issue tomorrow and that would be final. Whatever the outcome, I would at least have an explanation. Reality would be much better than ignorance. This was no bliss.

Pint finished, I trudged back to college. In the 'High', now almost deserted in winter, I remembered, it had been busy during the summer and autumn. Rachel had attached herself, in the summer, to a group of sightseers being lectured by a guide. Tall and stooped, white-haired, elbows, hands and fingers at all angles, he was wearing a grubby suit and what looked like egg on his tie. What sort of chap did this type of guided tour? A failed lecturer? A disgraced housemaster from a junior public school? A "resting" actor? He was surrounded by Japanese couples with cameras, Americans with Stetsons and dark glasses and Europeans with vacant expressions and was expounding eloquently on Shelly (whilst pointing to the memorial with his rolled, yellow umbrella.) Somewhere within his lecture he lost the plot and the next thing I heard, he was talking about Oscar Wilde, CS Lewis and Alice in Wonderland; the connection between the three escaped me. However, it was only when he started on Vera Lynn, Michael Caine and Glenn Miller that I finally gave up and whispered to Rachel, I would see her at Carfax Tower in about an hour. The last I saw of him, he was parading along with a 'High', umbrella lofted to the sky and the gaggle of tourists traipsing along behind.

In college, all I could manage was a snack in the Middle Common Room. Nobody bothered me.

The next day, Saturday, I'd go to London.

On the same Friday morning, Diane would have had her own worries to contend with. Reginald's mood had become erratic; one minute, hard-working; the next secretive (of course that went with the job but still…); then as bright as a button, smile on his face, off to London without a care in the world. This was not like him at all. He must be particularly preoccupied and even her reference to a non-existing warning from the doctor went unquestioned. She considered the matter. It was one thing to work, surrounded by colleagues, even if there were problems, it was quite another to sit at home not quite sure of what was happening. One thing she was certain of, or as certain as she could be, he was not playing away from home. He might be staying away from home tonight and tomorrow night, possibly even Sunday night; but playing away from home was out of the question. She decided to go into Cambridge and do some window shopping, perhaps even have a light lunch. But first breakfast; this morning he seemed tense; she'd made up an overnight bag.

They breakfasted in the conservatory in which the builders had thoughtfully provided central heating. Young had a scant appetite and Diane, who presumed the long silences of the previous evening and the somewhat restless night, was due to preoccupation with his work. She also knew it was better not to ask. He told her this morning; however, he would probably be away for the weekend but added quickly that work was heavy at present. (He wanted no misunderstanding.)

Diane was surprised at the sudden announcement. It was unusual for him to be away for a weekend and even more unusual to be told, so late and so abruptly. Obviously, this was important, and he needed her support and nothing else.

"Are you going out of London at all? Some emergency?"

"Yes, something needs clearing up and I'm not sure yet whether I'll be going out of London."

As she went upstairs, he acknowledged he was asking a lot of her; couldn't tell her what he was doing. He didn't want to mention anything. The burden she would carry would weigh heavily on him. He realised, not for the first time, how dependent upon her he was and how much she must imagine about his work. It may even be reasonable to suppose but it was more difficult to sit at home without knowing what's going on than being in the thick of things. He wondered if her patience came from years of being an officer's wife in the services or her commitment to the Church and her belief; probably both. She returned.

"I've left the case by the front door. You'll be alright?" A general question but asked with sincerity and a little fearfully. It didn't go unnoticed there was no unnecessary Inquisition and for that he was grateful.

"Thank you, Diane. Be in touch on Monday without fail, probably before." Then after a pause, "Church is it on Sunday?"

"And tomorrow afternoon. Bring and buy for funds again." She said, with a disguised sigh.

"Hope that goes well. Lock the doors at night…"

"We always do. And I will when you're away."

"Good. Good. That the driver then?" hearing the doorbell ring. As he left and gave her a peck on the cheek. Nothing too demonstrative. No need to overdo it.

"See you Monday, then," she said.

"Right you are. Or with any luck sooner. Thank you again, Diane." The car pulled away and he was gone.

It was Cyril again this morning, someone who knew Young's habits quite well and he was surprised to see the suitcase. Looked like an overnight bag only, but there you go.

"Staying in London tonight are you, Mr Young?"

"Probably Cyril. Won't need the services of your company tonight. Let them know when I'm back."

"Very good sir."

The conversation lapsed. Now he was on the road. Young was determined to move things along this weekend one way or another. Dammit, this blessed pandemic was getting nearer by the day and was going to need immense resources both monetary and personal to control it. The government seemed not to have woken up yet. Well, he couldn't do anything about that on his own but at least he could put his weight behind Bhatti's proposals, whatever they were. The 'services' could cope with Eleanor.

They were at the station before he realised it and his musings continued across London. He arrived at Whitehall, 10 am sharp.

"Good morning, Group Captain." Ms Guthrie was surprised at his early appearance. He swept past and was in his office before she could say another word; but she could think; *Well, I never,* she thought.

Before he left, he needed to speak to Franklin. He asked Ms Guthrie to get the Superintendent on the landline, no need for secrecy he reasoned.

"Everything alright is it, Reggie?" Ms Guthrie was still shell-shocked from his arrival this morning.

"Fine, fine thank you. And yourself?"

"Looking forward to the weekend." She chuckled. *What's got into her?* He wondered. "I'll get you the Superintendent."

"Morning Brian."

"Morning Reginald." Franklin's voice was as sharp as usual.

"Been mulling things over in my mind…"

"…so have I…" Franklin interrupted.

"…and decided this thing is getting more urgent by the day."

"I know that. Have you heard the news today? There is some talk of an exponential rise in cases worldwide now. Exponential! I'm not a mathematician but this is serious, and I think it's true to say that if there are 200 cases today, in 7-days' time there will be something like 25,600! And that's in only one location!"

"Brian! Brian! Hugely impressed and persuaded. As I see it, Brian, not only have we got to bring some urgency into the thinking upstairs, but there is also the matter of finding out what else is going on."

"I know." Franklin and Young knew what each other we're talking about but we're not saying it.

"I'm going to be away this coming weekend on business, you know. But the first thing Monday morning perhaps we can get together."

"Certainly. I'm going to be busy all over the weekend." To Young it came over as double talk. A nod was as good as a wink to a blind horse! And he was grateful yet again this morning. They disconnected.

Young pulled out his mobile and rang Ipswich. Finally, he got through to Gordon Baxter. He decided to arrive at Baxter's office and meet him that afternoon, say about 3 pm. He planned to be there or thereabouts for the whole weekend but whether he was on his own or not depended upon Gordon? They'd discuss that when he got there.

After a quick glance of his watch, Young grabbed his coat, picked up his small case and marched down the corridor towards reception.

"Ms Guthrie won't see you again. Going away on business this weekend. Thanks for your help."

"What about things upstairs? What happens if Lady Eleanor wants you?"

"Just tell her I'm away for a weekend; working; she'll understand." And with that, Young waved a hand nonchalantly in the air, and was out through the door before Ms Guthrie had time to bother him further. *Well, I never!* She thought *He's hurrying about. Wonder what's happened?* Then she started mithering about Lady Eleanor upstairs, and possible excuses.

Young burst from reception into Whitehall where the cold caught him unexpectedly. He quickened his step to get the circulation flowing and was almost at the Whitehall Theatre when the Audi saloon drew up alongside. He jumped into the car.

"Mikhail? Alright, are you?" The inside of the car was a welcome respite from the cold.

"Sure. Weekend job?" Mikhail was watching the traffic in his wing mirror; it was dense here around Trafalgar Square.

"You're free?" Young suddenly had a moment of unease. He needed Mikhail for the whole weekend.

"Sure. Free. Where to?"

"Just outside Ipswich" Young gave him the address and Mikhail switched on his Sat Nav.

"We'll go through Essex and on to Ipswich where we're meeting a fellow called Gordon Baxter. He's in management Border Control. How long do you think it will take us Mikhail?"

"The Sat Nav indicates about 3 hours, but I suppose it depends on the traffic, as always." Mikhail was a good and experienced driver and Young made himself comfortable and prepared to enjoy the ride. Central London was choked with Friday traffic; it was a matter of stop start; and the M25 not much better. But as soon as they turned onto the dual carriageway of the A12 Mikhail picked up speed as the traffic flowed more easily.

Young had never found the Essex countryside as beautiful as other parts of Britain, but it was pleasant enough. They passed the odd orchard; even a low slope of vines; gradually he became drowsy, and his impression of the journey was a series of visual pictures; a copse; and woods frosted; the trees bare, their branches fractured like broken limbs. Did the flattened fields promise green regeneration; trees bare like skeletons. On one occasion, Mikhail accelerated to pass a car and Young looked left to see a lady gripping her steering wheel, knuckles whitened with tension, floral hat askew. Or did he dream that? Clouds were gathering on the horizon; everywhere looked bitterly cold. Nevertheless, getting out of London and its tangled traffic and escaping from the office and confusing alliances came as more of a release than he had imagined. In his professional world, Eleanor Keenan had been at the centre, like a spider with a network around her. Her aim was not personal advancement in Whitehall; he reckoned she had an agenda which was more devious than that; but thank his lucky stars he could stand back from that now. He had no idea what her real intention was, but he considered her disloyal at best, deceitful at worst. Everything about her was a pretence as if there was no personal commitment at all. What about her unexplained behaviour away from work and at the hotel near Bedford? Didn't that reinforce his suspicions? But that was Marcia's problem now, and good luck to her!

His speculations were interrupted by Mikhail.

"Lunch boss?"

The car was slowing down and turning into a car park, and he looked out to see the promising view of a heavily beamed, thatched pub whose lights shone brightly from the tiny leaded windows. The sun was behind clouds that had spread up from the horizon; blue/grey heavy, casting deepening shadow. But Young was hopeful that rain or snow would hold off. It hadn't been forecast. But still, for early afternoon, it was decidedly gloomy.

"Eat?" Mikhail switched off the engine.

"Absolutely, and not before time." Young stretched his back, as he got out of the car. "Where are we?"

"It's a village off the main road, just south of Chelmsford. Half an hour here, and we'll make it to Ipswich by 3:00 pm, easy."

They went in. The bar had only just opened, and it was one of Young's favourite times in a pub. The landlord was still setting up; bottles were being wiped and stacked onto the shelves; the bar counter was shining. They sat precariously on bar stools, Young enjoying the smell of beer, hops and the cleaner's polish. The only sound was the clatter of bottles. A tortoiseshell cat stalked in, sniffed the air disdainfully, jumped onto the bench seat in the small bay window and proceeded with its ablutions. How quiet the place was. They waited. "Be right with you, Guv," the landlord called.

"No rush." Young was looking round the room; tables wiped, beer mats placed in front of four chairs to each table waiting for the customers to come and disrupt the order of things, only to be replaced again with unthinking precision later or at least before tomorrow. The one-arm bandits stood silent, waiting to come to life with the flick of a switch, when lights would rotate and leap about, incomprehensible noises would burp and throb their never-ending rhythms throughout the day. But now it was peaceful. That's as he liked it; he felt as if he owned the place.

"Right, what'll it be gents?" The landlord came towards them wiping his hands on a tea towel. Young ordered ploughman's and pint for himself, a pork pie and mineral water for Mikhail.

For some time, there was only Young and Mikhail but very slowly others drifted in—strangers intruding into their domain! Two young men in new suits, white shirts and new briefcases asked 'Eddie' for two pints 'of the usual special'. Young watched the barman pull two pints of strong lager and add an optic of vodka to each. The pair paid and went to the far end of the room. An elderly man wandered in, was served a half a bottle of champagne and one glass and, without saying a word, sat on the bench seat in the bay window, next to the cat that had finished its cleaning activities and was sound asleep. The old man pulled out and read a newspaper, the Daily Mail. Two young ladies arrived, obviously a couple, with defensive swaggers and aggressive make-up. Young felt his age. Then four bikers, soft drinks all round. Little by little the pub was filling. As he and Mikhail left, he felt strangely upset as if he had been excluded. This was someone else's local, not his. The bar had changed from being a welcome break to a local. Young was to find the experience good preparation for Fenlands in Norfolk that was famous, or notorious depending upon the way you viewed it, for being insular. Even exclusive. The matter had been exacerbated by the number of houses that had been bought as holiday homes, especially along the North Norfolk coast, where Dowson had lived. House prices had risen to such levels that the locals were unable to buy, and this led to resentment. Dowson would have unfortunately felt that. The extent Young would find out.

They arrived at Baxter's offices, near Ipswich, at quarter past three. The area was a nondescript chaos of single storey buildings, a row of garages with securely padlocked up-and-over doors and behind were large storage areas, patrolled by police (or was it army?) and guarded with barbed wire. Gordon welcomed them warmly and was gracious enough not to look at his watch but merely jumped in the car and directed them to his home. The house was on the outskirts of Ipswich, detached, in a new development, spacious and too large for a single chap. Young made no comment but the emptiness was uncomfortable, it was not homely.

They were shown into the lounge and Mikhail went to make tea, directed to the kitchen by Gordon. The lounge was furnished with a four-seater settee and armchairs, occasional tables and dominated by a 40-inch television set. The domesticity of the room only emphasised Gordon's loneliness. Young looked at him carefully and noted the thick dark hair and eyebrows we're now streaked with grey, and he appeared much older than 55. Not the smiling, jovial man that Young had known many years ago but a decidedly tired, sad and ageing man. Young felt desperately sorry for him.

"About Marjorie…" But before he could get further Gordon put up his hand; "It's alright, Reggie I'm over the worst now. Trouble was it was so sudden. Never for a moment thought anything was wrong. Got on well for perhaps 20-25 years. Then suddenly she met someone else, a rich farmer. Millionaire I've been told. The two boys sided with her although they're grown up. In fact, one of them is getting married next month; that's going to be tricky and make no mistake!" (Was that a flash of anger?) "I was working all hours God sent of course…perhaps that didn't help. The Border Force and Immigration are overwhelmed now, what with Brexit, drugs, immigration…and we've got a lot of deep seaports to deal with in the Haven Authority. Felixstowe has its own management problems. Largest container port in Great Britain, would you know. Four million containers every year. It's a hell of a job. Probably spent too much time on it. All you can see when you drive into Felixstowe are rows of giant cranes like sentries along the docks. Harwich is different; it's passenger ferries taking cars, vans, lorries and the like." Gordon gazed out of the window, quiet for a moment, lost for words. Then waking up again he went on. "Like I say, hell of a job!"

"Must be." Young sympathised. "What is it you do here, exactly, Gordon?"

"Well, 'exactly' is difficult. Generally, I coordinate the custom services in Haven's ports. Quite a bit of liaison with the police. Must be. We need their assistance a lot of the time. So, I've got a good relationship there; that's what prompted me to ring you. I knew you were working in Whitehall now and thought you probably come across this sort of thing now and again. But if I'm honest I didn't really know. Anyway, I decided to ring you about the car and the cargo just on the off chance; might even have been for old time's sake you can never tell."

"Of course, Gordon, of course. And I was pleased to hear from you anyway. Curiously enough it's something of interest to us." Young let Gordon continue; "The police bulletin, no more than routine really, caught my eye; there was a car abandoned in Harwich and I made enquiries. No one by the name of Dowson went through the port in December or January and not in February so far according to our records. But of course, he could have used a different name and passports and not always totally accurate, if you get my meaning!"

"I do. Oh yes, I do."

"Well, the plot thickened when one of the border officers reported he'd found some glass containers, insulated to keep cold, stored behind some insulating panels in a small van. Now here is the thing; they were addressed to this Dowson character; care of a storage depot in Norwich."

"Know what these glass jars contained?" Young asked.

"The description on the declaration forms was 'lipid/water emulsion. For chemical use'. We've not come across this sort of stuff before, and I really have no idea what it's for."

"And Dowson's name was on the cases? And bound for Norwich? Mikhail, tomorrow we'd better drive up to Norwich and look at this storage depot. Perhaps you could come with us, Gordon."

"I've already been up there with the police. Straightforward place, I think. Apparently, Dowson collected packages about once a month, sometimes quite big ones. Needed forklift truck and the like. I anticipated that you'd want to see the place so I've already called the local police and we can meet them about 1:00 pm. Tomorrow."

"Perfect, Gordon, perfect. Now, bugger all this work, let's go out and have something to eat and a little liquid refreshment. What do you say?"

"I'd say that was a good idea. I'll order a taxi and we can make an evening of it. Where are you staying? Here if you like." Gordon's voice was not as insistent as it might have been and Young surmised, correctly it turned out, that he was not really prepared for visitors staying overnight.

"Wouldn't think of it, Gordon. Take us to a decent pub, we'll make do there." By 6:00 pm, they were on their way to a very reasonable hotel on the outskirts of Ipswich. They feasted on rib-eye steaks and then settled down to make sure the beer on tap was up to scratch. In front of an open fire, they sat in deep armchairs stretching their legs and warming themselves recounted various experiences, some shared, over the previous few years. Mikhail was particularly interested in the tales of Cyprus; but many of the characters they talked about were unknown to him. "Remember that chap Shaw?" Young asked at one point.

"The mess rep.? Ran off with the mess funds, didn't he? I remember him alright."

"We called him Artie," "after that jazz wizard, Artie Shaw, remember? And not because of his expertise with a clarinet but something to do with the 'Artful' disappearance of money!" Young was enjoying the memories.

"He got drummed out, didn't he?" Gordon tried to remember.

"Sure. God knows what he's up to now. Dodgy car dealer wouldn't be surprised!"

Similar stories kept them amused but Young could see how Gordon struggled. There was no doubt he was a disappointed man. However, he did ask; "Diane. Good form?"

"Just the same Gordon. Just the same." Young cut the topic short and swiftly deflected thoughts elsewhere. By 10:00 pm, they had decided the beer was 'up to scratch' and had appraised it in sufficient quantities to make sleep easy, if not essential. They planned to meet at Gordon's place the following morning at about 10:00 am, pick up the Audi and explore Harwich and Norwich.

They all slept soundly.

Mikhail and Young came down to breakfast slowly. A lot of water and juice was drunk but a full English breakfast was not one of their priorities. However, they managed to call a taxi and get themselves to Gordon's house by 10:00 am, where he was waiting patiently for them. They collected the Audi, Young and Baxter sitting in the back, Mikhail drove into Harwich. The docks were a further mile. Admission went smoothly with Gordon's pass. The quayside was much busier than Young had expected even considering it was Saturday morning. Two big ferries were tied up. One was taking aboard passengers and traffic heading for Holland. Across the water, which was like a millpond and metallic-grey in colour, they could just make out the enormous line of cranes at Felixstowe, and several huge container ships tied up. Miles out to sea the wind farm could just be made out in the mist.

"There is a Harbour ferry that takes you around our deep-water ports, Ipswich, Felixstowe and so on. But the quickest way across to Felixstowe from here is the passenger-only ferry. The road between Harwich and Felixstowe is long; it takes about three-quarters of an hour to drive it," Gordon said. "Dowson's car was abandoned back in the town, so if he came to the docks, he would have had to walk. Unaided presumably. It is possible that Dowson crossed to Holland but it's a long trip, about 6 or 7 hours and we have no record of him passing through."

Young was thinking rapidly. If Dowson left the country for Holland through Harwich, then he got through without arousing interest. He might have used a false passport and name; or he could have boarded by ambulance, another car, or a van. But surely, they would have been checked. Young thought it highly unlikely he had left the country under his own steam, or unaided. That left the possibility of course that he hadn't left the country at all or left from somewhere else.

"We'll go on to the storage depot at Norwich if you've seen enough here," Gordon suggested. "It'll take about two hours, round the Haven then the A140 to Norwich."

In fact, it only took them an hour and three-quarters, the roads being unusually free for a Saturday morning. The storage depot appeared to be several well-built, brick constructions with intimidating barbed-wire fencing and plenty of CCTV cameras, prominently displayed.

"The storage units themselves are made of metal and attached to the back of the brick facades," Gordon explained. "The company takes all kinds of storage articles, large or small, and arrangements can be made for deliveries here, care of the company, to be picked up by the renters later. Each unit is securely locked and is guarded 24-hours a day, 7-days a week together with more than adequate CCTV coverage. The company depends upon its safety record for business, of course. Now we're a bit early so if you like, we can get a bite to eat at the site's canteen. I've decided to meet the police here at 2:00 pm. Is that alright?"

"Fine by us." Young was looking forward to his lunch having been abstemious over breakfast! The canteen was a single storey building, filled with lunchtime security guards and the menu was what you would expect, and each serving was accompanied by a mug of tea, sugar optional.

They returned to security storage 'A4' and found two uniformed constables and a detective Sergeant waiting for them. The civilian-dressed sergeant stepped forward and introduced herself as Glenda Eyles. "We meet at last." As Young shook hands with her he noticed the firm handshake, the blue eyes and chestnut-coloured hair. There were laughter lines around the corners of her eyes. They finally got to the 'A4' storage facility and were met by a smart security guard clutching the necessary paperwork that gained them entrance.

"Everything stored here is the property of the renter, in law, but I have their permission to open any unit for inspection. I'm afraid you can't remove any items stored here unless you have the necessary warrants."

"Here you are." Sergeant Elyes produced the paperwork and Young was duly impressed. *Worth keeping an eye on this young lady,* he thought. He exchanged a smile with her. The guard took the warrant and opened the door to Dowson's unit with his master key. He switched on the overhead light. They saw a large space, empty except for the cases that contained the vacuum jars filled with this curious oil/water emulsion.

"Normally empty like this, is it?" Young wanted to know.

"I've no idea. We don't usually enter the units."

"You don't inspect deliveries then?" Eyles queried.

"No. Not our job. As I said, these units store private property of the renter."

"And who rents this unit, is it Alexander Dowson?" Young asked.

The guard opened and inspected his-log book. "Company by the name of M.C.C.A."

"And who or what is M.C.C.A?" Young persisted.

"No idea. It means nothing to me." The guard didn't seem interested in the least, not part of his job.

"Well, it's not one of the big chemical companies," Young murmured. "Later on, better look it up."

"I've already done that," the ever-competent sergeant exclaimed. "Company trading out of a Mozambique port. Specialises in nanoparticles!"

"Nano what?" Young was lost.

Eyles went on to everyone's amazement; "Nano means, in scientific jargon; extremely small, smaller than a microscope can detect; and particles are what they say they are; particles!"

"Well, there you are!" Young was impressed. None the wiser really. "What the hell are they used for? Do you know Glenda?"

"I'm afraid not sir."

With that, they had reached the limit of the sergeant's knowledge. Young was left gazing at the four containers, thinking furiously. He'd need expert knowledge. And quickly. Forensics would analyse the stuff, but he needed to know what they were dealing with and what it was used for and quickly. He wondered about Linus Bhatti; he would know, that's for sure.

"I think that we have done as much as we can here today, so if the constables would be kind enough to take away one of the containers perhaps the police forensic department can analyse them," Young suggested.

"Gloves!" Eyles ordered the constables quickly. They complied.

"I think Gordon, if we still have enough energy we should go and look at Dowson's cottage by the sea. What do you think?"

"Fine by me," was the reply; "as you might expect I haven't got a lot on this afternoon." The resignation in Gordon's voice was unmistakable.

"And the sergeant?" Young looked hopefully at the wholesome Detective Sergeant. It would enhance his afternoon no end if she were to accompany them.

"I booked the whole afternoon for this, with inspector Craig. I'll be pleased to come." Glenda replied. "Thanks chaps," she addressed the constables; "if you take the containers in the police car and hand them over to forensics, that would be a great help. Assuming of course," she looked at Young, "if I can catch a lift."

Young was pleased.

Chapter 19

"I'll direct us out of Norwich, Mikhail, then turn onto the B1149 when I say, and North—no, not to Alaska!—to Holt." (*So, she's been round the block,* thought Young.) "Straight through Holt and follow the signs to the coast. Should take about an hour."

Glenda half-turned to talk with Young and Baxter. Young seized his chance to make inconsequential chat. "Sure this is ok? Saturday and all, I mean?"

"Certainly. I told Inspector Leeder I was meeting with Customs today with regards to our missing Mr Dowson. It's Leeder's weekend off, anyway, so I haven't got him to worry about. And for the moment business is slack."

Young looked well-pleased. To have her company was an unexpected bonus; furthermore, she was a mine of information.

"And you know the area?" Young asked.

"Oh yes, I was born and brought up here and hereabouts," she replied. "And I'm interested in my job. I was curious about this 'lipid/water emulsion' and what on earth it could be used for. So, I rang a friend of mine in Cambridge, studying chemistry, and asked him."

"Tell us then." Young was smiled.

"Apparently, these nanoparticles are extremely small clusters of atoms that can provide safe carriers for other substances doctors want to introduce into your body; for example, drugs for cancer; or possibly toxic substances. These substances are protected by the lipids masking it from the body's defensive system. Bit like a suit of armour; defends the chemical you want to get into the body without rejecting it."

"I see," said Young, not seeing at all. "So, what's that got to do with us, or more importantly Alexander Dowson and his disappearance?"

"I don't know. All I know is that he has been picking up these vacuum jars containing a most unusual mixture of fat, or lipid, mixed with water. More precisely, very cold water. Goodness knows where he takes them or what he does with them. My friend says they are widely used in commerce, paints, sun creams, stain-repellents and much more. The oil or 'lipid' ones are used in medicine."

Young turned to Gordon. "Connection with making those nasty drugs that are being used by everybody except me nowadays?"

"Not that I know of. This is all new to me." Gordon then lapsed into silence again and watched the countryside sliding past without seeing it. The landscape was monotonously flat, but he was clearly preoccupied. As Glenda had predicted, the road was remarkably clear, even for a Saturday afternoon, and they made good time. Mikhail was driving quickly, and the purr of the engine was hypnotic which helped Gordon relax into the corner of his back seat, gaze at the countryside. His head retracted into his shoulders, self-absorbed. Young sat quietly, knowing or at least imagining Gordon's misery. Young knew that if his own situation fell apart, he would be devastated in the same way. Certainly, Gordon's plight put his own domestic situation into perspective. But there were other considerations on his mind. He had to work out what Dowson was up to, where Dowson had gone?

Suddenly they were driving through Holt. He was reluctant to break Gordon's reverie, but as Mikhail slowed, Gordon sat up and re-joined them; "Holt! Nice place. I don't think I have been here in years. Woods near here. The boys loved it."

"Oh, it's nice alright!" Glenda giggled. "Tourist trap. Tea shops, antiques, bakeries, art shops. It's got the lot. And all around there are parks and walks and, like you say, woods and goodness know what. This is where I live."

Police sergeants shouldn't giggle, especially if they were CID, thought Young apropos nothing. 'Lovely lady though! They were through Holt before Young, or Baxter could have a good look and almost immediately they were winding their way into Dowson's village. So, this is where it all began'. Young mused, and a lovely Norfolk village into the bargain. The main coast road ran straight through, or at least wound its way through the village and was obviously the focus of the community. There were flint-pebble-and-brick cottages throughout, somewhat old fashioned.

"This is the nearest coastal village to where I live," Eyles announced. "I love the place. At the other end of the village, a few miles on, there's an old windmill which is a landmark around here and the cottages there act as Bed and Breakfast. The village itself is donkey's years old and it still has the Old Smokehouse where they still smoke bloaters, kippers and eels. There's a bookshop, delicatessen and teashop of course, a gallery for local artists, and a grocery store. The pub is farther down the road, just past the bend. The village is well provided for. In summertime crowded with tourists and passing traffic. But I still love it. The beach is only about two-hundred yards away, shingle but ideal for inshore fishing. I did a lot of that when I was younger. Once upon a time the village was on the sea, but marshland and reeds separate it now. There are plenty of paths through the reeds if you know your way about. Can be secretive."

Mikhail parked the car. Young looked puzzled. "Who would have thought it? A tiny village next to nowhere! Why would he choose to live here?" Mikhail stayed by the car whilst Glenda Eyles led them down a narrow lane that branched off the main road. The last cottage of the terrace of six houses, the one furthest from the road, was the cottage they had come to look at. The terrace was unattractive, built with flint-pebble and brick, each cottage had a door and narrow windows, the frames painted white. Opposite, a wall separated the approach path from a long neighbouring garden; shadow made the path and cottages dark. The cottage was padlocked, police warning tape had become detached and was fluttering redundantly in the breeze.

"I'm sorry we can't get in. The forensic boys have ordered that no one is to enter, in fact, next week they're coming to nail up the windows and the doors with corrugated iron and stick notices around declaring 'No Entry', and threatening dire consequences for anyone who disobeys. Quite what the palaver is all about I have no idea."

Young and Gordon peered in through the windows. The interior was completely empty.

"Cleared the place out, did they?" Young asked.

"Absolutely. But that was Dowson's employer, whoever that is. Not a stick of furniture left. Fumigated the place, or gave it a deep clean, or both would you believe, but that might just be rumour." Eyles seemed mystified by the whole business. "I've no idea why they did that."

"They didn't completely clear the place out, did they?" Gordon pointed. "There's still a picture hanging on the far wall." The remark went unheeded.

"Not much to be gained here, then." Young was disappointed. "If we could just take an amble up the main street and drop into the grocery store, see if anyone remembers Dowson."

"Certainly." Eyles led the way.

Back on the main street, they found the store only a short distance away. It turned out to be a general store. Small, but tightly stocked, the shop sold everything from eggs to jellied eels, from oil lamps to bread, from fishing tackle to model yachts. Young went in on his own. He loved the smell; dust, leather, a hint of spices; it was dark, musty and inviting. You never knew what treasure you might come across in here. He remembered a similar shop in his childhood, with his mother no doubt and forgotten all about it until now. The memory was of pleasure but at the edge of his mind he remembered crying. He couldn't remember why.

The shop assistant appeared behind a glass display cabinet. She was young, freckled, pretty and smiled at Young as she asked what he needed. Young looked around and his eye fell on a large cheddar cheese with the appropriate wire and wooden handle to cut slices. "I'll take a half pound of your cheddar, please." The girl expertly cut a portion, put it on the scales. It was 9 oz. Young approved of this skill and the imperial measurement.

"Just over half?" She asked.

"Perfect." Young was affable. "You've got a good eye, and that's for sure."

"Practice." She grinned.

"Your shop, is it?" Young risked.

"No. Belongs to Mum and Dad."

"Husband, not about today then?" Young had noticed the wedding ring.

"He's not here in the daytime. He drives the bus on the coast road. It's not too bad at the moment but in the summer with all the tourists he's tired when he gets in."

"Yes, a difficult day's work." Young was sympathetic.

"He has his days," was all she said.

"Knew a chap who lived in the Shingle Cottage, think it's called, down the lane opposite, until a few weeks ago. Know him by any chance?" Young inquired. "Alex Dowson by name."

"Oh yes, I remember him!" She was blushing furiously. "But I think he's moved away now."

"Know where he's gone by any chance?"

"No idea." She busied herself with rearranging some packs of butter, bacon, cheeses and yogurts in the display cabinet. Then suddenly; "Why? What's he to you?"

"Nothing. Nothing." Young said, fractionally too quickly. "Just heard that he had left, that's all."

"He certainly did." Her lips were drawn tightly together.

"Have many visitors, did he? Come in regularly to buy supplies, did he?"

"Enough." She was openly angry now. "Can I get you anything else?"

"Like some bread to go with this lovely cheese." Young was trying to calm her. Bread, sliced and ready wrapped, was banged on the counter.

"Thank you." Young paid then beat a hasty retreat. The three had wandered down the street and were gazing into the window of the local gallery; local scenes; quite well painted.

"Anything you fancy?" Young asked.

The three turned in unison. "Not sufficiently to buy," said Baxter.

"Shall we get back?" Mikhail was cold.

"How did you get on?" Glenda asked.

"Tell you in the car."

They started the journey back to Holt to drop off Glenda then on to the hotel.

"Mr Dowson was known, alright. From the looks of it, might have been known too well! The young lady in there is married and I think that our Mr Dowson might have been interrupting the blissful union." Young didn't sound perturbed.

"Really?" Glenda was interested.

"Well, she's a feisty young lady, full of spirit, and quick to anger. Appeared to be genuinely unsettled by the mention of Dowson's name. Husband, a bus driver, away quite a lot…" Young left the rest of the sentence unsaid. But relented. "Could have had her eye on Dowson."

"That right?" Glenda was all ears

"So, there we have it. Dyson makes a splash. Comes to the village, buys a property, probably no one else around here can afford. Maybe not popular; then, damn me, disappears without a goodbye, leaving a poor shop girl upset and angry. God knows what the bus driver must think. Did Cookson write this story?" At that moment, a single-decker bus passed them driving into the village. No one spoke. Glenda directed Mikhail through Holt to her house. The Audi pulled up at a cottage and Young noticed the tidy garden and a child's swing.

Michael set off for the last leg of the journey. Norwich, Ipswich, Hotel. They dropped Gordon at his house before returning to the hotel, for a light supper over which Young told Mikhail they had one more visit to make before they drove back to London. They'd see Dowson's supervisor at the East Anglia University.

"And where does he live?" Mikhail asked.

"Oh, Ipswich I believe," Young replied airily.

"Right," was all that Mikhail said.

They had a couple of nightcaps and retired early.

*** *** ***

They got up in the morning late, had a leisurely breakfast and went in search of Dr Crawford who supervised Dowson's postgraduate thesis at East Anglia University. As they passed University of East Anglia on the way up to Fackenham, all Young had seen was blocks of concrete and glass, shaped into cubes, cuboids with a few rounded edges. It was modern and utilitarian as far as he could see. Dr Crawford's house caught Young unawares. On the outskirts of Norwich, it was three-story brick built; no doubt previously the property of a wealthy merchant, but which was now neglected. There was a prominent security alarm below the eaves (probably for show only), paint was peeling. The front space, Young would hesitate to call it garden, was knee-high in grass and weeds and was surrounded by a laurel hedge about seven feet tall, badly in need of pruning. The front gate, one person wide, was tied up with a strong cord which when released allowed the gate to fall back onto the path that led to the front door, rather than swing open on hinges. There were no hinges. Young edged down the path and approached three steps that led to the porch and door. Odd that the university should be so new and bright, the supervisor's house so old and shabby. He rang the bell and immediately a cacophony of deep, frantic and menacing barking started up inside. After a while, the front door opened a few inches to reveal a middle-aged man in a loose cardigan, bent double holding a German shepherd dog by its collar. The dog was in a highly excited state. The man was finding life difficult.

"He's pleased to see you, really. Good dog. We thought it was the postman, didn't we Walter?" *Walter?* thought Young, bloody odd name for a dog. "He's as soft as they come. He's more likely to lick you to death than anything else."

"Take your word for that." Young mumbled.

"I'll just let him out the back." With that, Young was left standing in the dark hallway, the walls covered with smooth, dark brown, varnished wallpaper. He waited. The noise of the dog's barking diminished, presumably as he bounded down 'the back'.

Dr Crawford reappeared flustered and out of breath. He ushered Young into the lounge.

The lounge was not a lounge. It resembled a dilapidated second-hand bookshop; crowded with books on a multitude of shelves; books on the floor, books on the large desk in the window and books on every available horizontal surface. To the untrained eye, it was chaos. To the trained eye it was chaos.

"I'll move those papers." Crawford uncovered an uncomfortable-looking chair. "Sorry about the mess. Always going to get it in order. Never get round to it. You know how it is." Something moved behind a pile of journals. Young watched intently. To his relief, a Siamese cat appeared and looked at him suspiciously with a jaundiced eye.

"Take no notice of Fred. He's a bit standoffish. He'll go to sleep in a moment." Crawford found himself the chair by his desk. "Now, what can I do for you?"

Young, not an obsessional person himself, nevertheless was disconcerted by the confusion around him and for a moment couldn't remember why was there. He looked about, desperately seeking some form of normality that he could relate to.

"You've come to ask about Dowson?" Crawford helped him out.

"That's it. Dowson. Believe you were his supervisor here."

"For three years. Bright young feller, took a year off to do good works in Africa."

"Mozambique?"

"No. Doesn't bring a bell. More south, I think, I remember Kenya."

"What was he doing there?"

"He told me he was helping UNESCO. I suppose he was into some charity work or other. I'm not sure. All I do know is that he took a year out from his research. Not always a good idea. And I remember I told him that. Took no notice; off he went."

Crawford lent on his desk; all this talking seemed to have exhausted him. Walter started barking in the garden and Fred woke up and stalked out of the room, tail erect and angry.

"What was Dowson's thesis about?" Young inquired.

Crawford pulled himself together. "Interesting work. Mostly on the transport of foreign substances into the body. He had some good ideas, but he hadn't thought them through sufficiently. When he returned, it was a different story. Come to think of it, that was a trifle odd. Went off to help with a charity, came back full of ideas about his thesis. Break must have done him some good." Crawford dismissed Dowson's reorganisation. Young didn't. "Dowson was a new man. Worked solidly. Unfortunately, his thesis was mediocre; perfectly acceptable but without that cutting edge of serious innovation. Once he finished his research he left precipitously. Couldn't get away quickly enough. Disappeared."

"There was a change when he came back from Africa?" Young noted.

"Oh yes. He was always a live wire, but now he couldn't get on quick enough."

"Found that strange, did you?"

"Not really. Didn't give it much thought. I assumed he had plans outside academic world Commerce, pay's better, you know."

"Any idea which company?"

"No. Didn't ask me for a reference, presumably he'd already got the job."

Young had had enough. The conversation had confirmed his suspicions. And in any case, Walter was getting more desperate by the minute to come in.

"Thank you, Doctor Crawford, you have been most helpful."

"Not going, are you?" Crawford looked genuinely unhappy. "Thought I might show you around." (Whether that referred to the house or the university was not made clear. But what was clear was that Dr Crawford needed company.)

"Very good of you, I'm sure. But must get back. Driver a bit anxious." (Any excuse would do.) "But like I said, you have been very helpful. Thank you very much."

Young stood; they shook hands; and Young escaped before the dog could have a go at him. He tied up the gate as he left the front space.)

Mikhail had waited patiently.

"Home James. And don't spare the horses." Young clambered aboard.

"You what?"

"Never mind."

They made good time back to London, and Young was home by early evening.

"How nice to see you Reginald, I didn't expect you back until tomorrow. This is nice." Diane was all smiles.

"No need to stay away longer than was absolutely necessary." Diane poured a glass of dry sherry for herself, and a stiff gin-and-tonic for Reginald. "Travels satisfactory?" She asked. They settled themselves in front of a roaring fire and enjoyed a companionable evening. Even Rev. Charles' sermon sounded as if it had been completed without mishap.

Chapter 20

I woke, Saturday morning, and prepared to leave for London. There was no point reconsidering the issue. I just had to get on with it. I drove to the station; boarded the near-empty train; and took a taxi across London. As soon as I opened the door to Rachel's flat, I knew she had not been there for some time. Letters and circulars were piled on the rug unopened. But more than that. There was an unmistakable stillness and silence. Was there an unconscious awareness of space unoccupied? Had air not moved for some time? Had dust settled? Was there a subliminal threat? Whatever, I felt a frightening absence of somebody I cared about.

Wandering from room to room only reinforced this apprehension; the hairs on my neck really did stand up. I knew something was desperately wrong but recovering some composure I started to look around the flat more methodically. I opened drawers, cupboards, looked in suitcases; recognised some clothes hanging in the wardrobe. Of course, I could not be certain, but it appeared no clothes were missing, no suitcases taken. She had not packed and even her toiletry articles we're still in the bathroom. This was the deciding factor. She had disappeared and without preparation. I picked up the phone and rang the police.

*** *** ***

Regionalisation has often been cited as the cause of police ineptitude. But not in this case. The local Constabulary realised the person had been missing for at least seven days, her disappearance unexplained, therefore, to be taken seriously. Once the disappearance had been confirmed all police forces were notified by 'Missing Person List', officers came to the flat bringing forensic scientists with them. After taking my fingerprints and a swab from my mouth for DNA analysis they asked me to vacate the premises. Police forces nationally alerted, the eagle-eyed Glenda Eyles in Norfolk spotted the connection; I was the person who reported two widely separated disappearances in the last month.

*** *** ***

I had returned to Oxford Saturday evening and Glenda Eyles rang on Monday morning (11th.).

"This girl who's missing is the same one you were with when you met Alexandre Dowson in Paris?" Unless she was reading notes, he had a good memory. "That girl, is it?"

"It is."

"Rachel Harding?"

"Yes, Rachel."

"And we can assume, can we, the disappearance of Dowson and Miss Harding are unconnected?" Clearly, Sergeant Eyles did not want to offend me with any untoward suggestion.

"I am as sure as I can be that they haven't seen each other recently." Then I added; "Of course they knew each other a few years ago but again, as far as I know, there was no romantic connection between the two. In fact, they met in Tanzania some years ago—"

"Tanzania, you say sir?"

"I think it was Tanzania." Suddenly I was doubting my memory. "They were both working for a charity; children I think; possibly co-workers. I think the actual meeting was in Kenya. I'm not positive, that's how much notice I took." (I had now remembered.)

At that precise moment, I remembered the painting Alex had given Rachel, in Montmartre. It had been hanging above the phone in her flat. She'd had it framed. Inexplicably, I didn't mention that.

"You have not found any letters, notes, diary, calendar? Nothing like that?"

"I have not. But I must say that the local police have taken away unopened letters, some documents and books. They have logged them all. I'm not sure what they are. You can find out."

"Leave it, don't worry. I'll chase that up."

I was asking for reassurance. I said, "Is this where you say, 'don't worry, normally people turn up'?"

"Well, not exactly. But two weeks is quite a long time."

Then almost to herself she said, "She is in employment, and happy as far as we know, and no planned departure. Put it this way, we'll investigate it."

I liked this police officer. She spoke confidently and was reassuring, if non-committal; however…I didn't let my thoughts run on. There was no more to say at present, and we put the phones down.

*** *** ***

The same morning (11th.) Superintendent Franklin was handed a note by his secretary. He rang Fakenham immediately and was put straight through to Inspector Leeder.

"Leeder."

"Inspector!" (Franklin realised belatedly that he didn't know Leeder's full name, that is if he'd ever been told.) "Brian Franklin here, London. You rang?"

"Superintendent, thank you for ringing me back." (Formal Franklin noticed.) "There's been a complication in the disappearance of Mr Dowson. Do you remember the case that I'm talking about, sir?"

"Mr Dowson? Connection with a chap I know down here?"

"That's the one. Left a house he was buying, locked and padlocked on the outside, and empty on the inside. Strange business, sir. He works in an establishment near Norwich. There was also some query about a package sent from Africa—(pause)—I think Mozambique. Altogether, rather complicated and something has been added to the mix."

"Go on."

"The added complication is this, sir. A girl he met in Paris, a Miss Rachel Harding, has gone missing. She lives in the same neck of the woods as yourself sir, that is, London. Kennington. That's you, sir?" (Franklin wondered if Leeder really no idea how big London had was!) "The extraordinary thing, though, the same person, a man living in Oxford of all places, reported both Dowson and Harding as missing."

"Did he by God?"

"Curious that, don't you think? And living so far apart; the lady in London and the gentleman in Norfolk, odd, don't you think? And reported by a man in Oxford."

Franklin considered the matter. The connections were too strong to ignore. He'd ring the Met at Kennington police station straight away.

"I'll give the local police station a ring and find out what's going on. I'll try and ring you back today. You'll be about?"

"All day."

"Right."

*** *** ***

I was in my flat in Oxford on Monday afternoon(11th.) when the phone rang. I gave the number, nothing else.

"Superintendent Franklin. Who am I speaking to?" A male voice, London accent, not Alex that was sure. I gave my name.

"Good afternoon, sir. I wondered whether I could have a word."

"Certainly Superintendent." Superintendent? They were taking this seriously.

"The first thing to say is how sorry I am to learn of the disappearance of Miss Harding, your fiancé?"

"Thank you, but there's nothing official yet but certainly that was our intention. I can't understand her disappearance at all."

"Quite so, sir."

I believe policemen often call one 'sir': sometimes it is obliquely aggressive; sometimes disquietingly differential; but in this case, I felt it was reassuringly polite.

He went on; "I believe you know Inspector Leeder of the Norfolk Constabulary and there is the curious coincidence that two young persons you know should disappear within such a short time of each other. And you are the one person to report them both."

He paused for a moment. Of course, I understood the link and the implication was obvious. And yet, I could not bring myself to countenance an amorous relationship between Rachel and Alex. Surely, I knew Rachel far too well to discover…

"Still there sir?" Franklin interrupted my musings.

"Still here."

"I think it might be to our mutual advantages, if we could meet to discuss this matter further. You see, forensics have found nothing significant from either Dowson's cottage in Norfolk, or Ms Harding's flat in Kennington. I have a feeling, and it is certainly no more than that, there is more in this matter than meets the eye. And, we have another complication from Felixstowe which I might discuss with you further."

"Felixstowe? What the hell's that place got to do with Rachel?"

"Exactly sir. What indeed? Possibly nothing at all but it may be connected somehow."

"I'll help you anyway I can, but I don't see any relevance. But you know best."

"We could all communicate online, even visually, but I much prefer face-to-face meetings. What about you, sir?"

"I am willing to meet with you and any interested party that will help trace Rachel."

"Excellent. Leave it with me sir. I'll get back to you tomorrow if that's alright?" He rang off.

Chapter 21

Young was up and away early on Monday morning (February 10th). He had a meeting with Brian Franklin and Nigel Mountford arranged for 10:30 am and this was an important appointment. Unaccountably he felt more enthusiastic than usual. The sharp, bright February morning, or Cyril's particularly chatty mood, or the train that was not over-packed with commuters may have contributed to his unusually buoyant mood. Nothing particularly, he could put his finger on. The weekend had been of mixed fortunes; Gordon was understandably perplexed by his wife's behaviour; forensics might find something of interest in the glass containers found at the depository; Fisherman's Cottage was curiously empty, deep cleaned and padlocked; Alexander Dowson had been a bit of a lad, which might explain his involvement with Rachel. It was all something and nothing. Nevertheless, he felt optimistic.

Young took the Circle line to the embankment, exiting the station with a light step, which he interrupted to hand £2 to 'The Big Issue' seller, with a grin. On his walk along the embankment, he stopped at a newspaper kiosk, cheerfully passed the time of day with the seller and bought a national paper. The Thames look grey and lethargic, the plane trees along the embankment naked with patches of thin bark discarded, pale and somewhat tired. Between the trees benches encouraged pedestrians to sit and watch the world go by. Young accepted the invitation and sat for a while watching some passenger boats, almost empty at this time of the year, a couple of low-slung cargo barges and a polished police boat go past on their business. There was a constant slow movement on the water but more scurrying and hurrying along the towpath. Men with briefcases, occasionally the odd one wearing a bowler hat, and ladies with impossibly high heels and hair blowing attractively in the light breeze, making their way to important occupations.

He sighed. Much to be admired in London. Here, it was London at its best. The centre of his world now and a lot of other people's as well. He stood up abruptly, turned and strode purposefully to his Whitehall office. As he approached his office, he realised why he was in such a good mood.

"Clarissa!" He exclaimed as he entered reception. "How lovely to see you! Truly beautiful!"

"Steady, Reggie. I'm practically engaged."

"Engaged? Practically? You can't be impractically engaged, can you?"

"Reggie," Clarissa was exasperated. "What are you on about? I'm back, that's all."

"And God be praised. The devil has been banished!"

"The devil? Banished? Have you finally lost touch with reality?" Clarissa was worried.

"Not at all. Just gladdened by your presence. And the realisation that you are a wonderful receptionist!"

"I am?" Clarissa knew she had certain shortcomings as a receptionist but felt this was not the time to draw Reggie's attention to them.

"You are such an improvement on that Guthrie woman."

"Oh, that old bat," Clarissa suddenly realised what Reggie was referring to.

"Clarissa! She can't be dismissed as 'an old bat'. Damn it, the woman was a walking nightmare!"

"That bad"

"Worse! Shall we go to the office? Bring the diary with you."

They marched down the corridor and settled themselves in the office.

"Ok. How did it go? The rugby tour of the Scottish Highlands?"

"God, it's cold in Scotland. I was freezing most of the time. And hotels were no better. We got off to a bad start. The first game was against a public school's old boys' side somewhere near Inverness. There were these wooden planks put down—I think they're called duckboards for some extraordinary reason. I can't imagine ducks using them—anyway at least they kept my feet dry, but my heels kept getting stuck in the cracks."

"Heels? At a rugby match? In Scotland?"

"Well, l didn't know any better at the start, did I? Anyway, I'd made his red, blue, yellow and white uniform clean and pressed—"

"Kit."

"Yes, kit; I mean kit."

"Clean and pressed for rugby?"

"Well, yes. Silly me! Anyway, Sinclair looked all tall and handsome and was running down the field with the ball…or is it called pill? Such an ugly word…minding his own business and this great hairy monster jumped on him. It wasn't as if Sinclair had done anything; he was just running along minding his own business, and there he was, next second, flattened into the mud for no reason. 'Dirty bastard', I shouted, and everyone laughed. Well, anyway, all the rest of the chaps playing ran over and started grabbing and holding each other, with poor Sinclair underneath the lot. Suddenly the ball, or is it a pill, emerged and some other fellow ran off with it. All those who had piled on top of poor Sinclair let go of each other and chased after this other guy. Took no notice of Sinclair face down in the mud; and do you know what?"

"No, what?"

"Sinclair got up and said to this great hairy monster that had jumped on him; 'Well played, Andrew'. Well played! And after the other fellow had flattened him!"

"Did it get better after that?"

"I don't know, I couldn't bear to watch. It was all quite nasty. There didn't seem to be any rules at all and by the time they stopped to suck lemons—"

"Half-time."

"…whatever! They were all filthy. You couldn't tell one side from the other. And to make matters worse the referee, or umpire, or judge or whatever you call him, came over and told me to stop calling players naughty names. And all I said was 'dirty bastard'!"

"So, who won?" This was a genuine enquiry from Young.

"No idea. They seemed to give out points quite randomly."

"Were many watching?"

"Yes. All Sinclair's team brought girls or wives—one chap brought a fellow, but nobody said anything—and on the other side of the field all the boys from the school were there but not many of them were watching. Just larking about really. Anyway, afterwards we got the most miserable tea you can imagine in a huge, cold hall with long tables and benches down the side—have you ever tried getting onto a bench without showing your knickers—"

"Don't think so, no."

"Well, it is quite soul-destroying. Anyway, in the evening both teams met in the hotel bar and a great deal of beer and whisky was drunk. Things got a bit frisky; they started throwing chairs about!"

"Oh yes I can understand that" said Young, who had played the odd game of rugby himself.

"I went to bed. Sinclair didn't come up until the police had gone. Do you know what he showed me?"

"Think I can hazard a guess." smiled Young.

"Don't be rude, Reginald!" Clarissa scolded. "He showed me his bruises. He even seemed proud of them! The trouble was, he fell asleep straight away. I think it was all the beer."

"But the team got through the whole of the tour, did they?"

"Well, for the last game we only had twelve. One made the excuse that he had a broken finger, and one couldn't run because a nail had come up through his boot and into his foot and caused an infection. And one was in hospital. I don't think that was necessary; he only had a kick on the head, and he could sit up later the same evening. It wasn't that bad. Personally, I think he was malingering. One of the women wanted to play but I think really, she just wanted to grab hold of a few blokes."

"Yes," said Young thoughtfully. "You're not a real fan of rugby then."

"Not likely."

"It's wonderful to have you back."

"I'm glad to be back." Clarissa smiled. "Been busy?"

She put her mind to business.

"Just a bit."

"I've had a look in the diary, and you've got an ANCOM this Thursday, that's the 13th. There's something in here about Franklin, but I can't read it, and there's something about, is it Leeder? If it is, she can't spell Leader." Young said nothing. "And Eyles? I don't know who they are. And yes, there's a mobile number here. I don't know who that is."

"Let me see." Young reached for the diary. "Right, I know that number. I'll deal with it myself." "It was in fact for Mikhail Stephanopoulos. Might be a bit urgent. I'll deal with that. Thanks Clarissa, oh, and put the tour down to experience."

"An experience I could have done without." And having reported the tour rather breathlessly, Clarissa went back to reception.

*** *** ***

Clarissa rang at 10:20 am. "Brian Franklin has asked to see you in his own office rather than here. Is that, ok?"

"Yes, that's ok." Young realised the need for discretion. "I'll take a taxi over. Get me one, will you Clarissa?"

The cab dropped Young in Holborn and he made his way to Superintendent Franklin's office, arriving on the dot at 10:30 am.

"Come in Reginald." Franklin stood up. "Nigel Mountford said he preferred to meet here. He's coming over shortly, a bit held up just now."

Young settled himself.

Franklin poured coffee and they prepared for a long session.

"Now Reginald, how was Norfolk?"

"Yes. Satisfactory. Met up with Gordon Baxter; chewed over old times. Divorced now. A bugger. Went to the storage facility in Norwich Alexander Dowson had been using and it was empty except for two or three glass vacuum jars, filled with this mysterious emulsion. Taken to forensics. That sergeant Eyles had all the paperwork ready. Keep an eye on her Brian, she's smart. His storage space is totally empty now. Then we moved on to Dowson's cottage. Now, that place was much more interesting. First, Dowson's employers have removed everything from the house; not a stick of furniture left and damn me if it's not deep-cleaned, padlocked and with the intention to nail corrugated iron across the windows and door. God knows why! Distinctly odd I'd say. Then I went into the nearest shop. As far as I can make out, our Mr Dowson was a bit of a womaniser, might have been involved with a married lass in the village. Lots to report, but little concrete evidence of anything out of the way, if you get my meaning. How did you get on?"

Superintendent Franklin took a sip of coffee and composed himself. Young knew what was coming was to be significant. "I've already spoken to Nigel Mountford but here's the gist. I've checked into the background of Stacey Donato and Lady Eleanor Keenan in some detail. Nigel's brainwave of putting Richard Cobb into 'The Lawns' has paid dividends in spades." Young noticed the mangled metaphors but said nothing.

"In any case," Franklin went on; "I think we need to move quickly. As I say, I investigated the background of Donato and Keenan and found that there is more to them than meets the casual eye"

"For goodness' sake Brian, get to the point." Young poured himself another coffee in frustration!

"Ok, Lady Eleanor is quite the landed gentlewoman. Daughter of the Earl of Kingsford, no less. He had large estates and a castle in Dorset. The Earl died and his estates in Dorset were inherited by his only son, Eleanor's older brother who took the title; but the old boy also had large holdings of land, even villages, in Yorkshire, and he left those in his will to his daughter, Lady Eleanor. She grew up in Dorset hence she knows the area very well of course. The Earl's estates and castle are within walking distance of Lewesdon Hill, a famous beauty spot, from the top of which one can see Devon, Somerset and on a clear day the sea."

"Brian! Brian! You're not here as an ambassador for 'Beautiful Britain'!"

"Ok, Ok. Eventually, she went to Cambridge, got a third in PPE, (don't they all?), and whilst in Cambridge she bumped into our Stacey. Stacey was the manager of a large hotel on the outskirts of Cambridge where students who could afford it, frequently enjoyed themselves at weekends. Manicured gardens, rooms to hire for dances' parties, 'private meetings', the usual. By the sounds of it was a 4 or 5-star hotel. It's closed now oddly enough. Anyway, Lady Eleanor," Franklin went on, "became friendly with Stacey, or just possibly putting it another way, Stacey made a point of befriending a rich young lady, well-connected and a socialite. Whichever, to cut a long story short, Stacey was offered the management of a string of hotels in Dorset all owned by the Earl of Kingsworth. Whether there was anything more to that friendship between Eleanor and Stacey is a matter of pure speculation."

"Many of them were there, the hotels I mean, in Dorset?" Young wanted to know.

Franklin wondered for a moment if Young habitually used such tortured sentences, or whether this was his deliberate attempt at affectation. Never mind. He resumed; "To the best of my knowledge there are six hotels in the chain, all large country houses, Michelin-starred restaurants, saunas, pony riding, large ladies pummelling guests on the pretext of improving muscle tone. It seems that Stacey managed the Earl's hotels very efficiently."

"Anyway, in the meantime Lady Eleanor decides to get herself married and picks a stockbroker, a Mr, Keenan who luckily lives in Dorset and is rich beyond your dreams."

"Did well for herself then, did she?" Young muttered.

"Put it this way, she was born with a silver spoon in her mouth and made sure that it didn't get tarnished! The Kenans lived in Dorset, as you would imagine, in a nouveau riche monstrosity but there were no children of the union and gradually Lady Eleanor spent more and more time away from the matrimonial home. In fact, most of the time on the estates that 'Daddy' had left her in Yorkshire. Now, for all intents and purposes, the couple's marriage was over. Then in 2014, or thereabouts, Lady Eleanor was offered a job in government offices of Whitehall, and she moved down to a large flat in Belgravia where she now lives. I think you know about that already, Reginald."

"I do."

"Then it gets interesting." Young knew this was what he had been waiting for. The principal revelation.

"Lady Eleanor has resumed her friendship, if that's all it is, with the hotelier, Stacey Donato and got the same Donato appointed House Administrator of The Lawns', a government project, and part of Lady Eleanor's responsibility. Somewhere along the way our Stacey had got married to a guy called, would you believe, Alfred Dowson. They subsequently divorced and she now calls herself by her maiden name, Donato!"

Young was a man who prided it himself on his ability to hide emotions. He had used this skill to further his finances in the services by playing poker. But the revelation that Stacey Donato was in fact Stacey Dowson, nee Donato, caused his mouth to drop open.

At this point, Nigel Mountford burst into the office, out of breath arms all random movement. "I'm sorry I'm so late," he was flustered. "We had a routine section meeting this morning which held me up. I'm sorry. Where have we got to Brian?" He helped himself to coffee.

Franklin gave an abbreviated account of his conversation with Young.

"So, you have covered the two salient points." Mountford interposed. "Keegan and Donato have known each other for years and Donato's married name was Dowson, and she had a baby boy, Alexander."

"Alexander Dowson is her son?" Young spoke quietly.

"We have Richard Cobb to thank for much of this information." Mountford reported. "If I might add," holding up his hand, "Richard has been a mine of information."

"Well, it's certainly coming together." Young was stunned, but if he were to be honest with himself not unduly surprised. He'd suspected something along those lines for ages. Ignoring for the moment the contribution of Mr Cobb, he declared; "So we have a flow of information. Keenan to Donato (previously

Dowson) to Alexander Dowson. Add to that, Alex Dowson goes missing. A transmission of information that's difficult to follow."

"There's more." Franklin couldn't help but smile smugly. "Donato and Keenan meet regularly in the hotel near Bedford and on occasions are joined by a German chap, name at present unknown. A briefcase has been seen to change hands."

Young debated with himself whether to mention his knowledge of the meetings. He decided to keep his mouth shut. The three of them sat silently for some time trying to come to terms with all this. Whether this was of national importance or not, remained to be seen. Young spoke: "Before much longer we'll need the advice of Professor Bhatti. Ask him for the conclusions of the conference, if that is allowed. Do they compromise the county's safety? Could Donato possibly have passed them to Keenan? Has she passed them to her son? What has Keenan done with all the information? How many copies of the original are there? Who the devil is this, German?"

"This is where Richard Cobb is extremely useful." Mountford remarked. "He's already engaged with those questions and it's only a matter of time before he gets in touch."

Young, voiced satisfaction. His suspicions all along had been confirmed. "We can assume with a degree of confidence," he reflected, "that there is a leak of information and the people involved are Keenan and Donato. What is now critical, is what is the nature of the information?"

"Quite. And what has Alex Dowson got to do with it all?" This was Mountford. "We certainly have the resources to tie up the matter completely."

"There is no time to waste." Young summed up their feelings. "Can we meet again on Wednesday, and I think it's imperative that we include Stanton. Adrian Oakwell of the special branch needs to be in on it. In the meantime, I'll get hold of Professor Bhatti for more information on what we might be losing. Thanks very much indeed, Brian and Nigel, I think you have brought the whole thing to a head."

Young left.

*** *** ***

Franklin rang Young straight away and reported the latest.

"I'll find this guy's address in Oxford, and I think we better go down there tomorrow if you're free."

"Tell me the time and I'll be ready." They rang off.

*** *** ***

"Glenda Eyles rang me on Monday (10th) and confirmed that Rachel Harding and Alexander Dowson were the two missing persons of interest. Inspector Leeder had said so!" She rang off.

That afternoon I answered the phone again. "Superintendent Franklin. Who am I speaking to?" A male voice, London accent, not Alex that was sure. I gave my name.

"Good afternoon, sir. Superintendent Franklin. I wondered whether I could have a word or two with you sir."

"Certainly Superintendent." Superintendent? They were taking this seriously.

"The first thing to say is how sorry I am to learn of the disappearance of Miss Harding, your fiancée?"

"Thank you, but there's nothing official as yet but certainly that was our intention. I can't understand her disappearance at all."

"Quite so, sir."

Policemen often call one 'sir': sometimes it is obliquely aggressive; sometimes disquietingly differential: but in this case, I felt it was reassuringly competent.

He went on; "I believe you know Inspector Leeder of the Norfolk Constabulary and it is a curious coincidence that two young person's you know should disappear within such a short time of each other. And you are the one person to report them both."

He paused for a moment. Of course, I understood the link and the implication was obvious. But, Rachel and Alex? Surely, I knew Rachel far too well to discover…

"Still there sir?" Franklin interrupted my musings.

"Still here."

"I think it might be to our mutual advantages if we could meet to discuss this matter further. You see, forensics have found nothing significant in either Norfolk, or the flat in Kennington. I have a feeling, and it is certainly no more than that, there is more in this matter. And we have another complication from Felixstowe which I might discuss with you further."

"Felixstowe? What the hell's that place got to do with Rachel?"

"Exactly sir. What indeed? Possibly nothing at all but it may be connected somehow."

"I'll help you anyway I can, but I don't see any relevance. But you know best."

"We could all communicate online, even visually, but I much prefer face-to-face personal meetings. I would like to meet tomorrow, if that is convenient. May I bring a colleague, Group Captain Young? Nothing to be alarmed over. Captain Young is interested in a related matter."

"Fine by me."

"If we say 10:30 am, will that be acceptable?"

"Certainly."

Chapter 22

I watched the black, unmarked 4x4 Land Rover pull onto the gravel in front of the house. It was Thursday afternoon 2:00 pm almost precisely. The driver was in police uniform, but the two men in the back we're both in civilian clothes. One of the men bent and spoke to the driver; they looked at their watches, then the driver pulled back onto the approach road and drove away out of sight. The two men came to the house and rang my bell. As I went downstairs to let them in, I panicked, quite unnecessarily, that I had not prepared anything to eat. I opened the door.

"Good afternoon, sir. I'm Brian Franklin and this is my colleague, Group Captain Young. I apologise that we are slightly late but stopped at a self-service station on the M40 for a bite to eat. Sorry about that."

First impressions are important, but in my experience often wrong. However, I saw Franklin as the typically burly and large policeman of some rank. The group captain (how on earth did the RAF get into this?) older, grey haired, clipped moustache and bright eyes. *Much shorter, rotund and,* I thought, *more cheerful.*

"Come in, please." I stood back and waved them up the stairs. At the top I took their coats and we made ourselves comfortable in the lounge, whose large window gave us a spectacular view of Oxford.

"My goodness sir, what a view!" The superintendent gazed out of the window overlooking the city. "College fellow I hear"

"Only a junior fellow I'm a friend. Not very distinguished." Then I remembered my manners. "Can I get you a drink? Tea? Coffee?"

"If you, have it, please. Milk, no sugar." Franklin said.

"Milk, two sugars please." The Group Captain gave his order.

I scurried off and made their tea. No tray. No biscuits. Never mind, I had more important things to worry about. When I got back into the lounge and we had all started on our drinks, Superintendent Franklin began; "I always think it's better to meet face to face, sir. Gives everyone a better picture of what's going on. Perhaps I should explain that the Group Captain here works in Whitehall and has some connections, rather tenuous I would agree, with both cases which brings us to Oxford today. I hope you don't mind him sitting in."

"Not at all." I sat in an armchair and gave myself some time to assess the situation. There seemed to be no suspicious undercurrents. It appeared to be a routine and enquiry between friends about the temporary absence of another.

"How long have you lived here?"

"Well, I came to Oxford University when I was 18, that would be in 2018 and I've been here ever since, although living in this flat for only the last two or three years."

"Research sir?"

"Yes, mostly. But I also do some tutorials and lectures during term time."

"Must be rewarding, sir. Not had the advantage of a college education myself. I often regret it." It didn't look as if Franklin regretted it at all. Group Captain Young said nothing.

"And you met the young lady, Miss Harding, last year sir?"

"Yes, at a pharmaceutical conference in London. The dreadful affair—the conference I mean!" I hastened to add in case of misunderstanding.

"Indeed sir."

There was a delicate change of atmosphere. Nothing more. The questioning became more direct, more intrusive. Our relationship was being examined closely.

"And other friends?" For a moment I didn't understand what he meant but the question seemed innocent enough. "Do you mean Alex?" I asked.

"No sir, we'll come to Mr Dowson in a moment." I realised now that I had immediately connected Alex with Rachel and perhaps this was a mistake. "What I meant, actually," he continued, "was, did you meet with any of her other friends, colleagues, acquaintances…anyone else she knew in London?"

I thought carefully and suddenly realised that I had not met anyone who knew her in London at all. This came as a bit of a shock. I knew of her work with children and child psychology but no…no friends. "Now that you mention it, I've never met any of her friends."

"Would you say that's odd?" Franklin showed no particular interest in the matter, it sounded just a casual enquiry. Young said nothing.

"Well, I suppose, now you say it…" But now I was fully alert. Again, there had been this subtle, almost imperceptible change of tone. I was now on my guard. I had nothing to hide but it felt as if I was hiding something.

"Perhaps we will come back to that later." Now there could be no doubt that Franklin had introduced an element of tension. "Let's move on for a moment. This Mr Dowson. Known him for a long time, have you sir?"

I told them of my time together with Alex Dowson when we were in college and how he had left for East Anglia once he had graduated, and I stayed in Oxford. I went on to say that we had lost touch but that we met accidentally in Paris last year ear and curiously enough I was with Rachel at the time. I also told them that this was a completely chance occurrence.

"Good spirits, was he?" Franklin wanted to know.

"Just the same as always. Slightly larger than life. Generous." I sounded as if I was defending him, but this was completely unintentional.

Then we went over what had happened in Africa, but I had nothing to add to what I had already told Craig. I had not even known that Alex was in Tanzania until Rachel (or was it Alex?) mentioned it in Paris. For the first and only time Young took an active part in the proceedings.

"Is Miss Harding still in touch with Tanzania…the charity I mean?"

"Not as far as I know. Certainly, he has never mentioned it."

"Does she ever receive letters or messages from the charity do you know?"

"I don't think so."

"And Mr Dowson? Does she ever hear from him, do you know?"

"I will have absolutely no idea whatsoever." I was slightly cross. "I really have no idea of Alex's movements or correspondence or work since leaving Oxford. I don't even know what he does now."

"Right you are. Surely there is nothing there." Young sat back and prepared to listen again.

Franklin took over again. "You were saying that Mr Dowson was generous. I believe that he bought Miss Harding a painting." By 'generous', I meant that he was generous in spirit, friendliness, and companionship: not the interpretation Franklin was putting on it. But I let it pass.

"About the picture that he gave her, I saw it in her flat only on Saturday. As far as I know it's still there."

"Is the picture pretty?" Group Captain Young asked, rather naively I thought.

"Not pretty, exactly, more of an impression—but not in an impressionist style. It's called, if I remember correctly 'A Dream' and the title sums it up." I had done my best.

"Yes," was all the Group Captain could manage. Was he lost?

"And the meeting in Paris. This was a meeting by accident, surprising, out of the blue, that sort of thing?" Franklin was questioning again.

"As far as I could tell it was." For some reason, I couldn't quite define, possibly to protect her, I didn't mention my fleeting impression that there was some hesitancy on her part. I felt that the meeting this afternoon had become tense, the room a little warmer. To relieve that I offered to make more tea.

"Not at the moment sir, thank you." Franklin may have picked up on my anxiety. Perhaps not. He thought for a moment and then, quite abruptly, changed the subject. "Know anything of his work in East Anglia sir? Biochemist, was he?"

"I don't know what he is working on at present, but I think he's employed by a private company somehow connected with pharmacology or virology or something."

"Quite a shift from biochemistry to virology isn't it sir?"

"Well, yes and no. The two have much in common although the synthesis of proteins is the main concern of virologists with the study of DNA and RNA, and their potentially harmful effects."

"I'm afraid that you have lost me sir." Franklin didn't look as if he was lost nor did the Group Captain. The three of us stopped talking and the silence lengthened. At last, Franklin broke it saying, "We're looking at his work situation now. So far without a great deal of success. But we will persevere."

"Good." I said rather weakly.

It has been a much longer afternoon than I had expected and already the sky had darkened, and Oxford was hardly visible under a gathering mist. Lights were coming on in the city and some of the spires were floodlit. I looked at my watch.

"Yes sir." Franklin had noticed this. "We have taken up too much of your time, but it has been very useful. I'll call our driver—what do you think, Reginald?"

The Group Captain was obviously Reginald and he readily agreed that they should be getting back to London. No sooner had Franklin put away his mobile than the familiar crunch of tyres on the gravel in front of the house announced the driver had arrived and the car awaited their return. They got up, shook my hand and thanked me again for my time.

"We'll be in touch with any developments directly. You can rest assured of that." Franklin was back to his genial self and Young was smiling. As I closed the door behind them, for the very first time, I had a dreadful feeling of loss. I was on my own in this flat.

*** *** ***

The police driver had an easy journey back on the M40. By this time, early evening, all the traffic seemed to be leaving London and driving North, a constant column of headlights going in the opposite direction, whilst they had a free run into London. They were back in Whitehall by 6 pm.

"Want to come in for a while?" Young offered and Franklin dismissed the driver and told him he could return the car to the police station. The 4 by 4 disappeared quickly into the evening traffic of Whitehall.

Inside the building young found Clarissa had left already; no surprise there. Most of the lights have been turned off and they made themselves at home in the deep armchairs of Young's office. As if by magic, a bottle of single malt and two glasses appeared on Young's desk. Glasses having been charged they chorused 'cheers' in unison and relaxed.

"So, what do you make of it all?" Franklin asked.

Young savoured his whisky slowly and considered the matter. "Well, first I'm pretty sure if anything is going on that fellow in Oxford, he's not part of it. Secondly, it's my opinion, the association between Miss Harding and Dr Dowson was just a fling, if anything; just a short fling in Tanzania or wherever they were, but nothing serious. An awkward memory may have embarrassed the girl in Paris, but we don't even have any proof of that; nor are we likely to get any."

"That's true enough." Franklin responded. "But let's assume just for the moment, that they were both attracted to some project or development or reform movement or political upset or something in Africa that was not directly connected with the charity but which they both became involved…" he didn't finish the sentence. Probably he couldn't yet.

Young could see where this was going. "Either that or their focus was purely on some action, possibly political, but their interests in it we're not the same and their interpersonal relationship was not strong enough to endure."

"Most of this is supposition." Franklin wanted to get it straight. "What we know is this; they knew each other in Tanzania; they met again in Paris; they both knew some bloke in Oxford; they both disappeared at the same time. We might be able to add, and I say might, that Dowson received a package from Mozambique of all places. We can't even be sure of that. But it is possible. And the Donato/Keenan connection still poses a problem."

"Dammit! I don't know about you, but I've had enough for one day." Young recharged the glasses and they watched out of the window the moon, blue with a haze of frost around it move slowly across the sky. For some reason, they jointly felt that a hurdle had been cleared. Quite what it was they had no idea but there did seem to be a glimmer of understanding at the edge of their thinking. They needed more time; more evidence; more investigation. But they're optimistic if tired.

Chapter 23

Clarissa was satisfied with life. No, that was an understatement, and she didn't deal in understatements. Scotland had come and gone; exciting and boring by turns; bloody cold throughout. But worthwhile. Afterwards, she moved into Sinclair's flat in London. (To the disapproval of her parents.) And that was working out very well. As she walked cheerfully towards reception on this brisk, bracing and refreshing February morning, she was not concerned with world politics: nor epidemics: nor pandemics (whatever that was): nor the state of the economy. She had more important matters to consider.

Was Sinclair going to propose marriage?

As she bounced up the steps to the doorway to reception, she smiled happily at the policeman on duty and when she got inside even wished the morose and spotty internal security officer a bright 'good morning'. She received no indication that her presence had been recognised. Behind her desk she straightened her appointment book, checked her emails and shuffled through the mail. Nothing grabbed her attention. The telephone rang. Konrad Taylor wanted to speak to the Group Captain. Well, he'd have to wait until Reggie came in, wouldn't he?

Young reached his office at 10 am. Clarissa welcomed him and told him that Konrad Taylor had rung earlier, and she would put him through as soon as she could find him. He merely smiled and acknowledged the message. No sooner had he sat down at his desk than the telephone rang.

"Reggie." It was Clarissa. "Konrad Taylor was on the phone for you."

"That was quick!" Reginald snapped. Then: "Sorry Clarissa. Put him through, will you?"

What's wrong with him? Just about managed to acknowledge me, now barks at me. But she put Taylor through.

"Reginald. Konrad here. I thought you ought to be made aware of the latest developments in this Covid-19 business."

"Yes Konrad. Of course."

"On January the 20th, there were 282 known cases worldwide of this wretched COVID infection. By January the 30th, there were 7800 and at that rate there will be nearly 80,000 cases by the end of February. Nearly a week ago the cruise ship, Diamond Princess was quarantined in Japan. This is getting serious."

Young reflected upon these numbers. "Worrying."

"I'd say it was critical. WHO declared this infection to be a Public Health Emergency of International Concern about a month ago. They're going to announce a pandemic any day now."

"Does it make any real difference what they call it?"

"Only that they've raised the awareness from bad to bloody dangerous!"

Konrad had never sworn in Young's presence before. It made Young sit up. Konrad continued; "S.A.G.E. have been meeting regularly and I believe they are going to meet again soon. I've been told they are recommending wholesale shut down, schools, universities, travel, shops and social contacts. It would be a drastic step and there are no specific agreements from government, because there is a genuine fear that the population will either be unnecessarily frightened, or resistant to social isolation, or both. And as well as that, the politicians are forever worrying about the National Economy and the effect that any shut-down would have on trade—both internal and external. And that means votes. Naturally enough, the government wants to avoid drastic measures, but the scientists are much more pessimistic. This is the classical health/financial conflict. It is essential now ANCOM must act expediently to ensure the special recommendations from 'The Lawns' Conference are taken seriously."

Young agreed. The spread of this illness was at a critical level and rising; also, if Keenan and Donato were deliberately mislaying or leaking information abroad, that only increased the potential danger. He and ANCOM must sound an alarm.

"Konrad, listen. Several things I must do today; meetings planned. But we need an ANCOM as soon as possible. I'll get Clarissa to let you know the details."

"Thank you, Reginald. I'll bring Matthew."

"Yes, do." Young put the phone down.

An ANCOM was all very well, but his office was by no means safe. He'd have to give that some consideration. He sat alone and tried to visualise the impact of this pandemic, for surely that's what it was, but the numbers were too large for casual contemplation.

"Clarissa." He spoke on the internal phone. "I need to speak to Prof Bhatti. Can you get hold of him for me?"

"I'll do my best."

10-minutes later Clarissa told him the Prof was at The Lawns. Young gave the matter considerable thought and then decided he should go over there. Why not? Donato suspected nothing.

"Get me a cab Clarissa. I'll go over there."

He was met at the door of The Lawns by Richard Cobb and underwent the usual search where he surrendered his mobile and all metal objects. No expression of recognition passed between them, and customary professionalism was maintained.

"Ms Donato will see you directly, Group Captain." Cobb said as he returned to his office to enter Young's name in the Ledger.

"Group Captain!" Stacey Donato beamed as she greeted him warmly. "Please come in." They were in the spacious lounge, and she indicated two armchairs facing the gardens. "I'll get you some coffee." She pressed a button on the wall and politely as one of the catering staff for coffee. "Let's sit and enjoy the garden; I always think it looks so spectacular with the leaves frosted white as they are at the moment." So did Young, but that was not the reason for the visit. "Now then," she said, "how can I help you? At present we are between conferences but the next one starts in 10 days' time. Cybernetics! I can't even spell it!" A modest chuckle. Young had prepared himself carefully for this meeting. He would be companionable and complement her efficient management of the conference. To begin with he sat comfortably and composed himself but noted that she had not invited him upstairs to the flat. That was not necessarily significant as the last time she had visited she made him feel unwelcome, to go to the other extreme would be inconsistent.

"I agree about the garden." Young said. "I live in the country, near Audley End although you would probably have heard of Saffron Walden which is quite close and better known. The frost has really got hold of the bushes in the countryside and I watched a robin darting about aggressively to make sure he was in charge, only the other day."

"How delightful. I'm certain I saw a brown squirrel last week, but everyone laughed at me." Donato's modesty knew no bounds.

Whether the modesty was because she couldn't distinguish grey from brown, or grey were more numerous than brown. Wasn't defined. In any case, Young wasn't interested.

"I believe snow is forecast in the fairly near future," he continued. (Strange how British people have the extraordinary inclination to talk about the weather, he thought. It was as if they had the horror of silence, so they filled it with inconsequential chitchat. Perhaps it was avoidance of confrontation or more likely they didn't have to think. Whatever purpose it served; it suited his purpose very well for the moment.

"Beautiful though your gardens are Stacey, I've not come just to appreciate the view."

"I thought not, Group Captain."

He immediately detected a changing atmosphere between them. He could not be sure what it was about her posture but there was absolutely no doubt that she was fully alert.

"The reason that I'm here in fact is that I need to see Professor Bhatti and I've been told that he is somewhere on the premises. I haven't yet received the summary of the Professor's conference." Young looked out of the window, apparently relaxed. It took Donato a few seconds to collect her thoughts. "My apologies, Group Captain, but that's not really my concern, that is an inter-secretarial responsibility in which I have no role."

"You have no part in the transport of data then?"

"Goodness no. I wouldn't know where to begin, never mind understanding a word of scientific jargon." Her answer had come quickly.

"So, you don't know where the information goes?"

Donato considered the question. A speck of dust on her skirt attracted intense scrutiny. She was of course, in a quandary. She could hardly deny outright any knowledge as to where the data went, that would be verging on the absurd. Finally, she declared; "No, that's not my responsibility, although I *believe* it's sent to your department."

"Well, you are correct in your belief. The data does come to our department in Whitehall. I should have had a copy by now, but it seems to have gone missing. Do you know anyone in my department, at all? Someone who might perhaps know where all the papers have gone?"

"No. How would I?"

"Exactly. That's what I thought. In fact, I should have had a copy of the summary, but it seems to have gone missing and really that's why I'm here, to have a word with Professor Bhatti about that very matter." Young had to admit, she was good. Not any indication of discomfiture, not a bead sweat, not a tremor of a hand. He felt that he ought to leave it there for the moment and change tack. "Stacey, could I take a peep at the secretarial department?" But again, not a movement. She looked at him directly.

"Group Captain, that is completely beyond my control. You would have to make enquiries with, I think, the head of the secretarial department, Jill, that would be her province."

She was saying from further embarrassment by a squawk from her in-house bleeper which was calling her to the nearest phone. "Oh, sorry," she said, indicating the bleeper in her pocket.

"Please don't apologise. Obviously, a busy lady." Young smiled. "I'll just see if I can get hold of Prof Bhatti."

"When I've answered this break, I'll ring the switchboard and get him to come and see you."

"Thank you very much very kind indeed."

Young settled to wait, while Donato answered the phone.

After a few moments, Stacey Donato called across the room.

"Group Captain, Professor Bhatti is on his way."

"Morning Professor. Am I glad to see you!" Young stood and extended his hand. Professor Bhatti put his briefcase on the floor and sat on the edge of an armchair.

"Sorry to surprise you at such short notice."

The Professor smiled. "If I can help…"

"Nothing to do with you personally you understand, but I have not received a summary of the conference. Wondered where it had got to. Much to report was there?"

Bhatti considered how best to answer the question, without arousing disproportionate alarm. That proved difficult. "First of all, I apologise for any inconvenience the secretarial staff have inflicted upon you. With regards to the content of the final reports that have been passed to Lady Eleanor, there are really two separate lines of research that concern us. How to produce a modification in the virus that would make it deadlier and easier to transmit, what we call all in virology" 'gain-of-function' research, colloquially known as GOF. "And the second line of investigation is about how best to protect ourselves and the population from a widespread viral illness; either by vaccination or medication or social isolation or general immunity, popularly known as 'herd immunity', or by a combination of all four. The resources of the NHS as it is at present will be sorely tried unless emergency measures are taken."

"The symposium, in other words, was very far-reaching, Professor. Perhaps we could discuss that little further back at Whitehall. I can get Cobb to order a taxi. Go back to my place, what do you say?"

"I've done all I can hear today, with young Jill's help of course."

"Of course." Young agreed, man to man!

As they left the lounge together, Stacey Donato called out; "Goodbye. Finished for today?"

"Yes. Thank you very much Stacey. I'm quite satisfied now; just giving Professor Bharti a lift." Young called back. *That should cover it,* he thought. Should cover any qualms. Perhaps. It didn't.

In the taxi together, Young felt it easier to speak freely. Certainly, at The Lawns he couldn't be sure speaking confidentially and his office probably wasn't safe any longer. The taxi would do very well.

"To put all that in a nutshell you have been considering how Britain can develop viral warfare and how to protect us from someone else who develops such nasty viruses."

"Briefly, yes. Of course, it is vastly more complicated than that but…"

Young interjected. "With the greatest of respect, Professor, we need to deal with the bigger picture, not the microscopic elements that make up the picture. Without going into the details that I wouldn't understand in any case, did the conference make direct recommendations on the manufacture of variants or mutations of lethal viruses?"

"Certainly. The recommendation was to expand the research facilities at universities, or specialised establishments, let's say Porton Down, with considerable injection of funds. Again, defence against such viruses is crucial and significant sums of money ought to be ploughed into the programs of research at Oxford, Cambridge and London University where there are well-developed research departments already. Furthermore, private industry, particularly pharmaceutical companies should be encouraged to participate. Already that is in progress. It is an extremely positive way of using both government and private money. Incidentally, we are not the only country researching the manufacture of variants. China certainly is developing viral modification manufacture, almost probably at their laboratory in Wuhan, and Russia will be similarly engaged in viral research. And America, and many other countries."

"Your recommendations, when were they passed on to Lady Eleanor?"

"I fear I do not have the exact date, but certainly we have completed our reports."

"That is excellent, Professor." Young did not want to arouse any suspicions in the good Professor. "Happen to know how the finalised reports were transmitted to Lady Eleanor?"

"Again, I fear I do not know exactly. That is not my concern."

"Of course not, Professor of course not." The Professor had been extremely useful and reinforced Young's belief that the line of communication between 'The Lawns' and Eleanor Keenan was insecure. The actual transmission of information from one to the other and its destination was still unknown. "Thank you, Professor. We are arranging an ANCOM for Thursday this week and perhaps if you are not too busy you could attend. I'll get Clarissa to give you the details."

They arrived at Whitehall, Young very satisfied with his morning's work.

*** *** ***

Young wondered if he should take the rest of the day off or would this set alarm bells ringing. Probably not, he doubted if his absence would be noticed.

He picked up the phone. "Clarissa."

"Yes Reginald? What can I do for you?" She wasn't sure of his mood.

"Thinking of taking the rest of the day off. Act as long stop, will you?"

"Long-stop? Some position on a cricket field?"

"Well done, Clarissa. It means anything gets away from the main man."

"Really Reggie! If you mean, can I answer any questions about your absence by saying that you're pursuing some notion that you've got hold of, I'll do that."

"Clarissa you're a genius."

"I am?"

"You could not have put it better."

"I couldn't? Well, I'm pleased about that." She cut the connection somewhat bewildered. Be that as it may, she could live with 'genius'.

Reginald went home. As he walked along the embankment, he became sure that no one was either following or watching them. He felt free and confident that the conclusion of this business was nigh.

Part Four
Explanations

Chapter 24

Clarissa's morning was peaceful. Yesterday evening, Sinclair had taken her 'to see a show' and afterwards they had dined in a fashionable hotel. It had been quite splendid. This morning, reception was calm. No messages; no important emails; no walking about that was so irritating. Even the traffic outside seemed to be less intrusive. Peaceful.

She sighed.

Two things changed all that. At 10:00 am sharp, Reggie bustled in, nodded briefly and almost shouted at the security man before diving down the corridor and into his office. 10:05 am, the telephone rang. Stratton for the Group Captain. She put the call through. At 10:07 am, the telephone rang again. Mountford for the Group Captain. "Well, you'd have to wait until Stratton's finished." No, he couldn't wait, he was on his way in. Dear me, it was all go.

She sighed.

Whatever Stratton wanted didn't take long. The phone was disconnected within 2 or 3 minutes. Clarissa was wondering what that was all about, when the door was flung open, and Mountford shot through reception without a word to Clarissa and straight past the security guard with hardly a glance. 'Security' jumped up and chased after him down the corridor. *My goodness,* thought Clarissa.

She sighed.

Young had no sooner put down the phone than the door of his office burst open, and an agitated Mountford announced his presence with; "Group Captain. A word!" He stopped abruptly at Young's desk and 'security' bumped into him, unable to stop in time.

"What the—? Oh, it's you Nigel."

"We're going out!" Mountford was forceful.

"Out, you say?" Young was startled.

"We are." Mountford removed Young's coat from the hanger, holding it out to him. "You'll need this."

"I will?" Young struggled into his coat and the two of them made for the door, catching 'security' unprepared with the sudden about turn. "Just a minute. Just a minute!" 'Security' was struggling to get a notebook out of his pocket and at the same time trying to stop the departure of the two of them. He got his notebook out, but the two of them disappeared. As they shot through reception Mountford called out to Clarissa; "We're going out. We may be some time." Clarissa was sure that she had heard that expression before.

She sighed.

What 'security' wrote in his notebook and to what use he put that note was never recorded and remains a mystery. Two weeks later he left his employment in Whitehall and was last heard of serving beer in a pub in Handsworth.

Mountford drove quickly, and happily without sudden movements of his body or arms that were, to him, so usual. They arrived at the safe house in Streatham within 20 minutes or so; parked; walked briskly through the kitchen as before (this time a young lady sat on a stool reading a cookery book and as they went past didn't even look up.) Arriving on the first floor, Mountford opened a door, and they entered the same room as Young had visited previously. Marcia greeted them with a thin smile.

"Group Captain, and Mr Mountford, come in, do."

The same attic room, the same standard lamp casting a dim, yellowish light. This time seven chairs were placed in an arc facing another, to which Reginald was directed. "Please, sit down and make yourself comfortable." Young wondered whether to express surprise and inconvenience at this unscheduled meeting but looking at Marcia today, in a trouser suit, glasses and a serious face, he realised she meant business. He decided against making a complaint. "Thank you." He sat.

Marcia looked around; "You know everyone, I think. Mr Stratton. Mr Mountford. Mr Taylor. Mr Oakfield. And joining us today someone who I'm sure you've met before, Mr Cobb." Young nodded to each in turn. Cobb was a surprise, but he didn't let it show. Was the spare chair for our mystery guest? Young wondered. He would find out soon enough if it was. Crossing her legs and taking off her glasses Marcia sat back and gazed at Young thoughtfully. "Have you made any headway in the baffling disappearance of Mr Dowson? You know who I mean of course?"

Young was puzzled. Why had there been such an extraordinary hurry to get him here and now confront him with a question about Alexander Dowson who had disappeared two months ago. Perhaps Dowson had been found.

"Baffling occurrence, I would agree," he said. "Has he reappeared?"

"I regret, that is not the case." Marcia continued to gaze at him.

Young gave the matter some thought. Seemed straightforward. "Well, if we look at the usual reasons for vanishing acts, there are several possibilities. Mr Dowson was well known as a lady's man, and when I went to the village, I found a young, married lady who I think had a relationship with him of which her husband was unaware. On enquiry, she was as puzzled as we all are about his sudden departure, and she was angry about it, into the bargain. Then money worries; his finances seem stable. Paid money into his bank at regular intervals, in cash, so we can't trace the origin. Police enquiries also have been frustrated by lack of information from the Department of Works and Pensions, or HM Revenue and Customs. Mortgage is paid regularly, no outstanding debts, as far as I know, in the village. Police tell me he owns his car, has insurance, tax and MOT. Might have gone on extended holiday. Might have returned to Africa. Dowson, by all accounts, often made snap decisions, without much forethought. Mildly eccentric. Could be any of those things—or none!"

"Just one thing. His superior (Doctor Crawford) told me Dowson had been given a year's sabbatical in Africa and when he returned, he was a changed man. Wanted to give up university. More interested in commerce, apparently."

"Yes." Marcia lengthened the word to indicate her deep thought on the subject.

"Of course," Young continued, "there are more sinister explanations or possibilities. Illness, death, leaving Norfolk. Even the country? You name it, it could be a reason. But I've not found any reason!"

"That leaves us with a problem, wouldn't you say? His place of employment is still unknown?"

"That's true. But not for the want of trying." Young spoke sharply.

"And I think you tried very hard. It has come to our attention that you have been in contact with the Border Force in Harwich and have traced a package, or packages, from there to a storage depot in Norwich from which our absent Mr Dowson collected them subsequently. Is that not the case?" *If they knew all this already why bother asking*, Young wondered. "And you visited the storage depot in Norwich, we believe."

"Yes."

"And some articles were removed by the local police for examination?"

"Yes."

"Know what was found in the glass containers?"

"No."

"Mm." Again, Marcia lengthened the syllable to indicate deep thought. "I suppose we might speculate that Mr Dowson's departure and the contents and the merchandise found in Norwich storage are in some way linked. What do you think?"

"Possible. No way of knowing." There was a pause in the proceedings and Young looked around the shadowed faces before him. Mountford fidgeted discreetly. Stratton sat without a movement. Taylor found yet more interest in the standard lamp. Cobb was next to the empty chair which Young imagined gave off an air of menace. As if it were waiting.

"Yes." Marcia brought him back from his preoccupation with the chair. "I think there is a good reason to believe in such a link." She paused again, and taking a breath changed the subject. "Did you learn anything of Dowson's adventures in Africa? What was it? Two or three years ago?"

Was this the time I'm to talk of his visit with Dr Crawford? Young wondered. *Or had he overstepped the mark again?* Young reflected briefly. He could see no harm.

"Spoke with a Dr Crawford who supervised Dowson's degree thesis at East Anglia University."

"How meticulous of you." A note of sarcasm?

"Yes. Well. Couldn't find out much there. Was told he took a year off to help with a charity. Dr Crawford wasn't that bothered or interested."

"Like I said, he was a changed man when he came back."

"So, our Mr Dowson took a year from his research…oh by the way, what was he researching?"

"Not sure. Not in detail anyway. Seemed to me that Crawford wasn't much interested in discovering what friend Dowson was up to in Africa, or about his laboratory work; said next to nothing about it to me. So no, I don't think I can tell you anything on that subject."

"Very well, Group Captain. You have been most helpful and as we advised, what was it? Two or three weeks ago? You have made no direct enquiries into the chemical laboratory in which, as you so informally put it, 'friend' Dowson worked. For that, we thank you."

Young felt enormously relieved. He wasn't sure why. He had only followed up information that had been thrust upon him, he had next to no axe to grind with secret services, apart from the officious Marcia opposite. He relaxed. But his relaxation was short-lived.

"However." Never had a word sounded with such gravitas upon his ears. It had the ring of a sombre sound like a funeral bell, announcing doom. "There is another matter which exercises our minds," Marcia continued, "and one in which you are deeply involved."

"There is?"

"Indeed. May I ask you? How were you recruited to Whitehall?"

"Oh, that would have been years ago. About 2015, just before I left the RAF. Chap came to see me called Jeremy Gould. Offered me the management of a group that was to meet in Whitehall. It had been noted that I was discreet. Could manage personnel. Quite complimentary." Young realised he was being immodest. But it was said.

"Jeremy Gould, you say." Marcia seemed fascinated by the name, but no one was writing notes nor far as Young could see, was there any recording equipment. "Personable young man?"

"Yes, as I say complimentary. He spoke of liberal policies and the possible instability of Europe, or Brexit and its effects, and America. Took a strong line in equality of gender and race."

"And did you agree with this broad-minded approach?"

"To a certain extent. The armed forces are not known for their permissive approach to society. But within reason…" The sentence was not completed.

"I see. And therefore, after that, you began working in Whitehall, developing a group which is known as ANCOM."

"Yes."

"And your immediate boss is Lady Eleanor?"

"Not quite boss. Apparently, she was the person who resurrected the group, I think because the consensus was that increased cooperation between the secret services at all levels was beneficial to the overall efficiency."

"Quite so." Marcia pondered. "Could you remind us? Why did you become suspicious of Lady Eleanor? Or is suspicion too strong a word?"

"Well, I think a more appropriate word would be wondered. There was some talk, early on, of increased traffic count in the region of Hartwell, a sensitive area, atomic research or some such thing. Soon after that discussion, Rice from an annexe of Vauxhall Cross, was murdered. Lady Eleanor's reaction to that murder made me wonder. No more."

"Wonder? How wonder?"

"She seemed to dismiss it rather too eagerly."

"How perceptive of you, Group Captain." Marcia put her glasses on. "And you engaged a young Cypriot lad, Mikhail Stephanopoulos, to investigate?"

"I did." And Young couldn't resist it. "'The lady and her infant in' Muriel's Cakes reported that to you. So, you know all about it."

"Quite so." Marcia now tilted her head forward, making her glasses redundant, and peered over them at Young. "Perhaps we can move along."

Young waited.

"We believe you visited Oxford two days ago to talk with a friend of Alexander Dowson and another missing person, a young lady, named Harding."

"Yes."

"With Superintendent Brian Franklin of the Metropolitan Police, we believe."

"Yes."

"Now, leaving aside for a moment the young college fellow's fiancé, Ms Harding, did you discover any substantial information that would help us determine the whereabouts of Mr Dowson?"

"No. It was my impression that the young man was as surprised as anyone else. He did tell us however that Dowson was to visit him in Oxford at Christmas but that had called off because of 'flu."

"Yes, I think that would coincide with his disappearance from Norfolk. Nothing since?"

"Not a word."

"All very worrying. It has been my experience that people don't just vanish. And his cottage in Norfolk is locked and bolted, even deep cleaned. Any thoughts on cleanliness?" A thin smile.

"None." Young was too tired for any banter.

"No, I thought not." (*Hell did she mean by that?* wondered Young.) "But now, let us turn to yesterday. You visited The Lawns?" Here, she looked at Richard Cobb who nodded affirmation. "You spoke with Ms Donato and, I believe, left with Professor Bhatti. What was that all about?" Young was anticipating this and was not at all worried. Why should he be? He spoke confidently; "Yes. I needed a word with the Professor and was told that he was at The Lawns. I went, merely, to catch up with him. Hadn't received a summary from the symposium he held the previous week. Was wondering where it had got to."

"Now, that is interesting." Marcia's glasses had been taken off and placed carefully on her lap. "No summary, you say. And you have not had sight of the original manuscript detailing the deliberations of the eminent scientists."

"No. That's why I went to see him. Just said so."

"But surely you could have telephoned?"

"I didn't think that was secure."

"You mean that you did not want anyone to know of your interest in the original papers?"

"Not exactly. Wondered where they got to. Didn't want to start a panic."

The glasses went on again and Marcia sat forward. Obviously, there was more to come. "I think Mr Cobb and Mr Mountford have some news for you, Group Captain." Now she sat back. Richard Cobb spoke; "As soon as you left yesterday, Ms Donato went to her flat, packed a suitcase and left the premises. She drove off."

"She did?" Young was amazed.

"And we were able to track her," Nigel Mountford added. "She travelled to Lady Eleanor's flat in Belgravia and spent the night there. This morning, both left early in Lady Eleanor's car, and my watchers tell me that Keenan has also taken a suitcase."

Marcia butted in. "There's more. We are reliably informed that Kenan and Donato are on the M20 making for Folkestone."

Young was speechless. Perhaps for the first time in his life. "You seemed to have created something of a stir." Marcia looked at him. "Perhaps you have said more to Ms Donato than you have revealed here. Would that be the case?"

"No, it bloody wouldn't!" Young spook robustly. "If you are insinuating that I warned Stacey Donato of the interests of the Secret Service, I could have done that as soon as Mountford told me, when was it? Last week?"

The room was totally silent. No one moved. Had it got darker? Or was it Young's imagination?

.

After a few moments, a quiet voice. "We are in the process of closing down the whole section of Whitehall where Lady Eleanor, her secretaries and your office are situated." The quiet voice seemed almost apologetic. It was the first time Young could remember Special Branch speaking in any meeting. Oakfield went on; "I must advise you, Group Captain, that you must under no circumstances go back to your office or the government buildings of Whitehall. Mr Mountford or a deputy can take you directly home from here. I hope I have made myself clear."

"I apologise for the nature of this discussion. It has been protracted but necessary." Marcia stood. "We will be in touch, Group Captain. I would like to thank you for your patient attendance here today."

Hell! Patient attendance! Couldn't the woman speak English? Young fumed to himself as he was accompanied to the door by Nigel Mountford.

*** *** ***

Diane was surprised at Reginald's early return. There was a lot he needed to think over. And he needed to censor the day's events for Diane.

Chapter 25

Young was struggling with his breakfast. On Friday, 14th. Feb but by happy chance, he had ordered flowers the day before—before, that is, Marcia's interrogation. Diane never forgot St Valentine's Day! Reginald was in no mood to celebrate. The doorbell sounded.

"I wonder who that is. At this early hour?" Diane rushed off in hope rather than expectation, returning seconds later with flowers and a broad smile. "Dear, how wonderful. I'll get Mrs Braithwaite to put them in some water. Thank you, Reginald."

"Pleasure, Diane." Reginald continued to butter his toast. If he supposed for one moment that his wife did not notice his singular preoccupation, he was much mistaken. Diane had noticed but shrewdly kept quiet. She returned to the breakfast table still smiling.

The phone rang. Diane answered it. "For you." Diane handed over the phone.

"Young."

"Good morning, sir." The voice, cultured, precise and bright forced Reginald to believe the caller was educated, young and decidedly sober. "I have instructions to advise you of a day's leave, owed to you, according to our records. I have instructions to advise you to take that leave today sir; further, you are strenuously advised not to contact any person or persons at Whitehall. I am not to engage in conversation nor dispute, only most strongly advise. You can be assured this message is genuine."

"What? Office closed? Whitehall nuked? You relaying this message from authority? Not a practical joke? Not some demented administrator?"

"None of those things, sir. Just the message."

The line went dead. Young looked at the phone and caught himself acting as if in a bad B movie, if such things still existed.

"Problem Reginald?" Diane was scraping marmalade onto her toast.

"Not at all. In fact, quite the reverse. Got a day off, or more accurately ordered me to take a day off."

"They're not sacking you are they, nothing like that?"

"I don't think so. Given me the day off. Perhaps we'll make the most of it; go into Cambridge. See if that reopened hotel does a decent lunch. Let's make a day of it, what do you say?"

"I say, 'yes'."

*** *** ***

In reception, at Whitehall, Clarissa had realised by mid-morning something was wrong. Reggie wasn't in; Lady Eleanor Muck upstairs wasn't in; her appointment book at reception had been confiscated by a tight-lipped, but rather handsome young man, who had not even bothered to look at her. Next, they were ransacking Lady Eleanor's room, and taking away boxes filled with papers, files, laptops, cell phones, books and goodness knows what else. After that, it was the turn of the secretaries and their room. Then she was asked to accompany the young man to Young's office and had to countersign for any documents he took away. Finally, on pain of imprisonment for a very long time in very unpleasant circumstances, she was told (politely) to keep her mouth shut. She did so until she spoke to Sinclair later in the evening.

The afternoon was no better. Not a peep from Young, no messages from Stratton, Mountford, Franklin or Uncle Tom Cobley and by home-time at 5:30 pm she was a bundle of nerves. Even the purr of Justin's car on the way to his flat did not completely dispel her worries. It might even mean the end of her job. But she couldn't understand it. As far as she knew she had done nothing. Perhaps that was the problem.

*** *** ***

On a hot, sunny day in late August 2019, the late Phillipson Rice had emerged from a heavy door of an establishment known as 'The House' and walked to Whitehall for a meeting of ANCOM, chaired by Group Captain Reginald Young. It was through that very same door today, nearly six months later, the 14th of February 2020 that Hugo Stratton ushered in an elegant, gentleman of serious demeanour, resplendent in a light-blue suit with a yellow rose in the buttonhole. His shoes were highly polished. His briefcase very thin.

Inside, Stratton led the guest to his office and once inside, closed the door firmly and turned on the soundless, but effective, anti-audio surveillance system. They sat at Stratton's desk. The discussion centred around finance. Linden Manheimer was an expert on money, particularly the global transfer of funds. It was due to him and his team that a reticent banking system had been uncovered in Asia, and it was that system that had facilitated the transfer of funds to Al-Qaeda terrorists around the world. More than that, MI6 had become aware of entrepreneurs who managed money for weapons, arms, biological warfare, bioterrorism and the like. Not only were these commodities sold to terrorists but governments. Astronomical sums of money were involved; and many had become exceedingly rich. Stratton's hope was that following just one trail of corruption would not only expose a global network but enhance National Security.

The discussions took some time, but useful avenues of investigation were identified.

At Vauxhall, Cross lights burned during the afternoon. Nothing new there. But in one room, carefully secluded below ground level, a group of earnest men and women sat round a large table. Copious amounts of coffee were consumed, and secretaries took notes in a hand which certainly was not Pitman shorthand nor any other recognised shorthand system, whilst a machine recorded every word uttered and without human intervention translated it into a language like no other on the planet.

"Stratton. Satisfied?" The man at the head of the table asked.

"Absolutely sir. No doubt we have stemmed the flow."

"Stemmed the flow? What does that mean?"

"Prevented more misappropriation of sensitive information, sir."

"Well, say so, damn it. Anyway, they shouldn't have mislaid it in the first place. What's the minister going to say, or worse, do?" The man who spoke, wore a suit with a discrete pinstripe and had thick white hair which was carefully styled to touch his collar without causing alarm; he had a smooth, clean-shaven face (even late in the day), lightly powdered, was heavy of jowl, the epitome of a patrician. He glared around the table, but no one spoke, or was prepared to catch his eye. The question remained unanswered. Nevertheless, he continued; "And how serious is this business, Stratton?"

"Of the first order, sir."

"First order? Do speak English Stratton. What do you mean by 'first order'?"

"Top secret sir. Not only is there the possibility of very sensitive scientific data falling into the wrong hands but there seems to be a coordinated criminality if not treason."

"Bugger."

"Today, I've been engaged in detailed discussion with a financial advisor to the government, and in point of fact, to our own service."

"Feller's name?"

"Manheimer, sir."

"How are you spelling that Stratton? I'm hearing a European friend."

"Charterhouse, Cambridge and Merchant Bank, sir."

"Mm."

"As you know, sir, the international scene of finance is extraordinarily complicated. An overview was, in my opinion, necessary sir."

"Mm."

Around the table there was a shuffling of papers, an occasional cautious cough and even the scrape of a chair.

"Right. It's getting late." He looked around the room. "Time to wrap this up, as far as possible that is. Stratton, take Marcia here with you, go visit this Captain Young. Tie that end up, will you? After all, we don't want him talking to the world, do we? Friends on the other side of the water might get cross. Can't have that, can we?"

Stratton and Marcia agreed; stood; left and started their drive to Audley End.

*** *** ***

Later the same evening, Diane and Reginald returned to Plantagenet House having enjoyed a substantial lunch at their chosen Hotel and thereafter browsing through many of the shops in Cambridge. Throughout the expedition Young had been distracted. Which of course has not gone unnoticed. By 5 pm, they judged it was time to return home. They arrived at the front door of their home just before total darkness, and they could feel the cold beginning to bite in the air. Inside, the house was warm and comfortable. Young helped himself to a liberal gin and tonic, eased himself into his favourite armchair and looked forward to an evening of peace and quiet, even if there were matters yet unresolved.

The doorbell rang. Surely, the sound of a doorbell should not quicken the pulse. However Young sat up, wide awake. Diane went to the door. It was 8 pm exactly.

She opened the door and the safety light illuminated two heavily clad figures huddled against the cold. The taller of the two, an impressive lady of a size comparable to Diane, spoke; "Mrs Diane Young, I believe." She extended her hand, having first removed the leather glove which covered it. "My name is Marcia, and my colleague is Mr Hugo Stratton, for this evening my companion and driver. We wondered if we could be so bold as to have a few words with your husband."

Diane was not slow to recognise seniority and immediately stood back to receive the visitors into her home with her best, welcoming smile.

"Reginald," she called. "Two visitors to see you."

Young stood at once. Diane entered followed by Hugo Stratton, and of all people, Marcia!

"Reginald." Stratton was apologising. "Sorry to interrupt your evening. But Marcia," said with due deference to the lady, "would like a few words."

Marcia stepped forward. "Group Captain. We meet again. I sincerely apologise for bursting in like this, but I needed a word with you rather urgently and it is in everyone's best interest that we speak person to person."

Young was not at all pleased. He'd had enough with this woman, but he tried desperately not to let it show. She continued; "Would it be too much of a burden to ask to talk to you in private?"

"Of course." Diane spoke quickly, having detected a certain, unfortunate hesitation in her husband's attitude. "Reginald, why don't you go up to your study with this lady?" (She could hardly call her 'Marcia'—they hadn't been formally introduced, had they?) "You can be quite private there."

"An excellent idea if I may say so, Mrs Young. Group Captain, if you would be so kind as to lead the way I will follow." The arrangement was concluded without Young's participation. Marcia followed the somewhat reluctant Young out of the room and up to his study. As they entered his study, Reginald, remembering his manners, invited Marcia to take a comfortable chair and asked if she cared to join him in a drink. Politely, she asked him for a gin and tonic. As Young busied himself at his private store of alcohol, Marcia looked around the room taking note of the bookcases, the desk, the laptop and the telephones.

"Thank you." She accepted the drink and placed it on the coaster provided on a convenient table next to her chair.

"Before we start, how did you know I was home?" Young asked, with a mildly belligerent expression.

"I apologise most sincerely. We have known of your movements for some time now."

"You had me followed?" He frowned.

"To a degree. As I say, I apologise most sincerely. However, we are dealing here with a matter of National Security, and all avenues of enquiry must be followed vigorously."

"I'm suspected of something?"

"Group Captain!" Marcia seemed to think the question either unimportant or avoided answering it deliberately and changed the subject. She continued; "You have a delightful study. Very private. A loft conversion. If I'm not mistaken."

"I like it."

"You have a spacious house, Group Captain, and from what I hear, a garden of equally ample proportions."

Young bridled. "My wife inherited this house from her father, the founder of a successful chain store company. You may have heard of him."

"Indeed, Group Captain, I believe I have heard mention of the name, as I think most families in Britain have." Marcia seemed in no hurry.

Young was still irritated. The visit this evening was an intrusion into his private life which was, as far as he was concerned, completely unwarranted and he had now discovered he had been watched for some time. And though he didn't know it now, worse was to come. When all said and done, he'd been instrumental in exposing Keenan's original deception. Why should anyone think it necessary to doubt his loyalty?

Marcia continued; "I can understand your surprise at our unexpected visit. Let me just put you into the picture, as far as I am allowed. I must tell you now, in absolute confidence, that we have been suspicious of Lady Keenan for some time. Your appointment was, therefore, of great interest to us; hence the unfortunate intrusions that we have made upon yourself and your wife. We naturally were aware of your comfortable circumstances and as you will see shortly were keen to know how your recruitment to Whitehall came about. We now understand your independent financial position, through your wife I mean."

"You've investigated my, no, our finances?" Young was furious.

"Although at first you may consider this an unforgivable encroachment into your privacy, as you will shortly understand, it was necessary. We have believed Lady Keenan is, in some way, associated with a foreign consortium of million- or billionaires that offers weapons, arms, biotechnology, and so on, to individuals, governments and terrorists worldwide. The amount of money that is involved is quite staggering, I can assure you. What has caught our attention is the connection between The Lawns, and its highly secretive advice to government, Lady Eleanor and even your ANCOM. (Such an ugly acronym, don't you think?) When it became known, in part, through your good self, that information may be moving from Ms Donato to Lady Eleanor to a foreign gentleman, we took a lot of notice. Well, you would, wouldn't you?"

This was not particularly new to Young; he had been supposing something along those lines. But the foreign consortium was new, the immense commercial venture was new and now he realised the potential danger. To some extent he began to calm down.

"Our increasing interest in Lady Eleanor, was the reason for our involvement in your affairs, nothing more. Moving on from our immediate concerns, it will be the task of our overseas operatives, of which Mr Stratton is one, to discover where this misappropriated intelligence has ended up. If we can trace it to the consortium, that would be a considerable triumph. Don't you agree?"

Young agreed.

"Advancing from that aspect of the matter, we have taken into consideration the part played by Alexander Dowson and the startling discovery that he is Ms Donato's son. Fascinating, don't you agree?"

Young agreed it was fascinating.

"At this point, we must begin to speculate a little. Dowson graduated from Oxford with a first, the subject being biochemistry. He then studied for a higher degree at the University of East Anglia University, from which, interestingly, he took a year sabbatical leave in Africa, you may remember."

Young remembered.

"He then was employed by a rather mysterious firm working out of a large house situated in Norfolk. We have subsequently found this establishment abandoned, but it has every sign of having been used as a laboratory for bacterial or viral research: possibly for the development of bioweapons of some sort or another. Are you with me, Group Captain?"

The Group Captain was with her.

"Finally, we come to the last piece of the puzzle, one that may hold the key to the complex, multinational organisation in which we are so interested. That piece of the puzzle is Africa. Although the personnel of MI6 have for a long time had sight of various international intrigues in African states, two things have recently exercised their minds more than usual. Firstly, the increasing interest that China, Russia and possibly Asia have taken in the financial politics of that region. Secondly, we in Britain have taken notice of the development of infectious diseases particularly of viral diseases of which Africa has unfortunately a large number. When one of our specialists goes to the continent for a year, no matter what the pretext, we take note. Dowson was one such individual. And, lo and behold, by quite another route, one of pure chance, you identified the same individual as of interest. Isn't that strange?"

Young agreed it was strange.

"That interest in infectious diseases has been intensified by the epidemic (dare we say pandemic?), threatening our very existence. It has become a matter of considerable importance. Was there a leak of viruses from a laboratory, or was it a consequence of evolution? These questions are immensely important now, and as yet there are no definitive answers. Now, you must see the importance (should I say, urgency?) of our work."

It sounded as if Marcia had finished, and Young stood and extended his hand to take her glass to replenish it. If it was a gesture of reconciliation, it was rejected.

"No thank you. I must advise you that the Whitehall department in which Lady Eleanor worked, has been closed and you must take leave of absence as from today. Your remuneration will continue for now without interruption. I'm sorry, Group Captain, Mr Stratton and I have much to do yet this evening and so I must reluctantly refuse. I have taken up a considerable amount of your time and for that, I am truly sorry. Perhaps we can go on downstairs and re-join the others…" The sentence was not completed but the two of them descended the stairs where they found Diane and Hugo Stratton in animated conversation. Soon Marcia and Stratton left.

Once they had gone, Diane started to make tracks for bed. Young said that he needed time to sit and think for a while and have a couple of drinks although he didn't mention that.

"Follow you up."

"Don't be too long dear." She disappeared upstairs.

Young poured himself another drink and deliberated upon the evening. Much of what Marcia 'no name' had said, or lectured, made sense. He felt he had been exonerated, but from what, he wasn't quite sure. One thing was sure in his mind, ANCOM had been useful, but perhaps not in the way that Keenan had meant it to be. He would no doubt in due course hear from Clarissa of the closure of the department. That all meant that he was free to spend time at home. Good, as far as it went; but he was too young just to sit and read the Sunday Supplements. However, come to think of it, there was something remarkable about the evening at a more personal level. There had been no mention of Rachel Harding. Now, there was a thing!

He retired to bed.

No sooner had he got into bed than Diane spoke. "Marcia, no other name?"

"Not that I know of," Young replied.

"Doesn't matter. Cultured sort of lady, wouldn't you say?"

"I suppose," Reginald answered. "Not given the matter much thought."

"And Hugo Stratton is a remarkably entertaining person." Diane sighed. "He was telling me a little about his education. A grammar school student, later attended the University of…" But Young had fallen asleep. If he dreamt that night, he didn't remember it in the morning.

*** *** ***

Vagaries of human behaviour sometimes defy understanding. The Volkswagen 4 by 4 had left Belgravia and been driven to a hotel in Folkestone the previous day, but the two ladies had spent the night of 13th in a hotel. Today, February 14th, they appeared at ease or if they were nervous, they didn't show it. Presumably they were unaware that they had been accompanied by four police officers. The police watching Keenan and Donato could not understand why they had not attempted to board the cross-channel ferry on Thursday the 13th when they arrived in Folkestone. Still puzzled the police watched them as they passed the day at the hotel: about 8:30 pm all was revealed for they were joined by a Mr Willem Maessen in the lounge of the hotel and then the three motored at a leisurely pace towards Dover. Their car followed by the police moved at steady speed until it met with congestion on the approach to the Eastern Port where finally it came to a standstill. It was here that four plain-clothed officers surrounded the car and with quiet, but insistent persuasion, persuaded the two ladies and the gentleman leave their car. They were escorted back to one of the police vehicles. A uniformed officer from the Dover Police Force climbed into the driving seat of the now vacant Volkswagen. All this was carried out with such precision and with minimal commotion, that only a boy of eight in an adjacent car even noticed. His excitement, however, failed to draw their attention to these activities of the 'big men and two ladies' and he started crying. Well, it had been a long journey from Walsall, hadn't it? His crying was stopped by a sharp word from his father and a sweet from his mother; a little later, seeing the 'ginormous boats', together with their 'fairy lights', he forgot the incident altogether.

The three fugitives were taken into custody and at Dover police station advised of their rights and the reason for their arrest. Keenan and Donato were suspected of breaking the official secrets act and Mr Maessen suspected of espionage. They were to spend the night in Dover before being transferred to London for further questioning.

Lady Keenan had not spent a comfortable night in Dover police station. The room in which she had been held (she had eschewed the term 'cell', it was so vulgar!) was by any standards, cramped and ill-furnished. On the other hand, Stacey had found a degree of relief, her fears of arrest were over. She had been arrested! Her concern was for her son and his welfare. Whatever was to come, his protection was of in paramount importance. William Maessen was angry and when he was angry, he tended to shout and bluster. His language became unseemly and as the night progressed more obscene. The custody officer, thoroughly fed up with being equated with an animal of the swine family, withdrew whatever sympathy he had for him. And so, the long night dragged by, until after a meagre breakfast, the three were escorted, still separated, to London.

Chapter 26

The three were taken to Kent Police Station (Dover) and interviewed separately by the desk sergeant. They were each informed of their rights and placed in custody on suspicion of breaching the official secrets Act 1989 and/or espionage. They were searched quite intimately and although allowed to keep their clothes, jewellery, watches and all other personal possessions were removed. They were further informed that they would be held in Dover overnight and transferred to a London police station tomorrow, Saturday, morning.

Lady Eleanor responded with dignity, as one might expect. The cell in which she was confined, was rather less unpleasant than she had been led to believe from watching television dramas. She settled for the night, having determined that she would say nothing until her own solicitor was present the following morning, and then only after taking his advice. Stacey Donato was more disquieted; at first relieved with the arrest, she came to resent it. She found the accommodation cold and uncomfortable and without her watch she lay awake all night, the light constantly burning in her cell and listening to various random footsteps and shouts from the police and detainees alike. Regularly through the night, a viewing panel would open in the door, and an eye would peer at her, then just as quickly disappear. The whole experience was 'quite appalling'. And even worse, she could hear the continual tirade emanating from Willem Maessen's cell. He was a handful. A large man, with an unrivalled vocabulary of obscenity and additional threatening behaviour to match, he was most unpleasant. The police persons on duty that night were pleased to see him on his way to London on the Saturday morning.

As he drove into London, Roger Selby was not pleased. His Saturday mornings were a welcome relief from the grind of his solicitors' practice and were usually spent in some relaxing form of recreation, un-associated with The Law or interpretations of The Law. Today, however, he had been called to a police station (a place he would avoid at all costs, if possible) to advise a Lady

Eleanor Keenan on legal matters relating to the Official Secrets Act 1989. Generally, such requests would be passed to a junior member of the firm, but as the appeal had been made on behalf of Lady Eleanor he had been left with little choice in the matter. He knew Lady Eleanor, or at least her brother, 'Bags Boscombe' (now the Earl of Kingsworth) at Eton, and again up at Oxford, although they had lost touch over the years. He wondered idly where 'Old Bags Boscombe' had got to. He had never met the sister, younger by 10 years if memory served. But intriguing. The Official Secrets Act? Well, there you are!

At last, he pulled into the police station and entered the building.

The custody sergeant eyed him cautiously. "Sir?"

"Roger Selby. Solicitor. Here to advise Lady Keenan, whom I believe you have within these premises."

"We do indeed sir, and very glad we are to see you. There are three people here already who would like to meet with you before you interview Lady Keenan. A word of warning sir."

"Warning? What on earth do you mean Sergeant?"

"Yes sir, a warning. I think they are not one of us, sir, if you take my meaning."

"Not one of us? What, are they, three of them?"

"Well, in a way. How can I put it? Not regulars more, shall we say, irregulars. From across the river, you understand. Vauxhall Cross."

"Good God, this is serious!"

"Yes sir, I would say it is serious."

Selby was escorted by a constable along a short corridor to a door marked 'Chief Inspector'. The young bobby knocked, and receiving no answer, opened the door and ushered the solicitor into the room, closing the door behind him. Inside, Selby found Marcia sat, with Hugo Stratton on one side and Nigel Mountford on the other. Stratton remained motionless; Mountford crossed his legs and plunged his hands deep into his trouser pockets.

"Mr Roger Selby, we presume." Marcia stated the solicitor's name, as if possibly he had forgotten it.

"Solicitor. Here to advise Lady Eleanor Keenan. And you are?"

"My name is Marcia," the imperious lady stated, making it abundantly clear that was as much information as she was willing to divulge, "and these are my colleagues, from sister secret services. Hugo Stratton and Nigel Mountford."

Neither of these gentlemen spoke nor did they smile. Marcia, Stratton and Mountford gazed at Selby.

Selby spoke. "Well, I will make my position perfectly clear. I am here to advise Lady Keenan to make no statement nor answer any questions until I instruct her otherwise. Indeed, as yet I have no knowledge as to why she is being detained at this police station although I assume that will become clear."

"Well said Mr Selby." Marcia lent forward to emphasise her point and beamed for the first time. "Forgive me if I say so how wise your words are. I am sure your advice will be of the utmost relevance to both the police and Lady Keenan."

"Good. That's straight then." Selby was relieved, if a little surprised. But he had reached that optimism prematurely.

"You understand, Mr Selby, we are not here to interrogate your client, nor to question her. That is for the police. Goodness me, we would not think of interfering with the proper procedures of lawful prosecution. We are here on a quite separate errand. You see Hugo and Nigel are both acquaintances, I can say friends of Lady Keenan; they know her well. They have worked with her I might even say for her. No, we are here to offer our support and understanding."

So, they are 'regulars' to the sergeant, 'agents' to me and now, I'm informed, they're 'concerned colleagues' of Lady Keenan. Rubbish! Thought Selby. At that very moment, the door opened, and Chief Inspector Talbot entered carrying a tray laden with cups of coffee, a bowl of sugar, milk in a jug and biscuits. "Not for me," Selby said, holding up his hand, which was just as well because Talbot had no idea Selby was in the office.

"Inspector," Marcia spoke, "this is Roger Selby, solicitor, here to represent the interests of your Lady Eleanor. And if I am any judge…" here she paused to ensure the inspector fully understood that she was an excellent judge (of what was not defined)…"a very capable gentleman. I am sure Lady Eleanor will be given extremely professional counsel."

"Thank you," Inspector Talbot said.

"Now, if you have no objections Inspector, might I be allowed to see Lady Eleanor and pass on our best wishes and support to her. I am sure Mr Selby will want to accompany me and perhaps it would be fitting if you have an officer free and who would also like to be in attendance."

Talbot nodded. Not usual practice but with a police officer present and solicitor Selby to protect Lady Eleanor from intrusive questioning he could see no reason to be obstructive.

He reached for the phone and asked if Sergeant Savage would step into his office. Detective Sergeant Savage arrived promptly and introduced herself as 'Barbara'. She, together with solicitor Selby and Marcia went to talk with Lady Eleanor. Stratton and Mountford exchanged pleasantries with Inspector Talbot and waited for their return.

*** *** ***

Marcia concluded her interview with Lady Eleanor remarkably quickly, and she, Stratton and Mountford left the police station and were chauffeur-driven towards Whitehall. She informed them, on the journey, they were due for a meeting billed as a 'working lunch' but as she said "the committee provided the work, we must provide our own lunch. Something to do with the latest economic awareness memorandum." Accordingly, she ordered the chauffeur to pull up at a Pret a Manger and buy a selection of sandwiches, savoury pastries and takeaway coffees. They then proceeded towards Whitehall, driven quickly and expertly, eventually turning into a side street off Whitehall and pulling into an underground car park where the three alighted and approached a door leading to the lift. The lift shot upwards with such smoothness that when they arrived and the doors silently opened, they had no idea on which floor they had arrived. Before them stretched a long, deep red and luxurious carpet which led to a black door that was shut and highly varnished. Marcio knocked and they entered.

The room was only medium-sized, windowless and disconcertingly still. A quiet hum emanated from hidden air-conditioning; lighting being also hidden. No pictures adorned the walls, the carpet was thicker even than the one on the approach corridor and the heating a trifle more than was justly comfortable. This was the Ministerial Liaison Committee room. Jocelyn Carstairs at the far end of the table that stretched virtually the length of the room, unwound from his seat to welcome them.

"Marcia. How are you? I see you bring two lieutenants. Draw up chairs and join us."

With a managerial sweep of an arm, he indicated those present as a Private Secretary to the ministry (which ministry was not declared), two newly elected members of Parliament 'with special interest in national security', a financial advisor from the economics division, two civil servants of mature years and whose appointments were undisclosed and Jocelyn's secretary 'the glorious Annette'. Stratton, trained to observe, observed a flush spreading across Annette's perfect complexion.

Marcia pulled up a chair. Stratton and Mountford sat as far as possible from her, perhaps to show independence, or to emphasise Marcia's importance. Who knows? Jocelyn regained his place at the top of the table, gently laying his right hand on Annette's free hand. She removed her hand slowly as not to attract attention but also to indicate displeasure to her boss. Marcia stared at Jocelyn. And he stared back. There was almost a moment of competition. But not quite: both were too diplomatic for that.

"As you know Marcia, this committee is enjoined to consider and recommend any action of a substantial nature that may be important and possibly financially onerous. Part of the 'value for money' drive we are all labouring under at present," Jocelyn looked around the table garnering some subdued murmurs. Marcia, on the other hand, was silent. It was not her obligation to justify the service's proposal; only to emphasise its importance.

"I assume" she said somewhat disdainfully, "you have read and circulated the dossier, on the subject of treachery within Lady Keenan's department. And I assume also, so that you realise the immense importance of this treachery."

"Of course, Marcia, of course. And let me say at this early juncture of the proceedings, how impressed we are, not only with your quite extraordinarily success in revealing the miscreant, but your grasp of the wider, may I say(?), global consequences." Jocelyn had been embarrassed by the frontal attack. There was some general movement in the room as members investigated their lunch and boxes with intense scrutiny, a general unease. He needed to pull this committee together and legitimise any recommendation they may make to the Minister.

"Marcia, let's begin by revisiting the timeline of the treachery. Might best be the way to strengthen your submission, wouldn't you agree? And of course, give us a better view of the danger that lurks within!" He looked around the committee members. If he was expecting applause or even assent, he was mistaken. Marcia was here to convince the committee members that her submission for action was justified. She had brought her presentation dossier with her (or at least a copy) but it lay before her unopened.

"This business started some 6 years ago with the appointment of Lady Eleanor Keenan to within the structure of the civil service in Whitehall and, as normal, she was vetted by us as normal procedure. Not in depth, you understand, as we would one of our own agents, but enough to find her neutral in matters politic and with an unblemished police record. We merely noted her appointment. Then, 4 years ago, much to our surprise, she reawakened a committee long considered obsolete; this committee, unhappily named ANCOM, was to facilitate the free exchange of information between junior members our intelligent services, GCHQ, Metropolitan Police, Counter-terrorist branch and Special branch. In her wisdom, she recruited a Group Captain Reginald Young who was about to leave the RAF after a long and distinguished service and a person eager to continue some form of employment. Again, he was vetted by us, and we found no reason to take more than a cursory interest. Later, it transpired that his appointment was Lady Keenan's first mistake. He was rather perceptive."

Trying desperately to conceal his boredom (a yawn poorly disguised as a cough) one of the junior MPs said, "So a low-grade committee. Of little importance. But your agents, are they spies(?), were there to report back."

"Mr Evans," Marcia spoke after slowly looking around the members of the committee and her eyes at last coming to gaze intently at the young MP; "I am not going to burden you with unnecessary knowledge of my agents; but would point out that rather than, as you say, 'report back', they took an active part in the committee."

The rebuke was so politely expressed but no one dared question it. Or speak. Or even move. If anyone had died at that time, the room was so quiet no one would have noticed. Stratton smiled to himself.

"Please, Marcia, please…" and with much hand waving Jocelyn implored her to continue.

"Thank you, Jocelyn," Marcia again took up the story. "I have said that Lady Keenan's first mistake was to appoint Group Captain Young as chairperson. Her second mistake was a direct result of that." Now, she had the committee's full focus. "For some reason, as yet unexplained, Lady Keenan saw fit to send Nigel Mountford," again and nod of the head in Mountford's direction, "a note, headed 'Home Office, urgent reply required'. Perhaps you'll be good enough to explain Nigel."

All the heads turned to Nigel Mountford as he began to speak. "It must have been in November or thereabouts that I had a communication from the home office that there was some difficulty in traffic flow on the A34 near Culham and Harlow, experimental atomic sites. An area of high security. Curiously, the police had no knowledge of this, but it was deemed important enough to be referred to higher authority. The committee we're not particularly excited."

Marcia spoke again. "Our representative, at that stage, on the ANCOM was a promising and newly promoted man named Phillipson Rice. Within a month of this announcement of traffic difficulties, he was murdered." She allowed a pause. "The police were involved, of course, and the usual difficulties between our services arose to the frustration of both parties. The police have been unable to bring the miscreant to Justice so far, and we are completely at a loss to understand the murder. We have discovered incontrovertible evidence that no information had been leaked abroad by Phillipson Rice. Now we come to the crunch. Our vigilant Group Captain urged Lady Eleanor to search for a leak or a misappropriation of information or indeed some interest. He found she would have none of it and advised him most strongly to leave the matter to the police. Cutting a long story short, Group Captain Young felt so uneasy, that he enlisted the assistance of someone he had known previously in the RAF to uncover more of Lady Eleanor's activities. By now, we had also become aware that something unusual was being played out at Whitehall and when we discovered that Group Captain Young (or his associate) was trailing Lady Keenan, we became positively alarmed. This might seriously impede our enquiries and our own investigations might be compromised."

"Now a serious complication arose. The government had long decided that a highly sophisticated planning and research facility was required to advise them of the latest developments in natural national security such as biowarfare, cybernetic interference, poisons, false information, satellite interference and of course advanced armaments together with others. A conference centre named 'The Lawns' was provided with the secure facilities and modern information exchange. This interested us considerably and we sent one of our agents to act as caretaker, if you will, and report to us his observations. Our suspicions were confirmed when Lady Eleanor appointed the chairman of ANCOM, Group Captain Young as liaison officer to 'The Lawns'."

Now we were positive that Lady Keenan was taking more than a casual interest in these parallel schemes.

"Almost always in these complicated sagas a stroke of luck occurred which led us to suspect even closer links between the ANCOM and 'The Lawns'. It sent the whole investigation into overdrive."

During this monologue, Jocelyn's hand strayed once more towards that of his secretary and as it approached, accompanied by a sudden movement and loud cough, her hand was withdrawn in rebuff. Stratton noticed and smiled once again. Marcia didn't notice, or if she did, she did not smile.

"You were saying," Jocelyn, either covering his embarrassment or wanting to hear his own voice or both, interjected; "This bit of luck. It was luck, was it not?" Marcia said nothing and an uncomfortable silence spread among the members. "As I was saying," she continued patiently, "we were helped by an accidental meeting in Paris—to be precise, Montmartre."

"Oh yes. I love Montmartre. Don't we all?" Jocelyn was determined to remind the members of his presence. "Those scents of coffee, perfumes, French bread. The noise and bustle…" he's sentence tailed off, the committee seemingly uninterested in his olfactory and auditory senses. Marcia waited until she was sure his reminisces had come to an end and then; "This accidental meeting was between a chap from Oxford, quite unconnected to us or Whitehall, and one Alexander Dowson. What's more, his fiancé had met Dowson some years previously in Kenya." She turned to Jocelyn. "In Africa, you know."

Jocelyn remained silent but flushed. "It appeared Dowson's work was research in a chemical factory in Norfolk and one that we had been keeping an eye on, as it was funded mysteriously by a group notionally registered in Mozambique, but we believed also in Kenya. Then, Dowson disappears. Our friend in Oxford notified the police and quite naturally they became excited and on the meagre evidence they had they called on the good offices of a town in Norfolk's police to investigate. They then interviewed our feller from Oxford but made little headway in finding Dowson. Meanwhile, Group Captain Young was running around the countryside or at least his agent was and discovering that the lady managing 'The Lawns' is a friend of Lady Keenan and that they met privately in a hotel in Bedford. It is further thought that documents are passed between the two. There might even have been another gentleman present on one or two occasions."

"Finally, comes the proof if more is needed. With further searches, it is discovered that Alexander Dowson is the son of the manager of 'The Lawns' and so we have a direct line from an extremely sensitive scientific establishment through Stacey Donato to Lady Keenan and possibly a foreign national. Furthermore, Stacey Donato's son works at a very dubious chemical plant subsidised by East African states or those within those states and we are certain that information is being passed abroad."

"Marcia," Jocelyn, positively joyful, almost clapped his hands. "How perfectly your submission is in accordance with your acumen. I am sure that the committee is now sufficiently briefed on the importance of this work. Thank you."

Stratton looked from Jocelyn to Marcia and back, although there seemed no overt animosity, the air undoubtedly crackled with energy between them. Marcia allowed the silence to stretch. The members were either intent on reading parts of their dossier or seriously considering the submission, sat unmoving. Nigel dropped his pen. The interruption drifted away, and Marcia continued to let her address sink in. Then she leant forward:

"You will all have concluded by now that something is missing." Not a sound. "There is something that lifts this from yet another espionage enquiry into a unique challenge." Still not a sound. "That is one word; URGENCY."

The relief was palpable; even if the statement was not understood, at least it had been supplied for them.

"Last night and this morning Lady Keenan, Stacey Donato and a South African gentleman Willem Maessen have been taken into custody. There is no doubt in my mind that all three will be charged with espionage, the misappropriation of information essential to National Security. The information is the latest research available in this country on several aspects of virology. The research is from the isolation of the most dangerous and easily spread viruses in the world, to the manufacture of viruses and their variants; to vaccines that will protect our population and the latest research on antiviral medications. All this has been sent abroad. This you might say is but science fiction: IT IS NOT. We know that in Tanzania, Mozambique and probably Kenya consortia of extremely rich entrepreneurs deal in such projects. There was even an attempt to develop a rogue laboratory in Norfolk. DOWSON WORKS FOR SUCH AN ORGANISATION. It is of vital importance that we trace him and from him, those factories and this lethal trade. And as soon as possible."

"You may have noticed that WHO and our own SAGE committee are predicting an exponential rise in pneumonias worldwide all from an outbreak in Wuhan, China. In December last year just 2 months ago, to an estimated 100,000 cases globally and 40 deaths by the end of this month. In just over a year, it is estimated that there will be 200 million people infected globally and there will have been 4 million deaths. What we desperately need is research on viruses, vaccines and antiviral medicines."

"Dowson, and possibly the laboratory facilities in Africa and elsewhere, are working on unknown types of viruses; Keenan/Donato misappropriation of separate but parallel research means that this investigation is VITAL. WE NEED TO KNOW NOW."

And with that Marcia concluded her submission. Both Stratton and Mountford we're impressed with her brevity but also her emotional involvement. They were in no doubt of the urgency of this investigation, but would these members be impressed? Would they even understand? Or worst of all, would they be interested? Marcia, Stratton and Mountford stood. "We have no time for questions," Marcia pronounced and all three left.

*** *** ***

The abrupt departure said more than a million words. It meant action was needed and immediately! As Stratton left the building, he realised how Marcia had come to leave the interview at the police station so quickly. All she needed was a connection to South Africa, or at least an African country, for the whole business to fall into place. There was no need to labour the point.

Chapter 27

Mid-morning the following day (Saturday, 15th.February) Reginald was standing at the conservatory window gazing at the large garden. His mood was pensive, the weather cold. He looked up at the palest blue-white sky and involuntarily shivered. Clasping his hands behind his back, he stretched his shoulders. The interviews with Marcia on Thursday, and again, last night, had left him in no doubt; he was redundant; at least from Whitehall. Whilst he slept last night and pondered this morning, he had gradually come to terms with the fact that his life had changed, and he was determined this was to be for the better. Diane had remained remarkably calm; she must now be reassured. If he was dispensable in Whitehall, he wasn't here. He would talk with Diane, and they would construct an interesting life together. They would need interests. Some, shared, some individual. Buy a dog? Play more golf? Build a small library in his study? And the pair of them? They'd seen enough of the world in the service; there was Britain to explore. Why not? How best to do that?

"Reginald," a commanding voice, "what are you doing?"

Yes, he would need an active hobby. He'd resign. That, at least, was a positive decision; his decision not someone else's decree. Once the idea had formed, it became a challenge.

"Just thinking, Diane, just thinking."

He walked with a lighter step into the lounge.

Two days later Reginald wrote and posted his letter of resignation. If he imagined that such definitive action would release him from guilt, worry or disappointment he was mistaken. He meandered around the large house, lost. He was restless and, for the first time in his life, unemployed. Idleness did not sit easily upon him. His sleep was particularly troublesome. He had never suffered from insomnia, never lain awake tossing and turning continually racking his brains for ideas or solutions but now he couldn't stop it. Nightmares in which he was repeatedly lost in a town he knew well but somehow couldn't find his way home became common. He knew the streets; was familiar with the buildings but was lost. He was also in a hurry, late for a meeting but didn't know how to get there or what the meeting was about. Then suddenly the setting would jump unexpectedly but without surprise as they often did in dreams and now, he was being led to an execution chamber but had killed no one. Innocent. But no one would listen.

In the morning after a particularly vivid nightmare, he would be sweating profusely, and would be told that during the night he thrashed his arms about and shouted incoherently.

"Most unlike you," Diana almost scolded him.

So frequent were the nightmares he was beginning to fear going to bed; days and daylight were a relief. But even when Diane was away at the hospital or Church function, and he was on his own in the house, he was unable to feel at ease, constantly pacing, unable to settle. He would sort books ineffectually in his study or look at the garden in minute detail without doing anything to it. Once he sat in the conservatory just listlessly trying to reconstruct the meetings of the ANCOM and blaming himself for sluggishness or incompetence or even negligence. Then he became ashamed of these imaginings, stood up and berated himself for such nonsense. He must engage in an activity. Stop this nonsense. It was at this point he remembered. Buy a dog! That was not just two walks a day but the welfare of the creature and the bonding and training between the two of them. A satisfying partnership. Diane was bound to agree. Wasn't she? Then a determined effort to undertake a joint project with her. Find out what they could enjoy together. He'd start with her input as soon as she was home.

*** *** ***

During the remaining days of February, as Diane and Reginald came to terms with 'final' retirement, and beginning their new life together, elsewhere the activities of MI5 and MI6 escalated dramatically. The leak of sensitive information from the now defunct 'Lawns' and the defection (or attempted defection) of Lady Eleanor and Stacey Donato had caused considerable embarrassment to many. In several offices, the ancient and proverbial air-conditioning systems were used to remove waste matter that had hit them. A gentleman of aristocratic bearing with longish white hair and a short temper, needed the calming ministrations of his secretary rather more frequently than she deemed necessary. Marcia, on the other hand, rallied her agents and set about assessing and then repairing whatever damage had been occasioned by the collapse of The Lawns and ANCOM.

Throughout February it had been alternately colder and warmer than usual, but slowly and surely snow fell across Britain, first in Scotland and the North, then the East of England and finally on the night of February 26/27 London experienced its first snowfall. Even though the forecasters had warned of the winter weather approaching in Whitehall, hurrying pedestrians were ill-equipped to deal with the snow that was falling. There were few umbrellas and pedestrians seemed to prefer snow to settle on their heads and coats before brushing them off, rather than taking elementary precautions. Many were slipping unsteadily on the dirty snow piled irregularly on the paths and vehicles drove on treacherous roads, sliding between ridges of snow, skidding into huge puddles that drenched the unwary.

A policeman stood stoically outside the door leading to the reception area that Young knew so well. Occasionally he stamped his feet and blew into his gloves, to keep warm. Inside all was quiet; the large desk was unattended and stripped of telephones, computers, intercoms, appointment book and, sadly, of Clarissa. Young's office had fared no better and Eleanor's room above was completely bare (except that an unexpected visitor would have noticed, kneeling quietly in one corner, a technician removing a small microphone from behind and wainscoting.)

Lady Eleanor Keenan's department was closed. Permanently.

In a small room at Thames House on the embankment, Richard Cobb was interviewed by two men of intense demeanour. He was being questioned closely on every detail he could remember of daily life at The Lawns.

"And visitors, had many of those, did she?" He was asked by one of the young men with an irritating nasal accent.

"You mean Ms Donato? Of course. Plenty. Mostly tradesmen or reps, that sort of thing."

"Any she invited up to her flat?"

Cobb thought. There were one or two men she had invited upstairs, none of them had struck him as anything out of the ordinary. Perhaps even meetings of an amorous nature. Let's face it, even Young had gone upstairs once. But of course, they knew that, he suddenly recalled. The flat was under constant surveillance.

"You know very well who she invited to the flat, what they did, what they said, how long they stayed, what they took away. Why ask me?" Cobb spoke abruptly.

"Of course, Richard. Just crossing the t's and dotting the i's. You know how it is…" The sentence was left unfinished.

"I suppose," Richard replied shortly.

"And of course, you lived on the premises 24-hours a day, more or less."

"I went out occasionally." Cobb hadn't completely recovered his composure.

"Of course, Richard of course. Just getting the picture. Go anywhere we should know about?"

"Usually the local pub, which was about two miles away! Did I meet anyone regularly? No, I didn't."

The taller (and thinner) of the two continued, "To the best of your knowledge, did Alexander Dowson ever visit?"

"I'm not personally acquainted with this Alexander Dowson, so I wouldn't recognise him if I saw him." Richard answered after a brief pause.

"This is the person in question, or at least a photograph of him!" Again, it was the taller of the two that spoke and pushed a photograph of Alexander Dowson across the table. It was a colour reproduction, full face, size A4.

Cobb studied the photograph with some care before pushing it back. "I don't know that person. I've never seen him nor, to the best of my knowledge, did he visit."

The questioning continued for some time, but nothing of importance was added to what was already known. Richard left about midday.

Nigel Mountford in Thames House and Hugo Stratton in 'The House' were also questioned, but the thrust of the inquiries put to them centred rather more on ANCOM than anything else. Neither was able to advance any information that was not already known, except to add detail to Young's apparent bonhomie. Similarly, Adrian Oakfield of Special Branch and Les Morgan of the Counter-terrorist Branch were unable to add any new facts.

The whole unfortunate affair might affect several Ministers of the Crown and their departments, and they needed to be briefed in detail on the possible consequences of the betrayal. Who decided to convene a wide-ranging investigation was not made clear, but certainly Marcia took a leading role. It was accepted that a line needed to be drawn under the nasty business and if possible, to limit any damage to the state. It had to be remembered that the UK acted within

Western Alliances and the maintenance of confidence (particularly that of the Americans) was crucial. It was because of these worries that civil servants, permanent (or otherwise) undersecretaries to government departments involved and so on, met with scientists, who were held in the highest regard, to hear evidence and decide upon recommendations to Central Government.

Professor Linus Bhatti was invited to address such a gathering.

He entered a government building near the Embankment on Thursday afternoon, 27th February and was taken in a lift down perhaps 100 feet. He was escorted through a long corridor by a polite gentleman of upright bearing and few words. He was asked to sit and wait. The door before him had seen better days; it had lost much varnish and, with that, much formality. However, it looked solid if nothing else. After only a couple of minutes, this door swung open, and Bhatti was escorted into a large room containing desks arranged in an open square; behind these desks sat perhaps 20 or 30 individuals of grave countenance. His chair faced the gathering, and he was asked to sit. Marcia directed the proceedings, and she was clearly the chairperson. He looked around and recognised no one save for two scientists he knew to be members of the SAGE committee. The chairperson spoke:

"Good afternoon, Professor. May I apologise immediately on behalf of myself and all present on the imposition we have inflicted upon you this afternoon. Unfortunately, however, as you are no doubt fully aware, vital documents originating from your conferences at 'The Lawns' have been misappropriated and we are anxious to know in detail the implications of the facts they contained. Perhaps you would be good enough to answer any queries our members have pertaining to the nature of these facts, after you have given us an outline of the salient proposals your papers contain. It might just be as well to add that we have all had a chance to read copies of your final reports, which were fortuitously, not deleted from your secretaries' machines."

Professor Bhatti had prepared himself for such an interview and he was confident that he would be able to explain the main research recommendations, succinctly. They fell into two broad groups.

The first was the development of combined viruses that could make them more lethal and more contagious. The merger, for example, of the deadly Ebola virus with the contagious 'flu' virus might produce a pathogen more dangerous than on its own. And secondly, research for a 'universal' defence against viruses, one that would protect the population against any virus or variant, either by programs of vaccination or by using antiviral drugs or both.

He set about outlining these programs of research and the approximate cost of each form of research. His opening statement was short and to the point, but questions took up a considerable length of time. At 5:30 pm, Marcia announced the committee had exhausted their questions and brought the session to a close:

"Professor Bhatti, it remains for us to determine the political and economic implications of your excellent papers before we finalise our report. Thank you for your lucid explanation of such a complex matter. We are grateful."

As he was leaving the room, one of the senior members of the committee caught hold of his arm.

"Professor. May I introduce myself? Brendan Forsythe. After such a long and concentrated meeting, it is my custom to refresh myself at an establishment known only to a carefully selected group of influential businessmen and women. I wonder, *Can I offer you some relaxation for, shall we say, half an hour?"*

Professor Bhatti did not drink alcohol, not because of any religious prohibition but because it was his belief that alcohol was deleterious to health. A period of quiet relaxation, however, was very tempting. He agreed.

"Transport awaits us," was the reply, and they climbed into a chauffeur-driven car and were taken to this 'establishment' in a London that was quickly becoming white under snow.

They arrived within minutes at the 'establishment', which turned out to be a newly built condominium. On each storey, there was only one apartment with space for several bedrooms, lounges, a dining room and, of course, accommodation for servants. The top floor was not, as Bhatti expected a penthouse suite but a spacious room with magnificent views over the capital and Hyde Park. It acted as a very, very private club for the owners of the apartments below. Around the room several groups lounged on deeply cushioned couches and easy chairs. Conversation was subdued.

No sooner had they chosen to relax in armchairs, than one of the most beautiful Asian girls Bhatti had ever seen, asked if she could bring them some refreshment. Forsythe ordered a Glenfiddich ("Bring a bottle, my dear.") and Bhatti, sparkling water.

"There are hundreds of these condominiums in capitals worldwide," Forsythe murmured, "privately owned by the wealthiest ladies and gentlemen of the planet. If you look around, you will see the membership is cosmopolitan, representing China, Russia, the Arab States and more recently, African Countries and the American continent north and south." Then in a quieter voice, "Some who deny allegiance to any country or even continent. All enjoy a lifestyle of opulence and opportunity that is quite extraordinary. Of course, they are always on the lookout to invest their millions and reap the rewards. An extremely lucrative investment at present is the supply of instruments of aggression, or if you will, warfare. These are not necessarily conventional armaments or weaponry, but increasingly other forms antagonism is being tried, all used by various countries even terrorists of the right or left persuasion. In your own field of expertise, you have been recently studying viral pathogens that might be used for hostile purposes. A pandemic would lead to global deaths and economic meltdown; imagine the effects of an epidemic on a specific geographic region and limited to that region. As well as that, increasingly cybernetic technology and space satellites are being bought and sold as tools for hostility. Some, I don't say all, but some of the magnates you see here deal in such commodities. The investment is beyond the financial means of most businessmen, even some governments, but for the gentlemen you see around you such limitations don't exist. The outlay may be enormous, but the rewards may change global markets. Profits are beyond your ordinary man's conception. It is known that some within the whole consortium some act independently and for their sole advantage, no matter what the overall opinion is; so be it. But believe me, it is far more profitable to pool resources. Working for this consortium can be very worthwhile. It is a hugely lucrative business."

Chapter 28

Marcia's abrupt termination of the strategic Finance/Committees meeting did not have the desired effect of impressing urgency on Jocelyn Carstairs, the civil service or any of the other members of the committee. Days drifted by and interviews with Cobb, Stratton, Mountford and Professor Bhatti postponed any definitive action. Marcia had asked for urgency, there was no time for unnecessary delay. Dowson was probably in Kenya, but knowing of Willem Maessen from Johannesburg, the search may have to be widened. Similarly, exposing consortia selling arms or biowarfare diminished with any delays. She called Stratton to the office and told him that she had had decided the investigation should go ahead irrespective of bureaucratic impediment. The redoubtable Marcia would limit damage as far as possible.

She required the services of Rachel Harding. The young lady was an accomplished child protection officer but also a member of Britain's intelligence service. She had originally been sent to Africa, during the summer of 2016, to manage charitable assistance to rural areas in Tanzania. However, her other purpose was to examine and report the activities of an Alexander Dowson. Any notable scientist visiting Africa, especially with interest in viruses was of interest to the intelligence services. Activities in East Africa, including Mozambique, had attracted attention; funds were being supplied to numerous laboratories from China, Russia and the Middle East; even more interestingly, it was believed there was a consortium of extraordinarily wealthy financiers throughout the world jointly engaged with supplying vast funds for buying then selling hostile biotechnology and weaponry. The profits from such transactions were astronomical. This exercised the minds of some in Vauxhall House, and Rachel had been instructed to make the acquaintance of graduates from British universities that might be employed by such a group; hence her appearance at the pharmaceutical conference I attended in London in 2019, although I had no personal commitment to such an organisation and our meeting was accidental.

Later, it was similarly by chance we encountered Dowson in Montmartre; Dowson's disappearance from Norfolk later was enough to send Ms Harding to a safe house for her own protection. No one was sure if Dowson had died or been killed. It was something, however, that left me desperately abandoned.

The day Hugo Stratton came to release Rachel from the purgatory of the safe house in High Wycombe (March 5th), it was snowing again. Not a blizzard, but silent specks of white, floating and twisting from a flat, grey sky. Two months of daily newspapers, cryptic crosswords, killer Sudokus and brief conversations with an uncommunicative pair of lady guardians, had been hard work and in anticipation of her release, Rachel had put on a new coat, white in colour to match the snow, heavy, wool for warmth. Stratton was oblivious to its attractiveness.

They drove to an RAF airfield and took a night flight, landing in Mombasa in the early morning. As they disembarked, the heat enveloped them like a blanket. A second assistant (commercial) from the British and Embassy in Nairobi had flown all this way to facilitate Stratton and Harding's passage through customs. An unhappy young man, he had unfortunately blotted his copybook by becoming too friendly with an ambassador's wife previously resulting in this posting, which he resented; London had ordered him to meet these 'specials', which he resented. He had no time for that lot from 'the Bridge', He supposed that they spent all day hanging about bars and then sending coded and mysterious messages to God knows who. Whatever they did, he couldn't put up with them. Unfortunately, it showed.

Eventually, Stratton and Harding managed to reach one of the grand beach hotels that dotted the coastal sands of Mombasa. Rachel chose it, having spent many weekends here a few years ago, when she befriended Dowson. She knew it to be the watering hole of the local and international newsmen/-women and one that offered meticulous service but negligible intrusion. They booked a room with twin beds and slept the afternoon away. The hotel receptionist hardly noticed them. Restored, they descended for a drink at the beach bar to find reporters and many of the regulars Rachel remembered. And here came Harry Gaskell rushing over; or moving as quickly as his state of advanced intoxication allowed.

"As I live and breathe and bugger me, if it's not that beautiful and talented Rachel Harding! God bless you and keep you safely away from these reprobates and rogues." He waved an arm round the bar.

"Harry, how are you?" She asked.

"As always. As always. Eager for action but damned by ill-fortune. The scoop of a lifetime avoids me, and I stumble on the edge of an abyss."

"Not you Harry."

"And who is this handsome, ne'er-do-well I see before my eyes?" But before Stratton could answer; "Is that, upon your finger, a ring advertising the blissful state of matrimony?" Harry came to an abrupt halt, hand to his mouth.

"Oh, if you're worried about Alex, don't. That was over long ago."

Harry Gaskell gave himself a moment for reflection by taking a large gulp of whisky. "You've not heard?" His voce became deferential.

"Heard?"

"Heard about the…incident?"

"Incident? What incident? What are you on about Harry?"

"So, you've not heard?" He repeated rather lamely. Harry looked to Stratton for help, or at least guidance. He received none. Nodding to a new high-rise block of apartments he continued; "Got in with that lot. All billionaires I'm told. They say he joined them, but I don't rightly understand it, he hadn't got two pennies to rub together, as far as I know. Seems there was some sort of party; got out of hand; someone had a gun. Alex got shot or something. Accident they said. Course I was sniffing round there quick as you like. Couldn't find anything. Warned off. Makes you think."

"Anymore? When was this?"

"Earlier this year; must have been. Heard the odd story. Perhaps it was over a girl. God knows. Was told to leave it alone in no uncertain terms; not that I took much notice of that. But couldn't find a bloody thing! Police gave up. No report or arrest. Nothing. Pity but this is Kenya. Anyway, that monstrosity of apartments is closed and empty. No idea what's going to happen. I know one thing; I can't afford to buy one of them." He had given them the news they least wanted to hear. Now he seemed to lose interest in Alex. "Here long?" But he'd become bored already; needed another drink; didn't wait long enough for an answer. "Stay good, there's my girl." He turned on his heel, it must be said rather unsteadily, and made his way back to the crowd of reporters.

"Well, sod it! Marcia won't be best pleased, that's for sure. Always like that is he?" Stratton frowned.

"Of an evening."

*** *** ***

They stayed three days. Neither staff nor news-hungry reporters had much to say about the block of apartments except that all the owners (if that's what they were) left without leaving forwarding addresses. If anyone knew anything more, they weren't saying. But there was real speculation about the amount of money pouring into Tanzania over the border to the south, and possibly Mozambique. It seemed that China was investing finance and workforce; ports were being enlarged and money pumped into Tanzania's infrastructure of roads and rail. Although Kenya had its own super-rich, increasingly, eyes and minds, we're turning to the south and what prosperity might accrue from closer political and economic links. On experiments with bugs, not a word, apart from indeterminate references 'to chemicals further South. Mozambique direction?'

"And to the North?" Stratton mused; "Well, that would be Russia wouldn't it," came the vague reply.

Rachel had reached the end of her road. On the other side of Mombasa, rubbish dumps swarmed with Kenyans living in absolute poverty and existing solely on festering garbage. She had seen poverty before but not in such proximity to obscene wealth. She resigned from the service (heeding the warning of a lifetime controlled by The Official Secrets Act) and worked earnestly in heart-breaking circumstances for UNISEF.

Stratton returned to Britain. Marcia looked forward to a meeting with Jocelyn.

*** *** ***

When the decision was taken to close ANCOM, little thought was given to the effect this would have on its members. Because of the association with Keenan, ANCOM had become an embarrassment. It had to go. Full stop!

D-notices flew about like confetti, whilst at the same time Keenan and Donato languished at Her Majesty's pleasure, where they had undergone intensive questioning by highly trained interrogators who unfortunately elicited no further details of their treason, for whom they worked, nor why. The two concurred, however, that they had known each other since meeting in Cambridge, and that Dowson was Donato's son, but of a hotel in Bedford, and meeting with a foreign person, possibly of German or South African nationality, they knew nothing (or at least refused to say anything.) It was two years later Lord Kingsworth (Lady Keenan's brother) was reported absent, the castle and estates sold, and the funds secreted in various banks and offshore havens. By then, it was too late.

Brian Franklin had plenty to do. He missed Young who he thought of as a friend. But policing the capital was going to be difficult; the country was bracing itself for a lockdown. They were going to have to use strategies as 'Engage, Explain, Encourage' and if necessary, "Enforce" lockdown measures if they became law. Mountford and Stratton disappeared into the murky world of counterespionage.

In Norfolk, Superintendent Fitzwilliam, Inspector Leeder and Sergeant Eyles went about their business as usual. They were no longer investigating the cottage on the coast and the disappearance of Dowson. Some rather unfriendly officials came from London and explained, "This was a matter security, and they would deal with it." The large house in the wooded area near Norwich lay deserted until a demolition squad, dressed in personal protection uniforms, obliterated it. Baxter, still unhappy, continued to work in the Haven Ports; he lost touch with Group Captain Young again. Pity. On impulse, Glenda Eyles rang me of all people! She was to take a week's leave and suggested she might like to visit Oxford.

An increasing number of eminent scientists continued to pester the government on the dangers of the COVID pandemic and the SAGE committee advocated social isolation measures to prevent catastrophic death rates in Britain. The government was reluctant to close the economy down but soon lockdown was inevitable. On March 20th, 2020, Boris Johnson announced the closures of schools and three days later Monday the 23rd of March he announced total lockdown across the United Kingdom. Schools, universities, sports, pubs, restaurants and cafes were closed; all non-essential services and shops were to close; citizens were ordered to stay indoors except for exercise or shopping for food or medicine once a day or essential work. Gatherings of any sort were not to be allowed, with limited exceptions that involved essential services or National Security. The government dreamed up slogans easy to remember such as 'stay at home—protect the NHS—save lives' or more personally 'wash hands and face—give space'. Much debate ensued as to whether a democratic Society would accept such draconian methods of lockdown; we were not China when all said and done. But amazingly on March 23rd Britain came to halt. Franklin drove through Trafalgar Square at 9 am. on Monday the 23rd of March 2020 and found it deserted. He'd never seen anything like it. It was like the newsreels of Hiroshima post-bomb but with buildings still upright. There was nothing living in sight. Open spaces devoid of humans or any visible movement engenders horror or terror as the film industry knows very well. Edward Hopper, the American 20th century artist, used rooms at night deserted save for a single person to suggest loneliness, isolation, or solitude. Depression. And fear. And think Alfred Hitchcock.

Britain came to a rather frightened standstill.

Franklin was astounded. The population was remarkably compliant. COVID infection rate soared; hospitals found the influx of patients tested resources to the full. The number of deaths was frightening. The treasury was almost trying to keep the economy afloat but at great expense. In the first year of lockdown, the rate of criminal damage and robbery fell, sexual offences were unchanged but there was an epidemic of dog snatching, fraud related to COVID, and worst of all domestic abuse rose alarmingly. The rule of 6 in households on the 21st of June caused confusion but basic services and nightclubs opened again, and Britain returned to something approaching normal. However, Boris Johnson still left the final decision of facemasks, social mixing, opening of windows and so on to the individual. It was most unsatisfactory. Every aspect of life had changed, the economy, the welfare state, the mental and physical health of the nation. The effect of a world pandemic, man-made or otherwise, was catastrophic.

Curiously there was a distinct reluctance try limited freedom but by August or September 2021 when rules started to relax people began to visit pubs, shops, even go on holiday in Britain. Stay-at-home holidays became remarkably popular after quarantine measures were put in place for passengers moving to or from areas of high risk.

Then came the mutation of the COVID virus. The rate of hospitalisation and deaths rose. Another wave of uncertainty hit the world, changing behaviour probably for ever. Brilliantly, Oxford produced safe vaccination giving protection against the virus pandemic and other institutions and pharmaceutical firms also developed vaccines and antiviral drugs. The population (in Britain) was vaccinated with remarkable efficiency and life became more secure. Nevertheless, the world had woken up to the terror of pandemics. Manufactured or not.

The doors of the Home and Foreign Office are substantial. Once closed, they can easily give a false impression of security. Information is now extremely technical and carries extraordinary power. Misappropriation of information is a major concern. Misinformation is almost as dangerous. It has become clear from cases like the one discussed in this book that espionage and must include many aspects of modern life that traditionally it had not been associated. Marcia, Stratton and Mountford remained vigilant. The lessons learnt from the treachery of Keenan and Donato must not be forgotten. Although they had no conclusive proof (yet) of the consortium that dealt with death and the vast social/economic consequences of biowarfare, they had directed more resources and incentive into that aspect of National security. The episode was a useful catalyst. Undoubtedly, there would be more global crises and the Service must be prepared.

*** *** ***

You deserve an explanation. I have learned of the actions in and around Whitehall, recounted in this book because of my new association with Detective Glenda Eyles. She rang me when the social restrictions of the pandemic were lifted and invited herself for a weekend. Subsequently she has visited regularly, and our relationship has developed. Her parents sold their house in Holt and now reside permanently in a care facility, thus releasing her from daily responsibility for their welfare.

Glenda, of course, knew Young and had communicated with him after his retirement. He now travels the length and breadth of Britain with his good lady wife, Diane. They are recording, for posterity, villages, historically interesting churches, relaxing and picturesque walks, (hostelries of unusually welcoming atmosphere, whenever Reginald can) and especially agreeable hotels. Reginald has told Glenda the story related here (although with judicious summation) ANCOM and 'The Lawns' are closed; Clarissa, as far as can be discovered, is married and lives in Northumberland (no doubt gradually overcoming her shock of the kilt.) Rachel wrote a guarded letter to me about her work in Africa, and more freely of her sorrow at our separation. There was no address given for a reply.

The virus seemed to have passed us by, except for Gordon Baxter who died. Reginald declared that Gordon had lost his will to live, so that might have made him more susceptible. Who knows?

Without being too philosophical, I sometimes wonder if the treachery in Whitehall and related in this book in some ways mirrors the bigger international conspiracies, I hope not.

*** *** ***

The beach is wide and the sand yellow, warm and dry between the toes. A middle-aged man, tall and of aristocratic bearing, ambled from the crystal-clear sea and made for his huge beach house, which was partially screened from the tropical heat and unwanted scrutiny, by closely planted palm trees. As he climbed the steps to the veranda, his mobile called his attention. He answered it.

"Boscombe."

"And good day to you, sir." A familiar voice. "All well, there in paradise, is it? Would you say?"

"That you, Forsythe? Is that London calling?"

"At your service, my lord. And with good news. Your apartment overlooking Hyde Park awaits your approbation, as does the Consortium. This time a substantial investment would be judicious, but the return beyond your dreams, sir. We meet a week on Saturday, 20 December, to be precise."

"Book me in, Forsythe."

The line disconnected. The Earl of Kingsworth took a seat on the veranda. The members must have come up with a new programme. He watched the sea splashing against the sand. It was very warm.

Ingram Content Group UK Ltd.
Milton Keynes UK
UKHW021914120323
418425UK00006BA/108